BELOVED OUTLAW

Abby took a deep breath. The only way she could get the truth would be to take Chase by surprise. "Did you or did you not say last night that you wanted me in your bed?"

"Abby, for God's sake . . ." he stalked away, cursing low under his breath.

"Well, do you? Like I want you in mine?"

Chase grew rigid. He'd neither touch her nor would he retreat.

Abby knew it was up to her. She closed the distance between them. "I've waited for you all my life, Chase," she dared to breathe. "All my life. I love you."

The outlaw closed his eyes, a pained sound coming from his throat. "You can't love someone you don't know, Abby. And believe me when I tell you you don't know me."

She smoothed her hand along the side of his face, her fingertips tracing the line of his jaw. "I know all I need to know." She brushed her lips against his. "I know I love you."

With a groan, Chase crushed her to him, rained kisses across her forehead, her cheeks, her eyes. He tasted her, gloried in her sweetness, succumbing to the warmth, the magic that was Abby . . .

MIDNIGHT CHASE

LINDA BENJAMIN

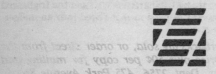

ZEBRA BOOKS
KENSINGTON PUBLISHING CORP.

ZEBRA BOOKS

are published by

Kensington Publishing Corp.
475 Park Avenue South
New York, NY 10016

First printing: September, 1989

Printed in the United States of America

To My Favorite Aunt and Uncle—Mary Ann and Bill

Chapter One

Chase Cordell sat astride his sorrel gelding and checked the cylinder on his Colt .44. Six shots. A full load. He didn't expect to use the gun when he robbed the Willow Springs stagecoach this afternoon, but he wanted to be ready just in case.

From his position on the rim of the bluff, Chase eyed the dirt road that ribboned across the wide, flat eastern Colorado plain toward the creek sluicing by below. In less than an hour a telltale plume of dust to the north would signal the approach of the stage. The driver would have to slow to cross the creek. That was the moment Chase was waiting for. Chase and the three other members of the Cordell gang.

Simple. Quick.

Nothing could go wrong.

Then why did the tightness in his gut persist? Why did this one feel different from the others?

Chase grimaced, the gesture tightening the line of his jaw, stubbled now with a three-day growth of dark beard. He supposed he could still be reacting to what happened two weeks ago in Rimrock, but somehow he didn't think so.

It was more than that. Something intangible, elusive. Something in the wind that just didn't feel right. Something that could get them all killed.

With a low curse Chase reholstered the Colt. Maybe he should call it off. Maybe . . . no, they were all but out of money. The others had been grumbling for days. And there was money on that stage, money and Luther Breckenridge. Luther Breckenridge owed Chase Cordell. Chase intended to collect.

He leaned forward to pat the sorrel's neck. "Maybe this'll be the last one, eh, Red?" The horse snorted and shook its head, the motion ruffling its flaxen mane. Chase cursed again.

The gelding had been shaking off a fly, but the truth remained that Chase was fooling no one, not even himself. This would not be his last holdup. Unless, of course, he got careless and the shotgun messenger put a bullet in his head.

His lips thinned and he dismounted. There was no sense transferring his rising agitation to the horse. Nor did he want to alert the others to his unaccustomed misgivings. A quick glance told him Josey and the Kid were hunkered down in front of a massive boulder with a pair of dice. Gantry was off by himself as usual, flat on his belly, peering over the bluff.

As if he could feel Chase looking at him, Gantry turned, the man's coal black eyes for an instant openly contemptuous, challenging. And then, with a calculated indifference, he returned his attention to the road.

Chase resisted the impulse to throw the bastard off the bluff head first. The time for a showdown between the two was coming. But not today. They still needed each other for the stage.

Catching up the sorrel's reins, Chase led the gelding down the sloping southside of the rocky upthrust, his spurs jingling as he walked. He inhaled the clean scent of water and wildflowers and crossed to the line of willows that bordered the meandering stream. He didn't worry about being exposed should the stage be early. An elbow curve in the watercourse would make him invisible from the road. Besides, of the dozen or so stagecoaches he'd robbed in the last two years, he'd never known one to be early. The thought brought a ghost of a smile to his lips that quickly vanished.

Letting the reins trail, he ground-tied the horse, then sank down beside the tree, his back enjoying the rough support of the willow's trunk. Tugging off his gloves, he shoved them in the waistband of his Levis, then lifted his Stetson to rake a hand through sweat-damp dark brown hair that shagged nearly to his shoulders. The mid-August day was hot, but tolerable, and he swiped indifferently at a trail of sweat that stung his eyes.

Long lashes gave those smoke blue eyes a sensual air that had attracted more than one woman in his thirty-odd years. But none had lingered, soon discovering the cynicism in those eyes was no surface pretension, but a character trait that ran bone deep.

Not that he minded their hasty retreats. On his own since he was twelve, he had nothing to offer a woman but a fiddle-footed nature and a checkered past. Which was why he neither expected nor sought out anything that could not be bought and paid for and left behind in any saloon, anywhere. A respectable woman wanted roots. He had none to give. And he told himself he liked it that way.

Forcing himself to concentrate, Chase again ran through his plans for the stage. He and Gantry would ride out from behind the bluff, while Josey and the Kid would come at the coach from the opposite side of the road. If nobody on the stage got any ideas about being a hero, the Concord would be on its way again in ten minutes. With Willow Springs some twenty miles south, it would be hours before the law could mount any pursuit, hours that would give Chase and his men ample time to hide their trail.

Even knowing that, the tension in him persisted, fueling an almost palpable feeling that something would go dangerously wrong. Angrily, he shoved the thought away. Things had been twitchy ever since Rimrock. All four of them had nearly bought a spot on boot hill when that bank job went sour.

Afterward, Noah Gantry had not opted for subtlety. He placed the blame squarely on Chase. Hell, Gantry had been itching for a showdown for weeks, even before Rimrock. Chase was becoming more and more eager to oblige him.

But for now, Chase couldn't afford to let himself be distracted by his foul-tempered confederate. Leaning his head back, he let out a long, weary sigh. God, he was tired, tired to the center of his soul. Gazing up through the weaving branches, he stared at the stark blue of the cloudless Colorado sky. How had it come to this anyway? How had he so easily slipped into the life of an outlaw? That until two years ago he'd spent his life on the shadowed edges of the law was one thing, but to actually have crossed over the line . . .

Against his will he reached into the pocket of the calfskin vest he wore and extracted a battered piece of metal, the star misshapen now, but the deep-cut letters still all too visible—SPECIAL DEPUTY. For long minutes he sat there turning the badge over and over in his palm.

He had made his own choice. He had no one to blame but himself. But sometimes he wondered just how different things might have been if—

Booted footfalls on the hard-packed earth jerked his thoughts from their most unwelcome direction. Quickly he stuffed the badge back into his pocket.

"Gettin' nervous, boss?" Josiah Vinson asked.

Chase studied this oldest member of his ragtag outfit. Snow-white hair topped grizzled features as rawhide-tough as saddle leather. Bowed legs attested to a half century spent on horseback. Chase admitted a mild surprise even to see the man on foot. The creek was at least twenty yards from where Josey and the Kid had been absorbed in their dice game. Distance enough to require the services of the mangy roan Josey had yet to convince Chase was a horse. In fact, dice might be the only time Josey Vinson ever parted company with that mule-eared beast. That and to stock up on his supply of Wedding Cake, the ever-present tobacco that puffed up his bewhiskered left cheek like a ground squirrel's.

"Not nervous," Chase allowed finally. "Cautious. I like to rethink everything before a job. I don't need anything going wrong."

"Like Rimrock?"

Chase bristled. "What about Rimrock?" He'd heard enough on the subject from Gantry. Until now,

11

though, Josey had offered no opinion on the abortive holdup attempt.

"I just want you to know," Josey said, apparently taking no offense at Chase's tone, "that me and the Kid don't put none of the blame on you for what happened. Nobody coulda knowed that bank vault was on some newfangled time lock. Or that the marshal would come back so soon from that wild goose hunt you sent him on."

Chase said nothing. He and Josey had ridden together some twenty months, but that didn't make them friends. They would watch each other's backs in a holdup, split the take fair and equal, but never had Chase expected friendship from the man. Nor did he want it. Friendship suggested loyalty; loyalty could be betrayed.

"What could go wrong with this one anyways?" Josey went on. "You've got the creek here," he pronounced it *crick,* "to make sure the stage pulls up. And we got the bluff to block the driver's view of where we're gonna ride out and throw down on 'em. It'll be slicker'n a crooked game of three card monte, and twice as easy."

"Yeah, easy," Chase gritted, rising to his feet. "Just remember, I don't want anybody gettin' hurt. Us or them."

Josey snorted. "You're an odd one. I've ridden with my share of hombres, but I never seen none so picky about keepin' his bullets in his gun."

"I steal money, not lives. And maybe I just don't want to hang."

"You don't give a hoot about hangin'. You just got no stomach for killin'. But you ain't soft neither. You sure ain't soft."

Chase pulled out the makings and rolled himself a smoke. Striking a match on his thigh, he touched the flame to the end of the cigarette and inhaled deeply, then snuffed out the match and again eyed Josey Vinson. "You got your part in this straight? That stage will be here inside of an hour."

"I got it straight. I keep my gun on the driver and the guard. The Kid'll watch the passengers. And Gantry . . ." Josey spat a wad of juice into the dirt, "Gantry will likely get somebody killed."

Chase took a last drag on the cigarette, then flipped it in a high arc to land with a hiss in the creek. "If you'll recall, it wasn't my idea to have Gantry along."

"Didn't say it was." Josey turned and slapped aside a trailing willow branch, starting up the rise toward his horse. He paused briefly, speaking over his left shoulder. "Just sayin' that sometimes his mouth has more of a hair trigger than his gun. The man could rile a statue."

Chase snorted his assent, while Josey continued toward his roan. The grizzled outlaw mounted and rode the remaining few steps to where his dice companion now stood staring intently over the bluff. Leaning over the saddlehorn, Josey spoke in low, earnest tones to the Kid, words Chase could not hear. The peach-fuzzed blond nodded vigorously, looking back down the slope toward Chase. But when he saw Chase looking at him, his gaze darted quickly — guiltily? — away.

Chase's eyes narrowed. Cal Talbot — no one ever called him anything but The Kid — was about as cut out for lawbreaking as a schoolmarm was for steer roping, but he was also extremely impressionable and he worshipped the ground Josey walked on. Chase didn't think the Kid, or Josey either for that matter, would try anything mutinous, but if this stage job didn't go right today, things could change in a hurry.

Chase recalled the first time he'd seen the reed thin nineteen-year-old. The Kid had been one of the passengers on a stage that had thrown a wheel outside of Leadville some eleven months back. He'd gotten such a kick out of watching Chase and Josey steal everyone's valuables, that he'd cut the traces off one of the lead horses and followed after them. The passengers of the disabled stage probably thought he was going for help.

They would've had a long wait. The Kid caught up to Chase and Josey and inside of five minutes had talked himself into joining up with them.

Between Josey and the Kid things had gone fairly smoothly for months. Neither was trigger happy, nor were they excessively greedy.

And then six weeks ago Noah Gantry had ridden into their lives, ridden in guns blazing. Gantry helped Chase and the others shoot their way out of a fracas with a band of Mexican pistoleros near the border. At the time Chase had been grateful. It didn't take long to realize that Gantry had thrown in with Chase and the others not out of any sense of which side was right or wrong, but because he hated Mexicans.

Chestnut-haired and square-jawed, Gantry likely would have been considered handsome by most of the women he met, if not for the vicious scar that jagged up the left side of his face from jawline to hairline, a souvenir of a long ago encounter with a Shoshone.

14

Chase had not asked what had become of the Indian; Noah had eagerly volunteered it. Chase's stomach had remained unsettled for two days.

Gantry's temper had proved explosive and unpredictable. Two weeks ago Chase had had to stop him from beating his horse half to death, when the animal had gone lame. That had not been the first time Chase suggested they part company.

Three weeks after Noah had signed on, the four of them had stopped a payroll wagon headed for Cheyenne. But there was no payroll, the wagon merely a diversion. An enraged Noah had levelled his Colt on the disarmed driver. Only Chase's desperate lunge, catching Noah's arm, had made Noah's shot go wild. Livid, Chase ordered Noah gone.

And he would have been. Gone or dead. But to Chase's surprise and irritation, Josey and the Kid had come to Noah's defense. Noah had been edgy, they said. It was Noah's first job with them, after all. It wouldn't happen again. Too, Chase knew, Josey and the Kid had been increasingly swayed by Noah's grandiose plans for more lucrative robberies. Noah himself made assurances that he'd acted without thinking, that next time he would follow orders. Against his better judgment Chase had allowed the man to stay.

Then he'd lived to regret it. His gaze flicked to where Gantry now sat astride a bay gelding, his attention still riveted on the road north. Again the outlaw seemed to have eyes in the back of his head. He turned, a slow smirk twisting his already twisted features. Nudging the bay into a walk, he headed toward Chase.

"I still say hitting this stage is penny ante stuff, Cordell." The man made no attempt to disguise his contempt. "We could've taken the bank in town easy."

"There's someone on that stage who owes me something," Chase said, even as his temper slipped a notch. He was sick to death of Gantry's baiting.

"Or maybe you're just scared of banks after Rimrock."

Chase straightened, holding on to the last threads of his temper by sheer force of will. "As I recall, it was your job to make sure the sheriff stayed on that phoney trail of yours another four hours. Instead, you circled back early and led him straight to town."

Gantry swore viciously. "He gave up! How could I have—"

Chase cut him off. "He followed you. I checked your supposedly covered-up trail back to town. A three-year-old could've followed it."

Noah's hand jerked instinctively toward the Navy Colt strapped to his thigh. But before he even touched the handle Chase had his own Colt drawn and centered on Noah's chest, hammer thumbed back. Seconds ticked by. Noah didn't move, didn't breathe, his gaze never straying from the barrel of Chase's gun.

"Do it, Cordell," Noah gritted. "I would."

More seconds ticked by. Every instinct in Chase's body told him to squeeze the trigger. But though he faced a murderer, he could not commit murder. Tilting the barrel upward, he eased down the hammer. "Ride out. Now. I never want to see your face again."

Color rose in Gantry's sun bronzed features. "If you think you can—"

Suddenly the Kid spurred his horse between them,

16

pointing northward. "The stage is comin'. I see the dust. It's comin', I tell ya!"

Neither Chase nor Gantry moved.

"You know," Josey put in mildly, "I don't much give a damn who stays and who goes. But I'd just as soon git it settled after the stage. I want me some money. I ain't had me a woman in over three weeks."

"Me neither," the Kid groused.

Chase knew if Noah rode out now, the man would make certain he alerted the stage to their presence. But better that than to suffer the man's unpredictable behavior during the robbery. Still, he owed some consideration to Josey and the Kid.

"It's your call, Gantry. You ride out of here right now, or you swear you'll take orders from me when we take the stage."

"I guess I ain't got much choice, *boss* man," he sneered. "If I'm ridin' out on my own, I'll be needin' a stake."

Chase reholstered his Colt. "Then let's do it." Crossing to his sorrel, he mounted, then reached back into his saddlebag and pulled out a small gunny sack. Yanking it over his head, he adjusted the eye slits, the coarse spun material prickling the stubble of his beard. The others did the same. The stage was less than a mile away now. Chase could see the Concord buck and sway to the whim of the ruts and bumps in the road. Its great orange wheels churned up considerable dust as the driver cracked his whip, shouting encouragement and a fair share of obscenities to his six horse team.

Chase reined his sorrel alongside Gantry. They were all business now. The Kid and Josey guided their

17

horses down the slope and across the road, ducking out of sight behind a stand of cottonwoods.

Chase's focus narrowed, his heart thudding with more anticipation than he usually felt before a job. For now at least he put aside his problems with Gantry. In five minutes the stage would be here, five minutes to Luther Breckenridge. Chase still couldn't believe the blind luck that had placed such sweet revenge in his path. He had been putting away a cold beer in the Lone Tree Saloon in Willow Springs, when a clerk had come in looking for some big shot citizen with a message that the Diamond B rancher would be travelling through town on his way to Denver. In that moment Chase had decided to rob the stage instead of the Willow Springs bank.

That he'd stolen from Breckenridge before didn't matter. He would relish stealing from him again. Two years ago Breckenridge had hired him — or more rightly hired his gun — to rid his range of illegal homesteaders. The squatters had been no problem. Chase had quickly convinced them to pull up stakes and try their luck elsewhere. If they didn't, he assured them, Luther Breckenridge would bring in fifty more guns — and the only part of their land they'd have left was the six feet they'd be buried under. The complication Chase hadn't foreseen had not come from the squatters, but from Breckenridge himself — in the form of his wife.

Violet-eyed, voluptuous and thirty years younger than her sixtyish husband, Felicity Breckenridge was as seductive as she was beautiful, a woman who could have charmed the halo off a saint. She made her interest in Chase known from the first minute they

18

met. A virgin couldn't have misinterpreted the look she sent him. Time and again she attempted to maneuver him into a private meeting. Always Chase made certain another ranch hand accompanied him. For a time he found her persistence amusing. When he grew tired of it, he quit answering her summons at all. Chase Cordell was far from qualifying for a halo, but he had never bedded another man's wife.

Then one night Felicity rode out alone to his campsite. She'd been drinking and when he again refused her, she slapped him, screamed obscenities at him. Livid, Chase stalked away, planning to mount up and get the hell away from her. In the dark she stumbled and fell, pitching headlong into a clump of sagebrush.

Her screams of pain brought Chase bolting back to her. He did the best he could to clean and dress the mass of cuts on her face, but even more than her terror of what might become of her looks, she feared the wrath of a jealous husband. Chase calmed her down, suggesting she tell him she'd fallen from her horse; then he took her home.

Felicity's tale of faulty horsemanship rang false from the moment she opened her mouth. In a panic she sobbed that Chase had attacked her, threatened her if she dared tell Luther the truth. Chase was given no chance to tell his side of the story. Breckenridge's ranchhands took turns beating him, then Luther ordered him spread-eagled between two posts. . . .

Chase tightened his fist on the sorrel's reins, making the gelding snort and shy.

Gantry cursed. "You want to just send up smoke signals? Let 'em know we're here?"

Chase settled the horse, wishing he could as easily settle the rage searing through him. Breckenridge had all but whipped the flesh from his back, then dumped him on the range to die—with no food, no water, no horse.

But Chase had not died. And Luther Breckenridge became the first man Chase Cordell had ever stolen anything from in his life. Though it seemed scarcely equitable, it was the perfect revenge. Even above his lovely wife, Luther Breckenridge valued money. And Chase had helped himself to a considerable sum.

Unfortunately, the stealing got easier after that. Trains, stagecoaches—Chase was building himself quite a reputation. He'd heard the reward on his head now topped a thousand dollars, most of it posted by Breckenridge. The rancher had labeled him an out-law; Chase had obliged him by becoming one.

Chase grimaced beneath his mask, shaking off the distracting thoughts. Instead he concentrated on waiting for Josey's hand signal from across the road. The jangle of wheels and harness was closer now. He heard the driver shouting "whoa up" to his team. Josey raised his arm. The stage was crossing the creek. Chase drove his heels into the sorrel's sides. The horse plunged around the bluff's edge. Reining in almost at once, Chase pointed his gun skyward and fired off two quick shots. "Hands up!" he barked. "Nobody move."

The driver stood in the box, yanking back savagely on the reins. The already slowing coach came to a quick standstill. Both the driver and the guard raised their hands. "Don't shoot, mister!" he shouted. "We got women on board."

20

"Just do as you're told and nobody gets hurt," Chase growled, careful to keep his voice low, indistinct. He didn't want to chance Breckenridge recognizing it.

Guns drawn, Josey and the Kid maneuvered their mounts into the middle of the road, shutting off any notion the driver might have of escape.

Chase dismounted, Noah following on his heels. Cautiously, Chase stalked to the stage door and yanked it open. He counted four passengers—three women, one man. "Everybody out," he said. "Hands where I can see 'em."

Gripping the stage for support, an older woman of about fifty, wearing a wool travelling suit, exited. Her gray eyes darted nervously from Chase to Gantry and back again. A golden haired girl of about thirteen followed. "Please," the woman murmured, "don't hurt us."

"Just do what we say, ma'am," Chase assured her, "and you'll be on your way in ten minutes."

Gantry herded the woman and girl toward the driver's boot. Josey had already ordered the driver and guard to the ground and they stood with their hands in the air.

Chase kept his gun trained on the coach's interior. "You inside," he called again, "Get out here. Hands empty."

The hands were empty. Big bear paw hands attached to a once bear-sized man. Chase stared, stunned. The bear paw hands shook. The wide-set eyes that had once gleamed with arrogance born of a lifetime of living by his own rules were dull and sunken.

21

"Don't shoot," Breckenridge rasped, his chest heaving as a spasm of hacking coughs doubled him over.

"Don't shoot," Gantry mocked, laughing wildly and poking his gun in the rancher's ribs, as he checked the man for weapons.

Breckenridge continued to choke and gasp.

Chase felt a rush of savage satisfaction to see what time had wrought on this man who had cheated him, beaten him, left him for dead. He managed to resist the urge to drive his fist into the man's quivering jowls, but otherwise felt no remorse for the pleasure he took at the man's discomfort.

He turned then, his attention drawn to the final passenger emerging from the coach. With a jolt Chase recognized Felicity. He'd had no idea she would be travelling with her husband.

She was still lovely, dressed as she was in blue silk and white lace. The long ago cuts on her cheeks had left only a faint scar or two, not enough to mar such exquisite beauty. But the lusty vitality once evident in those violet eyes was gone, replaced by a lifelessness that on first glance seemed the same as the sickness-induced look of her husband. But hers, Chase sensed, was more a lifelessness of spirit.

"My, my," Gantry said, taking his eyes off Breckenridge long enough to notice Felicity. "A little bonus for our trouble, eh, compadres?" He crossed over to her, even as she instinctively shrank back. But she was blocked by the coach. "Very nice," he said, chucking the barrel of his gun under her chin. "Maybe I'll let my associates keep whatever money we find. I'll take you."

Her eyes darted fearfully toward her husband.

"Please, I'm a married woman."

"Leave her be," Chase snapped. When Gantry only shifted to run a hand insolently along the bodice of Felicity's dress, Chase levered back the hammer of his Colt. "Get away from her. Now."

Chase sensed Gantry's fury at being ordered about in front of the woman, but he must have also considered the outcome of defying Chase with a .44 aimed at his spine. "Anything you say, boss man," he said, taking a step back from Felicity.

"Now drop your gun," Chase said.

Gantry stiffened. "What?"

"You heard me. Drop it." Chase knew he could no longer turn his back on the man. "You've got three seconds. One . . ."

For the space of a heartbeat Gantry's grip tightened on the handle of his sixgun.

"Two."

Gantry dropped the gun, the heavy weapon making a dull thud on the dirt road.

Chase walked over and retrieved it, shoving it into the waistband of his denims. He then continued to speak to Gantry in clipped tones. "You stay right where I can see you. If you move, I'll kill you."

Rage rolled off Gantry in waves, every muscle in his body bowstring tight. But he didn't move.

"You," Chase snapped, pointing at Josey, "get the money belt off this man." He indicated Breckenridge.

Josey moved at once to comply.

"You ladies get back in the stage," Chase said, gesturing toward the older woman and the girl, who had stood virtually unmoving since they'd exited the coach. To the driver he said, "You and the guard get

23

back up top and get ready to drive out of here." Chase wanted all of these people gone. He wanted to deal with Gantry once and for all. The outlaw was riding out of here on his saddle or over it—it made no difference to Chase.

The woman and young girl hurried aboard. Chase turned to Felicity. "You too, ma'am," he said, catching up her elbow and helping her into the coach.

He winced at the pitiful gratitude that came into her eyes. "Thank you for keeping that man away from me," she whispered, then looked quickly toward her husband, as though fearing he had overheard.

Chase wondered at the perversity of fate that he should be feeling sorry for this woman. Maybe Luther had publicly believed her story about Chase, but privately he must have made her life hell. Her gaze darted toward Josey, watching as the outlaw pushed back her husband's coat, then ripped open the buttons of his shirt to reveal a thick money belt beneath. "Jackpot!" Josey yelped.

"Do you think that man might kill my husband?" Felicity asked, her hands twisting in the folds of her skirts. Chase's eyes widened beneath his mask as he caught the threading of hope in that question. "We're not planning to kill anyone, ma'am."

"Oh." She sagged back, no longer looking at him.

Even in his debilitated state Breckenridge lunged at Josey, who was holding up fistfuls of hundred dollar bills. "Mine!" the man choked. "You'll not have it! It's mine!"

Chase gripped Breckenridge by the scruff of the neck and propelled him toward the Concord. "Be glad it's only money we're taking from you, old man. Be glad it's not your life."

In that instant Chase's gaze caught Felicity's. She looked directly into his eyes.

"Cordell." She mouthed the word, not saying it aloud, and her lips formed an almost imperceptible smile.

Chase gave her no time for any further reaction. Shoving Breckenridge into the coach, Chase jumped back and secured the door. "Get the hell out of here!" he yelled at the driver, who immediately lifted his whip and cracked it above the heads of his team. In seconds the stage thundered out of sight.

Before the coach's dust had settled, Gantry whirled on Chase. "You had no right to treat me that way, Cordell!" he hissed, flinging his hat to the ground and whipping off his mask to reveal scarred features contorted with rage. "You're a dead man. You hear me? Dead!"

Chase, too, removed his mask. "You should've left the lady alone. Get on your horse and get out."

"I'm not leaving without my share of the money."

"You get nothing."

Noah's face purpled. "You don't give me orders any more, Cordell. Not ever again! And maybe not them either." He jerked a finger toward Josey and the Kid.

Though he obviously expected it, neither Josey nor the Kid made any move to side with Gantry. But neither did they offer any encouragement to Chase.

Chase and Gantry—two lobo wolves—fighting for leadership of the pack. Josey and the Kid would follow the survivor, no questions, no regrets.

"You had your chance to kill me earlier, Gantry. You lost. I won. Get out." Chase kept his gun on the scar-faced outlaw.

Gantry's fists clenched and unclenched at his sides. "Do I get to take my gun?" he asked stiffly.

"No."

"My hat?" His voice dripped with sarcasm.

Chase shrugged. "Your choice."

Slowly, Gantry bent to retrieve his Stetson, his hand grazing the powdery dust of the roadbed. "We'll meet again, Cordell. I promise. We'll meet again."

"Not if—"

Like a snake, Gantry struck, flinging the dirt at Chase's face. Reflexively, Chase threw up his left hand, even as he reminded himself Gantry was unarmed. Too late a warning bell sounded in his head.

He felt the sting in his side before he heard the shot, before he saw the gun. A palm gun, its tiny barrel smoking in Gantry's hand.

"No, Cordell, you lose," Gantry snarled. "You're dead."

Chase staggered back a step, one hand instinctively reaching toward the blood spreading outward on his shirt, while the other sought to bring his own gun to bear. But the wound slowed him just enough. Gantry fired again. Chase knew an instant of blinding pain, his brain seeming to explode inside his skull, and then he knew nothing, nothing at all.

Chapter Two

Abigail Graham slammed shut the endgate of the Conestoga, nearly slamming it on her fingers as well. But she scarcely noticed. Catching up a loosened cord that served to anchor the canvas top to the wagon bed, she just missed tying it off to the apron that protected her blue calico dress. But she took little note of that either. She was too excited.

This was the day, the day she'd been waiting for since she'd left Illinois some seven weeks earlier. Today she, Aunt Winifred and Uncle Ethan would part company with the wagon train and begin the last leg of the journey that would take them to a whole new life.

Just thirty more miles, Abby thought, *thirty more miles to Willow Springs.* Sight unseen, she had accepted the post of schoolteacher in the small frontier town, and she couldn't wait to get started. She would be the only teacher in fifty square miles and that was exactly the kind of challenge she wanted, *needed* in her life right now.

Excitement shone through in her hazel eyes, shone

27

through in the lightly tanned complexion she had tried so hard to shield from the ubiquitous sun. Stray wisps of cinnamon brown hair poked free of the hurried braid into which she'd woven it this morning. Her token attempts to pin the plait into submission failed. "I suppose I should count myself blessed that I didn't tie it to the wagon, too," she muttered, then managed a rueful smile.

All around her in the steadily lightening day were the sights and sounds of her fellow travellers making ready for the day's trek. Twenty families in all were under wagonmaster Jeb Matson's guidance. Leaving so late in the season, most were planning to winter in various towns along the trail. Some, though, would travel north and finish the journey via the Central Pacific. Though the transcontinental railroad had been completed nearly ten years before, Abby had deliberately opted for the more uncertain wagon route, telling herself she wanted to experience first hand the rigors of earlier pioneers.

And maybe prove something to yourself in the bargain? the thought intruded. But she refused to dwell on it, reminding herself that a wagon would have been an eventual necessity anyway. No railroad spur yet existed to Willow Springs.

Pre-dawn shadows shifted and flickered beneath a scattering of already dissipating clouds. It was going to be another warm day on the plains. She took a deep, steadying breath, pausing to survey the treeless, grass-covered land all around her. Stubbled intermittently with lonely buttes and crosscut by sandy bottomed creeks it was a far cry from the forested hills of the Mississippi Valley. Far to the west, but in sight

28

now for days, rose the snowcapped peaks of the Rockies, buttressed to the timberline with thick carpets of aspen and pine.

Sometimes she could scarcely believe she was here, that she had actually come west at last. Until now she'd known this land and its people only through books.

Thoughts of books sent a familiar spark of mischief rippling through her. Casting a furtive glance around her, Abby first made certain she was alone. Assuring herself that she was, she quickly lifted her apron and pulled free the orange paperbound book she'd tucked into the pocket of her dress: *The Luckless Trapper; or, The Haunted Hunter* by William R. Eyster, one of many similar titles she had ferreted away beneath her petticoats in her trunk in the back of the wagon.

Abby hugged the dime novel to her chest. Cowboys, Indians, scouts, road agents, white-hatted lawmen — tales of the Wild West — *this* was where life was lived to the fullest. Here she could fulfill her other lifelong dream — to write her own dime novel. She had written to the publishers — Beadle and Adams of New York City — over a year ago, asking for specific instructions about submitting a manuscript. All she need do, they'd replied, was to write out her book in a neat hand and send it to them. They would then read it and decide if it passed muster. If it did, they would pay her two hundred dollars for the rights to publish her work.

Pay *her* to publish her work? Abby remembered shaking her head in astonishment. She would have been happy to pay *them* — just for the thrill of holding her own published novel in her hands. And who knew what could happen after that? If they bought one book, they just might buy another. And another. She had enough ideas already for twenty novels. And she was certain she could come up with twenty more.

Abby tucked Eyster's book back into her pocket. Heaven help her if Aunt Winnie should see it. Even at age twenty-four Abby was not exempt from her aunt's lectures on what did and did not soil young minds.

Besides, if ever there was a day for the proper exercise of restraint and reassurance with her beloved aunt and uncle, this was it. A glance toward the head of the wagon train told her Winnie and Ethan had not yet finished their latest visit with Jeb Matson. Though they would admit no such thing, Abby knew they had gone to see the wagonmaster to have him recount yet again his detailed directions to Willow Springs. How many times had it been? At least a dozen. Not that Winnie and Ethan were at all anxious about travelling across these last three days of wilderness alone. . . .

Abby smiled indulgently. No matter how overcautious her aunt and uncle might be, she was achingly glad they had sold their mercantile back in Moline and made the journey with her. Winifred and Ethan Graham had been her parents since Abby was three years old.

The Larinbee sisters, Agatha and Winifred, had married the Graham brothers, Jonathon and Ethan, in a double ceremony two years before Abby was born. Winnie and Ethan Graham had shared the same house with Agatha and Jonathon Graham.

"When Aggie and Jon caught the cholera and died," Winnie had said on more than one occasion,

30

"it was only natural that Ethan and I raise you as our own. We already loved you as though you were."

And the feeling had been thoroughly mutual.

Continuing her check of the wagon, Abby walked to its near side and made certain the water barrel was secure. They had plenty to last them the entire thirty miles, if necessary. But Matson had mentioned a creek they should reach by this evening. It would be good to freshen their supply.

The wheels, the harness, the horses' hooves—all received similar attention. Everything was in order. Catching up her pale blue sunbonnet from where she'd left it the night before dangling from the brake handle on the wagon box, Abby quickly tied it off under her chin. Yes, she decided, it was going to be a wonderful day.

Clambering onto the hub of the left front wheel, Abby reached for and retrieved a small rectangular metal box from under the seat, then hopped back to the ground. Opening the box, she pulled out a leatherbound book. Her eyes brightening with anticipation, she flipped the book open, past several already handwritten pages, to stop at the first blank page.

Tex Trueblood, Texas Ranger Extraordinaire—her novel, her very first novel, or at least the first forty-two pages of it. Clutching the manuscript, she rummaged through the box to find her bottle of indigo ink and a pen. She had time for a few quick notes at least.

Stepping over to the side of the wagon, Abby set the book, pen and ink on a small ledge beside the water barrel. She started to open the ink bottle, then frowned, noticing a slight ridge, six inches square, on the blank page of her book. Curious, she turned the page to see what had made the indentation.

Abby gasped, a surge of bittersweet pain sweeping through her. She lifted the pink envelope, her fingers trembling as they trailed across the lovely script that spelled out her own name and address. A letter. A letter from Lisa. The last one Abby had ever received. She had forgotten she'd put it in the book.

Biting her lip, Abby opened the letter, then just as quickly shoved it back inside its envelope. *No,* she thought fiercely, she wasn't going to give in to any sad thoughts now. Not this morning. Lisa wouldn't have wanted it that way. In fact, Lisa would have been the first to forbid any pall to be cast upon such a momentous occasion. Still, it hurt to think about her, about a lifetime of warm and wonderful memories that only best friends could share. Had she really been dead six months now?

A congenial call of "Good morning!" distracted Abby, made her lift her head and smile in acknowledgement to the passing Hugh Griffin, who was leading his team of horses toward the wagon just ahead of Abby's own. Father to a passel of racketing youngsters, Hugh and his wife, Jenny, had proved amiable company these past weeks.

"You take care now!" Hugh called, tipping his broadbrimmed hat and smiling through a thick growth of blond beard. "Give my best to your aunt and uncle!"

"I'll do that," Abby called back, her sudden melancholy mood exacerbated as she thought of never seeing the Griffins again. They had shared a meal of rabbit stew and cornbread last night, but none of them had spoken of the day's parting. Some things, Abby supposed, were better felt than said. Her buoyant mood shattered, she put everything back into the metal box and returned it to its place beneath the driver's seat. Tex would have to wait.

"Oh, my my," a familiar voice clucked, interrupting Abby's painful musings, "you didn't clear up all the breakfast things by yourself, did you, dear?"

Abby forced a smile. "I wanted to do it, Aunt Winnie. I need to keep busy this morning." Abby kept the smile on her face, even as she felt her heart twist at how tired Winnie looked. Her aunt's graying brown hair seemed grayer still, the usual twinkle in her green eyes dimmed with weariness. The overland trek had proved more strenuous to Winifred Graham than Abby could have predicted. Just past fifty, Winnie had spent a lifetime minding a general store with her husband. She had never been on so much as an overnight campout before this trip.

"I want you to ride in the wagon today, Aunt Winnie," Abby said, taking her aunt's arm and gently urging her toward the front of the Conestoga. "And I won't hear any arguments. I want you fresh and rested when we get to Willow Springs, so you can help me decorate our new home."

Winnie only nodded, and Abby's worry mounted. Normally Winnie would have protested any special treatment. Each of them took turns walking during the day to spare the horses. But not today. Winnie allowed Abby to give her a hand up into the wagon box.

"Where's Uncle Ethan?" Abby asked, as her aunt

sagged into the driver's seat.

"He's still talking to Mr. Matson," Winnie said. "He wants to be certain of the directions. We're going to be all alone, you know." Winnie's gaze skittered away from Abby's, tracking nervously across the plain.

"We'll be fine," Abby assured her, "Mr. Matson can't spare a scout, but his directions were very precise." Abby had cataloged every twist and turn in the road, every landmark the wagonmaster had mentioned in his first and only instructions to her three days ago. She was certain it was only for Winnie's peace of mind that Ethan had again sought out Matson.

"It's only ten miles to the creek Mr. Matson mentioned, remember?" Abby prompted. "We'll stop for awhile, take a bath. Won't that be nice?"

Winnie nodded. "It'll be wonderful, dear."

Unable to bear Winnie's obvious apprehension any longer, Abby walked ahead a few steps, pausing beside the left side lead bay. Absently, she patted the horse's neck, her gaze tracking into the distance. She had made the right choice, hadn't she? Not only for her aunt and uncle, but for herself. She was right to come west, come to Willow Springs?

"This is all your doing, Lisa," she murmured aloud, her mouth curving into a pained smile. "You told me you knew me better than I knew myself. Well, we're surely going to find out, aren't we?"

Blond-haired, blue-eyed Lisa Montgomery had cavorted into Abby's life when they were both four years old and Lisa's family moved into the house next door on Sixth Street in Moline. Companions of mischief

34

and mirth, they had quickly proved inseparable, despite the fact that Lisa was often confined to bed with a debilitating cough. The yellow-haired moppet's sober practicality complemented perfectly Abby's oft irrepressible curiosity about the world and everything in it. They had laughed together, cried together, schemed and planned together, certain the world stood by, patient, waiting to fulfill their every whim.

How often they had hidden in the storage room of Winnie and Ethan's General Store and read lurid half-dime novels by candlelight. Tales of western desperadoes and courageous lawmen battling cruel, but noble savages had held them rapt for hours. Often they would act out the most dramatic scenes together.

Young girl imaginings of being hied off by Indians grew into adolescent tragedies of Shakespearean proportions. At fourteen Abby remembered vividly the day she'd played the part of a Comanche captive, forced to watch as her husband was staked out on an ant hill and smothered with honey. Only Abby's brilliant notion of smearing honey on the Comanches as well spared her beloved a fate worse than death.

"I hope your husband appreciated your selfless courage," Lisa said, pretending to swoon. "I wouldn't have been able to go near those bloodthirsty savages."

"It was the only way to save his life," Abby intoned solemnly. "He would have done the same for me."

They fell to the floor then, convulsed in laughter.

And then there was the time Winnie had discovered them.

Abby had been standing atop a wooden crate in the middle of the storeroom. Lisa, her willing audience, sat on a smaller box some six feet away. For the two dozenth time Abby was caught up in the fervor of *Malaeska, Indian Wife of the White Hunter,* rereading her favorite passage aloud, where the beautiful Indian girl comes across the mortally wounded Danforth, the white hunter, whom she loves with all her heart.

" 'The poor Indian girl heard the voice,' " Abby read, the back of her hand pressed dramatically against her forehead, " 'and with a cry, half of frenzied joy and half of fear, sprang to his side. She flung her child on the grass and lifted her dying husband to her heart, and kissed his damp forehead in a wild, eager agony of sorrow.' "

Lisa dabbed at the tears flowing down her cheeks. "Oh, Abby, isn't this part just so tragic! So sad!"

Abby swiped at her own tears as she reached that tenderest moment of all, when Danforth was about to die.

" 'Kiss me, Malaeska,' " she read.

" 'The request was faint as a breath of air, but Malaeska heard it. She flung herself on his bosom with a passionate burst of grief, and her lips clung to his as if they would have drawn him back from the very grave. She felt the cold lips moving beneath the despairing pressure of hers—' "

The storeroom door burst open. "Abigail Graham!" Winnie cried. "What in heaven's name are you reading?"

Abby whirled, nearly tumbling from the crate, her eyes wide with dismay. "It's . . . it's . . ." she stammered, her mind racing to seize upon something, anything that might sound plausible to Winnie, yet wouldn't be a lie.

Nothing came to her. Instead she whipped the book behind her back, even as she scrambled down from the crate. "We were . . . we were just . . ."

Winnie marched straight toward her, her normally pleasant features pinched with stern disapproval. "Hand it over. This instant."

With a sigh Abby did so.

"I sent you two in here to sweep up," Winnie said, her eyes widening with horror as she thumbed through the slim, orange paperbound book. "And this is what you spend your time doing? Reading trash?"

"We're sorry, Mrs. Graham," Lisa piped up, coughing, as she often did when she got too excited. "We won't do it again."

"I should hope not. Now get to work, the both of you. Heaven knows what extra prayers I'll have to say, knowing your young minds have been soiled by this filth."

"But it's adventure, Aunt Winnie," Abby protested. "And romance." Her eyes grew misty, as she clutched her hands to her breast. "Malaeska is such a noble savage. She—"

"Enough!" Winnie said. "I'm going to have to have a long talk with your Uncle Ethan about selling these dreaded things in the store." With that Winnie had stalked out.

"What do you think your uncle will say?" Lisa asked worriedly, her coughing subsiding a little. "Do you think he'll be as mad as your aunt?"

"He'll say boys love to read 'em, especially the boys off fightin' for the Union. It lets 'em take their mind off gettin' shot at, at least for awhile. And the books

37

make money for the store." Abby automatically patted her friend on the back to help ease her cough. She had grown used to Lisa's more delicate health, and they rarely let it interfere with any of their make-believe adventures. "And besides, if he doesn't order them, he won't be able to read them himself! Who do you think snuck me a copy of *The Prairie Rangers?*"

Both girls giggled again.

"Aunt Winnie just doesn't understand," Abby said, as she picked up the broom and began sweeping the floor. "She's never even read one of the novels. I bet if she did—"

"Oh, Abby!" Lisa interrupted. "She never would. Never!"

"Someday," Abby said firmly, "someday she will. And then she'll see for herself. Just because something is popular doesn't mean it's bad."

Abby continued sweeping, while Lisa rested.

And as always they made plans—such plans they made to see the world.

"We'll go to Paris and London and Madrid," Lisa would say, "and just for you, Abby, we'll stop off in some wild, primitive place where you can educate the noble savages and fall in love with the sheriff."

"And he'll be tall and handsome and ride a white horse," Abby sighed. "It would be ever so romantical."

When they reached sixteen and gained their teaching certificates, it mattered not a whit that they had to postpone their plans for a year or two as they made up the one oversight that had escaped them—the need for money.

And then had come another year and another. Even

when Lisa had confided her growing love for farmer Ezechiel Stone, they had never forfeited their dreams of future adventure.

In fact, it was twenty-year-old Lisa's doe-eyed mooning over farmer Stone that had prompted Abby to answer a newspaper advertisement for a school-teacher in some unheard of town called Willow Springs, Colorado. She sent them Lisa's name — partly as a prank, and partly because she hoped the idea of leaving Moline would remind her friend of the many plans they had made.

Instead, Lisa accepted Zeke's proposal, and sent a demurely worded letter of regret to the Willow Springs school board.

"If you wanted to teach in some cow town, you should have sent in your own name," Lisa sniffed, pacing back and forth in the finely appointed parlor of the Graham home.

"I didn't want either one of us to teach there," Abby said. "I wanted you to stop and think before you got married to Zeke and ruined everything."

"Well, thank you very much." Lisa's blue eyes were tinged with hurt. "I love Zeke. And I don't want to go to any cow town."

"Or London or Paris either! You never really wanted to go anywhere, did you?" Abby accused.

Lisa grew serious. "Maybe I didn't. Maybe the pretending was enough for me." She gripped Abby's hand. "But it isn't enough for you. Oh, Abby, you take the job."

"Give up my work here? Leave you and Winnie and Ethan? I couldn't!"

"But it's all you ever talked about, Abby. Or don't

39

you really want to go either?"

Abby winced, turning her back on her friend. "It's just that I have too many other responsibilities right now, that's all."

"You'll always have responsibilities, Abby," Lisa said gently. "But to me they sound like excuses. Maybe you just don't want to admit you're getting the urge to settle down yourself. I know Daniel Bergstrom's had his eye on you."

Abby rolled her eyes. "That man doesn't want a wife. He wants a brood mare! Ten sons, he told me. Ten sons to help him build up his farm." Daniel owned a prosperous acreage just across the Mississippi in Davenport, Iowa. His vision was to make it the most productive farm in the state. Whether in crops or offspring, Abby had yet to fully ascertain. "He absolutely detests my earning a salary. No wife of his would hold a job, he says. No, Lisa, being Mrs. Daniel Bergstrom is not in my future."

But Lisa had married Zeke. Soon after, he purchased some prime farmland fifty miles east of Moline. Abby and Lisa continued their friendship through a warm and delightful correspondence, writing each other three times a week. Abby continued to teach. But more and more Abby felt a growing sense of dissatisfaction, though she could discern no particular reason for it.

It was Christmas of last year when Lisa came home for what was to be her final visit. They were taking tea in the parlor, when Lisa suddenly set down her cup and faced Abby squarely. "I've been reading between the lines of your letters, Abby. You have to leave here. It's killing you to stay."

"Nonsense! I have a fine job. I love my students."

"But I can see the restlessness in you, Abby. It's always been there. With me it was more . . . I don't know, wishful thinking, I guess. I love Zeke. I love the farm and my life here." She coughed for several minutes, terrifying Abby when she seemed unable to catch her breath.

"I didn't know it had gotten so bad."

"It's difficult sometimes. But you and I have both known that it would happen some day . . ."

"No! Don't you dare talk that way. I don't even want to think of such a thing."

"That's because I'm the realist and you're the grown woman still reading dime novels."

Abby grimaced. "I have to read them. Some day I'm going to write one."

"About a noble savage and a captive schoolteacher?" Lisa teased.

"About a Texas Ranger named Tex Trueblood. He'll track down horrid outlaws and hang them from the nearest tree." She smiled slightly. "Or at least wish that he could."

Lisa laughed. "It sounds wonderful. I want to read it before you send it to the publisher."

Abby walked over to her desk and pulled out a leatherbound book. "I sent for this special," she said, caressing the hand-tooled cover. "Winnie thinks I'm writing a journal." She giggled. "But I've already written out the first three pages of my book."

Eagerly, Lisa read them, her blue eyes widening. "Tex shoots three desperadoes on the first page?"

"They shot at him," Abby insisted defensively, thinking Lisa disapproved.

"Oh, no, it's wonderful! I just wish that fourth varmint hadn't gotten away!"

"That's the one Tex has to track down the rest of the book. He killed Tex's sweetheart." Abby heaved a dramatic sigh. "Tex is heartbroken and bent on revenge. But, don't worry, he's going to meet a pretty young storekeeper's daughter, who'll help him get over his lost love."

"Anyone I know?"

Abby smiled, then grew serious. "I do so miss having you here like this. There's no one else I can even share my book with. The school board would be scandalized. And so would Aunt Winnie. And I just can't bring myself to show it to Uncle Ethan, even though I know he would understand."

It was Lisa's turn to grow quiet, then finally she said, "I know you better than anyone, maybe better than you know yourself. You may be very angry with me, but . . ." She handed the book back to Abby. "I think you should finish your book . . . in Willow Springs."

Abby blinked. "Where?"

"Willow Springs, Colorado. You remember that little town that you sent my name about a teaching position four years ago? Well, it seems they need a new teacher again. And now the worm has turned and I sent them your name."

"You didn't!"

Lisa looked a trifle smug. "They remembered me and wrote and asked for my recommendation. You can write to me every day and tell me how wonderful the journey is. Indians, road agents, handsome lawmen. It'll be just like when we were girls reading the yellowbacks."

"I can't leave here! I've told you that before—"

"If you hate it, come home. But you won't hate it, Abby. There are children there with no teacher at all. You could develop your own study program. You have to fight the board here on everything. You remember when you dared tell Daniel Bergstrom's little brother to pursue his interest in art instead of work the farm? My heavens, I thought the board would burn you at the stake."

"Daniel would have lit the match."

"He asked you to marry him, didn't he?"

"I . . . I was getting around to telling you."

"Weren't you the one who gave me several reasons about why you'd never marry him? And now you're considering it?"

"He's a practical, sensible man."

"And you're not in love with him."

"I'm twenty-four years old," Abby snapped. "It's time I got a little practical and sensible myself."

"I love being settled and comfortable." Lisa coughed again. "It's time you admitted, my dearest friend, that you don't. Stop living your life the way I live mine. We're not little girls any more. You can do what you want, Abby," an odd look came in her eyes, "I'm terrified that if you don't, you're going to turn into a bitter old woman." Lisa pulled a letter out of her reticule. "Hiram Perkins has accepted you as Willow Springs schoolteacher."

Abby took the letter, scanned its contents and shook her head. "This is impossible. I would worry about you every minute. And Winnie . . . she'd die if I left."

43

Lisa looked sad, but didn't press the issue. They had finished their visit, and did not bring up the subject again.

Lisa returned home. Abby penned her regrets to Hiram Perkins, explaining that she wouldn't be able to take the position after all. But for reasons she didn't quite understand, she resisted posting the letter, instead leaving it lying on her desk.

A week passed without a letter from Lisa. Then two weeks, then three. Abby sent off several worried missives that went unanswered. Terrified, she took a leave of absence, boarded a coach and headed east for an unannounced visit.

She found Lisa confined to bed, the once bright blue eyes glazed, her features deathly pale.

"I wanted to spare you this," Lisa said softly. "I made Zeke promise not to tell you."

"How could you not!" Abby nearly shouted. "Oh, Lisa, if you had —" The word "died" caught in her throat, as she hurried over to Lisa's bedside.

"I guess my adventure is about over, dear friend."

"No!"

"Oh, Abby, please don't grieve so. I've had a good life. I've known the love of a good man. And had the best friend any woman could ever have."

"Lisa . . ."

"I want you to promise me something."

Abby couldn't speak.

"I want you to promise you'll live your adventure. The one in Willow Springs, or whatever one you choose. Where doesn't matter, just that you do it."

"We can still make plans together, Lisa. When you get better, you and Zeke and I . . ."

44

"You can write Mr. Perkins and cancel. I know you haven't yet. Or you can accept this last gift from me, Abby. I'm giving you your adventure, the one you were forever too responsible to take, but the one you wanted in your heart more than anything."

Lisa had died three days later.

Back home Abby went through the motions of teaching. So many times something would happen and she would think to make a note so she could write about it in a letter to Lisa, and then remember Lisa was not there. In bed at night she reread Malaeska. She hurt. She cried. She remembered. And went on with her life. But the feeling of emptiness she'd been feeling for a long time now magnified, and grew impossible to ignore.

She'd all but forgotten Lisa's "gift," until she came across the letter of acceptance Lisa had left behind at Christmas. Abby's hands trembled as she read:

My dear Miss Graham,

We of the Willow Springs school board have found your credentials to be impeccable, your eight years teaching experience more than adequate, and your superbly articulate reasons for consideration of school teacher most acceptable. Your response that you would accept our offer is simply splendid. We look forward to meeting you. As promised we will provide a house for you as part of your accommodations for accepting the post. Your salary will be the $40 a month as agreed.

Abby paused, managing a wistful smile. Lisa

had gotten her a raise! Abby only made $35 a month from the Moline school district.

Our small town certainly could use your educational influence. As the town mayor, undertaker and head of the school board I will provide any and all assistance you might require upon your arrival. My precious daughter, Penelope, will be a treasured addition to your classroom. My son, Russell, will be your student as well. I'm certain the boy will come around under your firm tutelage. The other children of the town and surrounding ranches are, however, to be blunt, in desperate need of your services. We look forward eagerly to the school session ahead.

With kind regards, Hiram Perkins

A challenge. An adventure.

Lisa's legacy.

It was late spring. School was out. Abby had not yet announced her intention to return in the fall. She took a long walk along the wooded banks of the Mississippi, listening to the mournful notes of passing steamboats. It was at moments like this that she missed Lisa the most. Their quiet time to sit and talk about life, about the future.

Abby sat down under a huge cottonwood, its dark green leaves lustrous in the May sun. Dare she go through with the Willow Springs offer? She would have to decide soon. The journey would take seven to eight weeks, depending on the weather. And she would want to arrive early, meet people, get her classroom ready.

How could she leave Winnie and Ethan? They had been desperately worried about her in the weeks following Lisa's death. No doubt they were just waiting for her to accept Daniel's proposal, settle down, give them grandchildren.

Abby plucked at a foot-high blade of grass. It would be foolish to give up a sensible, practical life with Daniel Bergstrom for the sake of some childhood fantasy she should have long since outgrown.

Wouldn't it?

Her heart thudded painfully in her chest. "I'm afraid, Lisa," she said aloud. "After all the talk for all the years, I'm afraid. What if I don't have it in me to teach at this new school? What if the first rabbit that jumps out from behind a sagebrush frightens me to death? And what if there aren't any handsome sheriffs riding white horses?"

She twined the grass through her fingers, swiping at an unwelcome tear. Maybe it was just past time she grew up. With a sigh she stood, knowing that tonight at dinner she would have to give Daniel an answer. He would be put off no longer. To marry him would surely be the wise thing, the safe thing. She started back up the slope toward where she'd tied off her horse and buggy.

A breeze stirred her hair, cool, wet, coming off the river. *Take your adventure, Abby. Live it. For both of us.*

Abby stopped, looked behind her. But Lisa was not there.

Live your dreams, Abby.

To marry Daniel was to close the door forever on those dreams, dreams she had spun her entire life.

Didn't she owe herself this one chance? This one dream?

She drew in a deep lungful of air and let it out. Yes, by heaven, she did! She rushed home and tore up her letter of regret to Hiram Perkins, then quickly penned him a confirmation of her acceptance. Before any of the hundred reasons why she shouldn't go could rise to taunt her, she hurried to the post office and mailed the letter. Then she broke the news to Daniel.

"You're being a fool," the tall Swede said, his generous mouth twisted in a derisive sneer. "You'll be back inside of a month, begging me to forgive you. Then see if I'll take you back."

At least most of his anger was directed at her foolhardiness. He didn't seem in the least heartbroken that they wouldn't be married. The harder task lay ahead. She had to tell Winnie and Ethan. She caught them just as they were about to sit down for supper.

"I thought you were dining with Daniel tonight," Winnie said.

"I was, but . . ." She hesitated. "I have something important that I have to tell you."

They both looked at her expectantly, and, Abby noted to her horror, with shadings of distress in their eyes. Had Lisa told them about Willow Springs? There was no help for it now. "I've decided to leave Moline," she said quickly. "I've taken a job in Willow Springs, Colorado."

To her astonishment Winnie and Ethan both rose from their chairs and rushed over to give her a fierce hug. "How wonderful!" Ethan said, his brown eyes twinkling behind his spectacles.

Abby blinked, bewildered, and maybe just a shade

hurt. "You're not upset?"

"When you said you had an important decision to tell us," Ethan said, giving her a teasing wink, "we were terrified you were going to tell us you were going to marry Daniel Bergstrom."

Abby's mouth dropped open in astonishment. They had never said a word against Daniel. Ever. But obviously their opinion of him as husband material matched Lisa's. Abby found herself laughing hysterically.

"But what about the two of you?" she said, sobering. "I don't know if I can bear leaving you."

"And we couldn't bear it either, my dear," Winnie said. "That's why it's settled."

"What's settled?"

"We'll make out the order blanks for supplies to our new store in Willow Springs. We're going with you."

And just like that they had.

That had been seven weeks ago, and now they were only three days from the end of their journey.

The sound of men's voices snapped Abby out of her reverie. She gave the bay horse a final pat and turned to see her uncle approaching, Jeb Matson at his side. Two more different-looking men Abby couldn't imagine. Ethan was short, round, and bespectacled with a perennial twinkle in his eye and his balding pate perpetually protected by a floppy-brimmed felt hat. Jeb was tall, lean, almost gaunt, with a full beard and thick brown hair shot with gray. His fringed buckskins and wide-brimmed Stetson made him look every inch the heroic frontiersman of the Beadle novels. The sixguns he wore strapped to both thighs bespoke the danger and high adventure Abby sought between the pages of her books, but had never before encountered in person. His often dour facial expressions, she had discovered, belied a quick wit.

"We're gonna miss you around here, Miss Abby," Jeb said, doffing his hat.

"I'll miss you too, Mr. Matson."

"I never could get you to call me Jeb." The man chuckled. "I've said my good-byes to your lovely aunt and uncle, but I wanted to talk to you once, too, before you left."

"I know the directions, Mr. Matson," Abby said. "Honestly."

He chuckled again. "The three of you should be able to draw a life-size map from the times I've—" He coughed, looking abashed as his gaze slid from Abby to Winnie. "Anyways, that ain't why I come by. Remember, last week when you were inquirin' about the trail scout I knowed once who wrestled grizzlies. . . . ?"

It was Abby's turn to cough, as she watched Winnie's eyes grow wide as saucers. "You don't need to go into that right—"

"Hank Larson was his name. Bigger'n a black bear himself. Why one time—"

Abby caught Matson by the arm and propelled him away from her aunt and uncle. "I'm sorry," she supplied quickly at his perplexed look, "but you see I'm working on a . . . a special project to surprise my aunt and uncle with one day. I don't want to give it away just yet."

Matson grinned through tobacco stained teeth. "Ethan told me you was writin' a yellowback. Used to read 'em myself durin' the war and lots of times when

I was alone up in the mountains."

"Uncle Ethan knows about my book?" Abby squeaked.

"He told me you left some roughed out page of it on the counter of his store once."

Abby felt her cheeks heat. She had thought she just lost it. A valuable lesson learned, considering the miserable time she'd had re-creating the missing page. "Did he say if my aunt . . . ?" Abby couldn't finish.

Jeb allowed a slow grin. "He never told her."

Abby relaxed.

"Now about your grizzly wrestler . . ."

"He's a Texas Ranger."

"Tweren't no Texas Rangers during the time of your book, Miss Abby."

"Oh. I could move it a decade or two."

"And there's somethin' else. Not too many grizzly bears in Texas either."

Abby made a face. "Could he wrestle something else?"

"A puma, maybe. Or a rattlesnake." Matson waited a beat. "But it would make a might more sense if'n he just shot it."

Abby felt color rise in her cheeks again. Yet when she was certain Matson wasn't making fun of her, she couldn't help laughing herself. "I suppose you're right, Mr. Matson. But Tex has been disarmed at this point in my book by the villainous Jackson 'Snakeyes' Benteen."

"Then I reckon ol' Tex can wrestle whatever the heck makes him happy." His tobacco stained whiskers split into a wide grin. "I surely am going to miss you, Miss Abby."

51

"And I'm going to miss your kindness and your patience with us greenhorns. I know we made things difficult for you sometimes."

"You're a good learner, Miss Abby. You'll do fine." He stuck out his hand.

Abby grinned and accepted the handshake, the first she'd ever had in her life. "Good-bye, Mr. Matson." With that she hurried back to the wagon, carefully avoiding the teasing glint in Ethan's eyes.

"Get those grizzlies straightened out, sweetheart?"

"Yes, Uncle Ethan," Abby said primly. "Everything's just fine, thank you."

"Grizzlies," Winnie sniffed. "I do hope there aren't any between here and Willow Springs."

"I'm sure not," Abby said, climbing into the wagon box beside her aunt and uncle. Lifting the reins, Ethan clucked softly to the horses and the wagon headed away from the others.

She drew in a deep, cleansing breath, tasting the subtle scent of wildflower and sage drifting on an early morning breeze. *This is it, Lisa,* Abby thought, *for both of us.*

An eerie feeling stole over her then, and with it the sure and certain knowledge that from this point forward her life would never be the same. And that no matter how she might come to wish it, there could be no turning back.

Chapter Three

Abby guided the wagon into a stand of willows and reined the team to a halt. The terrain here was exactly as Matson had described it — from the meandering creek to the bluff that rose abruptly beyond it. She allowed herself a smug smile. Lewis and Clark could have used her. Of course, the fact that she'd followed some kind of wagon road the last five miles or so hadn't hurt any.

"Oh, it's lovely!" Winnie sighed, and Abby was pleased to hear a renewed animation in her aunt's voice. Winnie had dozed most of the day, while Ethan and Abby took turns walking beside the wagon.

They would eat supper here, but Abby knew they would have to move on before nightfall. Jeb Matson had warned them about camping too near water. All variety of creatures could come to drink at the creek tonight. But for now it would be the perfect setting for a meal of venison stew and wild onions.

A single discordant note disrupted the tranquil scene — a large bird, squawking shrilly high above them. Abby shaded her eyes and studied the angry, black slash that circled against a cobalt blue sky. She frowned.

A buzzard.

A dark-winged interloper to upstage the soothing tumble of water over rock.

"What do you make of it?" she asked her uncle, as she climbed down from the wagon box.

"Likely looking to make a meal of some poor, dead creature," he said, giving the bird no more than a passing glance.

"I do hope it isn't upwind," Winnie said, delicately testing the air. "I wouldn't want supper ruined."

"Maybe we could have buzzard pie for dessert," Ethan said, grinning.

"Ethan Graham!" Winnie huffed, "I'll not have such talk before supper."

Ethan chuckled and set about gathering wood for a fire.

"I'll fetch some fresh water," Abby said, as she helped her aunt to the ground.

"That'll be fine, dear. I'll start peeling the potatoes."

Unaccountably Abby's gaze again tracked to where the buzzard dipped and glided above them. She knew the winged beast was only serving its natural purpose, but still she found its presence unsettling.

Annoyed that she should concern herself with such superstitious nonsense, she stalked to the back of the wagon, grabbed up two buckets and headed for the creek. The grass along its banks was high and lush, and she delighted in the rainbow profusion of late summer wildflowers nestled amongst the greenery.

Dropping to her knees, Abby dipped first one, then

the other of the buckets into the softly shooshing water, then sat back, allowing herself a quiet moment to just enjoy how lovely it was here, how peaceful.

Her brows furrowed, her gaze shifting to where the road angled away from her line of vision. Had she heard something? Some sound out of sync with the gently flowing stream? She listened hard, then shook her head. She was being silly. Winnie's fretfulness about travelling alone was beginning to feed into Abby's own too fertile imagination.

Climbing to her feet, she picked up the buckets, one in each hand. She'd best get this water back before . . .

The sound came again, an odd rasping sound, that reminded Abby of nothing so much as Lisa, when she'd had trouble breathing. Not wanting to, Abby again looked skyward, a slight gasp escaping her throat. A second buzzard had joined the first.

A chill prickled along her spine and she shivered despite the day's heat.

Abby set the buckets down. Now she really was being foolish. No doubt some animal lay near death from predators or disease. Perhaps she should fetch Ethan's rifle and put the beast out of its misery, rather than let the birds feast on it while it still lived.

Turning, she walked quickly along the creek to the road. First she would have to know what and where this animal was. Lifting her skirts and stepping gingerly, she used several badger-sized stones as a pathway across the inches deep water, then hurried to the far side of the wheel-rutted road. The noise had seemed to come from this direction.

A quick glance behind her assured her Winnie and

Ethan had not yet wondered at her absence. She had no wish to worry them.

Cautiously she stepped into the waist-high weeds that grew amongst the cottonwoods bordering the road. If some animal was hurt or wounded, it might strike out at her. She took a wary step, then another, listening.

She heard only the sluicing of the water, the steady hum of insects. And the buzzards.

She took a steadying breath. Perhaps she had imagined it. Perhaps . . .

There! Straight ahead. Deep, rasping . . . *pained.*

She crept forward, hunching low, fearful of startling what she was now certain was a wounded animal. She would pinpoint its location, then go back to camp for the gun.

Low, guttural, the sound came again—this time more distinct, recognizable. A sigh? A moan? My God! That was no animal. Abby bolted forward, then stopped dead.

She had all but stepped on him.

The man lay at her feet, sprawled on his belly, his stockinged feet bare inches from her own. In the space of a heartbeat the gruesome scene seared itself in her mind, mingling details significant and superfluous—dusty denim pants, gray chambray shirt, blue bandana, and dark tousled hair thick with congealed blood. His right hand was flung forward, his fingers twined in a fistful of grass as though he'd tried and failed to lever himself up. The sleeves of his shirt were sunbleached lighter than the back, suggesting a missing vest. The pockets of his trousers were turned out. And his face! Merciful heaven, did he even have a

56

face?

Abby's hand flew to her mouth, as she tried desperately not to be sick. And failed.

Turning, she stumbled back several steps and retched into the grass. The world spun crazily and she had to sink to her knees to keep from fainting.

The man was dead. He had to be. No one could lose so much blood and still be alive. The buzzards circled to feast on the body of a dead man. Again Abby covered her mouth, taking in deep, unsteady lungfuls of air. Never in all the books she had ever read, in all the imaginings she'd ever imagined, never had the fiction prepared her for the reality of a dead human being.

Tears tracked unheeded down her cheeks, and she was suddenly ashamed. Deeply, agonizingly ashamed. And afraid. Terrified. Unlike the heroine of her book, she had no idea what to do.

"No . . . uh . . . no . . ."

Her eyes widened. The man!

Forcing her legs to move, she staggered back to him, sagging to the grass beside him. She swallowed hard, her breath coming in short, shallow gasps. "I'm sorry," she murmured. "I'm so sorry."

She wasn't even sure why she was apologizing—for his pain or for her cowardice. But it suddenly didn't matter. It only mattered that she help him.

Her fingers trembling, Abby reached toward him, fighting a resurgent nausea as her stomach reacted to the cloying scent of blood that mixed with the more tolerable smells of leather and sweat. Gently, she drew back the blood stiffened strands of his hair. She closed her eyes, a shudder of relief coursing through her. His face was covered with blood, but his features were intact.

Only then did she notice the source of the blood — an ugly, oozing hole along the side of his head. A bullet wound. She stiffened, her gaze again taking in his turned out pockets, his bootless feet. This man had been robbed!

Abby's lips thinned, indignation rippling through her. The poor man was the unfortunate victim of ruthless road agents!

"It's all right," she soothed, even knowing he couldn't hear her. "You're going to be all right."

She cast a worried look around her. Surely, whoever had done this was long gone. But she couldn't suppress a stab of fear. Bending low, she whispered, "I'll be right back. I'm going to get help."

Climbing to her feet, she raced back to camp. Her terror must have shown clearly on her face. One look at her and Ethan threw down the armful of twigs he was carrying to their already crackling campfire. In one motion he crossed to the rear of the wagon, grabbed his rifle and levered a cartridge into the chamber. "What is it, Abby?" he demanded.

"A man. He's been shot."

"Merciful heaven!" Winnie cried, the potato she'd been peeling falling from nerveless fingers. "Indians?"

"Of course not, Aunt Winnie," Abby soothed, her own fear thrumming rapidly through her veins. She wasn't at all certain whether it was or was not Indians. But right now it didn't seem to matter. "We have to hurry; he's hurt very badly."

Abby led the way, Ethan close behind. Winnie followed after them both. When Abby and her uncle reached the man, Abby crossed over to the man's left side and again sank to her knees beside him in the soft grass. Ethan remained on his feet, his gaze tracking back to where Winnie had stopped some several yards distant.

"Go back to the fire, Winnie," Ethan said firmly. "Now."

Winnie's face was ashen, her hands twisting and untwisting in the folds of her apron.

"Uncle Ethan," Abby said urgently, "please, the man—"

"Go back to the fire, Winnie," Ethan repeated, not taking his eyes from his wife.

Winnie blinked, seeming to shake herself, then took a deep breath and turned, hurrying away.

Only then did Ethan kneel beside the injured man. "He's been shot all right," he muttered, laying down his rifle and taking hold of the man's shoulders. Gently, he eased him onto his back.

The man's bloodied face lolled to one side. Despite a deep tan that spoke of a life spent outdoors, his strongly carved features were unnaturally pale beneath the dark stubble of several days' growth of beard.

"Sweet Savior," Ethan murmured. "Two bullets."

Abby tore her gaze from the stranger's face and stared in disbelief at her uncle's bloodied hand, where it had come away from the man's right side. Sudden tears burned her eyes, as she stared at the blackened hole just above the stranger's belt line. "He's going to die, isn't he?"

"That's for the Lord to decide," Ethan said. "You

and I need to tend these wounds."

Abby found comfort in her uncle's steady, no-nonsense tone. She took a deep breath. "Tell me what you want me to do."

"Get some water and find something to use for bandages."

Abby rose to her feet and hurried off to retrieve the buckets she'd left by the creek. By the time she returned, Ethan had rolled up his shirtsleeves and was in the process of untying the blue bandana from the injured man's throat. Using it as a cloth, he dipped it into one of the buckets she set beside him. According herself as much modesty as the situation allowed, Abby quickly wriggled out of one of her petticoats and began to tear it into strips.

"We'd best bind up the wound in his side first," Ethan said. "It seems to be the one that's still bleeding." With deft fingers he unbuttoned the man's shirt. But before he exposed the wound he sat back, gazing at her levelly. "I'm not sure it's proper for you to be here. Your aunt will have my hide."

Abby kept her own gaze steady. She couldn't have explained it to her uncle, but it was desperately important that she assist him. All of her life she had fantasized herself in crisis situations in which she acted heroically, and yet her first reaction to this poor man's plight had been to throw up. "I'm staying," she said quietly.

He did not object; in fact, she was almost certain she saw a warm glow of approval in his soft brown eyes before he again turned his attention to the wounded man.

Ethan lay the shirt open. Abby tried hard to concentrate on the wound, but as her uncle used the bandana to dab carefully at the six-inch gash in the man's side, Abby couldn't seem to stop her eyes from straying to the rest of the man's bare chest. A fine mat of dark hair curled across that broad expanse, then arrowed down a lean, flat stomach to disappear into the waistband of his trousers. Nor did she miss the inch-wide, four-inch-long scar that marred his flesh some three inches above his left nipple.

Abby felt her cheeks fire red hot at the boldness of her scrutiny and she had to forcibly will her attention back to the wound. The bullet had gouged out a deep furrow in the meaty part of his side, but otherwise seemed to have done no serious damage.

"Bullet passed on through," Ethan affirmed. "Should heal up pretty quick."

Abby folded up several of the strips she'd torn from her petticoat and packed them against the injury, her pulses disconcertingly reacting to where her fingertips came in contact with the man's overwarm skin. Praying her uncle didn't notice her discomfiture, Abby held the bandage in place, while Ethan wrapped several more lengths of the material around the man's middle to anchor the bandage.

"From the look of him," Ethan said, "this likely happened yesterday. No care, no water—he must be one strong young man to still be breathing." He shook his head. "We'll have to camp here for tonight. We shouldn't move him until we get some nourishment into him."

Abby thought of Jeb Matson's warnings about camping near water, but knew there was no help for it. They would just have to keep the fire built up

61

throughout the night and hope for the best.

"Think you're up to dressing that head wound?" Ethan asked, casting a worried glance toward camp.

Abby knew he was concerned about Winnie. "I'll be fine," she assured him. "You go ahead."

Ethan gave her a grateful look, then rose to his feet and started back toward camp. "After I see to Winnie," he called back, "I'll drive the wagon over and reset up our camp on this side of the creek. The man shouldn't be moved any more than necessary."

Abby nodded, then took up the blue bandana and dipped it into the second water bucket. Somehow the act of doing the work, rather than watching Ethan, had a positive effect on her nerves. She felt calmer, more confident as she cleaned and bandaged the fearsome wound and rinsed as much of the blood from the man's hair as she could. She then rebuttoned his shirt. Finishing, she sat back and surveyed her handiwork. He certainly looked much improved from when she'd first found him. Tex Trueblood's sweetheart couldn't have done better.

"You're going to be all right," she said, the words more prayer than statement. "You're going to be just fine."

Reaching over, she brushed back a straying lock of dark hair from where it spilled over the bandage. She noticed then how parched and dry his lips looked. Though the surrounding trees had no doubt provided some shade, at least part of the day he'd been exposed to the overhead sun. He probably was badly dehydrated. But how in the world could she get water into an unconscious person?

Deciding she had to try, she went back to the creek

for more water; then, using a fresh strip of petticoat she soaked it thoroughly and held it against his lips, squeezing water into his mouth a few drops at a time. She watched most of it dribble uselessly down either side of his face.

"You're not cooperating," she fretted, attempting vainly to mask the odd pain she felt at how helpless, how vulnerable he looked. Again and again she drew the cloth across his lips. Time passed, but she had little awareness of it, except to look up briefly to see the sun disappearing in a blaze of reds and purples. She was certain she'd gotten no more than half a cupful of water into him, but it was more than he'd had.

Exhausted, she sank back on her heels. Dipping her hand in what was left of the water, she splashed some over her own face. Then almost against her will, she smoothed her wet hand across his forehead, along his beard-stubbled cheeks, again speaking soft words of encouragement. She found herself wondering who he was, where he was from, what business he'd been on when he was ambushed. Perhaps he was a nearby rancher, or a townsman. Heaven knew, she could tell precious little from his attire. He dressed the way she'd seen dozens of range riders dress since they'd left home.

He could be married, have children. Abby thought of a woman alone somewhere frantic with worry. Was he late coming home? Had a search party already been organized?

"How's he doing?"

Startled, Abby looked up to see her uncle standing next to her. She'd been so absorbed in her musings about the stranger that she hadn't even heard his approach. He'd driven the Conestoga to this side of the creek, setting up a new camp barely thirty feet from where she sat. "No change," she managed. "How's Aunt Winnie?"

"She'll be fine. Just the shock, that's all."

The lightness in her uncle's voice seemed forced, but Abby supposed he just didn't want to worry her.

"After I get the fire started," he went on, "I'll bring a blanket. We can slide it under him, use it to pull him closer to camp."

Abby nodded, settling down to wait, never taking her eyes from the sometimes ragged rise and fall of the man's chest. It was almost as though some part of her believed that as long as she kept watching, the man by some unspoken agreement would have to keep breathing.

A half hour later Ethan returned with the blanket. It was now full dark. Together she and her uncle eased the woolen blanket beneath the man's dead weight. He didn't stir, didn't even moan.

Abby started to lever herself up, so that she could help drag him, when suddenly her finger snagged on something hidden in the flattened grasses. She let out a pained yelp, sticking the finger in her mouth and tasting her own blood. Scowling, she reached down and picked up the offending object, examining it as much by feel as by the light of the fire some fifteen feet away.

"A badge," she said. "Uncle Ethan, look! It's a badge. This man's a lawman!"

"We can see it better by the fire. Come on, let's get him over there."

Quickly, Abby and her uncle maneuvered the stranger to within four feet of the flames. As Abby got him resettled, Ethan squinted closely at the misshapen metal. "Special Deputy," he read aloud. He then hunkered down to examine the man's shirtfront.

"What are you looking for?"

"Pin holes. A tear, something to show it was torn off him."

"He could've been wearing it on a vest." She explained the mismatched shadings in the shirt's color.

Ethan nodded, handing the badge back to her. "Maybe he was trailing the vermin that did this to him."

A lawman. Abby stared wonderingly at the darkhaired stranger. She had rescued a lawman. *Oh, Lisa,* she thought, *even Beadle and Adams wouldn't believe this one.* She bit her lip. Dark hair, a little over six feet tall, lean build . . . What color were his eyes, she wondered, unconsciously reaching one hand forward. Tex Trueblood's were—

"How's he doing, dear?"

Abby jumped, startled, her hand jerking back to her lap. "I . . . I didn't hear you coming, Aunt Winnie."

"I've been standing right here by the fire for ten minutes, heating the broth I'm making for the gentleman."

"I . . . I, well . . ." *Get hold of yourself, Abby.* She scrambled hastily to her feet, smoothing at her skirts. "I should probably spoon some out now, let it cool."

"Are you all right, dear?" Winnie said, catching Abby's wrist with one hand, while pressing her other lightly against Abby's forehead. "I do hope this hasn't

65

been too much for you. That you're not going to come down sick yourself."

"No, of course not."

"Maybe Ethan should sit with him for awhile."

"No! I mean, that won't be necessary. I'm fine, really." Abby picked up a tin cup and dipped it into the broth. "There. It'll start cooling." She turned back and again knelt beside the stranger.

Stranger. "I wish I had a name to call you," Abby said, not realizing she'd spoken aloud, until her aunt said, "Name or no name, if he doesn't wake by the time we reach Willow Springs, we're going to have to decide what to do with him."

"Take him in, of course," Abby said, as though the matter required no further thought.

"Abby . . ." Her aunt assumed a stiff, formal posture Abby knew too well. "You're an unmarried schoolteacher in a new town with new people. You have a reputation to consider."

"But you and Ethan would be there. You're not suggesting we turn him over to strangers."

"*He's* a stranger," Winnie said reasonably.

"But . . ."

"Now, now," Ethan interrupted, rising from the chair he'd set out for himself on the opposite side of the fire, "this is all a little premature. The first thing we'll do is get this man to a doctor, then let the doctor decide what's best."

Abby couldn't argue with that. Nor could Winnie.

"It's getting late," Ethan went on. "Come on, Winnie. We've got another long day ahead of us tomorrow. Longer even than today, if we try to push for town to get this man some medical attention."

Winnie did not protest as he guided her to the back of the wagon, then gave her a hand up inside. To Abby he said, "Call out if you need anything."

"I will." Abby made a point to spread out her blankets as usual under the wagon, but once she heard no further sounds from its interior, she quickly returned to the injured man's side.

Hugging her blankets around her like a shawl, she scooted close to him, touching the back of her fingers to his forehead. At least he had no fever to speak of. Not yet, anyway.

"You need a shave, you know that?" Maybe she would ask Ethan to do the honors in the morning. Surely it would make the man more comfortable not to have all that prickly stubble. Then she found herself envisioning what it would be like to do the honors herself.

She closed her eyes. She really had to call a halt to her more fanciful notions.

But then the whole situation had already gone well beyond fanciful. Here she was, Abigail Graham, schoolteacher and aspiring novelist, sitting next to a campfire in the middle of the Colorado plains caring for a wounded lawman.

"What color *are* your eyes?" she whispered. Brown? Blue? Tex Trueblood's were brown, a warm, trustworthy brown.

As though he could read her thoughts, his eyes fluttered open briefly. Abby leaned close, but in the dimness of the light, she could tell nothing about their color. "Sir?" she called, gently shaking his shoulder. "Sir, can you hear me?"

His eyes drifted closed once again.

"You're safe. You're among friends."

He made no response.

The night wore on, and Abby huddled deeper into her blankets, though she did not sleep. When the man shivered, she checked his hands beneath his blankets and found them cold. Quickly, she brought out another blanket. When he shivered again, she added her own.

Rubbing her arms, she moved closer to the fire, tossing fresh sticks into the flames. The man moaned softly, hunching his shoulders as though still trying to warm himself.

She touched his forehead. He was so cold. She had no more blankets.

"You can't do this," she said fiercely. "I want to know who you are. I want to know your name."

He only shivered more, his teeth chattering. She glanced toward the wagon, then at the man. There was no help for it. Taking a deep breath to fortify her courage, Abby lifted the blankets and settled herself next to him. The warmth of her own body was all she had left to give him. She would lie here, just for a little while, just long enough to help him stop shivering.

Her heart hammered. Never in her life had she experienced the feel of a man's body pressed against her own. As the minutes passed and she relaxed a little, she grew oddly more accustomed to it. And then she felt her body fire with embarrassment at the thought.

She grimaced. At least if she kept thinking these outrageous thoughts, she would have no trouble keeping both of them warm until morning. Reaching over, she touched her fingers to the pulse point in his neck. It felt stronger, steadier. His skin felt warmer.

"We'll take you to town," she said, speaking as though he could understand her every word, "and when you wake up you can give the sheriff a description of the desperadoes who did this to you." She had no doubt that whoever was in charge of law enforcement in Willow Springs would want to be on the trail of the beasts as soon as possible.

"No . . . uh . . . no . . ."

"It's all right." Abby tugged the blankets up under his chin. "You're safe now. It's all right."

"Can't . . . where . . . ?" He was making no sense.

"You're with friends," she said, more slowly, distinctly. "The bandit who shot you is gone. You're safe."

"Safe." He repeated the word and her hopes soared. He understood! He seemed then to try to raise his right hand, perhaps instinctively to examine the wound on his head. But her body's position prevented the movement. He didn't struggle, letting the hand relax between them.

In his sleep he shifted toward her. An odd tightness squeezed her heart at the boyish trust threading his voice as he nuzzled his head into the crook of her arm, again murmuring, "Safe."

Chapter 4

Abby struggled to open her eyes, resisting the urge to snuggle deeper beneath her blankets. For once the night chill hadn't seemed to permeate her bones. She wondered at the strange pre-dawn warmth, then stilled, remembering. She was warm beneath these blankets, because she was not alone.

Swallowing convulsively she scrambled to her feet, instinctively clutching the blankets to her bosom, even though she was fully clothed. Good heavens, she hadn't meant to fall asleep with the man! She'd only meant to stay with him until he was resting peacefully. Instead she had spent the entire night with him.

Her gaze shot toward the wagon. No one stirred. Abby let out a shaky sigh. Winnie and Ethan had retired well before she did. If she rose quickly, they would never have to know how badly she'd compromised herself. Not that they wouldn't understand, but there was no reason to distress them unnecessarily.

She looked again at the man at her feet, her cheeks flushing hotly. She was even more grateful that the stranger would never know. Lowering herself to her knees, she pulled the blankets up under his chin. He was so quiet. A sudden terror spiked through her. Too quiet. She yanked the blankets back, tugging open his shirt and placing her hand against his chest. She only relaxed when she felt the steady beat of his heart beneath her palm.

She should have pulled her hand back then, but felt a strange reluctance. An odd sense of reassurance pulsed through her at the life-affirming heat of his flesh. Never in her life had she touched a man so intimately.

In fact, only once before had she ever even seen a man's naked chest, and that was that infernal rapscallion Vernon Tawkey back home. Some years ago Vernon, then twenty-one and the youngest son of a Moline barber, had joked with his friends that he would ride through town bareback on the Fourth of July. No one thought anything of it, until he did precisely that. No only barebacked, but buck naked! The sheriff had arrested him for public drunkenness and indecent exposure.

All Abby remembered at the impressionable age of fifteen was being wretchedly disappointed at Vernon's spindly physique. She and Lisa had risked Winnie's considerable wrath to catch a glimpse of the errant Vernon. And neither one of them had been in the least impressed.

Abby's gaze skated again to the stranger. No, Vernon Tawkey looked nothing at all like this.

Mortified, she jerked her hand away. What was happening to her? She must have spent too much time in the sun yesterday.

The man groaned, and she all but leaped out of her

skin. Her breathing returned to normal only when she saw that he showed no signs of consciousness. He shifted slightly, as though again seeking her warmth.

Abruptly, Abby stood. She needed to build up the fire, get breakfast started, try again to get some nourishment into him.

She crossed to the wagon, pausing at the ledge beside the water barrel, where Winnie always left the skillet from the night before. Gathering everything she needed, Abby quickly got a breakfast going of bacon and cornbread. The familiarity of the everyday task calmed her a little, gave her a chance to recover from what she was now certain had been unforgivably scandalous behavior. No matter how cold the man had been last night, surely she could have thought of some other way to warm him.

But even now, as she stirred the sizzling bacon in the skillet, inhaled the invigorating aroma of brewing coffee, she could think of no effective alternative.

Sounds from the back of the wagon caught her attention. Winnie and Ethan were awake. Abby schooled her features into a carefully controlled mask. She could give away none of her inner turmoil to her aunt and uncle.

"Sleep well, dear?" Winnie asked, climbing down from the wagon and coming over to help with the cornbread.

"Just fine," Abby said, amazed at how matter of fact she sounded.

"And the gentleman?"

"No change."

Ethan ambled over to join them, tucking in his shirttail and adjusting his suspenders as he did so.

"Coffee ready?"

Abby nodded.

Ethan poured himself a cup. "We'd best eat, then get our patient into the wagon. If we start now, we just might make town before nightfall."

Abby ate hurriedly, tasting nothing. While her aunt and uncle broke camp, Abby tried and failed to get more broth into the wounded man. If anything, he was even more pale than he'd been yesterday. And considerably weaker. Two days without food, if Ethan's guess on the timing of the attack was correct. And very little water.

She touched the back of her hand to his forehead. Night chills had given way to fever.

He moaned then, his lips moving to form words she couldn't understand, syllables, fragments, nothing that made any sense. She bent low over him, straining to catch anything even vaguely coherent.

"Your name," she said, over and over. "Tell me your name." At least then she would have something useful to supply whoever was in charge of law enforcement in Willow Springs. The man's loved ones could be notified.

Though she couldn't be certain he was responding to her, or just thinking about going after the brigands who had attacked him, he mumbled a single, identifiable word. "Chase."

Her brows furrowed. Chase. It could be a name; it could be a random thought. But she found she liked the sound of it. If it was his name, it was a good one.

"Chase," she said, testing it aloud and liking it even better. She wasn't certain, but he'd seemed to turn toward her when she said it. She smiled. "Chase it is."

Ethan came over and hunkered down beside her. She told him about the name. Ethan shrugged. "Good as any, I guess." He laid a hand on Chase's forehead and grimaced.

"I felt it too," Abby said, unable to keep the anxiety out of her voice.

"Likely be delirious most of the day." Ethan looked at her, his eyes grave. "We're doing all we can, you know that, don't you?"

She nodded, though her heart thudded painfully against her ribs. Her uncle was by nature an optimist. If Chase's chances for survival were as bleak as Ethan looked. . . . Abby refused to finish the thought. Instead she rose to her feet. She would concentrate on the task at hand—getting Chase into the wagon.

It took the combined efforts of all three of them but within a few minutes they'd managed to settle him atop the freshly made up mattress that served as Ethan and Winnie's bed.

"I never knew an unconscious human being could be so heavy," Winnie said, sagging onto a trunk lid opposite the makeshift bed that was itself positioned atop several trunks full of things they'd brought west for their new home.

"Better check his wounds, Abby," Ethan said. "See that they didn't start bleeding again. I'll hitch up the team."

Abby quickly checked both of Chase's bandages, grateful to discover that neither wound had broken open. Still, he remained deathly pale. "I'm going to help Uncle Ethan with the horses, Aunt Winnie. The sooner we get started, the sooner we'll get to Willow Springs. Will you stay in the wagon? Sit with him?"

She gestured toward Chase.

A flicker of apprehension skittered across her aunt's features. Abby frowned. But then Winnie seemed to shake herself, according Chase a look that seemed at once oddly tender, yet pained. "Of course, dear."

Abby's frown deepened. "Are you all right, Aunt Winnie?"

"I'm fine, dear. You go ahead."

Instead Abby sat beside her aunt. "You haven't seemed quite yourself since we found this man. I know the blood upset you, but there's something else, isn't there?"

"It's nothing. Really."

Whatever it was, Winnie was obviously determined to keep it to herself, at least for now. And Abby had no time to press her. With a sigh she rose and went out to help her uncle. She almost asked Ethan about it, but knew instinctively he would shrug it off. Yet surely there was more to Winnie's mood than simple distaste for the sight of blood.

"You're being fanciful again," Abby muttered under her breath, as she helped Ethan settle the team in its traces. Finding Chase had put her imagination on overload. She had to be wary of making a tense situation worse by creating problems that didn't exist.

When they'd finished readying the horses, Ethan climbed into the driver's seat. Winnie joined him, while Abby took her aunt's place at Chase's bedside. As the wagon lurched into motion, Abby dipped a cloth into a bucket of fresh water, then ran it across Chase's overwarm forehead. "Hang on," she murmured. "We're going to get you to a doctor. Please,

75

hang on."

The miles rumbled by, but there was no change in him. At the nooning they didn't bother taking the time to build a fire, instead settling for a quick lunch of water and jerked beef. While Winnie and Ethan stretched their legs, Abby spent most of the brief respite trying to get more water into Chase.

"We'll be off again in a few minutes," Ethan said, climbing in beside her. "How's he doing?"

"His fever's higher." She hesitated, then asked, "I know this seems frivolous, but do you think shaving him would make him feel any cooler?"

Ethan stroked his chin thoughtfully. "Might. I never liked a beard in the summertime. I'll get a lather ready."

In minutes Ethan had a mugful of frothy soap that he applied to Chase's whiskers with a brush. He then pulled his straight-edged razor free of its leather holder. Settling himself beside the unconscious man, he tilted Chase's head to one side and positioned his razor above one lathered cheek. He was interrupted by Winnie's shrill call and the thunder of approaching hoofbeats.

"Did you hear me?" Winnie jerked aside the canvas flap at the back of the wagon. "Someone's coming! A stagecoach, I think."

Ethan handed the razor to Abby. "Maybe there's someone aboard the stage who could help." He hopped down to join Winnie.

Abby gripped the razor, wondering if she should wait for Ethan's return. But to do so, she reasoned, would allow the soap to dry out. Swallowing nervously, she positioned the razor carefully alongside

76

Chase's cheek. "You've already lost enough blood," she said, "you don't have to bother to shed any more, all right?"

After the first few awkward strokes, during which she scraped away far more soap than whiskers, she fell into a rhythm and soon removed the dark stubble. Wetting a towel she dabbed off the remaining soap, then scrutinized her first foray into barbering. Aside from the two tiny nicks just below his left jawline, she was relieved to see he'd survived her ministrations intact. And though it was likely only wishful thinking, he seemed to be resting more comfortably, too.

As she sat there, the finely sculpted lines of his face now clearly visible for the first time, she couldn't help but admire his looks. "Oh my, Chase," she said softly, her heart seeming to skip a beat, "you are most certainly a handsome man."

She was glad for the distraction of the stage pulling to a halt alongside the wagon. Above the creak of thoroughbraces and the stamp of hooves, she could hear her aunt and uncle exchanging greetings with someone. Abby stuck her head out in time to see a mountain-sized man in trail-stained clothing climb down from the driver's boot.

"Name's Hank Griswold," he said, catching her eye and tipping his equally trail-stained hat. He extended his right hand toward Ethan. "Where you pilgrims headed?"

Ethan accepted the handshake. "Willow Springs."

"Me, too," Griswold said. "No passengers this trip, though. Just the mail."

"We have a wounded man inside," Abby said, gesturing toward the wagon. "We found him near the creek about eight miles back."

Griswold's bushy eyebrows knitted together with sudden keen interest. "We had us a robbery there day before yesterday. I wasn't drivin', but a friend of mine was. Mind if I take a look?"

"Please do," Abby said. "Maybe you'll recognize him. He had no identification. Nothing."

Griswold hefted his great bulk into the wagon, emerging seconds later shaking his head. "Never seen him before. But it seems likely he got himself ambushed by the same bunch that robbed the stage."

"He's a lawman of some sort." Abby showed Griswold the badge she'd found near Chase.

"Maybe he was on their trail. Rumor hereabouts is that it was Cordell and his gang."

"Cordell?" Ethan queried.

"Gunfighter, thief." Griswold spat a wad of tobacco juice into the dirt. "Murderer, too, if you believe some you hear."

Abby shuddered. To think that Chase may have gone up against an entire gang of outlaws alone. "We're taking him to the doctor in Willow Springs."

"Ain't no doctor in the Springs, miss. None closer than Denver or Cheyenne. Take your pick, seventy-five miles south or north."

"But that can't be!" Abby gasped. "He could never survive such a trip! Surely someone in Willow Springs can help."

The man scratched at his whiskers. "I've heard tell of ol' Ezra down at the Silver Nugget pullin' a bullet or two outta cardsharps caught bottom dealin'."

Abby's hopes sank. A saloonkeeper was hardly her idea of a qualified physician.

"Is there some sort of boarding house?" Winnie asked. "Someone who could take him in?"

"Hotel, but a bachelor fella runs it. Widow Baines at the Baines House is on the far side of ninety, and she takes a nip now and then. She might forget he was there for a week or two."

"We can take care of him," Abby asserted. With the dearth of help available in Willow Springs, she saw no other choice. Just how primitive was this town she had chosen for her long-postponed "adventure"?

"Abby . . ." Winnie began, then stopped. She was obviously not going to discuss the relative wisdom of taking care of the man indefinitely, at least not in front of the stage driver.

"I'll tell Sheriff Devlin you folks'll be comin' in." Griswold climbed back into the boot.

"We appreciate that, Mr. Griswold," Abby said.

Griswold grinned through tobacco stained teeth. "My pleasure, little lady." He tipped his hat toward Abby and Winnie both. "You folks take care now!" With that he cracked his whip, setting his six-horse team in motion once again.

"Quite a character," Ethan commented, but Abby was already clambering back into the wagon.

No doctor. What in heaven's name were they going to do? She pressed her hand to Chase's brow. Even in the past few minutes his fever had spiked higher. She closed her eyes, fighting a surge of panic. "Please, God," she murmured, "please, God, help me know what to do."

Chase's head lolled from side to side. "Kill . . . no . . . Uh . . . no . . ."

Her heart twisted. The man had pleaded for his

life, pleaded with his assailants not to kill him.

"You're going to be all right," she said fervently, running the dampened cloth across his face. "Do you hear me? You're going to be all right."

The wagon rumbled forward.

"Hot." Chase licked his lips, his chest heaving.

She had to get the fever down. Somehow, some way she had to get it down. "Propriety be damned," she muttered, opening his shirt and running the cloth along his upper chest as well.

"Wa-ter . . ."

Abby blinked back tears, squeezing as much of the precious moisture into his mouth as he would take. And as he had done before, he seemed to relax under her hand, his ragged breathing easing, if only a little. But she could not suppress her growing terror that nothing she could do was enough. That he was dying.

Chase was on fire. Noah Gantry stood directly in front of him upending a canteen. Chase watched the lifesaving water mingle with the dirt. Hot . . . so damned hot . . . he was burning up. Noah threw back his head and laughed.

"Kill . . . no . . . uh . . ." Hate fired deep in Chase's vitals. "Kill Noah."

Chapter Five

The pain . . . the pain . . . Chase curled his body inward trying to escape the pain. He heard words, far away, but could make no sense of them. Nothing could penetrate the pain, except more pain. His father was beating him again. . . .

Chase was nine years old and Clete Cordell was roaring drunk. But then the curious thing would have been for Clete to be sober. Chase had never seen his father sober.

Trembling, Chase shrank back farther into the shadowed corner of the rat-infested room in the squalid El Paso boarding house. If he was quiet, really quiet, maybe Clete wouldn't find him this time.

A string of obscenities spewed from the mouth of the hulking figure in the middle of the room. Clete Cordell staggered nearer the corner in which Chase was trying so desperately to hide.

Bloodshot eyes squinted through tufts of straggling salt and pepper hair. "Where are you, boy?" the man bellowed, spittle dribbling unnoticed on his bearded chin. "You come when I call you, you hear? Lazy, good-for-nothin' brat. I'm your pa and you'll do whatever the hell I tell you, unnerstan'?" The words slurred together.

Chase hunkered down lower, feeling for all the world like a mouse cornered by a rabid cougar. Things had never been good for Clete Cordell, but overnight they had gotten considerably worse. Rosa was gone. And Clete was drunker than Chase had ever seen him. Meaner than Chase had ever seen him.

Rosa Velasquez had put up with Clete's drunken rages for nearly two years, but last night had been the end of it. Last night Clete had taken a belt to Angela, Rosa's seven-year-old daughter.

Chase had awakened at midnight to the sounds of their leaving. He'd begged Rosa to take him with her. He'd begged her.

"I'm so sorry, *niño*," Rosa had said, giving him a kiss on his cheek. "But your padre would follow us, if I did that. I do not wish to see him ever again."

"But I love you! I love Angela! She's like my sister! Pa would never follow you. He hates me!"

"I cannot take that chance, *niño*. Forgive me."

Chase had gripped her plump arm with all the strength he possessed, but in the end it had not been enough. With Angela clinging fearfully to her mother's skirts, Rosa had disappeared into the night.

Angrily, Chase swiped at the tears scalding his cheeks. He had to learn to stop being such a crybaby. After all, he should be used to being left behind. His own mother had abandoned him when she'd deserted Clete seven years ago.

She hadn't wanted him was the only conclusion that seemed to fit. At two years old, Chase couldn't have taken up too much room, or eaten too much. She hadn't wanted him, so she left him with a father who didn't have much use for him either.

Now Rosa was gone, and Chase was again left to bear Clete's wrath alone.

"Worthless bitch!" Clete roared to the four walls. "Does she think I can't get a half dozen just like her down at the El Diablo? Stinkin' whore! Who needs her and her whiny little bastard?"

I need her, Chase thought, but made no sound.

"I'm warnin' you, Charley!" Clete snarled.

Chase winced. God, how he detested the sound of his own name.

"I'll give you two seconds to get out where I can see you, boy. You don't, and when I get my hands on you, you'll wish you'd never been born."

Chase already wished that a dozen times over. He didn't move.

"Come on, boy." Clete's voice took on a wheedling tone. "I won't hurt ya. I was only funnin'. Come on. I want you to go down to the Diablo and pick me up a pint." He scratched his crotch. "I'm gettin' a powerful thirst. You can even keep a nickel for yourself."

Chase wasn't fooled. He'd heard that one before. He'd only had to fall for it once. Clete was either too drunk or too stupid or both that he didn't know he used the same story over and over.

His father unbuckled his belt. "You'd best get out here," he gritted. "Now!"

Chase looked longingly toward the door just six steps from where he cowered in the shadows, but those steps would take him within Clete's drunken grasp.

83

Clete lurched toward the table nearest Chase. Using it as a crutch to keep his swaying body on its feet, Clete inched toward the room's corner. Whether he saw him or not, Chase didn't know. But he dared not take the chance. Swallowing nervously, he edged away from the shadows. He didn't see the overturned tin cup on the floor, not until he'd accidentally kicked it, sending it clattering halfway across the room.

With a roar Clete lunged toward the sound. "Gotcha, you little guttersnipe!"

Chase bolted for the door. He would have made it if Clete hadn't stumbled, inadvertently throwing himself bodylong in Chase's path. With a curse the man gripped Chase by the hair and yanked him savagely back.

"When I tell you somethin', I expect you to listen. I'm your pa, and you'll do what I say." Each word was punctuated by a blow from the belt.

Somehow Chase tore free and streaked for the door. He threw it open, whirling only long enough to shriek, "I hate you! I hate you! I wish you were dead!" And then he was gone.

He stayed away five days that time, until the sheriff caught him sneaking food from the trash behind a cantina. "Don't take me back there, Sheriff Hines. Please, don't."

"It's there or the workhouse," the gruff-voiced lawman said, holding him by the scruff of the neck. "Take your pick, Charley."

"Don't call me that! I hate it. That's what *he* calls me, and I won't go by anything he calls me." Chase struggled to break free of the sheriff's grip. "Take me anywhere, but don't take me back to him."

The sheriff hadn't listened, depositing him back at the tumbledown boarding house. Chase went in only because he could see that his father was unconscious, lying in his own waste on a filthy pallet in the middle of the floor. He seemed not to have moved in the five days Chase had been gone.

His empty stomach overruling his better sense, Chase made himself a meal of stale bread and beans, jumping when a voice slurred, "Get me a drink, boy."

Chase hesitated a moment, then did so, handing his father a half empty bottle of tequila.

"Good boy. That's a good boy. Be nice to your old pa." Clete raised the bottle to his lips and drank deeply, then lurched to his feet. "I'll be gone for a little while. You take care of the place, hear?"

Watching him leave, Chase guessed Clete's "little while" would likely last for a week or more, as he scoured the town looking for a woman fool enough to share a bottle and a bed.

Chase picked up a piece of harness he'd started to work last week before Rosa left. When he finished, Mr. Aston down at the smithy's would pay him two bits. He would use the money to buy food for himself and his father.

He would try to be good, try to be extra good. Even though he knew being good didn't make much difference. He had learned that lesson only too well.

He was five years old the time Clete had taken him to a parsonage and dumped him off. A church couple took him in. They didn't have any children, and they so wanted a son. He was like a gift from God, they said. They were kind to him. They didn't beat him, and Chase had been the very best boy he knew how to be. But then the man and woman had a baby of their own and they brought him back. He was six years old, and he never forgot the acid pain of it.

Clete Cordell had not been pleased to get his son back. But the parson had made it clear that Clete would be in jail if he didn't own up to his responsibility. For a time things had been tolerable. And then Clete had lost another job. And blamed Chase.

"It's havin' a brat around that's kept me from bein' a success in my life. Always havin' to look after you. If I didn't have a good-for-nothin' whelp to worry about, I could've been somebody. Now get me another drink, boy."

Hot, so damned hot. Chase couldn't breathe. Something cool on his forehead. Words, soft, gentle. Hurt, hurt so damned much. Hurt . . .

Chase was six days shy of this thirteenth birthday, when his old man beat him for the last time. In between blows with the belt, Chase had curled his fingers into a fist and slugged Clete Cordell full in the face. Then Chase ran out the door. This time he never stopped running.

Drifting north and east, on foot and at times by hitching a ride with some passing traveller, Chase stayed alive over the next two years by doing chores, earning a few coins here and there, and making do with other people's leavings. He never stole anything. Not once.

Along the countryside, he heard vague rumblings that some sort of war had broken out, that the South had seceded from the Union. But it meant nothing to him. Sometimes a whole week would pass, though, when he met no travellers on the open road. Days punctuated by distant, sporadic gunfire became the norm, rather than the exception.

It was a cold, wet three-day spring rain that spawned the end of his self-imposed isolation. It had been nearly a week since he'd eaten anything. Exhausted, he stumbled upon a small rebel infantry patrol. They took pity on him, fed him, then took him to their commanding officer. "Major Murdock'll know what to do with ya, boy," a gaunt-faced corporal had said, delivering Chase to a rain-spattered gray canvas tent set back a half mile from the main battle line.

"I thank you for the food," Chase said, "but maybe I'd best be on my way." He was almost choking on the fear that this officer would somehow have the authority to send him back to his father.

The corporal jerked a thumb toward the tent. "Inside, boy. Now."

Chase brushed aside the entryflap and ducked into the tent. He stood there, shivering but defiant, staring at the ramrod straight back of a silver-haired Confederate major. It didn't matter what this man said. No one could send him back to Clete Cordell. Not ever again. The officer turned then, and Chase took an unconscious step back from the kindest eyes he had ever seen.

"Corporal Willoughby tells me you're a Texan." Major Quinton Murdock's voice was as mellow as rich cream, his accent a smooth Virginia drawl.

"El Pa—" Chase cut himself off. He wasn't going to make this easy for Murdock. The man might look friendly, but Chase had long since learned to trust no one.

"Want to tell me how you come to be in Tennessee?"

"I walked," he said warily. What was Murdock getting at? What did he want?

"How old are you, boy?"

"Eighteen," Chase lied.

"Why do I think fourteen would be closer to the truth?"

"I wouldn't know, *sir*." He mouthed the military formality with a defensive belligerence.

"Are your parents living?"

Chase bristled. "My pa is." He said nothing about his mother, long considering her dead.

"What if I sent word to your father and asked him how old you are?"

"He wouldn't answer, sir. He can't read. Not that he'd give a damn what I was doing anyway. Maybe he's dead."

If Murdock felt any censure toward the callousness of Chase's words, it didn't show in those eyes. "What's your name, boy?"

"Cordell, sir."

"That's it? Cordell?"

"That's it, sir."

Murdock walked behind a map-laden rectangular table and seated himself in a straight-backed chair. "How would you like to run dispatches for me, Cordell?"

Chase's eyes narrowed. "Sir?"

"You heard me."

"Would I get a uniform, sir?"

"You would."

Chase bit his lip. He wasn't sure where Murdock was headed with all this, but it was suddenly more than a little tempting. "What about food?" More and more of the farms he encountered these days were deserted, or run by women barely scraping together enough to feed their children.

"You'd get rations every day, Cordell."

"Then I'll do it, sir."

Murdock suppressed a smile. "Glad to hear it." He handed a leather pouch to Chase. "This is your first assignment, Private Cordell."

Chase felt a surge of pleasure at his new military title, a strange sense of belonging, which he tried without success to shake off. He listened intently as Murdock continued, "I need you to take a message to our supply headquarters." Murdock scowled. "That's currently six railcars on a spur outside of Nashville. Anyway, that train's got the food and ammunition I've been waitin' for for two weeks. Maybe my friendly little reminder," he pointed to the pouch, "will get those pencil pushin' supply officers off of their fat duffs and get my troops some bullets to fight this war. You got all that?"

"Yes, sir."

"Good, boy. Now have Willoughby fix you up with a uniform and a horse and be off with ya."

"Yes, sir." Chase turned to leave.

"Cordell . . . ?"

Chase paused. "Yes, sir?"

"Watch yourself out there."

Chase hurried away, eager to reach the supply train, hoping somewhere along the line there would be an extra meal in it for him. Within three hours he'd returned with a reply for Murdock. The major perused the missive then cocked an eyebrow at Chase.

"Good work, Cordell. We'll have what we need by morning. Maybe you'd like to be my official courier."

"Maybe I would, sir." Chase didn't want Murdock to think him too eager. He still didn't trust the man, but he was willing to transport his messages if it meant three meals a day.

Murdock stepped close, reaching out as though to touch Chase's shoulder. Chase instinctively flinched away. When he saw that Murdock meant him no harm, he coughed nervously, pretending to have stumbled. "Rock, sir," he said, pointing vaguely toward the ground.

"Of course." Murdock crossed to the table and rummaged through his haversack, pulling free a small wrapped bundle. He broke off a piece of a crumbly, whitish substance and handed some to Chase.

Chase accepted it, frowning. "What is it, sir?"

Murdock chuckled. "A praline, soldier."

"Sir?"

"Candy. You eat it."

Chase bit into the confection and chewed thoughtfully for several seconds, thoroughly enjoying the sweet taste though he allowed Murdock only a grudging, "Thanks."

The major snorted. "You're welcome." He handed Chase another dispatch. "Think you're up to it?"

"Yes, sir."

Murdock's gaze grew curious. "I get the feeling life hasn't always been kind to you, Private."

"My life ain't your concern, sir."

Murdock took on such a knowing look that Chase squirmed inwardly. It was almost as if the man could see inside him, see him for what he was. But the man said only, "I need an answer back on that dispatch before nightfall."

"Yes, sir."

Over the weeks that followed Chase stayed on as Murdock's messenger. During that time the South seemed to be making headway against the Army of the Potomac. But later, after word of Gettysburg came down, the rebel forces grew more and more chaotic. All around him now—awake or asleep—Chase heard the thunder of cannonfire, the roar of muskets, the agonized screams of the wounded and dying.

But through it all, somehow, Murdock's forces held together, moving on toward Virginia, digging in, gaining ground a bloody inch at a time. More than once Chase thought of bolting, heading west away from the war any way he could. He'd never officially enlisted, after all. But each time he thought of it, he thought of Murdock, and somehow he stayed. He never quite allowed himself to reason out why he stayed, but he stayed.

"This isn't the answer I sent for, Cordell," Murdock told him one morning, handing Chase back a message he'd just delivered.

"It was the one Colonel Reardon gave me, sir."

"This is the one I *sent* to Colonel Reardon, Private."

Chase flushed. "Oh."

"Read it to me."

Chase backed up a step. "What, sir?"

"I said read it to me," Murdock repeated levelly.

Chase felt the blood rise hot in his cheeks.

"All these weeks, you never said a word." Murdock

slammed a fist down on the table. "You can't read, can you, boy?"

Chase stiffened. "A lot of men can't read, sir."

"But men who want to make something of their lives learn."

"My father never much bothered about sending me to school." Damn, Chase hated how defensive he sounded. He'd never cared much one way or the other about being able to read. Until Quinton Murdock knew he didn't know how.

"Sit down, son."

"I ain't your son, sir."

A strange look scuttled across Murdock's granite carved features, but he only repeated, "Sit."

In the midst of a war Major Quinton Murdock taught Chase Cordell to read.

Chase proved a quick study. Within weeks he was devouring Murdock's copies of Hawthorne, Longfellow and Thoreau. From the body of a dead Union soldier he even appropriated a dog-eared edition of *Uncle Tom's Cabin*. When he finished the book, he took it to Murdock. "Do you have slaves, sir?"

Murdock looked up from his ever-present maps. "No."

"Then why do you fight for the South?"

Murdock stood and crossed over to him. "I don't consider slavery a major issue in this war, son. Slavery would have died the natural death it was meant to in another few years. To me this war is about economics, a state's right to choose its own destiny. I might ask you the same question. You're fighting for the South, aren't you?"

"When I was hungry, I ran into a rebel patrol. I

suppose I'd be a Yankee, if they'd fed me first."

Murdock grinned. "You're a real cynical bastard for fourteen, Cordell."

"Eighteen, sir."

"Right."

"Can I give you a little advice, son."

"You're a major, sir. You can do anything you want."

Murdock ignored that, saying, "Don't judge the whole world by what you've seen of it so far. Some day you'll find the right woman, have a family, find out what life's really all about."

"Life's been a belt on my back and rats in my bed, sir."

Murdock put his hand on Chase's shoulder. Chase did not pull away. "Not any more, Cordell. Not any more."

Chase headed out to the campfire and laid out his bedroll for the night. For long minutes he sat there and stared into the crackling flames, clutching the book in his hands. For the tiniest instant he allowed himself to wish that Quinton Murdock had been his father instead of Clete Cordell.

And then he cursed himself for being a fool.

Don't die, Murdock. Oh, God, please, don't die. The bullets, the fire . . . Murdock . . .

May 1864. The Wilderness of Virginia—the fighting and dying going on in tangles of brush so thick a man couldn't see six feet in front of him. Murdock himself was set to lead a charge on the Union lines at daybreak.

"Get this message to Colonel Reardon," Murdock told Chase. "We'll need his reinforcements here by noon or the Yankees will overrun us for certain."

"Let me stay here," Chase urged, a nameless fear goading him. "Let me fight. Let someone else take the dispatch." As a courier Chase had rarely engaged in combat. But he'd often practiced with Murdock's revolver.

"There's no one I'd trust to carry this message but you, Cordell."

"Major, please . . ."

"Go."

"Yes, sir. They'll be here, sir." Chase mounted a plucky bay and spurred the horse into a ground-eating canter, taking care to keep close to the cover of the trees. But it wasn't his own life that concerned him. He couldn't shake off the odd foreboding that had been with him all night.

Something caught his eye, something out of sync with the burgeoning green growth all around him. Chase reined in, his brows furrowing to see a strip of bright blue silk caught in the brambles bordering the woods. Quickly he dismounted, taking a closer look. He found himself face to face with a frightened young woman, clutching a small infant in her arms.

Her shoulder length brown hair was wildly dishevelled, her dress tattered and torn beyond repair. But it was the look in her eyes that gripped him, transported him back to a time and place he didn't want to be, a look of such abject terror that he felt for an instant as though he were looking into his own eyes as he'd cowered before his drunken father.

"I won't hurt you," he said softly, holding up a hand as though to calm her, although he made no move to close the six-foot distance that separated them.

"Don't shoot me!"

"No, ma'am." He dared a step toward her.

She stumbled backward, falling heavily, though her body shielded the sleeping infant. The baby snuffled slightly at the disturbance, but otherwise did not stir. Chase resisted the urge to help her to her feet, fearing that she would rush out into the open, get caught by a stray bullet.

"Are you going to rape me?" she whimpered.

"No, ma'am."

"Forgive me," the woman said, half sobbing. "I had to run for my life from some men—Union soldiers—a ways back. My coach was waylaid, my driver killed. The soldiers . . . the soldiers were shoving me from one to the other, trying to take my baby, trying to. . . ." Tears rolled down her cheeks. "I only escaped with my life when they were fired on and distracted."

"I'm sure they're long gone, ma'am. But I was thinking you and your baby might do better to get to a town, a farm." He glanced about, his heart thudding as he worried about delaying Murdock's message. If only there was a place to hide her until he could get to Reardon . . .

The woman continued to sob quietly. "I have no horse, no food."

Chase reached into his haversack and pulled out two pieces of jerked beef. "Don't have nothin' for the baby, ma'am."

"He's still nursing."

"Oh." Chase coughed. "Yes, ma'am." He lifted his cap and raked a hand through tousled dark hair. "I know where there's a Confederate field hospital. I think I could get you and your baby there. After that, you'd be on your own."

"I'd be ever so grateful."

"I can't take you now, though, not until after I deliver this dispatch." He patted the pouch looped through his belt.

The woman nodded, though her eyes were bleak. "I understand."

"I'll be back just as soon as I . . ."

The baby began to wail piteously. Chase closed his eyes. If the soldiers who'd attacked the woman earlier were anywhere about, they could hear the babe and find her again. Damn! What was he supposed to do? What would Murdock do?

With a low curse Chase helped the woman to her feet, then helped them both onto his horse. He mounted behind them. There was no help for it. They would have to come with him. He knew the extra weight would slow the horse. And he could not be as reckless with his passengers' lives, as he may have been with his own.

All told, Chase figured the woman and baby added an extra hour to the time it took to reach Reardon. As the colonel rounded up his troops to go to Murdock's aid, Chase hurriedly delivered the woman and baby to the field hospital. He turned at once to go, but she caught his arm.

"I can't thank you enough, Private."

"It's all right, ma'am."

The woman stood on tiptoe and gave him a kiss on his cheek. "It's good to know that in this hellish war a woman can still find a man of honor and decency."

Chase looked at the ground. "Safe journey to you and your baby, ma'am."

He hurried off then to ride with Reardon. Though the troops marched as fast as they dared, it was half past noon before they made it back to Murdock's camp.

By then the battle raged behind every bush, every tree, every blade of grass. Nowhere did Chase see Murdock. He looked past the soldiers to the vegetation-choked forest beyond. Peering into those woods was like trying to look through a wall. But he could hear the roar of muskets, knew there were soldiers warring in that maze. And already he could see smoke rising from the underbrush, fires set by the musket blasts, fires that cared not for the color of man's uniform.

Chase grabbed up a Colt from a dead sergeant and barreled headlong into the woods. Murdock was in there somewhere. Chase would find him.

Within minutes he could scarcely breathe, so thick was the smoke. He dropped to his knees and moved forward by feel. A bullet from nowhere ripped through his left shoulder, but he didn't stop, couldn't stop.

"Murdock!" Chase called his name until his voice gave out. He found more than one gray-uniformed body, and each time his heart wouldn't start beating again until he saw there was no major's insignia, no thatch of silver hair.

Until the last.

Chase found him belly-down in a tangle of haw-thorns, his Colt empty, bayonet drawn. Swallowing a sob, Chase turned him over, nearly gagging at the

97

gaping wound that had torn open his abdomen.

"Oh, God, oh, sweet God. Major, I'm sorry. I'm sorry."

Murdock stirred, gasping slightly. His eyes opened. "Cordell?"

"Yes, sir." Chase gripped his shirtfront. "Don't you worry, sir. I'm going to get you out of here."

"No . . . no time . . ."

"It's my fault," Chase sobbed. "All my fault. I'm sorry, sir. So sorry. I was late. I—"

"No, dammit . . . no . . ." Murdock seemed to draw on some last vestige of strength. "They overran us right after you left. No chance . . . no chance, boy . . . don't . . ." Murdock groped for the pocket of his uniform shirt and took out a small metal object, handing it to Chase. Chase stared at the badge, at the words Special Deputy carved into its surface. "Take it . . . want you to have it."

"Sir . . . I . . . sir, please."

"It was my son's," Murdock rasped.

Chase blinked, stunned. "Son?"

"He's dead . . . four years now." He coughed blood. "Stray bullet . . . breaking up saloon brawl."

"Don't talk, sir. Let me get you some help."

Murdock caught Chase's wrist. "I know you won't believe this . . . and in a lot of ways you're nothing alike . . . but there's something in you, something you hide and protect . . . that reminds me . . . of Edward."

"That was his name? Edward?"

Murdock nodded. "I wish I knew your name, boy."

"Don't have one, sir. Just Cordell."

"Man needs a first name for friends to call him."

"Don't have any fr . . ." He stopped, looking at Murdock. "I just don't have a name, sir. My father called me Charley. I won't let anyone ever call me that. I hate him. I hate him!"

Murdock's breathing grew more ragged. "I knew a Charles once. He went by Chase. It suited him. I think it would suit you, too. You call yourself Chase."

"I will if you say so, sir." Tears tracked down his ash-coated face.

"You're a good man, Chase Cordell. A good soldier. Friend . . ." His head lolled back, those eyes capable of such infinite kindness now wide, sightless.

A long, mournful cry escaped Chase's throat. And then he collapsed forward, feeling his own blood ebbing into the dirt.

He woke in a field hospital. "Take it easy, boy," a man was saying. "You're going to be fine."

He didn't want to be fine. He wanted to be dead. Murdock was dead.

"I'm Colonel Ben Hamilton," the man said. "I'm a doctor. You're in a Yankee field hospital."

"Yankee . . ." Chase didn't recognize the sound of his own voice.

"You inhaled a lot of smoke, son. Don't try to talk."

A woman came up beside Hamilton and for an instant Chase thought he must be dreaming. He'd never seen anyone so beautiful. Sun-colored hair, green eyes. She introduced herself as Hamilton's daughter, Stacey. "I'm afraid you're a prisoner of war, soldier. But don't worry, with my father as your doctor you couldn't be getting better care." She sat beside him, taking his hand in her own. "Is there anyone you want to write? Anyone you'd like to send word?"

He shook his head.

She continued to hold his hand, speaking gently, of everything, of nothing. And slowly, slowly he began to listen. "I want to be a doctor myself one day, you know," she said at one point.

Chase had never heard of a more fool notion than a woman doctor, but he didn't tell her that. He just listened. He listened then and over the days that followed. Listened as she spoke of a handsome cavalry captain named Joshua Steele, watched as her eyes grew warm, misty. In spite of himself Chase grew relaxed in her company and over time he found himself pouring out his grief to her about Murdock. "He was my . . . friend."

"You hold onto your memories of him," Stacey said. "Make him proud of you, Chase."

Chase. It sounded good to have Stacey call him that, and yet to most anyone else it was still Cordell. He felt oddly protective of the name. Though he thought of himself as Chase, he allowed its use by virtually no one.

As for making Murdock proud of him, he'd done a helluva poor job at that. He rode west after the war, finding work here and there, but quickly discovering he did best when the job included the use of sixgun. He rode herd up the Goodnight trail, rode shotgun with Wells Fargo, hired out as a troubleshooter with the transcontinental railroad. His reputation spread. He hired out for special jobs. He didn't much care if he crossed into gray areas of the law, though he always managed to stay just legal.

Until Breckenridge.

The pain in his head was like wildfire. Water. God, he needed some water. Burning . . . burning up. He forced his parched lips to move.

"Wah-ter."

Cool, wet, it slid down his throat. A hand stroked his forehead and someone was speaking gentle, soothing words. He imagined sun-colored hair and emerald green eyes and wondered if Stacey Hamilton ever found her captain.

Hurt . . . hurt . . . a bright light drifted toward him. The pain receded. Tired, so tired. Sleep.

Abby was scared to death. The man—Chase—was slipping farther and farther away, and there was nothing she could do to stop it. "Hang on," she whispered urgently, squeezing his hand. "Please, don't give up now. We're almost there. Please." His breathing had grown ominously more shallow the past few hours. And she'd scarcely been able to get any water into him at all.

"Willow Springs ahead, Abby!" Ethan called back.

Abby leaped up. Finally! Surely someone in town could help him. She poked her head out the front of the wagon, her sudden hopes fading as quickly as they had come.

Dusk was settling, but even the graying shadows did not disguise the primitive cut of many of the false-front buildings she saw lining the town's main street. She gave only a passing notice to the various trades represented—leatherworks, hostlery, cafe, undertaker, gunsmith, hotel, mercantile, barber, saloon—four of them—but not one shingle, not one sign, not one windowfront proclaimed the word she wished most to see — doctor.

Far off to her left, set apart from the town itself, they passed an impressive white building she guessed to be the school. But though she would have thought to feel some stirring of interest, curiosity, she felt only a numbing exhaustion — as she continued to worry about the man lying so still behind her.

"Best we find the sheriff's office," Ethan was saying. "He'll know what to do with our patient." Winnie nodded in silent agreement.

Ethan guided the team to a halt in front of a solid-looking building of dried mud and fieldstone, the only non-wooden structure in town. Narrow, barred windows along the side facing the alley announced its position as jail even before Abby noted the painted lettering of same on the front door.

She was about to climb down and knock, when a big rawboned man stepped out to greet them. He was tall, well over six feet, with broad shoulders that somehow enhanced his already imposing height. Hard-angled features were softened by a full, sensual mouth, partially hidden by a dark, well-groomed mustache. On his black leather vest he wore a tin star, not unlike the one she'd found near Chase.

All of this she took in in a heartbeat. "Please, Sheriff," she began, gesturing toward the back of the wagon, "we have an injured man —"

"I know," the lawman said, his voice as rich and deep as the laugh lines that crinkled about the corners of his brown eyes. "Hank Griswold filled me in when he brought in the stage this afternoon. Sorry I didn't ride out to meet up with you folks, but we had a little fracas over at the Silver Nugget. Nothin' serious. Only a couple of broken bones." He stuck out a hand toward Ethan. "Name's Sam Devlin."

Ethan leaned down, accepting the handshake and making introductions all around.

"Please," Abby interrupted, "the man—"

"Now don't you worry, Miss Graham," Devlin said, "if he's lived through the ride to town, he's probably already halfway along the road to recovery."

Abby frowned, planting her hands on her hips, not at all sure she appreciated this man's cavalier attitude toward bullet wounds. As she watched, Devlin tromped toward the back of the wagon. Quickly she ducked back inside, beating him to the rear flap and drawing it aside for him. "I believe this injured man is a law officer himself, Sheriff Devlin," Abby said, thinking to pique his concern for a comrade in arms.

"So Hank told me." Devlin climbed in beside her, squinting at Chase in the dim lanternlight. "Somethin' familiar about him all right. But I can't quite place him. You got the badge?"

Abby handed it to him.

Devlin shook his head. "Ain't no style I ever seen before."

"Please, does it really matter? We'll find out his name in time to carve it on his tombstone if we don't get him to a doctor and quickly."

"I'm sure Hank told you we don't have a doctor, Miss Graham."

Abby's lips thinned as she detected a sudden patronizing tone.

" 'Course," Devlin went on, "I could send for Ezra Weed. He's barkeep over at the Nugget. I hear he's gone lead minin' a time or two."

"Lead mining?" Patronizing or no, Abby felt her knees wobble just a bit.

"Forgive my rusty manners," Devlin said, his brown eyes growing suddenly serious. "I forgot you folks aren't likely used to our way of doin' just yet. And . . ." he looked a little sheepish, "I guess I forgot to tell you I sent a telegraph message to a doctor in Denver as soon as Griswold drove in. Doc Winthrop should be here sometime tomorrow afternoon."

Whether Devlin actually had or hadn't *forgotten* made no real difference to Abby. She was too busy being grateful for the doctor's impending arrival. "Thank you, Sheriff. Truly."

He grinned. "You're mighty welcome, ma'am. And please call me Sam."

Abby flushed under the intensity of his gaze. To distract him she said, "Your Mr. Perkins mentioned something about a house in his letter." She needed to get Chase settled for the night. And she was in desperate need of sleep herself.

"Sure. I'll take you there. One of the finest houses in town, in fact. Mr. Perkins figured nothing was too good for our new teacher."

The sheriff mounted a roan gelding and led them back up the main street to its intersection with a narrower side street. He rode for one block, then dismounted in front of the house on the leftside corner. "This is it."

Despite her wan state, Abby couldn't suppress a rush of genuine pleasure. In this at least Willow Springs had not proved a disappointment. The house was lovely, a large white frame building with a white picket fence surrounding both the front and back yards. The garden bordering the front porch was in serious need of weeding, but Abby could tell that with proper attention it could be quite lovely.

"It's delightful!" Winnie concurred, as Ethan helped her down from the wagon. "I can't wait to see it in the daylight."

Devlin helped Abby down, and she was more than a little certain his hands lingered on her waist a pulse-beat longer than necessary. But her thoughts were again with Chase. "Please, Sheriff, can we get him inside?"

Devlin barked orders to a passing stranger and together the sheriff and the burly man carried Chase into the house. Abby hurried ahead of them, scarcely noting a myriad of supplied furnishings. But she did notice the wide open sitting room to her right with its massive fieldstone hearth. The room to her left though was of primary interest. It had a bed. She gestured toward the two men. "Bring him in here."

Devlin and the stranger deposited Chase atop a musty patchwork quilt. Devlin thanked the stranger, who promptly left.

Abby struck a match and lit a bedside lantern.

"I've seen my share of gun-shot hombres, miss," Devlin said, taking a cursory look at Chase's wounds. "And this one doesn't look too good. He doesn't look too good at all." Abby felt her already flagging hopes sink lower still. "I'm sorry if I seemed to make light of it earlier. I'm afraid he may not last 'til the doctor gets here."

Chapter Six

Abby stood beside the bed, her fingers twisting in the folds of her skirts, as she watched Dr. Simon Winthrop pour a little more chloroform into the cloth he was holding above Chase's face. "This will keep him out," the medical man said. "It wouldn't do for him to wake up before I'm done operating."

Dr. Winthrop, a slightly built, no-nonsense individual with thinning gray hair and clear, sharp blue eyes, had arrived from Denver two hours before. During his first five minutes in the house, he'd given Chase a cursory examination, barked orders about boiling water, then laid out various potions and instruments from the black bag he carried. In the succeeding hour and fifty-five minutes he'd sweated and probed, cursed and commanded, all the while tending to Chase's wounds.

And now he was just about finished. Abby brought in another bucket of fresh water as the doctor tied off the last suture he'd applied to Chase's head wound. With a grunt that Abby charitably assumed was a thank you, the man stepped over to the refilled basin and washed his bloodied hands.

"Will he be all right?" she queried, her voice more tentative than she would have liked. Every time she'd opened her mouth, Winthrop had either grunted a brusque reply, glared at her, or not answered at all.

"He will or he won't be," Winthrop answered, toweling his hands dry, then crossing back to Chase to dress the wound.

"What does that mean?" Abby demanded. Now that the surgery was over, she was finding her own patience wearing thin with the man's less than congenial manner.

The doctor tied off the new bandage, then set about returning his cleansed instruments to his medical bag. When he was through, he snapped the bag shut and gazed levelly at Abby. "I mean just what I said, miss. I've done all I can. Now it's up to the good Lord and this man's own constitution, which, from the look of him, would seem to be a pretty good one." He started for the door.

"You're not leaving?" Abby gaped at the man, incredulous, even as she unconsciously moved to intercept him.

Winthrop halted, scowling darkly. "I have to get back. I have other patients to tend to."

"Can't you at least stay until he wakes up?"

Winthrop gave an indifferent shrug. "He may not wake up."

Abby's lips thinned. "He most certainly will. And he'll be fine."

For the first time the doctor smiled. "With a pretty nurse like you, I'd wake up too."

Abby rolled her eyes, but managed to hold her

tongue. She didn't want to offend the man. Chase might yet be in need of his services. "Will you be coming back to check on him?"

"Nope. He'll make it or he won't, like I said. There's nothing more I can do."

"Dr. Winthrop!" Abby huffed. "I hardly think that you're taking a proper attitude here . . ."

"Miss . . . forgive me, I've forgotten your name." His tone was now blatantly patronizing.

"Graham," Abby supplied tightly.

"Miss Graham," he said, sweeping a hand across his almost nonexistent hair, "I don't give a tinker's damn what you think about my attitude. And let me assure you of something else, my attitude isn't going to matter one whit to this patient either. What will matter is what *you* do for him."

"Me?"

"From what I've seen and heard you've already done considerable. You've gotten water into him, broth, kept him warm, cooled him down. There's nothing that could have been better. And now I've gotten the bullet out of him. The rest, as I said, is up to God and him. Of course, you could try and get some more soup into him, change the bandage every other day—making sure your hands are clean when you do so—and in fairly short order you should know whether he's going to live or die." He cast a glance back over his shoulder toward the bed. "Good young healthy body; from the looks of him, he's survived worse. 'Course from the location of that bullet in his head, he could—" He stopped, seeming to reconsider whatever he had been going to say. "Never mind. No sense borrowing trouble."

"What do you mean?"

"Just follow my instructions, and let nature take its course, all right?" With that Winthrop bid her good day, swept by her and was gone.

For a long minute Abby just stood there, feeling for all the world as if she'd just survived an unexpected storm. If it hadn't been for the fresh dressing banding Chase's head, she could well have convinced herself that Dr. Simon Winthrop had been some sort of bizarre hallucination brought on by lack of sleep.

But the man had been here, and he had been a doctor. And despite his crotchety disposition Abby was also certain that he was a very good doctor, that Chase couldn't have received better care even in the bigger cities back home.

Dismissing any further reflection about Winthrop as pointless, she crossed over to the bed, automatically adjusting the quilted coverlet to a higher position on Chase's bare chest. His arms rested atop the bedcovers, and she considered tucking them underneath. But the afternoon temperature was warm and she decided against it. Though she knew she shouldn't, especially with Winnie bustling in and out every fifteen minutes asking if more boiling water was needed, Abby seated herself on the bed and took Chase's hand in her own.

All last night and all this morning, before the doctor had come, she had sat with him, dozing off and on in a rocking chair she'd brought in beside the bed. Even Winnie's anxious objections did not dissuade her. He had grown so weak, his breathing so shallow that she had feared the worst.

"I can't let him be alone, Aunt Winnie," Abby had

said. "Please understand."

Winnie had left her then. And Abby had dozed fitfully overnight, waking with a start each time she did, always to assure herself that Chase still lived.

She sat there now, the surgery finished, knowing that his living or dying was still not decided, and she tightened her grip on his hand. "Stay," she said softly. "Please, stay. I want to know you. I want to know who you are."

She knew she was being fanciful, even — dare she admit it? — romantic. But she couldn't seem to help it. She thought about all the years she had never felt settled in Moline, and then all the times she'd wanted to leave, but couldn't. She thought about the thousand separate decisions that had led her to one particular creek on one particular day.

"Our lives were supposed to connect," she said, smoothing her palm along the back of his hand. "And it wasn't so I could watch you die. Please . . .

"Abby, dear . . ."

Abby turned to see her aunt framed in the doorway. Flustered, Abby rose to her feet. "I . . ."I just keep hoping he'll wake up."

Winnie stepped into the room. "Ethan and I spoke to the doctor before he left. Abby, you mustn't take this to heart so. I'm frightened by how much time and effort you've put into caring for this man. If he dies . . ."

"He won't die!" Abby snapped. "Don't say that!"

Winnie looked pained. "Oh, Abby, my dear . . ."

Abby closed her eyes. "Forgive me. Oh, Aunt Winnie, forgive me." She came over and gave her aunt a heartfelt hug. "I'm sorry. I don't know what's happening to me. These last two days have been a nightmare."

Winnie's gaze softened into one of warm understanding. "I know, dear. That's why Ethan and I are as worried about you as you seem to be about this young man. Please, won't you lie down . . . for just a little while? You've scarcely even seen your new bedroom."

"I'm too wound up to sleep, Aunt Winnie. I think you're right, though. I do need to get away from him for an hour or two. If you don't mind, I think I'll walk over and take a look at the school."

Winnie seemed to visibly relax. "I'll have supper waiting when you get back."

Abby found that just stepping outside helped. She inhaled the clean Colorado air as she headed toward the inviting white building scarcely fifty yards from the last building at the head of the block. She must remember to compliment Hiram Perkins on his thoughtfulness. A lovely house, a fine looking school—and both but a brisk walk from one another. She was halfway to the school, when booted footfalls behind her made her look back.

Sheriff Sam Devlin halted mid-stride and grinned. "I saw you leave your house, Miss Graham, and I couldn't resist catching up to you to say hello again."

Abby smiled. "Hello, Sheriff."

"How's the patient?"

"Come now, Sheriff," Abby said in a tone she might use on a naughty student, "do you mean to tell me the doctor didn't stop by your office and fill you in on every detail of the man's condition?"

Devlin's grin broadened. "You're a smart lady."

"I have to be, I'm a schoolteacher."

He stopped in front of her. "Can I walk you the rest of the way to the school?"

"If you like."

"I'd like it very much." He fell into step beside her and she was again struck by how very tall he was. She would barely reach mid-chest on the man.

"So what do you think of Willow Springs so far?" he prompted.

"This is only the first time I've left the house, Sheriff Devlin."

"Please, call me Sam."

"I hardly feel I know you well enough for that, Sheriff."

He stopped and she did the same. "That's easily taken care of. Have dinner with me."

Abby could feel her mouth dropping open in astonishment. "We've only just met. I scarcely think that would be appropriate."

"Maybe not appropriate," he agreed with that engaging grin of his, "but tactically wise, I assure you."

"Sir?" He had totally confounded her with that one.

"Tactics, Miss Graham," he explained reasonably. "I need to take you to dinner before all the other bachelors in town get a look at you. That way I can establish what we call out here a right of prior claim."

For the briefest instant Abby felt a flash of anger at his presumption that she was available for claiming, prior or otherwise, but the utter guilelessness with which he obviously said the words thoroughly disarmed her. She felt herself blushing. "I . . . I don't know what to say."

"Say I can call for you about seven."

"I . . ." She smiled. "Not tonight, really. I'm . . . it's been very tiring. And the injured man may need . . ."

He sighed, shaking his head. "It's enough to make a man go out and take a bullet, when I think of the kind of tendin' I'd get."

Abby could feel her blush deepen. "Sheriff Devlin, please."

"I'm sorry, ma'am, miss." He jerked his hat off his head, curling his fingers nervously into the brim. "I don't always get a chance to use my manners. Like I tried to tell you last night, they can get a little rusty. Forgive me if I was too blunt."

She laughed and reflexively patted his wrist. "You're forgiven. In fact, I'm flattered."

"You'll allow me to invite you to dinner another time then?"

"I'd look forward to it. Honestly."

He settled his hat back atop his head. "Another night it is, Miss Graham. Now if you'll excuse me, I'm sure you'd like to be alone for your first look at your new school."

Abby watched him stride away, and she wondered if she imagined the extra buoyancy in his step. The man certainly was not subtle. Yet she had been telling the truth. She found his obvious interest in her flattering.

She frowned slightly. Flattering, yes. But with no quickening of her pulse, no breathless anticipation, no "smile of the heart" as Lisa had often described her feelings for Zeke. But then what did she expect? She had only just met the poor man! And why on earth did such fanciful musings send her thoughts tripping back to another dark-haired stranger, one who had yet to say more than a single coherent word to her?

"You really do have to get some sleep tonight, Abigail," she grumbled aloud. "Aunt Winnie's right. You're coming undone."

With a rueful grimace she continued toward the school. The one-story frame structure looked sound on the outside. Making a quick circuit of the building she noted where the frayed, but still serviceable bell cord was, then found a working water pump in the back of the building, along with a nearly depleted woodpile that would have to be restocked before winter.

Returning to the front, she climbed the six wooden steps to the door. Taking a deep, anticipatory breath, she turned the latch and flung the door wide to take her first look at her new classroom.

She nearly dropped in her tracks.

Abby had seen tornado damage once back in Illinois. Uprooted trees, wagons tossed about like doll carts, houses smashed into match sticks. Somehow that same twister must have reformed, touched down here in the jumbled mess of this twenty-by-thirty-foot room. Surely a tornado was the only conceivable explanation for such utter chaos.

Abby walked, stunned, amid a tangle of overturned desks and smashed slates. Dark splotches spattered the wood floor, mute testimony to upended inkwells. Her shoes crackled and scraped across wide areas of scattered ashes from the overturned potbellied stove.

"Or maybe it was an earthquake," she said aloud, the sound of her own voice somehow calming in the stark void she felt here in this room. "An earthquake.

114

Yes, I like that. And it only hit in this room, nowhere else."

At least she would have preferred to ascribe the damages to something as absurd as a freakishly selective natural disaster. It was certainly more palatable than what had to be the truth. This had very likely been done by one or more students. The thought did not so much frighten as sadden her. How could they have come to hate their school so much?

Crossing to one long bench seat that still seemed sound, she managed to right it and sit down. All across the plains on her journey west she had thought about the new challenges she might face here in Willow Springs — slow readers, a class bully, math haters, pranksters. So many varied and wide ranging problems could come up in the course of a school year. But never once had she considered anything like this. Never once.

As she sat there, she found herself wondering if Sheriff Devlin had known what she was walking into. In fact, the more she thought about it, she couldn't imagine his *not* knowing. Why hadn't he come with her? Or at least warned her? Hinted that things might not be entirely in order.

But then who could prepare a person for this? It had to be seen to be believed. Surely, the townspeople didn't expect her to put the school in order all by herself?

She turned her head toward a flyspecked windowpane to her left. Had she detected movement on the other side of it? As though someone were peering in?

"Are you the new teacher?"

She jumped, startled, then relaxed to see two wide-

115

eyed youngsters standing in the doorway—a russet-haired boy of about nine and a dark-haired girl maybe two years younger. Both were dressed in the sturdy, practical clothes that bespoke farm life. It was the boy who'd spoken. "I'm the new teacher, yes," Abby said, coming over to greet them properly. "I'm Miss Abigail Graham. And who might you be?"

"I'm Keefer O'Banion and this is my sister, Molly."

"Come in, come in," Abby said, when they both hung back shyly. "Just watch your step, all right?" Maybe these youngsters could offer some explanation for what had happened here. At least give her some idea of *when* it happened, so that she might better know if this was some student's farewell to a previous teacher, or, more ominously, a warning to his replacement.

From the incredulous looks on both children this was not something they had seen before. To Abby that meant that the destruction of this room had not been the reason for any abrupt end to the previous school term.

As the children circled the room in horrified fascination, Abby followed, picking up a wood chip here, a piece of broken slate there, though the whole process was futile without a wheelbarrow and a shovel. "Will you children be coming to school here?"

"My sister will first off," Keefer said. "But me and my two older brothers have to help Pa finish with the harvest."

"Well, it'll be a pleasure to have you both in my classroom."

"Are we gonna have to sit on the floor?" Molly asked.

"Ma would have our hides if we ever put the house in such a state," Keefer said.

"It is a bit untidy," Abby agreed, picking up an eraser and setting it on the chalk ledge of the blackboard, only to watch it slide back to the floor from the tiptilted surface. She grimaced. "Was it anything like this when school ended last term?"

"Weren't no school last year."

Abby started. "What did you say?"

"Never had no teacher last year. Mrs. Perkins tried for a week or two, but she couldn't stand it. Mr. Perkins only lasted a day."

Abby returned to the bench seat and sat down. Mr. Perkins, it seemed, had been less than candid with her. She had been under the impression that the previous teacher was to stay on until the end of the term last April. She had no idea she would be dealing with students who had missed an entire year of schooling.

Well, she'd wanted a challenge, an adventure. And it certainly seemed she was in for one. She supposed it didn't really matter that they'd missed school last year. After all, there was no help for it now. It only served to make things all the more clear as to just how badly she was needed here.

"You won't leave, will you?" Molly asked, her blue eyes enchantingly innocent, eager.

"No," she assured them firmly, "I'm not leaving. In fact, I can't wait to get started."

"Not even if Zeb comes?" Molly asked, her voice tinged with an odd mix of wonder and doubt.

"Hush, Molly!" Keefer said.

Abby stood. "And who is Zeb?"

"Nobody to worry about, Miss Graham. Mr.

117

Perkins would never—"

"Mr. Perkins would never what?" a male voice boomed from the back of the room.

Keefer gasped, skittering backward so fast he started to trip over the bench on which Abby sat. Her arms shot out to catch him, but what concerned her more than the tumble was the way Keefer's gaze had darted suddenly toward the window. He looked for all the world as though he wanted to leap through it. She still had hold of him, and she could feel his body tremble along with his voice as he said, "Good afternoon, Mr. Perkins, sir."

"I hope my name wasn't being taken in vain," the man chuckled, though Abby detected no humor in the laughter. She watched as the blond-haired, brown-eyed man moved through the maze at his feet with barely a downward glance, as he made his way toward her. His patrician features were too delicate to be considered classically handsome. But he was a man who expected to be noticed and admired, of that she was certain.

He was dressed in a finely tailored blue frock coat with matching trousers. A silver brocade vest, white shirt and black string tie completed the dandified look so at odds with what Abby had seen so far of Willow Springs. At Perkins' side flounced—it was the word that came immediately to mind—a lovely blond-haired girl of about thirteen wearing an elaborately fashioned pink lawn dress with a looped overskirt and carrying a matching parasol.

Behind the man and girl walked an unassuming looking woman with dark blonde hair pulled into a severe bun. Her attire was in marked contrast to the others—a drab brown cotton dress that did nothing for the woman's already sallow complexion. Clinging to her skirts was a little boy of about eight. His clothes were on par with the gentleman's, but they did not seem to suit him at all.

"I take it you're Miss Abigail Graham?" the man asked.

"I am." Abby found it difficult to take her eyes off the odd little assemblage that followed in the man's wake.

"I'm Hiram Perkins, mayor, undertaker, and head of the school board of Willow Springs."

"How nice to meet you, Mr. Perkins." Abby nodded and looked expectantly toward the woman, but Perkins did not introduce her.

Keefer and Molly used Abby's diverted attention as an excuse to rush out the door. She frowned. She had wanted them to stay a little longer, partly because she wanted to get to know them better, and partly because she knew the instant she met Hiram Perkins, she would have a better chance of finding out about the school and its difficulties from the children, than she would from this man.

"The O'Banions are certainly sweet children," Abby said.

"Farmers!" the blond-haired girl next to Perkins sniffed, saying the word like an epithet. "Their folks are in town for supplies. Don't expect them to dress any better when school starts. Those were likely their Sunday go-to-meeting clothes."

Abby waited for either of the child's parents to correct the girl for her abominable lack of sensitivity, but no censure was forthcoming. In fact, Abby was almost certain she saw a shading of approval in Hiram Perkins' haughty features.

"Ah, Miss Graham," Perkins asked, "please forgive my faux pas."

Abby winced as the man gave the French phrase a strictly English pronunciation. "And what fox pass was that, Mr. Perkins?" she managed, taking a delightfully evil joy in discovering the man's cultivated manner was played out in exterior trappings only. His culture had apparently never made it to his brain.

"I neglected to introduce you to my delightful daughter, Penelope."

The girl curtsied demurely.

"Isn't she a delight? Talented, charming, brilliant. You'll find her to be your most advanced student. But," he gave that odd, humorless chuckle again, "let me assure you, I don't expect any preferential treatment for my dear Penelope. She won't need it."

"And the young man?" Abby asked, gesturing toward the boy, when Perkins showed no interest in introducing the other youngster.

Perkins made a dismissing gesture toward the boy. "My son, Russell. He'll be in your class too. Hopefully you can put the fear of God into him."

Abby bristled, as she watched Russell immediately flinch away from her. She was taking an immediate and very intense dislike to Hiram Perkins. She only hoped she had enough forbearance to give Penelope the benefit of the doubt. Perhaps the child wasn't quite spoiled beyond redemption.

Abby took matters into her own hands regarding the woman at Perkins' side. "I'm Abigail Graham," she said. "And you are . . .?"

"Grace Perkins," the woman said softly. "Pleased to meet you." She made no further comment.

"We heard you have some sort of injured drifter in your home," Perkins said, his disapproval evident in his tone.

"He's a law officer," Abby corrected testily. She had just about had it with this pompous oaf. School board member or no, the time for exchanging inane amenities was over. "Never mind my patient, Mr. Perkins. I want to know what on earth happened to this schoolroom?"

He shrugged. "Vandals. We meant to have it fixed up before you arrived. We had no idea you'd be three weeks early."

And what did that mean? Had the town been planning to hide the entire incident from her? Perkins had painted a very rosy picture of teaching in Willow Springs. Abby found herself wondering how many thorns he'd kept to himself.

"Why would anyone do this, Mr. Perkins? Do you have any idea? A personal vendetta? A deranged mind? Just what might I be facing here?"

"Tut, tut, my dear. I don't want you having an attack of the vapors or something. It's all been taken care of. None of this clutter will be here the day school starts, I assure you."

"I would hardly classify this mess as clutter, Mr. Perkins. This room has been destroyed by one or more very angry human beings. And I think I'm entitled to know why."

"It's been taken care of," he said again. "Don't worry about a thing."

The stove door, long hanging by a single hinge,

chose that moment to tear free and clatter to the floor.

"There's a new stove on order," Perkins said. "It should be here any day now."

"And what happens if someone wrecks that stove as well, Mr. Perkins?"

"It won't happen."

This time there was an inflection of something she couldn't read in that voice, a kind of veiled warning, but she dismissed it to her own rattled sensibilities. "I'm sorry. If you'll excuse me, I'd like to be alone here for awhile."

"Of course. Children . . ." The girl immediately fell in step beside him, but the boy wandered over to where Abby now stood beside the great oaken teacher's desk.

She traced her fingers along the deep carved letters "Z. T." in its mutilated surface. Russell looked up at her with big brown eyes, somehow wise beyond their years.

"Z-Zeb must have d-d-d-done that," he said.

"Stop that stuttering!" Hiram said sharply, taking a quick, almost threatening, step in the boy's direction.

Abby shifted her body between Perkins and his son, being careful to make the movement seem natural, unhurried. With a gentle smile she leaned down to put her arm around Russell. "And who is this Zeb I keep hearing about?"

"He's a terrible bully," Penelope put in. "And so ugly he could turn a herd of cattle with his face."

Abby squeezed Russell's shoulders and continued to smile at him. "I'll be looking forward to having you in my class."

"Th-th-thank you," the boy said, then flushed fiercely, casting a frightened glance at his father. Hiram gave the child a thunderous look.

"Zeb Tucker will not be in this school ever again," Perkins said, "so please don't concern yourself, my dear."

Perkins herded his family toward the door. "I'm sure we'll meet again before the term starts. My wife will send over an invitation to supper to you and your aunt and uncle."

"How lovely," Abby said, beginning at once to stockpile excuses as to why she wouldn't be able to make it. "It was a pleasure to meet you all." She said it, though she looked only at Russell.

Perkins stopped at the door. "You're still a spinster, are you not?" he asked suddenly.

"I'm a schoolteacher, Mr. Perkins."

"Of course. I meant no offense. But I strongly urge you to find other accommodations for your injured transient as soon as possible." With that he and his family were gone.

Abby sank onto the bench seat, trying very hard not to hate Hiram Perkins. How dare he issue ultimatums about Chase! She would have the man in her home as long as necessary. He was wounded, for heaven's sake. Hadn't Perkins ever heard of the Good Samaritan? She was doing what any human being with a conscience would do.

Then why did her heartbeat quicken just to think of him? A most unsettling phenomenon to say the least. Maybe Winnie was more right than she knew. Abby was spending too much time with him.

She forced herself to stay at the school, working

through supper without stopping. She would need to come back tomorrow with a mop and a bucket, but for now she could at least get started making the room habitable again.

Much later, when she stepped outside, she was surprised to find the sun setting. She hadn't realized she'd stayed that long. But the physical exertion had been good for her. She was ready for the Hiram Perkinses of the world again.

Still, despite her best efforts, it was not Hiram Perkins she was thinking of on the short walk home. She picked up her pace until she was all but running. She had to see Chase again. She had to know that he was all right.

Chapter Seven

Abby slammed through the front door, but stopped herself midway to the door of Chase's room. He was still alive or Winnie would have come to the school and gotten her. He was also still unconscious or Winnie would be in there with him.

She forced her gaze away from his room, as Winnie came in from the kitchen to greet her. "How were things at the school, dear?"

"Just fine," Abby said, too distracted to even realize what she was saying. "Where's Uncle Ethan?"

"He went to see about a store. Sheriff Devlin told him Gunther's Mercantile might be for sale at the right price. We could take over and not have to wait to build a new one."

"Oh, Aunt Winnie, that's wonderful," said Abby, genuinely pleased. She knew her aunt and uncle were happiest when they were working. "I get so worried sometimes that you're going to be sorry you left Illinois." Again her gaze strayed toward Chase's room, but she did not act on the almost overwhelming urge to go to him. She didn't want Winnie to get upset all over again.

"We miss our friends, certainly," Winnie said. "But we're not sorry we left, or we wouldn't have done it. Believe it or not, your uncle has long harbored a fondness for seeing the West himself."

"I'm just glad you're happy."

"Happy as clams," Winnie said. "Now come in the kitchen and help me with supper. We're eating late. I've been putting things away all afternoon. This house is already starting to look like a home."

"I should have stayed here to help."

"Nonsense. I like doing it, especially without Ethan about. The man actually wanted to put that buffalo skull he found on the plains over the mantel, can you imagine?"

Abby smiled, glad to see her aunt in good spirits again. "Aunt Winnie," she ventured, "how . . . I mean . . . has there been any change in Chase?" It couldn't hurt to *ask* about him at least.

"He's been mumbling a bit now and again, more sensible than before. I think he just may be waking up, slow but sure."

"That's wonderful." Impulsively, Abby started toward his room, then stopped. "I guess you'd like some help setting the table?"

"I would."

Winnie's tone made it patently evident she didn't want Abby in Chase's room. Meekly Abby followed Winnie into the kitchen.

As she set the table, she told her aunt about her meeting with the O'Banion children and the Perkinses, anything to take her mind off Chase. It wasn't making the least bit of sense not to sit with him. All she could do was think about him. More than once she thought she heard him cry out, but when she scurried to the door of his room it was only to find him lying quietly in his bed.

"I'm sorry," Abby said, returning from her third false alarm visit to Chase's doorway. "I just don't want him to wake up alone. He won't know where he is."

The front door opened and Ethan came in.

"Serve the potatoes, Abby," Winnie said.

Abby did so, adding roast chicken and fresh green beans to each plate as well. It was one of her favorite meals, but she found she had no appetite for it.

"I think we can be in Gunther's Mercantile by week's end," Ethan said, as he finished washing his hands and took his seat at the table. He seemed to take no notice of the renewed tension between Abby and her aunt. "Gunther and his wife are anxious to be on their way to California. They've got a daughter there, who's recently had a baby. And they've decided to make the move."

They ate supper, talking agreeably about plans for their new home, new business, new school. But again and again Abby's gaze trailed toward the front of the house, until finally Winnie lay down her fork.

"Go on and sit with him, dear. You're going to wear out your neck, if you don't."

Abby hurried from the room, but not before she planted a resounding kiss on Winnie's cheek. "You're a dear!"

"I'm going to live to regret this."

"Never."

Abby settled herself in the rocker beside Chase's bed, feeling an almost uncanny sense of relief as she did so. Until this moment she hadn't realized just how anxious she'd been about being away from him. Winnie was right. This wasn't healthy. But she couldn't seem to help it. Nor could she explain to anyone, herself included, how vital it was to her that she be with this man when he at last regained consciousness.

It was as though she were still bound by their unspoken agreement—that she would keep watch as long as he would keep breathing. And, in fact, it had somehow gone even a step further. She felt at times as though she had actually breathed *for* him, those times when his strength had been all but gone, when to take another breath had simply been too much to ask.

"We're linked, you and I," she murmured. "Somehow, some way, we're already a part of each other. It doesn't make any sense I know, but . . ." She pressed her fingers to her mouth. Dear God, was this how it started? Were these the words of a woman about to lose her mind? If Aunt Winnie ever heard her say such a thing . . .

Taking a deep breath, Abby pulled a small orange-bound book from her dressfront pocket. It would be best for all concerned if she just picked up where she'd left off in *The Luckless Trapper*. Refreshing her memory, she recalled she was at the point in the story where heroine Edith Van Payne was now the captive of War Hawk, the noble Indian chief. At least compared to the events of the last couple of days, even Winnie would have to find this sort of fantasy relatively harmless.

Daylight waned, Abby read to herself, *and the shadows deepened. In the west the crimson flames that flared over the mountains died away, and the night-stars began to shimmer in their field of blue. A moist, sweet wind came wandering up from the woods. Edith sat within her little prison-house alone.*

Abby didn't remember making any conscious choice to read the book aloud, but when she reached the part where War Hawk spoke to the captive Edith, whom he now called White Bird, she pulled the chair closer to the bed and shared the passage with Chase, some part of her hoping that one of these times he would awaken to the sound of her voice.

" 'The warriors of our tribe are not used to wooing as are the pale-faces,' *War Hawk said,* 'and if War Hawk had sought the fair one he loves as our warriors seek their squaws, she might have thought his grip was stronger yet. He has handled her tenderly and would ever do so; yet she should know that she *must* be his' . . . his voice grew harder and colder, and there was a ring of savage fierceness in it as he spoke — 'let her dream of her pale-faced lover no longer. If she should see him again it would be to destroy him, for he may not look on her face again and go away living.' "

Abby sagged back, her voice fading. " 'The War Hawk will let no eyes rest upon his pale-faced squaw in love.'

"Edith Van Payne realized more than ever the

129

depth to which she had stirred the heart of her dusky-visaged admirer."

Abby's eyes slid closed. She forced them open. " 'War Hawk, you have wasted time in your pursuit, and you seek what will never, never be yours. . . .' "

The small book slipped from Abby's fingers. She tried to reach for it, but she was simply too tired. Her head lolled back, her eyelids heavy, so very heavy.

She was dreaming. She knew she was dreaming, because Chase was awake and standing before her, garbed in the finest buckskins she had ever seen. In place of the bandage that swathed his head was a headdress of magnificent eagle feathers. "I want to thank you for saving my life, fair maiden," he said, bowing slightly and according her a lopsided grin.

Abby blushed shyly. Never had she seen a man so handsome, or known one more gallant, more charming. "It was my deepest pleasure, sir. I knew you were my one true love from the moment I saw you. I always knew I was destined to love a lawman."

"Thanks to you, heart of my heart, I will be able to trail the gang of villainous desperadoes who shot me down. After I see them all behind bars, I'll come back for you, my sweetest flower."

"But Chase, my dearest one," Abby cried, feeling as if she must swoon, "I've waited for you all my life, must I wait longer still?"

"Fear not, I will make all haste, beloved."

"But how can you? Didn't those desperadoes steal your favorite white horse, too?"

"Yes, my valiant steed, Whirlwind. But, never fear, I will rescue him from their evil clutches." He lifted her hand to his lips and gently kissed the backs of her fingers. "Be patient, my beloved, for when I return we will make plans for our wedding."

His dark head bent low then, his lips parted for a kiss not meant for the back of one's hand. . . .

Abby woke with a start, all but falling out of her chair. Scrambling to her feet, it took a moment for her to realize where she was. And when she did she had to fight down an overwhelming embarrassment. Thankfully Chase was still sleeping, or unconscious, it was difficult to tell which. Surely the man would have been able to read her mind had he seen her face just now. Kiss him! She simply must put an end to these outrageous fantasies.

Still shaking, she tucked the book back into the pocket of her dress and crossed to the lantern. Her brows furrowed to find Winnie's bible on the bedside table. Then she smiled. Winnie must have sat with Chase awhile herself. She wondered if Winnie had read aloud to him too. He was certainly getting a variety of literature.

Abby bent close then to wish him good night. She wasn't sure how it happened, but she suddenly leaned closer still and gave him a soft kiss on his forehead. Angrily, she berated herself. This was no way to put an end to her foolish fantasies about the man. She was about to blow out the lantern when she thought she heard a low moan. Again she peered at him.

"Chase?" She said his name with a fierce urgency, her own silly foibles forgotten. She had to wake him lest he slip away again.

He shifted, his eyelids fluttering. Her heartbeat

131

quickened. And then his eyes opened. For the first time she noted their color—blue, a deep smokey blue.

"Chase?"

He shifted groggily, blinking. Again and again she called his name.

He closed his eyes tight, then opened them again. He seemed to try to say something, but couldn't find the words.

"How are you feeling?" she prompted. No doubt he was confused. The last conscious thing he would've been aware of was being shot and left for dead by the stream.

He raised a hand slowly, feeling the bandage that wound round his head. He winced. Abby caught his hand then and lowered it back to his side. "You're still healing. You'd best not touch it."

He still was not looking at her. His gaze seemed focused on nothing.

She thought to run for Winnie and Ethan, but it was so late, past midnight. "Are you hungry, Cha—?" She stopped, suddenly not feeling right about calling him Chase, being on such familiar terms with a total stranger. She would wait until he supplied a surname. Though for all she knew she'd already been calling him by his last name. Or maybe Chase wasn't his name at all.

"Where . . . ?" he rasped. "Where . . . ?"

"You're in Willow Springs. Do you remember being robbed?"

His face was blank, devoid of expression. He rubbed his eyes. "Who . . . are . . ." with great effort

132

he finished the question, "you?"

"My name is Abigail Graham. Can you tell me your name?" She repeated the question several more times. She wanted to keep him awake, let him get his bearings, find out if the bullet wound had done any less visible damage.

His eyes drifted closed. Gently, Abby shook his shoulder. "Wake up!"

"Why . . . hell . . . creep . . . around . . ." Talking seemed such an effort for him. She was about to insist that he stop, until he added the words, "in . . . dark?"

Abby's brows furrowed. "What did you say?"

"Lamp, dammit." He licked his dry lips, squeezing his eyes shut yet again. "Turn up . . . damn lamp."

Abby was almost as disconcerted by his swearing, as by his request. He was already eroding her image of a genteel man of noble stock. More worrisome still was his demand that she turn up the lamp. Her gaze shifted to the softly glowing light on the table next to him.

His hand groped to either side of the bed. He found the table, then felt for and discovered the base of the lamp. "Give me . . . match. Do it . . . my . . . self."

Her heart thudding, Abby stepped close and waved her hand in front of his eyes. He made no reaction. "My God . . ." she whispered. "Oh, my God."

"What? What are you . . . ?" He sagged weakly back.

"Please, Mr. —, sir, I . . . blast! What *is* your name?"

133

He closed his eyes again, opened them. "Cor—" he began, then coughed, nearly choking himself. He fell silent.

"Excuse me? I didn't catch that." When he said nothing, she prompted him again. "Your name?"

His face twisted, as though pained. "Murdock," he said at last. "The name's . . . Murdock."

"I . . ." She frowned. "I'm sorry. When you were . . . delirious . . . I thought you said your name was Chase. I didn't know if it was a first name or a last name."

He stiffened, a sudden strange look on his face. "No . . . one . . . calls me that. The name's . . . Murdock. Chase Murdock. You call me Murdock."

Abby felt oddly bereft to have lost the name Chase. But she had no time to think about it. The man was struggling to sit up. He was mentally more alert than when he'd first awakened, but physically he was obviously weaker than he thought. He had to stop to rest long seconds between every tiny exertion.

"Light . . . the damned lamp, woman. Or give me some . . . damned matches."

"Mr. Murdock," she said slowly, "the lamp *is* lit."

He opened his mouth as if to dispute this, then grew very still. He reached a hand again toward the lamp base, then held his hand up toward where the chimney would be. She knew he could feel the heat radiate against his palm.

A trace of fear came into those smoke blue eyes, which she could actually see him suppress, as though embarrassed anyone should be witness to it.

She heard his barely audible, "No."

"Please, Mr. Murdock," she said, reaching toward his shoulder, wanting to touch him, reassure him somehow. But she stopped herself, her fingers curling into her palm. "I'm sure it's just a reaction to your injury. I . . . I'll send for the doctor. He'll know what to do. Please, don't worry. I'm sure it will clear up."

"Clear up?" he murmured hoarsely. "Clear up?" His fear was now a living thing he couldn't hide. "Sweet Jesus, I'm blind."

Chapter Eight

Blind. The word hung in the air between them. Abby couldn't bring herself to move as she stood beside the bed, staring at Chase Murdock. Blind. If *she* couldn't assimilate the full shock of the word, she could scarce imagine what the man himself was going through.

She wished she could think of something to say, do, that would take away the fear, the pain now etched in those blue eyes. "Mr. Murdock, I . . ." She faltered, grew still. She would wait, take her cue from him.

Chase closed his eyes, seeming to collect himself. When he opened them again, Abby was startled to see that the fear was gone. "Did a doctor do this?" He touched the bandage on his head.

"Yes. Dr. Winthrop from Denver."

"Did he say anything about blindness? Whether or not I'd ever see again?"

Abby could only marvel at how matter-of-factly he asked the question. How could a man find himself blind one minute, and then so rationally discuss the condition the next?

"He didn't mention it at all. I'm sorry."

He was silent a minute, and she would have given anything to know what he was thinking behind that expressionless mask.

Finally, he said, "What time is it?"

"Past midnight."

"Then I suppose you're heading to bed."

His voice disturbed her now. Such casualness could not be natural.

"I . . ." she caught herself, stung by a sudden fierce reluctance to admit she'd been sitting there reading to him. Worse, that she'd been fantasizing him to be some gallant amalgamation of War Hawk and Tex Trueblood. Embarrassment and, more disturbingly, a very real shyness rippled through her. Almost against her will she found herself disconcertingly aware of how drawn she had been to this man from the moment she'd found him by the creek. "I just came in to check on you," she managed, "before I retired. We were pretty worried when you were unconscious for so long."

"We?"

"My aunt and uncle. This is our home. They're asleep in another room."

"How did I get here?"

"Our wagon. We were travelling to town. We're new to—"

"Why don't you just go on to sleep yourself. I'm sure you're tired. Looking after me couldn't have been easy."

There was no emotion in his voice. None. Abby's brows furrowed. There was something wrong here. Very wrong. Certainly she didn't know this man, but no one could find himself blind and react so indifferently. With a studied nonchalance of her own, she rose to her feet. "If you're sure you'll be all right 'til morning . . . ?"

"I'll be fine. Just fine."

Abby crossed to the door, her anxiety mounting. Maybe she should at least wake Ethan. He might know what to say to this man better than she. "Good night then, Mr. Murdock."

"Good night."

She opened the door.

"Ah, miss . . . ma'am . . . ?" he called.

She turned. "The name's Abby, Mr. Murdock," she reminded him gently. "Abigail Graham."

"Is there . . . was there anything else I should know?"

"What do you mean?"

"When you found me . . ." He hesitated. "Was there . . . anyone else around?"

"You mean the beasts who did this to you?"

He seemed to stiffen just a little, but she decided it could have been a trick of the light. "No one."

He lay back, saying nothing.

"We reported it to the sheriff, of course."

"Sheriff?" His hand knotted in the coverlet. "Sheriff Devlin?"

"You know him?"

"No. We've never met. I've just . . . seen him

138

around." There was an undercurrent, something she couldn't read in his voice now.

"You're from around here then?"

"No."

The word was clipped, sharp. No doubt he was anxious to speak to the lawman, to find out if Devlin had uncovered anything about the men who attacked him. "I . . . I didn't mean to seem forward, Mr. Murdock." Blast! What was the matter with her? Why couldn't she speak to this man without stammering? She drew in a deep breath. "I only asked because I'll be sending a telegram in the morning to Dr. Winthrop about your vision." He didn't move, not a muscle. "And, well, if there's someone you'd like me to notify . . . ?"

"No one."

"Family? Your . . . wife?"

"No one," he said again.

Was there a hint of defensiveness in those words? She knew she should let him rest, sleep. But she couldn't seem to bring herself to leave, not yet. "Were you trailing the men who did this to you?"

"Trailing?"

"The outlaws who shot you. I . . . I found a badge beside you in the grass. I know you're a lawman yourself of some sort."

He closed his eyes again and sagged deeper against the pillow. "Yes, a lawman," he said, his voice strained, then added, "a very weary lawman, Miss Graham. If you don't mind . . ."

"Oh, dear, I'm sorry. I shouldn't have rattled on

139

so. I . . . yes, please, rest. I'll bring your breakfast by in the morning." She started out the door. "Is there anything special you'd like?"

"It doesn't matter."

"I'll see you in the morning then."

"Yeah. *See* you." He gave a bitter laugh.

She winced, regretting her choice of words, then left the room, leaving the door ajar. She walked several paces then turned back. The lantern still glowed beside the bedside table, Chase Murdock visible in its heavily shadowed light. She couldn't take her eyes off him. He looked not nearly so formidable and intimidating as he had seemed moments before. Instead he looked painfully vulnerable, alone. And she knew, *knew,* the fear he had shuttered away earlier had returned to those smoke blue eyes.

For a long minute Chase sat very still. He had heard the woman leave, but he wanted to give her time to get to her room, go to bed. And he wanted to give himself time, time to discover he wasn't awake at all, that this was just some grotesque nightmare. That soon now he would wake up and be lying in the grass beside the road, where Noah and the others had left him.

Blind.

Sweet Jesus, he couldn't be blind.

He groped a hand toward the table beside the bed, his heart thundering. This was a dream, a nightmare, and he was going to prove it. His fingers collided with something solid on the table. He grabbed for it, felt it skitter across the smooth surface and fall with a thud to the wood floor.

Without thinking he leaned down. A savage pain tore through him, starting deep in his right side and surging upward until he thought the top of his head was going to explode. For a long minute he didn't move, his body twisted, half on, half off the bed. Slowly, the pain ebbed, grew dull. Tolerable.

Cautiously, he righted himself, one hand pushing off the floor. His fingers brushed a firm rectangular object. Catching it up, he slumped back into the bed. His body shook, trembled. His side hurt; his head hurt. He felt weak, hollow.

This was no dream.

He gripped the object, held it up, willing himself to see it. Nothing. He ran a hand across it, smelled it. A book, leatherbound.

Ignoring the pain that again sliced through him, he shoved himself into a sitting position, groping about for the matches he'd heard the woman use earlier. She had turned down the lantern, that was all. That was why he couldn't see the book.

His fingers found a match. He stilled, fighting off a sudden cloying terror. What if . . . ? *Light it. Find out the woman had been the dream, that now he was awake*. He struck the match, heard it flare, smelled the sulphur.

And saw nothing.

Chase concentrated, his head pounding, as he

willed himself to see the flame. He swore, his hand jerking spasmodically, as the match burned down to his fingers. Quickly, he felt for it, uncertain if it had been out when he let go of it. He found the shriveled stick, closed his fist over it, fighting a sick despair.

Blind.

He swallowed hard and lay back, staring into nothing. *Relax, Cordell. Think.* This was just some kind of reaction to the bullet wound, that was all. It would clear up, go away. *Relax.* It might take a day or two. He would wait. He had to wait. He had no choice. The woman—what was her name? Abigail? She said she would send a message to the doctor. He would know what to do. Please, God, he would know.

He forced his mind to other things and noticed for the first time how hungry he was. He wished now he would have asked the woman to bring him something to eat before she went to bed. Not knowing the layout of the house, he didn't dare try to find anything himself. Besides, he wasn't sure he could trust his legs to support him.

He checked beneath the blankets and surmised he was dressed only in knee length drawers. The wound in his side, too, had been cleaned and bandaged. He reached a hand up, running it along his jaw. He'd had a shave, and not too long ago. Had the woman . . . ?

He tried to recall her voice. Soft, a little nervous at times, but pleasant, and strangely comforting.

142

Obviously she had no idea who he was. Thank God, he'd had the presence of mind not to tell her his name was Cordell. It may not have meant anything to her, but Sheriff Sam Devlin would have been sent scurrying to his reward dodgers.

So now he was Murdock, Chase Murdock. He hoped his old friend wasn't spinning in his grave, his name now tagged to an outlaw. He grimaced. How in the hell had the woman known his name was Chase anyway? He called himself Chase to no one.

Likely he had mumbled something when he was unconscious. He vaguely recalled fragmented images of Quinton Murdock and other less pleasant encounters from his past. He raked a hand through tumbled hair. What else had the woman heard? Had he said anything at all about Breckenridge? The stage? Gantry?

No. He couldn't have. He wouldn't be in a bed in some innocent family's house. Bullet wound or no, he would be in Devlin's jail.

Abigail Graham herself had inquired about the badge he carried. She had him pegged as a lawman. He shook his head. Chase Cordell, lawman. That was rich. What the hell? Let her think he was tracking outlaws. He'd stay here, get his strength back, then do some real tracking. He'd find Noah Gantry. And when he did, he'd kill him.

Find him? He closed his eyes. Right now he couldn't find the door.

His head hurt, the pain thudding in time to the beat of his heart. Maybe in the morning, he would see again. Maybe in the morning everything would be all right.

Abby lay in bed, afraid to sleep, fearing that if she did, Chase Murdock would wake again, need her. She had kept her vigil in his doorway until she was certain he'd fallen asleep. Only then had she gone to bed herself.

She'd watched him light the match, felt his fear, his frustration, when he obviously couldn't see the flame. It was all she could do not to bolt into the room when he'd burned his fingers. But greater than his fear, she sensed a need in him to sort through this, initially at least, on his own.

She would wire the doctor in the morning. Surely, there was something medically that could be done.

But what if there wasn't? What would become of Chase Murdock then?

She blushed, as she again thought of how she'd sat there holding his hand. What in the world had possessed her? Seemed still to possess her, as she thought of how vulnerable he'd looked, how lost? What was it about him that intrigued her so?

Her own foolish fantasies, that was what, she thought grimly. She was endowing this man with all manner of heroic characteristics that were bound to run afoul of who he really was. She wasn't being in the least bit fair to him.

"I'm sorry, Chase," she murmured. She would try to do better tomorrow.

Chase. He had asked her, *told* her, to call him Murdock. That was his right, of course. And she couldn't have presumed to address him informally anyway. But in her thoughts, he was still Chase. Whatever indefinable link she had formed with the man while he was unconscious, she had done so on a first name basis. And in the morning she would be there with him, when he dealt with his blindness for the first time in the full light of dawn.

Chapter Nine

Abby woke with a start. Chase! He was calling her name. She had to go to him. Throwing back the bedsheet, she was halfway across the room before she realized what she was doing. He was not calling at all. The house was silent. It was still dark. She'd been dreaming.

Barefoot, clad only in her cotton nightrail, Abby padded back to bed and sat down on the edge of the feather tick mattress. Never had she had a more vivid dream. Chase had been calling to her, but she couldn't find him. It was pitch dark, and all she could hear was the sound of his voice.

She'd followed the sound, called out to him, but he only continued to call her name. Stumbling into room after room, she was confronted again and again by darkness. She tried to light a lamp, but the matches didn't seem to work. And then she realized it wasn't the matches at all. She couldn't see, because she herself was blind.

Terrified, she screamed and Chase came to her. He caught her in his arms, pulled her to him, his

146

strength at once overwhelming and incredibly comforting.

"It's all right, Abby," he'd murmured. "I won't let anything hurt you. I'll never let anything hurt you."

And then he was gone, vanished.

She cried out his name, but he didn't answer. She was alone and blind. Chase had abandoned her, when she'd needed him most.

And then she heard him calling again. He was still lost. But this time she was afraid to find him.

Abby sat on her bed, hugging her arms tight against her, her heart hammering. Her waking moments were already consumed with thoughts of Chase Murdock, and now for the second time he had intruded on her dreams as well. It seemed the harder she tried to *stop* thinking about him, the more he proved to be all she *could* think about.

You just feel sorry for him, she reasoned a little desperately. Or maybe in a peculiar way she even felt responsible for him. After all, she'd saved his life.

But there was more to it than that. And she knew it only too well.

"Oh, Lisa," she murmured aloud, "I'll wager you saw it coming all along, didn't you? Abby Graham finds herself a wounded lawman and right away she writes herself into the poor man's life—his angel of mercy, the woman of his dreams."

She let out a shaky sigh. Being brutally honest, she reviewed her late night encounter with Chase Murdock. He had not been at all a charming and gallant knight in shining western armor. In fact, he'd

147

been rude, demanding and had a foul mouth to boot.

Of course, he'd also awakened to find himself blind. Hardly the sort of circumstance to put anyone in the best of humors. But, she reasoned primly, Tex Trueblood would rather have died than swear in the presence of a lady.

Thoughts of Tex prodded her to reach into the drawer of her nightstand and retrieve the metal box containing her manuscript. She'd scarcely had time to think about the book, let alone make any notes since finding Chase. Maybe she could make time for it today.

Right now, in fact. After all, dawn was still a half hour away. No doubt Chase was still sleeping. And even if he wasn't, she could scarcely visit him at this hour. Aunt Winnie would have her hide.

Quickly she skimmed the last two paragraphs, written several days before. Tex was hot on the trail of the man who killed his sweetheart.

"When I find that varmint, I'll take him to the nearest jail and hand him over for trial," Tex said, patting the mane of his faithful steed, *Valiant.*

Abby frowned. The words had sounded decent enough when she'd written them. Why didn't they seem so now?

Unwillingly she found herself wondering what Chase Murdock would do to a man who'd killed *his* sweetheart. *Hang him from the nearest tree,* came the equally unwilling answer.

Her frown deepened, sudden doubts assailing her,

as she closed the leatherbound volume and hugged it to her breasts. Could she have drawn Tex's character *too* heroically? Could it be he was no flesh and blood man at all? Would the editors at Beadle and Adams ever believe in a character as kind and true-hearted as Tex?

Her lips thinned, her eyes narrowing. She was doing it again! First, she was upset with herself for allowing Tex's personality to influence how she perceived the unconscious Chase Murdock. And now she was allowing the conscious, and thoroughly uncouth, Chase Murdock to sully the honor of the finest Texas Ranger who ever lived! And he did live! In her heart and in her mind. Because for a writer, that was the only way to write believable fiction.

Fuming, Abby returned her manuscript to the security of her nightstand. She might not be able to control her dreams, but she could certainly make a more conscious effort to control her thoughts now that she was awake. Toward that end, she decided it would be wise to think of her wounded patient as *Mr.* Murdock, not the much too familiar Chase. Conjuring first-name images of the man had only led to disaster.

Too, she had to make some allowances for him. After all, he'd been ambushed by outlaws, was in considerable pain, and may have lost his eyesight as well. Surely, his temperament would improve as his condition improved. But whether it did or did not could no longer be her concern. She would do everything she could to help the man recover. But after that, he was on his own.

That decided, Abby rose and crossed over to her wardrobe. She didn't wonder why such a sensible decision should sadden her so. She supposed reality just took a little getting used to. The aroma of frying bacon prodded her to hurry. Winnie was up and about.

Quickly, Abby selected a relatively new solferino pink and white striped lawn, trimmed with ruffles. She told herself it was because she wanted to make a good impression on any new townspeople she might meet today. Yet she couldn't help thinking she would also be taking Chase Murdock his breakfast attired in the flattering dress.

"Now you are being absurd, Abby," she muttered, fastening the final pearl button at the base of her throat. If the man's vision hadn't yet cleared, she could wear a gunny sack and it wouldn't matter.

But it would matter to me . . .

Rolling her eyes, Abby realized she had a battle on her hands. *Telling* herself not to think overmuch about Chase Murdock was one thing; *doing* it, it seemed, was going to be quite another. The battle joined, she marched toward the kitchen.

"Good morning, Aunt Winnie!" Abby said, smiling and giving her aunt a swift kiss on the cheek.

"Good morning, dear," Winnie said, continuing to stir a panful of scrambled eggs. "You certainly seem more chipper this morning."

"Well, I am and I'm not," Abby said. "Our patient finally woke up last night, which is wonderful,

150

but—"

"Just what time was that, dear?" Winnie interrupted.

Abby thought about hedging, but said, "Midnight."

Winnie removed the skillet from the heat. "Abby, dear . . . " she began, then faltered.

"Please, Aunt Winnie, he may be bl—"

"You're a woman grown," Winnie put in, "but there are still things proper and improper. You should have fetched me or Ethan."

"Maybe you're right," Abby allowed. "And I'm sorry. But it was very late. Anyway, that isn't important now. The man is blind, Aunt Winnie. The wound to his head . . . He can't see. The lamp was lit, and he couldn't see it at all."

"Merciful heaven." Winnie clasped a hand to her bosom. "The poor man. Oh, dear, oh, dear."

"What's all this?" Ethan asked, lumbering into the kitchen, straightening one of the suspenders that had slid off his shoulder. Abby quickly reiterated what she'd told Winnie.

Ethan settled himself into one of the straight-back chairs in front of the table. "Blind. Poor fellow! And no family. What's the boy going to do?"

"The first thing he needs is to get his strength back," Abby said. "And I thought I'd go down and send a telegraph message to Dr. Winthrop."

"Your aunt and I will do that. We have to go see Gunther about his store this morning anyway. We can close the deal."

151

"I don't know," Winnie said, worrying her lower lip. "If this Mr. Murdock is conscious, we can't both leave Abby alone with him."

"We won't be gone long," Ethan assured her. "And I want your opinion on the store, dear."

With obvious reluctance, Winnie relented.

While her aunt and uncle ate breakfast, Abby excused herself and went to see if Chase Murdock had yet awakened. Moving very quietly, so as not to disturb him if he was still asleep, she crossed to the open door of his room.

He was sitting up, his right hand splayed in front of his face, as though willing himself to see it. As she watched he let the hand drop to his lap, his fingers curling into a fist.

"You have to give it time," she said softly.

He jerked, startled. Abby didn't miss how his hand dropped instinctively to his right thigh — where the sheriff wore a gun.

"You shouldn't sneak up on a man like that," he all but snarled.

"I'm sorry," she said, flustered. "I didn't want to wake you, if . . . " She paused to steady herself, then continued evenly, "Do you want some breakfast?"

"I'm not hungry." A timely rumble of his stomach put the lie to his words.

"Would bacon and eggs be all right? Or something not so heavy?"

"I'm not hungry."

"I'll bring you some soup."

"That's great," he gritted. "I'm blind. You're deaf. I said I am not hungry."

Abby frowned, both at his sarcasm and because she knew full well he was lying. The man had to be half starved. She'd barely been able to get more than a cup of soup into him each of the last three days.

Deciding his ill humor was a result of his condition and had nothing at all to do with her, she said, "I'll be back in a few minutes." Giving him no further opportunity to protest, she returned to the kitchen and set about preparing a tray. "He's awake," she told her aunt and uncle, who were busily clearing away their own breakfast dishes. Abby didn't offer any further details about his condition or his mood, but she was quietly grim, expecting the worst, when Winnie and Ethan accompanied her back to the man's room.

"Mr. Murdock?" she announced, taking care this time not to be overly quiet. "I've brought your breakfast." Before he could offer his opinion—for good or ill—she quickly added, "I've also brought my aunt and uncle. May I introduce Winifred and Ethan Graham? This is Chase Murdock."

To Abby's surprise, when Winnie spoke, acknowledging his grunted "Good morning," Chase automatically pulled the blankets up to cover his half-exposed chest. Though she knew she was being absurd again, she found the gesture disarmingly sweet. The fact that he'd made no such acknowledgement to her own presence didn't matter. No doubt he could discern from Winnie's voice that she was a matronly woman and he had at least made an effort to conduct himself accordingly.

"You rest easy now, young fella," Ethan said. "Winnie and I have a few errands to run. And we'll get that message off to Dr. Winthrop first thing."

Chase maintained his grip on the coverlet. "Thank you."

Winnie exchanged a look with Ethan, and Abby knew her aunt was still not comfortable with the idea of leaving her alone with this man, but she nevertheless allowed Ethan to guide her from the room. Seconds later, Abby heard the front door open and shut. They were gone. She was alone in the house with Chase Murdock, whose indifferent features in the presence of her aunt and uncle had now darkened considerably again.

"I told you, I'm not hungry."

Abby had set the tray on the table beside the bed. She lifted the napkin and deliberately fanned the aroma of the food in his direction. She watched him swallow and involuntarily lick his lips.

"Can I help you sit up?" She reached to fluff the pillow for him. He flinched away when she accidentally brushed his arm.

"I'm blind, not crippled." He said the words through clenched teeth.

"I'm sorry." She bit her lip nervously, as the coverlet fell away to his waist when he struggled to a sitting position. Unwittingly, she remembered trailing her hand across that broad expanse. Her cheeks fired and for an instant she was actually grateful

154

that he couldn't see her.

Gingerly, she picked up the tray and set it on his lap. "I'll help you." She started to pick up the utensils.

"I can feed myself. I know where my mouth is."

"I . . . of course." She backed away, watching as he very cautiously felt his way around the tray with his right hand. She could feel him tense for a moment, when he couldn't locate the flatware, then relax a little when his fingers closed on a spoon.

He picked it up, then groped around further, cursing when he stuck his fingers in the soup. Very slowly, he said, "I'd appreciate it, if you'd leave me alone."

"I don't think that would be a very good idea."

He closed his eyes, a muscle in his jaw flexing, but he didn't ask again. He took up the spoon and again found the bowl of soup. Keeping his left hand on the rim of the bowl, he dipped the spoon into the steaming hot liquid. Carefully he brought the spoon toward his mouth, only to have the soup dribble off onto his chest.

A deathly quiet second passed. Then with an oath, Chase slammed down the spoon and upended the tray, sending everything flying. "Get out!" he roared. "Get out and leave me alone!"

Abby stood there, trembling with shock. She had never seen an enraged human being before. Angry, yes. But not this. He lay there, his hands balled into fists, his whole body shaking with fury.

Part of her knew she should go, let him deal with

this alone. And yet how could she? Bits of food were scattered everywhere. The bedding had to be changed. The soup had soaked through everything it touched. Picking up a napkin, Abby began to clean up the mess as best she could, all the while aware of how stiffly he was holding himself, as though if she so much as touched him he would explode.

When she'd finished with the food, she decided the bedding could wait. She couldn't very well remove the stained coverlet while he was still half naked beneath it.

She picked up the tray. "I'll get you some more soup."

"No."

"Mr. Murdock, you can't tell me you're not hungry. I'm going to get you some more soup."

In the kitchen she stood by the stove for long minutes, shaking violently, unbidden tears rimming her eyes. For a moment back in that room Chase Murdock had actually terrified her. She had a very hard time admitting that, but it was true. He had been so angry, that she had feared for her safety.

But he hadn't hurt her. And it really wouldn't have been all that difficult for him to get his hands on her if he'd wanted to, not even in his weakened state.

He was just frustrated, that's all. A man like that would be used to doing for himself. Being helpless no doubt went against everything in him. She would just have to be patient.

She poured more soup in a large cup, seining out the meat and vegetables, so that he could just drink

156

it, then she heaped the last of the scrambled eggs into another bowl. Returning to the bedroom, she found Chase standing, or rather leaning against a footpost of the bed. He turned his head toward her. "Where are my clothes?"

Abby stood stock still, staring at him. He was dressed only in his drawers.

He continued to glare in her direction, and for a moment Abby had to remind herself that he could see nothing.

"Are you going to answer me?" he demanded. "Where are my clothes?"

She set the food down and hurried to the wardrobe to retrieve his freshly laundered clothing. Keeping her eyes averted, she sidestepped toward him. "Here," she managed in a small voice.

He reached out, but did not connect with her outstretched hands. "What the hell . . . ? Give me my clothes."

"They're right in front of you," she squeaked.

"Why are you . . . ?" Sudden awareness shone in those sightless blue eyes. With a low curse he reached down to grab up a blanket from the bed. In one furious motion he wrapped it around his middle. "You could have said something."

"What?" she croaked.

"Right." He pressed a hand against his forehead, swaying slightly.

Abby rushed over to him. She put her arm around him and hurriedly assisted him back to bed, all the while trying to ignore the hard feel of solid muscle, the musky smell of his skin.

He took a few deep breaths to steady himself. "If the sight of this underwear offends you," he said, "I strongly suggest you leave. Or you're going to be really offended." He reached to loosen the drawstring.

"Wait!"

He paused.

"I'll be in the kitchen."

His temper seemed to settle to the simmering stage. "When you get back, you can take me to a hotel."

"But why? I mean, you said you have no one, no family. How could you manage? You're still so weak. You're in no condition to take care of yourself, Mr. Murdock."

"I can't stay here."

"Why not?"

He had no answer to that, finally saying, "I'm sure I've imposed on you and your family long enough."

"We don't mind. Honestly. At least here you have someone to take care of you. Until you're well," she added hastily.

His shoulders sagged. "How long do you think it will take to hear from that doctor?"

"I don't know. It depends on if he's made it back to Denver yet."

She brought the soup over to him. "I . . . took out the meat and vegetables, so you could just drink it, and . . . I put the scrambled eggs in a separate bowl."

He accepted the soup. "Thank you."

She smiled slightly at how grudgingly he said the words. He lifted the cup, took a sip, then drank the whole thing in a single gulp. Holding out the cup, he asked, "Could I trouble you for some more?"

"I'll get it." She started out.

"Ma'am . . . Miss Graham?"

She turned. "Yes?"

"My boots?"

"You weren't wearing any."

"My gun?"

She shook her head, then grimaced, realizing he couldn't very well see such a gesture. "You had nothing but the clothes you were wearing . . . and the badge."

"Ah, yes, my badge. Could I have it?"

She got it from the vanity and placed it in his hand. He turned it over in his palm. "Guess I won't be wearing this any time in the near future. Who needs a blind lawman, eh?"

"I'm sure Dr. Winthrop will offer some hope."

He chose not to respond to that, asking again for more soup, adding, "I'd still like to get dressed."

"Of course. If you need any help . . . ?"

"I'll manage." But again he was unsteady on his feet. Ignoring his protests, Abby helped him with his shirt.

"I'll put on my own pants, if that's all right?"

She blushed. "Please do. I'll get the soup." She fussed around in the kitchen for what she hoped was

159

a long enough time, then came back with soup and coffee.

Chase was sitting on the side of the bed, fully dressed except for his stockinged feet and unbuttoned shirt. Abby set down the tray, asking him to move long enough so that she could change the bedding. Swiftly she did so, then frowned, as she glanced at him and thought she noticed a fresh red stain on the bandage around his waist. She came over to him. "You may have broken open your wound."

"I don't think so."

"I'd feel better if you'd let me have a look."

He lay down on the bed atop the covers, crossing his legs at the ankles. "Whatever you say, ma'am."

His manner was so cold and distant that she found it difficult not to be hurt by it. But she steeled herself inwardly. No matter what his mood, she had to see to the wound.

She took a deep breath. She'd never done this while he was conscious before. Determined, she gathered up fresh strips of bandages, then lifted the side of his shirt away from the wound.

Her fingers trembled. She waited until they steadied. She didn't dare let him realize how nervous she was. Using a scissors, she cut away the old bandage, being careful not to apply any pressure to the area of the wound itself. As she worked, she dared a quick glance at his face. He lay there, totally impassive. He might as well have been unconscious.

She peeled away the layers of bandages and noted

with relief that while the wound had indeed bled a little, it was already clotting shut again. "Can you lift up?" she asked. "I need to pull the rest of the bandage out from under you and wrap you up again."

Wincing, he did so. Catching up his shirttail, he tugged it upward to the middle of his back so she could work freely. She had to lean close to wind the cloth around his waist. She found herself all too aware of him, his warm breath, the rise and fall of his chest. Working more rapidly than was necessary, she quickly tied off the new bandage. "There. That should hold you for awhile."

If she expected any thanks, it was not forthcoming.

"I might as well change the other bandage, too."

He made no objection, and she had the uneasy feeling that he had determined not to make any more requests of her, because she wasn't doing much of anything he asked anyway. Working swiftly, she rebandaged his head wound. "It's healing very nicely," she said.

He made no comment.

She sighed inwardly, then noticed again that his shirt was open. "Do you think you could button your shirt? My aunt and uncle could be back any time."

He must have been waiting for that one. In an acid drawl, he said, "It would certainly never do for them to find you in bed with your less than fully clothed patient, now would it?"

161

Abby shot to her feet, feeling a hot flush of hurt and shame. "That was uncalled for, Mr. Murdock. If that's any sample of your sense of humor, you'd do well to keep it to yourself."

To her surprise he expelled a snort of disgust, self-directed. "I'm sorry."

She had no time to wonder at the sincerity of his words. The front door was opening and she caught the sound of voices. She gasped, looking helplessly at Chase. "Please, it's my aunt and uncle. Your shirt . . ."

He gave a low curse, but worked the buttons as quickly as he could, just finishing the last one as Winnie and Ethan came into the room.

"I'm glad to see you've got some color back, boy," Ethan said.

But Winnie was silent, and Abby knew her aunt was worried about just how much assistance Chase had needed to get dressed.

"We know you need your rest," Ethan went on, "but I'm afraid we brought a visitor. He was very persistent."

Abby gazed toward the door, surprised to see Sam Devlin come into the room. "Sheriff," she began, frowning when Chase again winced visibly. He must be in more pain than he was letting on.

"This'll only take a minute, Miss Graham," Devlin assured her. He caught up a chair and pulled it over beside the bed, never taking his eyes off Chase. "I have a few questions that need answers, and I'm sure your patient won't mind providing them." Devlin sat

162

himself down. "Mr. . . . Murdock, is it?"

Chase nodded slowly.

"This is about a stage robbery, Mr. Murdock. And an outlaw named Cordell."

Chapter Ten

Chase hoped he appeared calm, because he certainly didn't feel that way. He hoped, too, that no one had been looking at his face, when Abigail Graham had said the word *sheriff*. He knew he hadn't been able to hide a sudden rush of apprehension. Maybe Sam Devlin knew more than he'd been letting on, maybe he'd only been allowing the Grahams to care for him until he regained consciousness. After all, it was pretty damned difficult to bring a dead man to trial.

He felt his pulse quicken. Maybe Felicity Breckenridge had given the sheriff a full description of one particular masked outlaw. . . .

Chase lay still, listening as Devlin scraped up a chair and sat down. Chase found himself noticing other sounds as well. Like the rustle of skirts. Miss Graham had not left the room. She was pacing back and forth, and though he hadn't the slightest idea what she looked like, he had a clear image of her wringing her hands, worried that Devlin's presence would tire her prize patient. He sensed too that

Winnie and Ethan Graham were still standing somewhere near the back of the room.

Chase noticed all this and more, and then Devlin said the name *Cordell*.

He was very careful not to flinch. He remembered the lawman clearly from that day in the Lone Tree Saloon when a clerk had brought in a message to some citizen about Breckenridge being on the stage. Devlin was a big man, tough looking, who wore a Colt .45 strapped to his right thigh. Chase had no doubt the man was watching him closely.

"Cordell," Chase said slowly. "Yeah, I know the name. What about him?"

"I've got a witness who puts Cordell and his gang at a stage holdup right about where you got yourself shot."

Chase wondered again if Felicity had given him up, or if she'd left that privilege to her husband. Not that it mattered. What mattered was that the Breckenridges were obviously no longer in town, or Devlin would have brought them along to identify him. The sheriff was fishing. It was up to Chase to make certain he didn't hook anything. Chase would have to bluff this out as best he could. "I was after Cordell myself," he said evenly.

"That's a pretty tough outfit for a man to take on alone."

Chase touched his bandaged head. "So I noticed."

"You threw down on the whole nest of 'em by yourself?" Devlin clearly saw such an act foolhardy at best. Perhaps even unbelievable.

165

"Overran 'em actually," Chase said. "Kind of accidental like." He was making this up as he went along, and he had no idea if Devlin was buying into a single word of it. He wished to heaven he could see the man's face.

"You want to explain that," Devlin said.

Chase manufactured an entire scenario about tracking the Cordell gang for nearly two weeks. "I didn't figure them to hold up the stage," he said. "It didn't seem like something Cordell would do."

"From what I hear he had it in for someone on that stage."

Chase shrugged. "I wouldn't know."

"So you just kinda stumbled into 'em?"

"Wasn't my lucky day. They shot me, left me for dead."

"It was Cordell who shot you then?" Devlin prompted.

"Actually it was one of the others." Chase couldn't risk naming Noah Gantry. No one but Chase, Josey and the Kid yet knew Gantry rode with the Cordell gang. Of course, his tale of trailing them for two weeks would give him a reason to know. But there was another reason for not naming the outlaw. To do so might somehow alert Gantry that Chase was still alive. He didn't want Gantry stalking him, at least not until he got his sight back. *If* he got his sight back . . . Chase gave himself a mental shake, forcing his attention back to the lawman.

"Miss Graham showed me a badge you were carrying," Devlin was saying. "You're some kind of spe-

166

cial deputy?"

Chase's mind raced, though his head hurt. How was he to get out of this one? "I was."

"I'm listenin'."

"I don't wear the badge any more, Sheriff. You see, I'm a little out of my jurisdiction. I quit when I went after Cordell and his bunch."

"Why's that?"

"Guess it's like Cordell and that man on the stagecoach. It's personal."

Chase could hear Devlin shift his weight on the chair, lean forward. "Who said Cordell was after a *man* on that stage, Murdock? Could've been a woman."

Chase tucked his thumbs into the waistband of his trousers, giving himself the second he needed to seem totally unconcerned with Devlin's heightened probing. "Like I said, Sheriff. I think I know Cordell, the way he thinks, at least a little. I've never known him to draw down on a woman."

Devlin's demeanor shifted, grew even more intense. "Didn't I see you in Willow Springs about a week back, Mr. Murdock?"

"I believe I stopped for a beer." Damn! Obviously the lawman had seen him in the Lone Tree.

"Is that all? Just a beer? No other business in town?"

"That was it, Sheriff."

"You'd think you would have looked me up, Murdock. Told me about your trackin' Cordell to my town."

167

"I work alone, Sheriff."

"You don't work at all, Murdock. Remember? You've got no jurisdiction here."

"I remember." Murdock was pressing hard now. Chase's head was throbbing. He worried he would make a mistake, contradict himself. He had to get the lawman out of here.

"You know, Murdock. There's something else I don't understand about that holdup . . ."

Chase allowed a low moan, his face twisting. As he'd hoped, the ever solicitous Miss Graham was instantly at his side.

"Please, Sheriff Devlin," she urged, "Mr. Murdock has been through quite an ordeal. I think he'd better rest now. You can ask him more questions some other time."

Devlin sighed, but agreed. "I guess I can't complain, Miss Graham. If I have to come back and talk to him, that means I'll get to see you again."

"Now, Sheriff . . ."

Chase caught a sudden flutter in Abigail Graham's voice, as though she were pleased by the sheriff's personal attention. The notion unaccountably soured his own mood even further.

"Please, Miss Graham," Devlin said, "I told you — I want you to call me Sam. And it would certainly please me mightily to call you Miss Abby."

Abigail Graham giggled. "I suppose that would be all right."

"And what about our dinner?"

"Would tomorrow night be all right?"

168

"Perfect."

The sheriff, Miss Graham's aunt and uncle, and Abigail herself then started out of the room. Chase heard the scrape of boots that told him Devlin had paused. "You rest easy now, Mr. Murdock," the lawman cautioned with just a trace of sarcasm. "I'll be back."

They then closed the door behind them.

Chase lay back, exhausted, numb. And worse than that — helpless. How the hell was he going to get out of here? He didn't know why Devlin was suspicious, but he was. The lawman wasn't going to stop digging until he hit what he was looking for.

Chase eased his legs over the side of the bed and sat up, the simple movement sending waves of nausea crashing through him. *Great.* Furious, he lay down again. He would have to hope he could ward off Devlin for a day or two at least. For now he had no choice but to let his body heal.

A knock sounded at the door. He frowned. "Come in."

He knew at once it was Abigail Graham, picking up the lightness of her step, the subtle suggestion of jasmine. "I thought I'd get some sleep, Miss Graham."

The way she halted, in mid-stride he guessed, he had disconcerted her with his identification.

"How did you know it was me?" she asked.

He shrugged, too tired for explanations. "Lucky guess."

"I just came in to see how you were doing. I know

169

Sheriff Devlin's questions were very tiring."

"I'm fine." He angled his head away from her, uncertain why he couldn't face her, when he couldn't see her anyway.

"Can I get you anything?"

"No, ma'am."

"It wouldn't be any trouble."

"Whether it's troublesome or not, I don't want anything." He could feel himself behaving like a jackass, but her constant hovering was getting on his nerves. Besides, he had yet to deal with this new helplessness. He didn't want her or anyone seeing him this way.

He sensed her come close, stop beside the bed. "I'm sorry," she said. "I don't mean to be patronizing. I know all of this must be very difficult for you, but I really am here if you need anything."

He laced his fingers together and blew out a long sigh. Though he still didn't face her, he said, "Maybe some coffee?"

"I'll get it for you." He could actually feel her smile.

She left then, and he found himself wondering what she looked like. Her voice was warm, soft. And Devlin was certainly interested.

Chase scowled darkly. Let him be. It was no concern of his. All he cared about was getting his sight back. Maybe he needed additional surgery. Or time. A few days, a week. Whatever it took, he would do. He had to see again; he had to get out of here.

He had to find Noah Gantry and kill him.

Abby stood in the front doorway and crushed the telegraph message in her fist. A young boy had brought it by the house just a minute before.

Ethan came up to her. "I take it the news from Winthrop isn't good."

Abby grimaced. "Dr. Winthrop is a most infuriating man." She handed the missive to her uncle. "According to the dear doctor, Mr. Murdock's sight will either come back or it won't. There's nothing more medically that can be done. Something about internal swelling." She looked helplessly at her uncle, then at Chase's room. "What am I going to tell him, Uncle Ethan?"

"The truth."

"What truth?" she demanded. "That we don't know any more now than we did before? I can just hear myself — 'I'm so sorry, Mr. Murdock,'" she spoke as though he were standing in front of her, "'but you may be blind for the rest of your life. Or maybe not. Maybe you'll regain your sight at some unknown date in the future. In any event, good-bye and good luck.'"

She pressed her fingers to her eyes. "How can I hurt him like that?"

"You're not hurting him," her uncle said gently, placing an arm about her shoulder. "You're telling him what the doctor said. After that, it's up to Mr. Murdock."

Her shoulders sagged. "It's just that I feel so

171

awful for him. He has no family, no one." She looked at Ethan. "I know you and Aunt Winnie are uncomfortable having him here, especially Aunt Winnie. But with this kind of news we can't just . . ."

"I think we'd best bring your aunt in on this," Ethan cut in, guiding Abby toward the parlor.

Winifred Graham looked up from the needlepoint sampler she was working. "You two certainly look grim," she said. "Out with it."

Abby repeated the contents of the telegram, then said, "I want to tell him it's all right if he stays here for awhile. At least until he gets his strength back."

Winnie's eyes were at once understanding and concerned. "I know you want to help the man, Abby. But you must have a care for your reputation, too. We're new to Willow Springs. I doubt Hiram Perkins is a man to take something like this lightly."

"You and Ethan live in this house too. And if being a Good Samaritan is bad for my reputation, then so be it."

"We can't just turn him out into the street, Winnie," Ethan agreed.

Reluctantly, Winnie made it unanimous.

"So now the only one who doesn't know is Mr. Murdock," Abby said.

"Do you want me to tell him?" Ethan asked. "He's still plenty shaky from those wounds. But I get the feeling he can be a bit moody."

Abby winced inwardly. Moody was an understatement. She recalled the scattered food tray, but said only, "I appreciate the offer, Uncle Ethan, but I need to be the one." She took a steadying breath, though it did nothing to slow the triphammer beat of her heart, then headed toward Chase's room. Outside his door she took another deep breath, then knocked.

There was a moment's hesitation, then a gruff, "Come in."

She was surprised to find him standing next to an open window. He was leaning against the wall, favoring his right side. His body anchored one of the gingham curtains, apparently to keep the breeze from riffling in it in his face. As she stepped nearer, he cocked a sightless glance toward her and sniffed the air, his voice maintaining its already too familiar acid tone. "What? No food for me to toss about?"

She ignored the taunt, knowing full well she was about to further blacken his mood. "I've just received a reply from Dr. Winthrop."

He stiffened.

Abby swallowed, holding the telegraph message up with trembling fingers. But she couldn't bring herself to read it.

"Well," Chase prompted, when she'd obviously stalled too long, "what the hell did he have to say?"

"It . . . I . . ."

Chase felt his way to the bed and sagged onto it. "There's no hope for it, is there? That's why you can't get the words out."

"No . . . I mean . . . I'm sorry, Mr. Murdock. The doctor just doesn't know."

A slight bit of hope crept into his face. "He'll

come back then, examine me?"

"No."

"Why the hell not!"

"He says there's nothing more he can do. Either you get your sight back, or you don't."

"How long before I know?" He stood abruptly, his breath catching as the sudden movement must have sent a shaft of agony lancing through him. "How long?" he repeated.

Abby pressed her hand to her lips, hurting for him. "He doesn't know that either. It could be weeks, months. If there's been no permanent damage, then you'll see again. Otherwise . . ."

"Otherwise, I'll be blind the rest of my life." He said it as though he already believed it.

"You mustn't think that way." She had to fight an overwhelming urge to touch him, to somehow reassure him, knowing he would reject her concern as pity.

He sat again, stretching out atop the bedcovers. "I think I'd better get some sleep."

"You can't sleep your life—" she stopped. "I'm sorry. I know the wounds are still bothersome. But please, if you need anything, anything at all, just ask."

"I don't *need* anything, Miss Graham. Except my eyesight. And since you can't bring that to me, I'd just like to be alone."

She stepped close to the bed. "I . . . we could talk. I don't know very much about you."

He closed his eyes. "There's nothing to know."

"My aunt and uncle and I haven't been in Willow Springs very long. In fact . . ."

"Look, Miss Graham," he cut in, "you said you didn't want to be patronizing, yet that is exactly what the hell you are being. Please, just get out and leave me the hell alone."

His voice was cold, hard, bitter. Abby bit her lip to keep the tears at bay.

"Abby, dear . . ." Winnie's voice reached her, tentative, nervous, from the open doorway.

Abby turned, praying her own voice didn't betray her distress. "Yes, Aunt Winnie?"

"Mr. Perkins is here to see you."

Abby sighed. That was all she needed. "Thank you, Aunt Winnie, I'll be right out."

Winnie looked from Abby to Chase Murdock and back again, her eyes pained, sad, but she nodded and left.

Abby again looked at Chase. "I'm very sorry, Mr. Murdock." He didn't open his eyes. "It's certainly not my intention to upset you, to make you feel worse than you already do."

When he said nothing, she went out to face Perkins.

She found him seated in the rose-hued Queen Anne's chair in the parlor, sipping tea Aunt Winnie had brought out for him. He stood when Abby entered the room. "Do forgive my untimely arrival, my dear," he said. "But at least it accorded me the opportunity to hear for myself what you've been up against, having to deal with such a rough sort as Mr.

175

Murdock."

"He's hurt, Mr. Perkins. And he's been blinded by outlaws. I doubt you'd be in the best of humors yourself in such a situation."

"In any event, Miss Graham, Mr. Murdock is not the primary reason I stopped by."

"Then what does bring you here, Mr. Perkins?"

"I've made arrangements for the other members of the town council to be at the schoolhouse tomorrow. We'll all be pitching in to get everything in order for the opening of school. And I thought it would be a good time for you to meet everyone."

"I appreciate that. I'll be there, of course. Now, if that's all, I'm afraid you'll have to excuse me. I'm very tired."

If Perkins was offended by her abrupt dismissal, he was careful not to show it. "I understand perfectly, my dear." He set aside his tea cup. "We'll all look forward to tomorrow then." He started toward the door, then paused. "Of course, I'm certain you'll be making arrangements soon that Mr. Murdock be sent to a facility better suited to care for him."

"And I'm certainly glad you're certain, Mr. Perkins," Abby said, showing the man out. "Good evening." With that she closed the door.

"Of all the arrogant so and so's," she muttered. But at least her irritation with Perkins helped assuage some of the stinging hurt she still felt from Chase Murdock's shutting her out. Maybe leaving the man to himself for awhile would help. She headed toward the kitchen to help Winnie with supper.

Not wanting her aunt and uncle to worry about her any more than they already did, Abby kept her voice light and animated throughout dinner. Then she cheerfully prepared a tray for Chase.

"Do you want me to take that to him?" Winnie offered. "You're wearing yourself out for that man."

"I'm fine, Aunt Winnie. Honestly. Besides, Mr. Murdock and I have a kind of rapport established about mealtimes." Abby almost choked as she remembered the exact nature of that rapport. But the image of Winnie having to confront Chase Murdock's towering temper kept Abby's courage up. One incident like that with Winnie and Chase would be out in the street for certain. Abby couldn't let that happen. Whether the man wanted to admit it or not, he was scared. And it was that knowledge that steadied her as she carried the tray to his room.

This time he barely acknowledged her presence, sitting sullenly on the bed. He refused to make any attempt to feed himself. She decided to wait him out, hoping his hunger would override his pride. When it did not, she cut his steak for him. Though she knew it galled him, he sat there and let her feed him.

She could feel his rage mount. When she used a napkin to dab away a bit of gravy on his chin, she thought he might knock away the tray again. But he didn't move. She stood, wanting only to put an end to this most unpleasant meal. "Is there anything else I can get you?"

177

"A gun."

She started. "I beg your pardon?"

"I want a gun. I feel naked without one."

"I . . . my uncle has a rifle and an old Dragoon Colt someone gave him years ago."

"I want a gun of my own, Miss Graham."

"You could hardly have much use for—" Her lips thinned. It was absurd to even discuss a gun. "I'll be going to the mercantile tomorrow. I could get you some boots. Do you know what size?"

"I don't have any money."

"You can pay me back later."

"When I get a job?" he sneered.

"You can't give up."

"Can't I? You haven't seen it from this side, lady. It's as black as hell in here."

"Please, your language."

He swore.

She sprang to her feet. "When you can behave like a gentleman, I'll be back."

"Then you won't be back, lady. I've never been a gentleman."

Abby felt her own temper nudge her. She had been nothing but kind to this man, and he was nothing but rude and sarcastic in return. Yet she held her tongue. It wouldn't be fair to take her own hurt feelings out on him. He'd been through so much already. She would try one last time. "I like to read before I retire. I often read aloud to my aunt and uncle. Would you like to join us this evening?"

The look on his face made her wish she hadn't

asked. "It's your house," he said.

Abby assisted him to the parlor and settled him on the divan with a blanket on his lap. She wasn't certain, but she thought she heard him mumble something about "damned invalid." She decided to give him the benefit of the doubt. When her aunt and uncle, too, were settled, Abby began reading aloud from Louisa May Alcott's *Little Women*.

An hour passed; Abby grew content, comfortable. She so enjoyed these times with her family. Ethan was lounging in the rocker, half dozing. Winnie worked her sampler by the light of the fire crackling in the hearth.

She continued to read, glancing up every now and then to see that Chase seemed more and more discomfited. Perhaps his wounds were bothering him. But the pain in his face seemed oddly not physical at all. She was about to ask him if he was all right, when suddenly he threw back the blanket, stood up and, keeping his arm outstretched, made his way out of the room.

"Mr. Murdock, please . . ." Abby started after him, fearful he would run into something.

"Leave him go," Ethan said. "He needs to be alone."

"I just want to help him."

"He needs to learn to get along without anybody's help."

Abby heard the door slam to Chase's room. "He's blind, Uncle Ethan. There are things he can't do any more."

"And things he can. New things he can learn."

Abby thought a moment. "I've been doing it all wrong, haven't I?"

Ethan leaned forward, the rocker creaking slightly. "I remember a soldier come back from the war. He'd lost his right leg at Bull Run. Every day I'd come across him on the street corner in front of the store, begging. I figured it was all the poor soul could do to get by any more. I'd always drop in a coin or two and be on my way.

"One day, when your aunt was home with you nursing a cold, I was starting to feel kinda poorly myself. I asked him to come in and mind the store for a few minutes, while I ran down to the doctor's office for a potion.

"When I got back, he was like a new man. He was helping customers, talking, happy. For the first time since he lost his leg he felt like he could do something again, something worthwhile to earn his own way. I figure Mr. Murdock has got a lot of the same feelings going on in his head right about now. His pride as a man is on the line, Abby. He needs to know he can still do for himself."

Abby worried her lower lip, considering the wisdom of her uncle's words. He was making a lot of sense. "Do you think a blind man could work in the store, Uncle Ethan?"

"I've been thinking about asking him, but I wanted to wait until he was stronger. But maybe I shouldn't have waited. I'll talk to him about it tomorrow."

Abby came over and kissed her uncle on the cheek. "You're wonderful, you know that."

"Why do you think your aunt married me? It wasn't for my looks."

Abby straightened with a renewed determination. "I'm going to help him too, Uncle Ethan. Tomorrow morning I'm going to help Chase Murdock help himself."

Chapter Eleven

The next morning Abby didn't waste any time. She quickly readied Chase's breakfast tray and took it to his room. She was bound and determined not to feel sorry for him a moment longer.

He was awake and more surly than ever, if such were possible. He sat there on the bed, waiting for her to feed him. Perversely, she drew up a chair and sat down, not touching the food tray. His lips thinned, and for a moment she feared he intended to outwait her. But his stomach defeated him. With a low curse he swung his legs over the side of the bed and felt for the tray himself.

Cautiously, he began to place the position of the food. He stuck his fingers in the applesauce.

Abby scooted close. "I have an idea."

He ignored her, continuing to feel his way around the tray full of food. He nearly upset the coffee. With an oath he pushed the tray away.

"You like watchin' this?" he hissed.

"You can eat it or wear it," she said, "it's up to you." She bit her lips, appalled by her own words.

She could feel the fury in him. She opened her mouth to apologize, but closed it again, as he carefully reached for the fork. As though the words had been tortured out of him, he asked, "What's your idea?"

Her heart thudded with new hope. "Think of the plate as the face of a clock. The steak is at 12:45, the potatoes at 12:15. The applesauce at 12:40."

"Steak at 12:45?" His lips twisted derisively.

"Exactly."

He picked up the fork and made a stab at the meat. "Feels more like 12:50 to me." He was still grumbling, but there was the tiniest trace of ruefulness in his voice now.

Abby allowed a slow smile, feeling for the first time as if the ice had been broken between them. While Chase concentrated on the food, she sat by, quietly watching him. Such a strong face, she thought wistfully. It seemed impossible that those remarkable blue eyes could see nothing. When he'd finished, she asked, "Would you like some more coffee?"

He nodded.

She poured it for him. "Do you like it?"

He shrugged. "It's all right. A little weak, maybe."

She settled in the chair again. Maybe she could finally get him to talk a little, tell her something about himself. She was still so very curious about him. "You know," she began haltingly, "most men chatter away endlessly about themselves. You haven't said a word."

"Nothing to say."

She worried about pressing him, but her curiosity won out. "Where did you grow up?"

"Here and there." He took a sip of the coffee.

"I thought I detected a little Texas drawl."

"That was a long time ago."

He was speaking grudgingly, but at least he was speaking. It was a start. "Were you born in Texas?"

A muscle in his jaw jumped. Why should he be touchy about where he was born? "I was."

"Are your parents still there?"

"I wouldn't know."

She blinked, disbelieving. "You don't know? How can that be?"

"How can that be, Miss Graham?" He set the coffee cup down and glared at her, an altogether unsettling glare, considering how accurate the direction of his gaze was and the fact that he couldn't see her at all. "Obviously you've never encountered the underbelly of life. Well, maybe it's time you did. My mother left my father when I was two years old. I don't remember her at all."

Now that he was talking, she wished fervently that he would stop. But he didn't. The words had evidently been caged inside him a very long time.

"My father was drunk and mean. And when he was sober, which was very rare, he was even meaner, because the only thing he cared about in the world was being drunk or getting drunk. I left home when I was twelve, and I never looked back."

"I'm sorry," she said. "Truly. I didn't mean to stir up such painful memories. I just wanted to know something about you."

"Forget it."

"No," she said quietly. "I won't do that."

He turned away. "Would you mind if I smoke?"

"If you must."

"I had the makings on me when I was shot. I don't suppose Cordell and his bunch left them behind."

"No, nothing. I still can't believe you took on those horrid outlaws all alone."

"Damned stupid," he agreed.

She stood. "I can pick up some tobacco for you at the store. I—" she had a sudden thought, "or you could come with me. The fresh air might do you good."

He started to decline, and she sensed his sudden nervousness. No doubt he chafed at the idea of being led about in public. But then he reconsidered. "I would like to get out of here for awhile. This room is like a blasted jail cell." He got to his feet. "Lead the way."

She caught his upper arm and they started toward the door. Abby tried hard to ignore the feel of bunched muscle beneath her palm. She halted abruptly. "Oh, dear," she cried, dismayed, "I completely forgot! I have to meet Hiram Perkins and the town council over at the school." She looked forlornly at Chase, who was trying hard to hide his disappointment. "I don't know how long it will take, I . . ."

He felt his way back to the bed. "Maybe later."

"Later I'm having dinner with Sam Devlin."

Chase stiffened.

"Tomorrow for certain, all right?" she prompted.

185

"Whatever." His voice was cold again, distant.

Abby collected the food tray, feeling as though the tiny bit of progress they'd made had just been dashed. He tried to feign indifference over being left behind, but she knew he was smarting. She vowed inwardly to make it up to him tomorrow.

Alone in his room, Chase again found the darkness overwhelming. Abby was gone. Abigail Graham with her soft, reassuring voice that brought an odd measure of comfort to his black void. Even when he was angry with her for hovering over him, he didn't want her to abandon him to this abyss.

Yet again and again he was rude to her, all but deliberately driving her away. And though he doubted she would believe it, being rude to a woman was not something that came naturally to Chase Cordell. Then why Abigail Graham? He supposed it could be her oversolicitude. Or just the fact that she could see, and he couldn't. Or both. Or neither. Or maybe it was more subtle still — a wariness in him of her very vitality, a joy in living that he hadn't felt or heard since Murdock.

And as he had with Murdock's paternal concern, Chase felt a compelling urge to run. Only it was very difficult to run, when one couldn't see where one was going.

He knew he was feeling intensely sorry for himself. But he couldn't seem to help it, stop it.

He crossed to the open window, listening. He caught the sound of jangling harness from a passing wagon, the excited voices of children at play, the song of birds, the drone of insects—the pulse of life all around him, but in his own frighteningly dark world he felt no life at all.

Physically, he was healing. His head throbbed occasionally, but not nearly as badly as it had when first he'd regained consciousness. The wound in his side was no more than a dull ache. Being up and about only made him all the more aware of how dependent he now was on the generosity of others.

And the knowledge ate at him as nothing ever had.

He moved away from the window. Perhaps he could at least learn the layout of the house. He took several steps forward and jammed his knee into the chair Abby had left near the bed. He swore, then straightened. He tried again to walk, holding his hand in front of him. He found a wall and felt along it for the door. But he must have gotten turned around. This wasn't the wall with the door.

He groped forward and found what must have been a vanity. He ran his hand over the top of it and accidentally sent something flying. He heard it shatter to bits on the wood floor. With a curse he swept his arm across the smooth surface, sending everything else shattering as well.

He stood there, shaking with an impotent rage. Who was he trying to fool? He couldn't live like this. Not Chase Cordell. He was like a horse with a broken leg. Just one thing to do. Put it out of its misery.

How long would it be before Devlin figured out who he was anyway? Maybe the lawman had already sent a message to Breckenridge. Luther would be only too happy to return to Willow Springs on the chance that he might be able to identify Cordell.

Then it would be prison. Or maybe he'd hang. There were those trying to pin unsolved murders on him. What did it matter now? He already felt like a dead man.

He made his way to the window, felt the sun on his face. He would never see it again. One less outlaw, one less no-account. He didn't know how long he sat there, but it had to be well past noon. He was hungry, but he didn't care.

Winifred Graham brought him his lunch. He ignored it, ignored her. She came back later and removed the fully laden tray.

Chase heard Abby come in, heard the sound of her voice outside his room. His pulse quickened, and he realized he was actually looking forward to her company. It would be good to hear her voice again, after listening too long to the brooding voice inside his head.

But she didn't come in. He waited. An hour passed, maybe two, and someone knocked on the front door.

Devlin. Calling for Abby. Chase had forgotten they were going out to supper.

Chase could hear the smile in her voice, as she talked to the sheriff about meeting the town council, about feeling a part of Willow Springs, about being happy she came here. Chase's heart thudded. Surely she would come in, bring him his supper before she left.

But the front door opened and closed again, and she was gone. Winnie brought his meal in soon after, leaving it on his bedside table. Again he said nothing, and she quickly left, closing the door behind her.

Trapped. He was trapped, a prisoner of his own body. He couldn't live this way. He smelled the food, but made no move to eat it. Winnie came, said something about his not eating. He made no comment. She took the tray away.

He sat there, staring at nothing.

Ethan has a rifle and an old Dragoon Colt. . . .

Chase waited, waited until he was certain Winnie and Ethan had retired to their bedroom. Very quietly he crept into the parlor. He had no idea where Ethan would have stored the revolver. It could even be in the bedroom.

Chase felt around, groping awkwardly, but being extra careful not to knock anything over. He didn't want to be interrupted. Not now.

He found the fireplace, his hand tracking above the mantel. Nothing. He found a large rolltop desk. He felt inside each drawer, his hand pausing when he reached into the top left hand drawer. The Colt.

With a strange eagerness he patted along the rest of the drawer until he found a small box. He opened it and extracted a single cylindrical object.

He broke open the sixgun and punched in the cartridge, adjusting the cylinder so that the bullet was in the first firing chamber. His heart hammering, he felt his way to the divan and sat down. He felt the cold steel of the barrel, the smooth wooden grip. His hands shook slightly, and he took a deep breath. He sat there, breathing harshly. *Get it over with. What are you waiting for?*

He heard a very deliberate cough from somewhere behind him, as though made with the full intention of not startling him. "You sure you want to do that, son?"

Ethan.

Chase's grip tightened on the gun. "Don't come near me, old man."

"I wasn't planning on it. That thing might go off. I got some livin' left in these old bones."

"I don't."

"Think not?"

"Don't give me any sermons."

Chase heard him walk over to the chair opposite the divan and sit down. "If you're gonna do it, could you give me five minutes?"

"Why?"

"Maybe time for me to leave the room, if I get a notion. I don't particularly want to see your brains hit that wall yonder."

Chase winced, but said nothing.

"In fact, you could be a mite more considerate and do it outside. Winnie will likely be pretty upset about the blood on her curtains."

Chase thumbed back the hammer.

"So you figure you got nothin' to live for, am I right, son?"

"You're right. I've got nothing to live for."

"You been blind long enough to know that for a fact?"

"What are you talking about?"

Ethan rose, and Chase stiffened. "Now don't worry, son. I'm not going to even think about taking that thing away from you. Understand?"

Chase continued to listen warily as the man seemed briefly to move away, then return.

"What I want you to do is hold out your left hand. I'm going to put something in it."

"Put what in it?"

"You tell me. Come on, hold out your hand."

Chase hesitated, then did so. Ethan plopped something round and solid into his palm.

"So what is it?" Ethan asked.

Chase felt it, brought it to his nose and smelled it. "An apple. So what?"

"So you got other senses, boy. Use 'em."

Ethan took the apple away and replaced it with a potato, then a paring knife, then a small wooden carving of a horse. Each time Chase identified the object using his other senses. "I know what you're trying to do, old man. It won't work."

"Come to the store with me tomorrow. Help me stock the shelves, count inventory. Can you work a harness?"

Chase let out a harsh laugh. "Yeah, I'm real good at fixing harness."

"Promise me you won't pull that trigger for thirty seconds?"

"Why?"

"I want to get something. Promise?"

Chase said nothing.

Ethan left. When he returned he placed a small

tangle of leather into Chase's hands. Chase curled his fingers around it.

"Tell me where it's bad."

Chase felt along the harness and found the frayed section. "This wouldn't be hard to mend."

"You want to do it?"

"Not particularly." Chase let go of the harness, broke the gun and pulled out the bullet. He then handed the gun butt first toward Graham. "At least now I know your niece comes by her gift for talking too much honestly."

"Abby means well, Mr. Murdock."

"Chase." It took a moment to even realize what he had just said, done. How long had it been since he'd asked anyone to call him by the first name Murdock had so long ago given him?

"Chase it is. You know somethin', boy? I don't think you would've—"

Chase cocked an ear toward the front door, knowing at once why Ethan had stopped. Abby was home, back from her evening with Devlin.

The door opened with Abby speaking softly to the lawman. "I had a lovely time, Sam. Thank you so much."

"You're mighty welcome, Miss Abby. I hope we can do it again real soon."

Chase heard her stop and knew that she was now aware of his presence in the parlor. If she questioned it at all, she did not acknowledge it aloud, saying only, "Mr. Murdock, you should hear some of the tall tales this man can spin."

"I'll bet." He rose.

Ethan cleared his throat. "I guess I'm through cleaning this Colt. I'll be off to bed."

"Good night, Mr. Graham," Chase said, after a slight pause adding, "Thanks."

"Don't mention it, son. Glad to be of help."

"Can I get either of you two men coffee?" Abby asked.

"I wouldn't want to intrude," Chase gritted.

"Oh, you wouldn't be. Honestly. Right, Sam?"

Devlin didn't answer right away. "I think I'll pass on that coffee, Miss Abby." He stopped in front of Chase. "You might want to think about leaving."

"Maybe I haven't worn out my welcome yet."

"And maybe you have, but you just don't know it."

Chase's head jerked in Abby's direction. Had she said as much to the sheriff this evening?

"I think you'd better go, Sam," Abby said.

"Good night again, Miss Abby." He showed himself out.

The silence was suddenly deafening. "Mr. Murdock," Abby began, "I don't know what you thought of Sam's remark, but let me assure you . . ."

"There's no need for explanations, ma'am." He stepped around her, stalked exactly ten paces, opened the door to his room and stepped inside, shutting the door behind him.

He stood there, wondering what had gotten into him. Why should it even matter if Abigail Graham wanted him gone? He could scarcely blame her if she did. She had a school term to prepare for; Winnie and Ethan had a new store to take care of; they certainly didn't need a blind man on their hands.

He heard her knock on the door, her voice softly calling his name. He didn't answer, but she opened the door and came in anyway.

"I am not going to let you stand there and think that I in any way hinted to Sam that you should leave. My aunt and uncle have discussed your situation and they sympathize totally with your circumstances."

"You mean you pity me."

"Sympathize," she said again. "We want you to stay as long as you're comfortable. Please." She stepped close and he caught the heady scent of jasmine.

"Did you enjoy your dinner with Devlin?"

"Very much."

"You'll be doing it again soon no doubt."

"No doubt."

He walked to the window, and breathed in the sweet night air. "You say your aunt and uncle don't mind if I stay. What do you say?"

She seemed to hesitate, then said bluntly, "I don't want you to go."

Maybe she was just feeling sorry for him, but then he had been doing a pretty good job of that himself these last couple of days. He turned toward her, suddenly overwhelmed with the need to know what she looked like—the face, the body that came with that incredibly warm, vital voice. And just like that he heard himself asking.

"I beg your pardon?" she murmured.

"I said, what do you look like, Miss Abigail Gra-

194

ham?"

He had the feeling that she shrugged, that the question made her uncomfortable. "My hair is brown, like cinnamon, I guess. My eyes are kind of hazel, sometimes green, sometimes not. Medium height and sort of medium looking."

"I'd like to decide that for myself."

"What do you mean?"

"Your uncle has been teaching me a thing or two. If you'd let me show you . . . ?"

She was standing just inside the door and he walked straight to her. "That's very good," she said, and he grinned, feeling he'd just been on the receiving end of the schoolteacher in Miss Abigail Graham.

"A-plus?" he prodded teasingly.

"A-plus," she answered.

He didn't miss the sudden shift in her voice. She was as aware as he was of how closely they were standing together. "Can I touch you?" he asked softly.

She gasped slightly and took a step back.

"Your face," he amended quickly. "I want to know what you look like."

"Oh. I . . . all right."

He closed that step between them and held up a hand, tentative. "If I poke you in the eye," he said, "I apologize in advance." She laughed and he relaxed a little. He'd made the remark as much for his sake, as hers. He was feeling damned nervous all at once. He'd never done this before.

He found her shoulder first, then traced his hand

upward, bringing his other hand over, so that both now rested on either side of her neck. Though he willed them to stop, his fingers trembled slightly as they tracked upward to trace the line of her jaw and across her cheeks to the bridge of her nose. He slid either palm along the side of her face, the tips of his fingers shifting to outline her eyebrows, feel the velvet tickle of her eyelashes.

Soft, her skin was so soft. His right hand moved down then to skate across her lips, parted slightly. He could feel her breath hot, moist.

He had touched her to "see," but something else had happened during his incredibly sensual exploration. He cleared his throat and stepped back, jamming his hands into the pockets of his trousers.

God, how he wanted to touch the rest of her, pull her into his arms. Swearing inwardly, he stalked back to the window.

Pretty, damned pretty. He had known she would be. "Thank you."

"You're . . . you're welcome," she whispered. "I'd think I'd best go to bed now."

"Good night, Miss Graham."

"Abby. Please call me Abby."

"Good night . . . Miss Graham."

He heard the door open and close. For long minutes he stood in front of the open window, breathing in the cool, night air. Pretty, so damned pretty. "Abby."

Chapter Twelve

Noah Gantry backhanded Cal Talbot across the face, sending the nineteen-year-old outlaw sprawling butt-first into the dirt. "I don't think I heard you right, Kid," Gantry snarled. "You can't be tellin' me you're thinkin' of backin' out on our little bank job. Everything's set. We ride into Rimrock in an hour."

The Kid made no move to rise, gingerly reaching up to touch his lower lip. He was visibly shaken when his fingers came away bloody. "You didn't have to hit me, Noah. I was only sayin' that maybe we shouldn't try Rimrock again so soon."

Josey Vinson stepped in front of the Kid. "He's right, Gantry, and you know it. That Rimrock sheriff'll be edgier than a penned bull in a corral full o' heifers."

"I don't recall askin' your opinion," Gantry said. "Or the Kid's either. I do the thinkin' around here now. Nobody else." Gantry stalked back and forth, swearing viciously. "Cowards! Every last one of you! Cowards!"

He eyed the four men staring stonily back at

him—the Kid, who had scooted back several yards before daring to climb to his feet; Josey Vinson, whom Gantry had never trusted, but who had the savvy it took to pull off a job like this; and two newcomers, J.D. "Buckshot" McKenzie and Frank Brown. McKenzie and Brown were both hardcases, the kind of men who gave up on honest wages the minute a better proposition came along. Gantry had offered the better proposition—after winning their grubstake in a poker game.

The five of them had been holed up in this undersized outcropping of dirt and rock for nearly a week, biding their time. Yesterday the local ranch and mine payrolls had come in. Today they would do what should have been done a month ago—clean out the Rimrock bank. Without Cordell around to raise a fuss about innocent bystanders, they should all be considerably richer by day's end.

Just thinking of Cordell deepened Gantry's scowl. He knew he still battled the man's ghost with Vinson and the Kid. The two had been willing enough to throw in with him after he'd finished the bastard off, but that didn't stop them from making comparisons about the way Gantry was now running things.

This bank job would be a test. Gantry had to handle these men, keep them in line, or afterwards they would ride their separate ways. And Gantry wasn't ready for that, not yet. He had plans for this band of renegades, plans that when the time was right would put the name Noah Gantry right up there with Jesse James.

"Listen," Gantry said, attempting a placating

tone, though the effort galled him, "don't you see? They'll never figure another holdup this soon. It's perfect."

Vinson looked Gantry straight in the eye. "Cordell wouldn't have done it."

Noah had his Colt in his hand, hammer drawn back. "I'd best never hear that name again. Unless you want some of what I gave him."

"Not especially."

Gantry had to give the old coot credit. Vinson didn't even break a sweat. Gantry's own palm itched, his hand curling and uncurling around the butt of the gun. He'd like to put a bullet in the old bastard's face just for the hell of it. But then he'd likely have to put one in the Kid too, leaving him short two guns when he rode into Rimrock.

With a contemptuous snort he holstered the Colt. "Cordell was a fool. A softheaded fool. Too soft to do this kind of work proper. He's better off dead, and we're better off without him." He grabbed up the reins of his bay. "Mount up. We got us a bank to rob."

Gantry rode out, setting the horse into an easy canter. The others quickly fell in behind him. His heartbeat quickened as he rode, his anticipation mounting. They would blame this one on Cordell. No one yet had any notion the man was dead. Gantry had made sure to leave nothing on the body to aid in its identification. For now it would work to his advantage to have the law continue its search for Cordell. Gantry could ride in and out of towns with impunity.

199

But eventually he wanted them to know, he wanted them all to know—Noah Gantry was a man to be reckoned with. A man to take what he wanted and kill anyone who got in his way.

Like that puffed up fool on the Willow Springs stage, Gantry thought irritably. He hadn't been able to get the man's engorged money belt out of his mind. After taking care of Cordell, Gantry had convinced the others to ride into Willow Springs with him, and find out the man's name. They'd found Luther Breckenridge in the Lone Tree Saloon wheezing out his story to anyone who would listen. His wife, it seemed had recognized one of the outlaws. Gantry listened as the consumptive rancher added another thousand dollars to the reward on Cordell's head—alive or dead. Gantry had almost been tempted to ride out and fetch the body.

But in Breckenridge he had seen the opportunity for much more than two thousand dollars. A man who carried the kind of money he had that day had to have access to much more. And as for the violet-eyed beauty at his side . . . Gantry's blood ran hot as he remembered the look of revulsion on Felicity Breckenridge's face when she'd chanced to look up and see him standing at the bar. One day, he'd vowed, she would regret that look.

Gantry smiled, a thoroughly unpleasant smile. Maybe after the bank, he and the others would ride north. He figured it to be a week's ride to the Diamond B with time added in for a day or two of whorin' around in Cheyenne.

He reined in then. They had reached the bluff that

overlooked Rimrock. Thoughts of what he was going to do to Felicity Breckenridge and her husband would have to wait. "You all know what you're supposed to do," he said, feeling no need to go over the plan again. "Inside of an hour we'll have more money than any of you can spend in a year."

"Or we'll be dead," Josey muttered under his breath, but Gantry paid him no mind. The man would do his part. With cash on the line, Vinson had proved himself to be just as greedy as the rest of them.

They split up then, each riding into town from a different route. A half hour later, Gantry and Vinson tied off at the hitchrail in front of the bank. Their simultaneous arrival would seem no more than coincidence to the casual eye. Behind the bank McKenzie dismounted, feigning a check of his gelding's right front shoe. Brown was already lounging on a chair on the boardwalk in front of the adjacent barber shop. He seemed to be dozing; Gantry knew that he was not. The Kid would ride in within the next two minutes and act as if he were meeting Brown. By then he and Vinson should have everything under control in the bank.

"This don't feel right," Josey said, as they headed inside. "I don't like not wearing a mask."

"Just shut up and do your job," Gantry said. "Ain't nobody going to be saying what we look like."

They paused inside the door. Gantry took note of two male customers in line at the teller's cage. Everett Turnquist, the man Gantry knew to be the bank's owner, was busy with a ledger book at his desk in

201

front of the vault.

Gantry drew his Colt. "Nobody move."

The customers and the teller immediately raised their hands. Turnquist's pudgy face reddened with anger as he rose to his feet. "You won't get away with this."

Gantry levered back the Colt's hammer. "Another word and it'll be your last."

The man's lips thinned, but he said nothing more. Quickly Gantry had the teller stuff money into a gunny sack. Turnquist added more cash from the vault.

The front door opened. "Drop 'em, gents," came a harsh male voice.

Josey's gun clattered to the floor.

Gantry raised his hands and turned, but he did not release the Colt.

"I said drop—"

Brown stepped in behind the man in the doorway, levelling a gun at his spine. The man, who wore a sheriff's star pinned to his vest, cursed low and dropped his gun.

"Glad you were fool enough to come alone, Sheriff," Gantry said silkily, then he put a bullet in the lawman's heart.

The sheriff crumpled soundlessly. The two customers dove for the floor, as did the teller. Turnquist sat rigid as stone at his desk. With a wicked grin Gantry picked up the money bags and motioned Vinson and Brown out the rear door, where McKenzie would have gathered all of their horses. Gantry then fired four more shots.

"What the hell was that shootin'?" Vinson demanded, when Gantry stepped outside to join them.

Gantry grabbed his bay's reins from McKenzie and vaulted into the saddle. "I told you no one would be sayin' what we looked like."

"You son-of-a-bitch!" Vinson exploded. "You killed — ?"

"Let's get the hell out of here," Gantry yelled, spurring his mount. "Or you'll be joinin' 'em!"

They rode hard the rest of the day and much of the night, using creekbeds to cover their trail. It wasn't until after dawn the next day that they paused long enough to divvy up the money.

"Me and the Kid are ridin' out, Gantry," Josey said, accepting his share of the loot. "Too many law dogs and bounty men interested in us now. Not to mention that even I've got my limits to the kind of scum I'll ride with."

"You're not goin' anywhere, less'n you want to be planted where you stand."

"I'm gettin' tired of your threats, Gantry."

Gantry pulled his gun. "And I'm real tired of your mouth, old man. You keep forgettin' who's ramroddin' this outfit."

"I didn't forget. I just don't give a damn. Me and the Kid are ridin' out. And you can go to hell." Josey started toward his horse. "C'mon, Kid."

Gantry cocked the Colt.

Josey whirled, his hand jerking toward his sixgun, but the weapon never cleared leather. Gantry shot the old gunman square in the face. "I guess it was him goin' to hell, eh boys?"

Nobody said a word. The Kid dropped to his knees beside Josey. Tears welled in his eyes, but he made no move to retaliate.

"Vinson was sayin' something about you ridin' out, Kid," Gantry said, his voice ever so mild. "I'm sure he was mistaken, wasn't he?"

The Kid closed his eyes, tears tracking down his ashen cheeks. Slowly, he nodded.

"Good boy. Now, let's see, I'm the leader. I get half. The rest of you get a fourth of what's left." He looked at Josey. "Make that a third. Any objections?"

There were none.

"You boys and I are gonna get along just fine, just fine. We'll rest the horses awhile, then ride on to Cheyenne. We'll have us a good ol' time. Then I've got another little job in mind for us." He had him a taste for that violet-eyed bitch that wouldn't go away. If he worked it right, they'd lay the blame for that one on Cordell, too.

Noah smiled. He liked that idea. He liked it a lot.

Chase walked the six steps to the wardrobe in his room and pulled out a clean shirt. In the two weeks he'd been in the Graham house, he'd committed every square inch of it to memory. And he was feeling pretty damned pleased with himself.

The Grahams, for their part, had gone out of their way to be helpful, making sure to always return things to specific places and never to move any furniture without telling him. His strength had returned almost a hundred percent, and though he had yet to wake a single morning without hoping his sight had returned as well, he was getting more and more used to his sightless world. Whether he liked it or not, he was going to have to face getting on with his life. And that meant leaving the Grahams. They couldn't go on playing nursemaid to him indefinitely.

Too, he had grown uncomfortably used to Abby's presence. Her spirit and vitality had at first been an untenable irritant as he wallowed in his pain and self-pity. But with the passage of days there had been a gradual shift in his attitude, until now the time she set aside for him was the time he looked forward to the most. And that reality unsettled him in ways he had not yet found the courage to examine.

Nor did he need to be sighted to know that Winifred Graham was becoming increasingly uneasy about the time Abby spent with him. He didn't want to be the cause of tension between Abby and her aunt. For Abby's sake he had to consider some way to get out on his own.

Ethan and Winnie had taken him to the store several times, and he had helped sort and stack merchandise on the shelves. The work had given his battered confidence a much needed boost. Ethan had even started to pay him a salary for his efforts. He could use that money to get a room at the hotel. It wouldn't take long to memorize a different route to the store.

All that was left was that he broach the subject with Abby. She was probably just as eager to have him out of the house as Winnie was, but she was too polite to tell him. Though she'd never said anything, she had to be concerned about what Hiram Perkins and other members of the school board might be thinking.

Chase crossed to the chair beside the bed and sat down, wondering what was keeping her anyway. He had stayed home from the store today, because she'd promised to come by for him. They were going to have lunch. According to his stomach, it had to be past noon.

His mind wandered and he found himself picturing her. He knew exactly what she looked like. He'd memorized every detail that night she'd allowed him to touch her face. Even now, his fingertips tingled, recalling the delicate arch of her eyebrows, the softness of her skin, the way her lips had parted . . .

Damn! He gave himself a mental shake. That was hardly the sort of thing he should be thinking when Abby walked through the door. It was hardly the sort of thing he should be thinking at all. The woman was kind to him. She felt sorry for him. There was no more to it than that.

Then why did some part of him cling to the fantasy that she too had been affected by his brief, but sensual exploration? That his touch had somehow created a heightened awareness in them both.

Is that why he continued to have her address him as Mr. Murdock? To maintain at least an illusion of emotional distance, when all he wanted to do was close it? She couldn't possibly know how exposed he would feel if she called him Chase. A long ago battlefield nurse had used the name, but it was new to him then, and he hadn't yet drawn it into himself, protected it. No woman since had ever called him by the name Murdock had gifted him with. But he knew if he stayed here much longer, Abby would. And it unnerved him in a way he didn't understand.

Annoyed, he rose and stalked to the window, swearing. He should have gone with Winnie and Ethan. This was not a day to be left to his own thoughts. Maybe Abby had changed her mind about lunch, figuring if he got hungry enough he would feed himself. Maybe she'd run into Sam Devlin. Maybe . . .

He heard a knock on the front door. Grateful for the distraction, he walked off the correct number of steps, stopped in front of the door and opened it. No one said anything, though he sensed someone standing there. "Who is it?"

"M-m-me."

Chase frowned at the child's voice. "Who's me?"

"R-R-Russell."

Chase recalled Abby's mentioning Perkins' son. She had been none too pleased by the way the man seemed to intimidate the boy. "Something I can do for you, Russell?"

"Is M-M-Miss Graham here?"

"She's at the school, I think."

"N-n-n-no, she isn't. I-I was just th-there."

Chase scowled. Maybe she had indeed run into Devlin. "She should be back soon enough. Do you want to wait for her inside?"

"Can I?"

"Sure. Come on in." He swung the door wide and

led the boy to the parlor. "Have a seat. Want an apple?"

When Chase heard no response, he realized the child must have nodded or shaken his head. "Want an apple?" he repeated.

"Yes."

Chase walked out to the kitchen and fetched one from the pantry, then took it back to the boy. "Here you go."

The child accepted the fruit and took a noisy bite. His muffled words told Chase his mouth was still partially full when he asked, "Something w-w-wrong with you, m-mister?"

"I can't see."

"Oh." Chase heard another crunch. "M-my pa says you're—" The boy stopped midsentence, and Chase had a feeling it had nothing to do with his stuttering.

"I'm what?" Chase sat beside Russell on the divan.

"N-n-n—" Russel couldn't get the word out.

"It's all right," Chase said. "Never mind." He was feeling a bit ill at ease all at once. He hadn't had that much experience with small children. And the son of Hiram Perkins wasn't the first child he would have chosen to practice on. He didn't want to wind up saying something that would get Abby into trouble. He decided on what he hoped was a safe topic. "Are you looking forward to school starting?"

"N-n-no."

"Why not?"

"The k-k-k-k-kids always l-l-laugh at me."

"How old are you?"

"Eight."

"Anybody ever teach you how to fight back?"

"N-n-n-no."

Chase didn't miss the sadness in the child's voice. "Would you like to know how?"

"I sure would!"

Chase grinned. Russell hadn't stammered on that sentence. "Come on over here," he said, rising and walking to the middle of the sitting room. "Hold up your hands like this." Chase assumed a boxing stance. "Got that?"

Chase figured the boy was nodding again. "You have to say your answers out loud, Russell," Chase said. "I can't see, remember?"

"And I c-c-can't talk so g-g-good."

"You talk better than I see." He felt ridiculously pleased when Russell laughed.

Chase taught the boy several punches and counterpunches, his light touches to the boy's ribcage setting off squeals of giggles. "You're not what m-m-my p-p-pa says at all," Russell pronounced some minutes later. "You're not some n-n-no-account drifter, are you?"

Chase chuckled. "Your pa's got a real way about him, doesn't he, Russell?"

The boy fell silent.

"What is it, boy?"

"M-m-my pa doesn't like me very much."

Chase felt a familiar stab in his own gut. "I think your pa likes you just fine, Russell."

"N-n-no. I s-s-s-stutter. He gets m-m-m-mad."

Chase reached out and ruffled the boy's hair, hunkering down in front of him. "Maybe he's just scared for you. He doesn't want you to miss out on things."

"He only likes P-P-P-P-Penel-Penelope. She's smart and she doesn't s-s-s-stutter."

"Sometimes fathers make mistakes. No matter what he ever says about you, you believe in yourself, you hear?" Chase's voice had grown fierce, and he had to consciously will himself to speak in a more neutral tone. "Now come on, let's get back to practice."

Russell threw a fearsome mock punch to Chase's mid-section. Chase pretended to be hurt, doubling over, groaning.

"What is going on here?" came a stern voice from the archway.

"Abby." Chase straightened, clearing his throat. "I didn't hear you come in."

"Obviously."

He had a perfect image of her standing there with her hands on her hips.

"Rusty and I were just teaching each other the finer points of boxing."

"G-g-g-good afternoon, M-M-M-iss Gr-Graham," Russell managed.

"I hardly think that boxing is an appropriate subject to be taught to a young child."

Chase listened as she marched her way across the wood floor to stop inches from where he stood. He made a guess as to where her arm was, reached out and missed, accidentally brushing her breast. "Sorry," he said. Not allowing either one of them time to be embarrassed, he caught her arm and pulled her to one side. "The boy is the butt of jokes at school. I figured he should be prepared to fight back."

"Teaching him to be a bully is no way to—"

He cut her off. "You can hardly label him a bully for defending himself."

"We'll discuss it later."

Chase grimaced, even as Abby turned her attention to the child. "Russell, what brought you by the house today?"

"The other day you s-s-s-said I could b-b-b-borrow that b-b-b-b-book . . . *Tom Sawyer*?"

"You're welcome to it, Russell. Don't worry if some of the words are too big, all right? I'll be glad to help you with it any time you like."

"I'm a g-g-g-g-good reader. T-t-to myself anyway," he added with a wistfulness that clutched at Chase's heart.

Abby quickly went to her room, returning with the book. "Here you are, young man."

"Th-th-thank you."

"You're welcome. Now you'd best get home before your family gets worried about you. And Russell . . ."

"Yes, m-m-ma'am?"

"Maybe it would be best not to mention your boxing lessons to your father, all right?"

"M-M-Mr. Murdock already said it was our little secret."

"Oh, he did, did he? Well, you enjoy the book and I'll see you in school on Monday, all right?" Chase listened as Abby showed the boy out. He waited.

211

One, two . . .

"You had no right to do that," she said, stalking back over to him.

"The boy has a right to defend himself."

"I'd appreciate it if you'd let me handle my students."

He felt his defenses rise. "And how does Russell handle insensitive brats? Or his father when you're not around? You can't always be there to handle things for your students. And maybe you don't always have the right answer, even when you are there."

"I'm an experienced teacher, Mr. Murdock."

"I had an experienced teacher once. She beat my legs with a willow switch until they bled because I didn't do my homework." He remembered vividly his two week stint in Elsa Harkness's classroom.

Abby didn't say anything for several minutes, and he had the disconcerting feeling that she was studying him much too closely, that she could somehow see inside him, see that frightened little boy. He kept his features impassive.

"Have you eaten?" she asked finally.

"I was waiting for you."

"I'm sorry. I ran into Sam and I guess the time just got away from me."

"Whatever." He failed to keep his voice impassive. He was astonished at the sudden rush of raw jealousy that surged through him. Thankfully, she didn't seem to notice.

"Come on in the kitchen, I'll fix you something, while I start supper."

"I can help."

"I'd like that."

Her voice was soft again, and he found himself aching to reach for her, touch her. He pushed the thoughts away as he took a chair beside the table.

"Here," she said, catching his hand and placing a paring knife in it. He made a face as he felt the potatoes she piled in front of him. Methodically, he began peeling. But again he could feel her eyes on him.

"Who made you so angry, Chase Murdock?"

The knife slipped, and he gouged a slice out of his thumb. Abby caught his hand. "Let me see."

He jerked free.

"Hold still! For heaven's sake, you're bleeding on the potatoes." Again she grabbed his hand.

Scowling, he submitted to her ministrations, though he held himself rigid as he did so. Again she had skated too near the subject of his past. Again he had provided no answers. Yet each time it grew harder and harder to say nothing. More and more he felt compelled to share parts of himself with her. A dangerously idiotic move, considering his circumstances. And so he got angry. If he got angry often enough, maybe she'd stop asking.

Yet to tell her, to have her understand . . . No! He didn't need her pity, or even her understanding. He was an outlaw, a man with a price on his head. He couldn't afford to get tangled up with some sweet little schoolmarm just because he was bored and scared. His sight would be back soon. It had to be.

Ethan and Winnie arrived home then and the conversation thankfully turned to safer subjects—the store, the weather, the next chapter of *Little Women*.

"Mr. Murdock and I started supper," Abby told them, "though he and I disagree on how to season potatoes."

Somehow even Abby's now very obvious understanding of his need *not* to talk about himself was stirring feelings in him he had never in his life had to deal with before. He stood, running a hand through his thick, shaggy hair. "I need some air."

"Mind if I go with you?" Abby asked.

He was going to say yes, that he minded very much, but the words came out altogether differently. "I'd like that." He crossed to the corner of the kitchen and hefted the hickory stick cane Ethan had fashioned for him last week.

"If you like," Abby said, "I could finally take you over and show you the school."

"Lead the way."

"You two take your time," Ethan called after them. "I'll help Winnie with supper."

"Thank you, Uncle Ethan," Abby said.

Chase couldn't be certain, but he could almost feel Ethan send Abby a wink. Maybe Winnie objected to her niece being too much in Chase's company, but apparently Ethan did not share his wife's disapproval. The thought, however mere wish, brought a strange tightness to his throat.

Outside, he revelled in the warmth of the afternoon sun, revelled too in the gentle pressure of Abby's hand on his left elbow, as she ever so subtly guided him forward. Despite the alarm bells going

214

off in his head, he was looking forward to their being alone together at the school.

"Afternoon, Miss Abby," Sam Devlin called from somewhere just ahead of them. Abby murmured a polite reply, halting and waiting for the lawman to reach them. To Chase the sheriff offered a grunted non-greeting.

Chase's own mood soured instantly. And more than that he felt a nudge of fear. Had Devlin made any more connections to Cordell?

"Talked to Elijah Adams, Murdock," Devlin was saying. "He was the stage driver held up the day you were shot. Adams says he's almost certain he heard a shot, maybe two as he drove away that day. He didn't turn back to check, because he felt responsible for his passengers' safety. Know anything about those shots, Murdock?"

"Can't imagine, Sheriff," Chase said, keeping his tone casual. "I was already half dead by then, remember?"

"So you said. By the way, I've been meaning to tell you about a bank robbery over to Rimrock a few days back. Five people gunned down, including the sheriff. Guess they didn't want any witnesses."

Abby gasped. "How horrid!"

"Why tell me?" Chase asked with a feigned indifference, though his heart thudded against his ribs. There was only one reason the sheriff would think him interested in a bank robbery.

"It was Cordell," Devlin said, and Chase could actually feel the man watching him for a reaction.

"Never knew Cordell to be so cold blooded."

215

Chase's own blood ran hot with fury. Gantry. The son-of-a-bitch had murdered five people. "Besides, if there were no witnesses—"

"They found a Cordell reward dodger on the banker's desk." Devlin seemed to be enjoying doling out this story one fact at a time. "Somebody stuck it there with a letter opener. On the bottom there was a message: 'I missed it last time. This time I made sure.' "

Chase considered the irony. Gantry's obvious plant to blame Cordell had inadvertently cleared him completely. Cordell couldn't possibly have robbed that bank, since he was two hundred miles away when it happened and stone blind to boot. Then why did Devlin's suspicions continue to seem centered on him? "Maybe someone just wanted Cordell blamed, Sheriff."

"I thought of that. Actually, rumor has it Cordell himself doesn't take part in the robberies any more, just makes the plans and calls the shots from wherever he's holed up."

"And why would he be holed up?"

"Another rumor has it he's not feelin' too good."

"That so," Chase said.

"Rough bunch," Devlin drawled. "But they'll still bleed when a bullet hits 'em. Or maybe two."

Blast! Why didn't the man just come right out with an accusation, instead of all this shadow boxing?

"Did they get away, Sam?" Abby asked, and Chase was at least grateful that she seemed to have picked up on none of the undercurrents between the sheriff and himself.

"For now they have, Abby. But don't you worry, their kind can't run forever. They'll make one mistake too many, and the law will have them. And they'll hang. They'll *all* hang."

Chase straightened.

"Hanging's too good for them," Abby said. "After what they did to—"

"I've changed my mind," Chase grated. "You go on to the school without me. I've got a headache." He turned and started back for the house. He could feel her watching him as he tapped his cane ahead of him, making his way back along the street. If she knew the truth, he wondered, would she slip the noose around his neck herself?

Chapter Thirteen

Abby slipped out of the taffeta dress she'd worn to church and pulled on a simple green calico. She wished she could have convinced Chase to accompany her to the service, but he'd only grunted a sullen "no thanks." He'd been in a foul temper ever since the meeting with Sam Devlin in the streets yesterday.

She supposed being reminded of those horrid beasts in the Cordell gang had upset him. And no wonder, considering what they'd done to him. They did deserve to hang! Every last one of them. Maybe Chase even felt an element of guilt. Cordell was getting farther and farther away, committing more and more atrocities. If things had gone differently that day by the creek, Chase could have put an end to the man's murdering ways.

She sighed. There was no help for it now. She just hoped Chase could come to accept that. Maybe she could take his mind off Cordell altogether. She wanted to stop by the school. Classes started tomorrow and she wanted everything to be in order. Perhaps she could get him to come with her.

Readying her classroom had also been the perfect excuse to decline the Perkins' invitation to Sunday dinner. Winnie and Ethan had gone ahead, but Abby had come home.

Stealing herself, she headed toward Chase's room. The man could be so temperamental sometimes. And yet she liked him, more and more every day—a thought that brought a quick flush of heat to her cheeks. In fact, at times she found his company downright pleasurable. He was getting along in his blindness better than she could have hoped, considering his reaction when he'd regained consciousness.

And there really was something about that husky voice of his, she thought, feeling a rush of shyness, even when he used it to growl at her. Besides, she was more than a little certain that he liked her too. She hadn't forgotten the featherlight touch of his hands on her face, nor the abrupt way he had stepped back from her that night, as though perhaps he'd wanted to explore more than her face.

Her blush deepened, and she was grateful he wouldn't notice. But more and more she did notice how the man consumed her thoughts. Her resolve not to think of him had long since proved an exercise in futility. Her heart leaped whenever she so much as caught a glimpse of him. Either he was the cause of some heretofore unknown physical ailment, or—

She took a steadying breath. She was falling in love with him.

The thought, acknowledged at last, brought with

219

it an odd mix of excitement and fear. She'd never been in love before. She wasn't even certain she wanted to be. And yet from what she remembered of Lisa's moon-eyed musings about Zeke, Abby was definitely beginning to exhibit similar symptoms.

What Chase would think of such a development she couldn't begin to guess. But she embraced the feeling, welcomed it, looked forward to the very challenge of it. For loving Chase Murdock — blind or sighted — she already sensed could prove a formidable challenge indeed. The man was over thirty, used to being on his own, and obviously a bit of a tumbleweed by nature. Loving him was no guarantee of ever having him.

But she already seemed to have no choice in the matter. Her heart, not her head, was in charge of this journey. Only time would tell where it would lead.

As usual her pulses quickened when she reached the door to his room. She knocked, but received no answer. She frowned. She knew he was in there, knew he was awake. It was past noon. "Mr. Murdock?" She knocked again and opened the door.

"I don't recall saying 'come in.' " He was sitting on a chair facing the window.

"I'd like to talk to you."

"I'm tired."

He wasn't tired, he was tense, but it was obvious he didn't want to admit to that. "Mr. Murdock, please . . ." Thunderation! How much longer was she going to have to call him that? It wouldn't be

220

proper to address him informally, since he'd specifically asked her not to, but surely he hadn't meant to continue the practice indefinitely. Still, something kept her from making the transition. "I'm going over to the school. I thought you could do with an outing."

"I said I'm tired."

She dragged another chair over and sat down next to him. "You're not tired, Mr. Murdock. You're grouchy."

His lips thinned. "Grouchy?"

She smiled. "Very, it seems."

He angled his face away from her. "I'm sorry. I guess I am pretty poor company right now. If you don't mind—"

"Oh, but I do. I want to show you the school. We never did make it over there yesterday."

His scowl was back. "I remember."

"Please come." She caught his wrist. "Please?"

He sighed. "If you're that determined to spend your afternoon with a grouch, who am I to stop you?" He stood and allowed her to lead the way.

At the school Abby set about showing Chase every square inch of her classroom, guiding him through the double row of patent desks with their varnished wood surfaces and black iron feet. A brand new potbellied stove centered the room, while at the front Abby's desk abutted a spanking new blackboard. "Mr. Perkins had all these new things in storage," she said. "He didn't want them set up until school was actually ready to start."

221

"Does he think whoever wrecked the place will do it again?" Chase asked, tracing his fingers along the pencil groove at the top of the children's desks.

"Actually, he's very closemouthed about the whole thing. I can't imagine why he wouldn't want the culprit caught and—"

The main door opened and Abby looked up to see Russell and Penelope Perkins come into the room. "Hello, children," she said, smiling.

"Good afternoon, Miss Graham," Penelope trilled. "Do you like my dress? My father ordered it from Paris, France."

Abby found the layered blue silk a bit affected for such a young girl. "The color suits you very nicely, dear."

Russell hung back, though time and again his gaze lifted shyly toward Chase.

Penelope, too, studied Chase, but she was not subtle about it. She marched straight up to him. "My father says you're a no-account drifter."

Abby opened her mouth to chastise the girl, but Chase responded first. "I guess your father is pretty close to right."

The girl blinked, obviously taken aback by his matter-of-factness.

"And just what else did your father have to say about me?"

Abby frowned. Chase's curiosity seemed genuine. Why would he care about anything Perkins said? Penelope didn't answer, walking over to seat herself in the desk nearest the stove. "This is where I should

222

sit. I have such delicate skin, you know. I could catch a chill in winter."

Chase continued to look vaguely troubled.

Russell stepped forward and handed Abby her copy of *Tom Sawyer*. "It was a . . ." he paused, his face pinching together, as he struggled to get the words out, "a...a...real good b-b-book."

"You read it all in one day, Russell?"

His eyes widened with sudden hurt. "I t-t-t-told you, I can read t-t-t-to myself real g-g-good. I don't st-st-stutter when I read."

"Oh, Russell," Abby said, stooping to put her arm around his shoulder, "I wasn't thinking about your stuttering. I was just surprised that a boy so young could read a book this long so quickly. You must be a very smart young man."

He beamed with such genuine surprise and pleasure that Abby wondered if the child had ever in his life received a compliment before. Bashfully, he ambled toward Chase. "Did you ever r-r-r-read it, Mis-Mis-Mister Murdock?"

"It's been awhile," Chase said. "But I remember I liked Injun Joe and the cave a lot."

Russell smiled. "It was r-r-reeaaalll scary, huh?"

"I couldn't sleep for two days."

"An absolutely horrid book," Penelope said. "If I was Becky Thatcher, I wouldn't have given that ruffian Sawyer boy the time of day."

Russell ignored his sister, stepping right up to Chase. "H-how-how-how could you read it, Mr. Mur-Murdock, if-if-if you're . . . if you can't s-s-s-see?"

"Don't be such a ninny, Russell," Penelope interjected in long-suffering tones, "he hasn't been blind all his life. Only since some other no-account put a bullet in his head."

"That's quite enough, Penelope," Abby said, her patience with the girl's utter rudeness gone. "If you and I are going to get along in my classroom, you're going to have to have a care for your manners."

Penelope's blue eyes grew wide. She was obviously not used to being corrected.

"W-w-will that ha-ha-happen to Zeb, too?" Russell asked.

"Will what happen to Zeb?" Abby asked, confused.

"M-my pa says Zeb's a n-n-no-account. Will someone shoot him, too?"

"Who is this Zeb I keep hearing about?"

"Zeb Tucker," Penelope said. "You don't have to worry about him, Miss Graham. My father says he isn't allowed to set foot in this school ever again. Besides, Zeb's father thinks school is a waste of time."

"What does Zeb think?"

"The same thing, I'm sure," the girl said, as though scarcely believing Abby could even ask such a fool question.

"N-no!" Russell put in. "Zeb likes sch-school. He told me so."

"Russell Perkins," Penelope scolded, "I'm going to box your ears if you tell another fib like that."

"It's not a fib!"

Abby gave Russell's small shoulder a reassuring squeeze. "How old is Zeb?"

"F-f-fourteen."

Abby frowned. She could hardly make a boy of such an age come to school, if he chose not to. "Maybe he has to help with the crops."

Penelope rolled her eyes. "The Tuckers don't have any crops, ma'am. They're pig farmers." She made a face. "With three pigs."

"Maybe I could have a talk with Zeb," Abby mused aloud. "Where does he live, anyway?"

Penelope looked aghast. "You wouldn't really go out there, Miss Graham? Not to the Tuckers? You couldn't!"

Abby was actually relieved to see a trace of real concern in the girl's eyes. Maybe there was hope for her yet. "I am. In fact, I think right now is as good a time as any." She turned toward Chase. "Will you come with me?"

"Wouldn't miss it."

Abby shooed the children out of the school, then she and Chase headed for the livery stable to hire a buggy. Chase assisted her into the seat, then climbed in beside her. "We'd better let Sam know where we're going," she said.

"Must we?"

Abby wanted to believe there was a trace of jealousy in Chase's reluctance to seek out the lawman. But there was something else, too, a tenseness that seemed to come over him every time Devlin's name was mentioned. Was there something neither man was telling her?

Even as she had acknowledged her deepening affection for Chase Murdock, she was reminded again of how very little she knew about him. Was it more than memories of an unpleasant childhood that kept him from talking about himself? Was he hiding something? He had said it was something personal that had set him on Cordell's trail. And it was Cordell's name that constantly seemed to come up when Sam talked to Chase. Perhaps if she made it a point to find out more about the outlaw . . .

She tucked the thought away as she reined in the buggy in front of the sheriff's office. Sam came out at once. His reaction to her plan was similar to Penelope's. Only more blunt. "Are you plumb out of your mind, Miss Abby?" he demanded." You can't go out there. Harley Tucker is one mean son-of-a—" he coughed, "Sorry."

"It's all right." She was beginning to appreciate the timely use of some of the more colorful phrases she'd been hearing of late.

"You can't go out there," Sam repeated. "At least not without protection."

"Mr. Murdock will be with me."

"A blind man is hardly my idea of protection, Miss Abby."

Abby felt Chase stiffen beside her. "We'll be fine, Sam."

"If you could just wait, then I could go along. But there's someone I'm expecting on the two o'clock stage."

"I want to get out there and back before supper. We'll be all right. Don't worry."

She left Sam muttering on the boardwalk, as she gigged the horse into a trot, heading north out of town. Within minutes she'd settled back, relaxed, pleased when Chase did the same. This could turn out to be a very pleasant afternoon indeed. More than once her right thigh bumped against Chase's left leg. She was not so naive that she didn't know he was aware of it too. Though he had a few more inches on his side of the seat, he made no move to shift away from her. She might never have a better time to find out more about him.

"Will you growl and snap if I ask you a question, Mr. Murdock?"

"You make me sound like a hound dog."

"The comparison occasionally suits you."

She watched his mouth, how hard he was trying not to smile. He failed. "What would you like to know, Miss Abby?"

"Nothing dramatic really. Just the general sort of information one person learns about another over time. I know you don't want to talk about your parents or your childhood, so how about your recent past? Why did you become a lawman? Is that how you got that other scar on your chest? The one near your left shoulder?"

"Souvenir of the war."

"Ethan said you have one on . . . your right thigh as well."

227

"Souvenir of a saloon brawl."

She supposed she should be glad that he'd answered at all and not mind that the answers were grudgingly given, despite his apparent good humor.

"You must have had some dreams for yourself growing up. Something that drew you to the law."

"I don't want to talk about it, Abby."

She sighed, ready to concede defeat. Then he surprised her by continuing.

"It's not because I don't want to tell you. I do, more than you know. But it just isn't very pleasant, all right?"

She sensed he truly didn't want to argue. "All right."

As if to reinforce his desire to talk, he asked a question of his own. "What dreams did you have, Abby?"

"That's easy enough. To travel the world. To be a good teacher. And . . ." She hesitated, suddenly shy, only then realizing just how difficult it could be to open yourself up to another human being about things kept close to the heart. "I read a lot of books growing up. Not just the ones I should have—like Shakespeare and the Brontës and Dickens. But . . ." she bit her lip, wondering if he would laugh at her. "I've read about Deadwood Dick and Malaeska and Buffalo Bill and all sorts of romantic heroes. I . . . I'm even working on my own novel. I hope to get it published one day."

The silence that followed terrified her. She looked at him, but couldn't tell what he was thinking. "You think I'm being foolish, don't you?"

"Not at all. I think you'll publish your book."

"You're just saying that. You certainly had to think about it long enough."

"What I was thinking," he said slowly, "was what it must have been like to be a child who had dreams. I couldn't tell you mine, because I didn't have any."

She pulled the horse to a stop. "I'm sorry. I shouldn't have brought it up."

"It's all right."

"You can't know how I've missed having someone to talk to about dreams, about life. Lisa and I could talk about anything."

"You have Winnie and Ethan."

"Of course, but . . ." she blushed, "there are certain things a girl just doesn't want to share with her parents."

"Such as?"

"She as the first time a beau kisses you, that sort of thing." She gasped, mortified. "Oh my, I didn't mean to say that."

"You been kissed a lot have you, Miss Abby?"

There was a teasing note in his voice she'd never heard before. It made her feel all warm, quivery. "I most certainly have not," she managed. "My teaching was much more important than such nonsense."

"Kissing is nonsense?"

"Of course not. I mean . . ." She grimaced. "You know what I mean. I didn't think I should have to be forced to choose between being married or being a teacher. Lisa finally made me understand that I had to live my own life, no one else's."

"It's good you came west. You fit in."

She considered that high praise. "I was really frightened sometimes on the way out. Who in the world did I think I was? Not only to bring myself, but to uproot my aunt and uncle as well."

"You've got guts, Abigail Graham. Sometimes you may not believe it. But you do. I can't think of too many ladies who would take on being nursemaid to some shot-up stranger."

"Anyone would have helped."

"Picked me up off the side of the road maybe, but dumped me off in the first town they came to."

"You can be a very cynical man, Mr. Murdock."

He turned toward her and she saw something in his face she couldn't read. "Somebody else told me that once," he said, a strange wistfulness in his voice. "I've been thinking . . ." There was a hesitancy in him now, a shyness that touched her deeply, "that maybe, if you want, you could call me Chase."

She sensed something very important had just happened, but didn't quite know what. "It's the way I think of you anyway, when you're not around."

"You think of me?"

She blushed. "I only meant . . . I . . ."

A smile tugged at one corner of that sensual mouth. "I think of you, too."

She was suddenly very nervous. To allay the feeling she gigged the horse forward once again, grateful to see the Tucker place come into view when they reached the crest of a small hill. She stared at the slat boarded shack and its ramshackle outbuildings. Surely, no human beings could live in this place. Perhaps the Tuckers had moved on.

As she reined the buggy to a halt in front of the sturdiest looking of the three dilapidated structures, she described the scene in detail to Chase. Rotting boards covered window openings. The place could never be warm in winter, never dry in the rain.

A short, grizzled man in soiled clothing lurched out of the shack. "Who the hell are you?" he slurred. "Get off my property. Now."

"Are you Harley Tucker?" Abby ventured.

"Ain't none of your damned business who I am, lady. Now get the hell off'n my land afore I shoot ya both for trespassin'."

A shaggy-haired boy of about fourteen emerged from the shack.

"Are you Zeb?" Abby asked.

"What if I am? Who are you?"

"I'm the new schoolteacher in Willow Springs. Abigail Graham." Even in the face of Harley Tucker's menacing glare, Abby climbed down from the buggy. Chase followed at once on her heels.

"I ain't goin' to no school no more. It's a waste of time." Even as he flung the words at her, there was a flicker of sadness, longing, in his eyes that he couldn't hide. Rusty had been right. This boy did want to come to school. Abby straightened her shoulders resolutely.

Harley Tucker wiped a dribble of tobacco juice from his chin. "No boy of mine is gonna waste good work time with cipherin' and readin' and fool stuff like that. So just get yer highfalutin' rump back in that buggy and get the hell off'n my place."

"You use a decent tone when you talk to the lady," Chase said, taking a step in Harley's direction. Abby had sensed a tenseness in him ever since Harley Tucker had first opened his mouth. Now it was more than tension. It was danger. Chase Murdock was a dangerously angry man. But Harley Tucker was too drunk to notice.

"And who the hell are you?" Harley muttered.

"The name doesn't matter," Chase said. "What I'm telling you does. That boy had best be in school tomorrow morning, or I'm coming out here to get him. And I don't much care if I have to go through you or over you to do it. Understand?"

Harley took a step back. "You don't scare me none."

Chase gripped Tucker's shirtfront so swiftly, the movement startled Abby. How had he . . . ? "You let your boy come to school tomorrow, or I'll crush your drunken skull! Now are you scared?"

Harley nodded, swallowing convulsively.

Chase tightened his grip. "Say it!" he snarled. "I want to hear you say it!"

"Yes, sir. He'll be there. You can count on it."

Chase let go of the man so roughly, Tucker stumbled back and fell heavily. Chase wiped his hands on his pants leg, as though the very act of touching the man's shirt sickened him.

Then Chase helped Abby climb back into the

232

buggy. He again turned toward Harley. "Remember what I said, Tucker. That boy had best be there." With that Chase climbed into the buggy, lifted the reins and to Abby's astonishment drove toward the road.

"How do you know where you're going?"

He shrugged, handing the reins over to her. "I don't. I reined the horse around and gave him his head. I figured he'd turn toward home."

"You really enjoyed yourself back there, didn't you?"

"I don't know if enjoyed is the right word."

"You took a strange pleasure in it then."

"Maybe I did," he admitted. "But the bas—" he swallowed the word, "the man had it coming. Drunken, worthless fool."

"When you grabbed him, it was almost as though you could see him. How did you do that?"

"I could smell him." His voice was harsh. "I could smell exactly where he was."

Abby fingered the reins. "He reminded you of your father, didn't he?"

Chase was silent for a moment, then said, "A little too much, I'm afraid. I'm sorry if I scared you."

"You didn't." She smiled. "But you certainly put the fear of God into Mr. Tucker!"

"I hope so."

"You can be quite outrageous."

"Thank you."

"It was not necessarily a compliment," she said primly.

"Oh." He took the reins and pulled up.

"What are you doing?"

"This is the first time I've been out of town since I was shot. I just thought I'd make the most of it. I hear water. There must be a creek nearby."

Abby looked about in surprise. "There is! About fifty yards east of us. I hadn't even been paying attention."

"Maybe we could take a swim."

"But I don't have anything to wear."

"That wouldn't really make much difference to me now, would it, Miss Abby?" he drawled.

She felt a telltale blush creep up her neck. "It would make a difference to me, Chase Murdock. Maybe we could just take a walk." She tied off the reins to the brake handle. "Mr. Tucker is the one who could really use a dip in that stream. Except that afterwards the animals wouldn't be able to drink out of it for a week."

Chase laughed with genuine amusement. "And you say I'm outrageous, Miss Abby?"

"I guess that was a bit uncharitable."

"But accurate." His gaze grew warm, as he seemed almost to look at her. "I wish I could see you smile," he said.

"You can." She lifted his fingers to her face, tracing his fingertips along her lips. Her smile widened, then froze, as she felt those fingers tremble ever so slightly.

"Abby . . ."

It was her body trembling now, staring into those

fathomless blue eyes. And in those eyes she watched passion flare, ignite. And suddenly it was not his fingers on her lips, but his mouth. Sweet, warm, wonderful, she tasted of him, gloried in the velvet soft feel of his mouth on hers.

He groaned, softly, his hand coming up to caress the side of her neck beneath her ear. Tantalizing, mesmerizing, he continued the honey sweet exploration of her mouth, until Abby became aware of how weak her whole body had become, deliciously weak and warm, so very warm.

He drew back, his blue eyes questioning.

"Could you . . . could you do that again?" she whispered.

"My pleasure," he murmured. With both hands he cupped either side of her face, his lips again claiming her own. "Sweet . . . oh, Abby, you taste so sweet . . ."

Her own hand came up and caressed the side of his face, felt the shadings of his day's growth of beard. She tucked a strand of his longish hair behind his ear, then traced the ear itself with her index finger. She felt him shudder, pull back, his breathing harsh, ragged.

He jerked his hat from his head, gripping it in his fist on his lap. "I'm sorry."

"No! Please . . . I . . ." She didn't know what to say, but she knew she didn't want him apologizing. But he had been right to pull away. If they'd continued to touch each other like that . . . "Maybe we should take that walk by the water?"

235

"Uh, no . . . I'll just sit here awhile."

"Please?"

"Give me a few minutes, all right. I'm a little tired all at once." He kept his hat clutched tightly on his lap.

Abby felt puzzled and a little hurt by his refusal to join her. But she climbed out of the buggy alone. "I won't be long."

She waded through hip deep grass to reach the water's edge, then sank to her knees. She was surprised her legs had supported her this far. Her whole body trembled mightily. Never had she felt this way. It was as if her whole being had suddenly caught fire, igniting parts of her, very private parts of her . . .

She looked back at Chase. He sat just where she'd left him. She wished she could read his mind. Did he regret the kiss? Wish it back? Had he been as stunned by its intensity as she had?

It was several minutes before she trusted her legs enough to return to the buggy. "Still tired?" she asked.

He nodded.

"Maybe we'd best start back."

"That might be a good idea."

She climbed in beside him and sat down. This time he shifted his body, so that they were no longer touching. "Chase, I . . ." It was the first time she'd called him that and it pained her to watch him close his eyes, as though he regretted inviting the intimacy. She longed to ask him about the kiss, what it meant,

236

if anything, but now she found she couldn't. Fighting the hurt, she clucked the horse into motion, her gaze tacking absently to the top of the bluff to the west. Two riders appeared. She told Chase.

"Recognize them?"

"No."

"Probably just drifting through."

"Probably." When he continued to sit so still she asked, "Are you all right?"

"Fine, just fine. We'd best hurry if we're going to get back by supper."

She snapped the reins, again glancing toward the ridge. There was something familiar about one of the riders, but it was hard to tell from this distance. Not that it mattered. She didn't want to think about the riders. Her thoughts were as before consumed by the man beside her.

"You didn't tell me we would be doing any saddle riding," the violet-eyed woman sniffed. "This is most uncomfortable, Sheriff."

"Sorry, Mrs. Breckenridge," Sam Devlin said. "I wanted you to get a good look at the man I wrote you about as soon as possible." He handed her a pair of binoculars. "Does he look familiar? Is that Cordell?"

Felicity studied Cordell. He was still as handsome as ever, maybe more so. Even blind the man retained an air of animal grace that two years ago had filled her nights with erotic fantasies. She'd wanted him

237

then. God, how she'd wanted him. And he'd refused her.

Felicity thought about telling Devlin. It would certainly be the perfect way to get even with Cordell for his callous rejection of her. But then she thought of her wheezing, near-dead husband and of the fortune she stood to inherit the moment Luther breathed his last. The man owed her for all those years of hell.

Maybe after Luther died, she could come back and have a little talk with Cordell. Surely, he'd be most attentive to anything she had to say—unless he wanted to wind up on the end of a rope.

"Is it Cordell or isn't it?" Devlin demanded.

Felicity Breckenridge looked at Sam Devlin and smiled.

Chapter Fourteen

Chase sat on the divan listening as Abby began to read from Louisa May Alcott's *Little Women*. They'd spoken little on the trip back to town, even less during supper. Ethan and Winnie had seemed aware of the strain, but chose to ignore it. Perhaps Winnie Graham was even pleased by it. Not that Chase could blame her. If he were in her place he would certainly do nothing to encourage Abby's relationship with him.

He supposed he should have stayed in his room or volunteered to go down to the store and do a little extra work. It certainly would have proved a more productive use of his time. But that would have meant not spending the evening with Abby. And that he couldn't, wouldn't, do. He closed his eyes and leaned back, finding a measure of contentment just listening to the sound of her voice.

Ethan sat next to him, puffing on his pipe. Chase inhaled the fragrant tobacco smoke, realizing he hadn't had a cigarette since just before the stage holdup. He had never smoked enough to call it a habit, but he would've enjoyed rolling one just then. Thoughts of the kiss he'd shared with Abby this afternoon kept him from pursuing the notion further. Though he knew he shouldn't, he couldn't help hoping a moment might somehow present itself when he could kiss her again.

Such pleasant musings had kept him oblivious to much of the plot of Miss Alcott's book, and so he frowned, puzzled, when he heard a sudden catch in Abby's voice, a sadness. He forced himself to listen more closely to the words. It took a few sentences for him to catch on. Someone named Beth was talking to a sister named Jo, and Beth was dying.

" ' . . . You must take my place, Jo,' " Abby read, " 'and be everything to Father and Mother when I'm gone. They will turn to you, don't fail them.' "

Abby's voice quivered, cracked. Chase sat up straighter on the divan. She was crying!

" 'And if it's hard to work alone,' " Abby continued to read, " 'remember that I don't forget you, and that you'll be happier in doing that than writing splendid books or seeing all the world; for love is the only thing that we can carry with us when we go, and it makes the end so easy.' "

Abby paused, sniffling. "I'm sorry," she said. "I know I'm being silly."

"Nonsense, dear," Winnie said, her own voice shaking. "I know precisely how you feel. That poor dear girl, after all she's already suffered."

Abby blew her nose. "Just give me a few minutes."

"I thought you'd read that book before," Chase

240

put in, thoroughly uncomfortable with the picture of tears streaming down Abby's face over a figment of some author's imagination.

"I have." She hiccoughed. "This is the fourth time actually."

"And you do this every time?" He hadn't meant the hint of incredulity that crept into his voice. Certainly he didn't want her to think he was making fun of her. But the damage was done.

"Obviously you can't appreciate the travails poor Beth has been through," Abby huffed, rising to her feet. "Here I've been reading this book aloud night after night and you don't give a care about it at all, do you? How anyone could sit there dry-eyed while Jo has to watch her dear sister meet her maker . . ." She stomped over to him, and he had an image of her face, pinched, tear-streaked and thoroughly furious. "Chase Murdock, you're nothing but a boorish oaf!"

He blinked, startled. He would've made some appropriate retort, if he could've thought of one. But before anything came to mind Abby had blazed from the room.

"Abby takes her *Little Women* kinda seriously," Ethan deadpanned, giving Chase's knee a sympathetic pat. "I should have warned you. After all, I'm the one who sent her out of the room sobbing the first time she read the blasted thing eight years ago."

Chase swallowed a snort. "I didn't mean to hurt her feelings," he said and meant it.

"She'll figure that out. Just give her a few min-

241

utes."

Chase sat there, feeling like a prize idiot. The evening had been so warm, so familial, and with his big mouth he'd gone and spoiled everything. "I really am sorry, Ethan."

Ethan stood, and Chase could hear the older man's joints crack slightly in an exaggerated stretch. Ethan then crossed the room and eased open one of the desk drawers. "I've got just the thing to take your mind off Beth and Jo." He withdrew what sounded like a heavy object. Chase knew what it was. The Dragoon Colt. "This thing hasn't been cleaned in an age. Would you mind?"

"Not a bit," Chase said, accepting the long-barreled sixgun and a bit of oil cloth. "I'll do it in my room. It's getting late, and Abby has school tomorrow. You want me at the store early, right?"

"Right. You're a real handy man to have around that store, son. I mean that."

"Not counting the keg o' nails I spilled all over the floor that first day?"

"And not counting the flour sack I split open last week."

Chase excused himself and went to his room. Even with Ethan he found himself dealing with feelings he thought he'd buried with Murdock. He was getting much too accustomed to this, all of it. Abby, her aunt and uncle, family meals, thoughtful conversation. He had to take a step back, remind himself that none of this was permanent. He would be leaving this house soon, leaving Willow Springs, too, if he had any sense. The way Devlin was sniffing around it wouldn't be long before the sheriff found him out. He seriously doubted Devlin would have any qualms about jailing a blind man.

His thoughts turned inevitably to Abby. He hoped she was all right. *Boorish oaf.* That was a new one. No one had ever called him that before. And strangely, he took no offense. In fact, he well deserved it. He hoped it didn't take her too long to forgive him. It wasn't that he hadn't recognized the quality of Miss Alcott's writing. The story had just been a bit sentimental for his taste. He recalled Murdock's giving him a copy of *Oliver Twist.* Now that was a proper book, even if the kid did go straight in the end.

To take his mind off Abby, he sat on the bed and set about disassembling the Colt. He'd cleaned enough weapons in his day to do the job strictly by feel. It was a good gun, well balanced. Ethan had included a box of shells, but Chase didn't load it. With school children stopping by at all hours it would only be borrowing trouble to keep a loaded gun in the house. Chase used the cartridges strictly to check the cylinder.

He was so engrossed in his work, he almost didn't hear her soft knock. His heart thudded. "Come in."

She stepped inside in the door, but didn't come near him.

He took a deep breath. *Just say it, Chase, get it over with.* "I'm sorry I'm a boorish oaf."

"No, you're not."

He managed a wry grin. "I'm not a boorish oaf, or I'm not sorry?"

"Both." She was pouting, but she had to work at it. His smile broadened. Damn, how could it feel so good just to be in the same room with her? "I'm sorry Beth died, all right?"

"Are you?" She didn't sound convinced.

"Well," he drawled, "not as sorry as you are."

"Chase Murdock!"

"I'm sorry," he said quickly. "Honestly. I'm sorry, because her dying hurt you."

"Oh. Thank you."

"You're welcome."

"Can I come in?"

"I'd like that."

"Do you mind if I light the lamp?"

He chuckled. "I hadn't noticed it was out."

He heard her give an exasperated laugh. He couldn't believe himself that he could joke about it. Part of him still believed somewhere in his soul that his blindness was only temporary. That some day he would get his sight back. And when that day came the very first person he would seek out was Abby. He wanted to look into those hazel eyes, and see what he hadn't been able to see this afternoon when he kissed her.

"I hope you're not worried about me and the gun," he said. "I'm only cleaning it."

"Why would I worry?" she asked, blowing out a match.

Chase's admiration for Ethan Graham went up

244

another notch.

"Would you like me to read you some more of *Robinson Crusoe*? Maybe he'll die and you can laugh."

"Does that mean you don't really forgive me?" he mocked gently.

She sighed. "Yes, I forgive you. But if it's all the same to you, I'll just finish *Little Women* for Aunt Winnie and me. I'll spare you and Uncle Ethan."

"Why don't you read from your own book, the one you told me about today?"

"I don't know if I could do that." He caught the sudden nervousness threading her voice.

"Why not?"

"I've never . . . shared my writing with anyone. Lisa read the first couple of pages, but . . . I couldn't even show it to her after that."

He shrugged, taking no offense. "It's up to you."

"Well, maybe . . ." She went to the door. "I'll be right back." She returned quickly, laying the leather-bound manuscript next to him on the bed. "I haven't had much time to work on it lately."

"What's it about?"

Haltingly at first, then with an infectious excitement she told him about Tex Trueblood.

"Sounds like a helluva man," Chase said, feeling a most peculiar jealousy ripple through him. "Is he your notion of an ideal man? The kind of man a respectable woman can happily spend her life with?"

"Of course! What woman couldn't be happy with Tex? He's such a gentleman. And he's always right

245

there fighting for justice . . ."

"And widows and orphans?" he muttered.

"Excuse me? I didn't catch that."

"Nothing."

"I hope you find a man like that some day, Abby. I really do. You don't deserve any less."

She was quiet then, and he could feel her gaze burning into him. *Do you see me, Abby?* he thought bleakly. *Do you see me for what I am?*

"I'm sorry," she murmured. "I can't read it to you. I thought I could, but I can't."

"It's all right. I understand."

"I think you really do."

"Are you all right? You don't sound like yourself." Was she thinking of the kiss they'd shared this afternoon?

"I guess I'm worried about school starting tomorrow."

He ignored a stab of disappointment. "You'll do fine. You've been teaching for years."

"But never in a school all by myself. I'm all these children have."

"Then they've got plenty."

"Thank you, Chase. Thank you very much." She came over and sat beside him on the bed. He almost bolted to his feet, but then the pieces of the gun would have spilled all over the floor. How could she be so nonchalant about it? If he reached over, he could press her down, rain kisses across her face, her neck, feel the swell of a breast beneath his palm. "Son of a bitch . . ."

246

Abby gasped, startled, leaping to her feet. "What is it?"

"I . . . I . . ." he stammered. Blast! "Nothing. I just thought I lost a piece to the gun. But it's right here." He held up the cylinder.

"Well that's hardly a reason to curse," she scolded indignantly.

"You're right." *Deep breaths, Cordell. That's it. Steady, man.*

"By the way, Chase Murdock, are you ever going to tell me why you decided to be a lawman?"

He swore inwardly. He'd hoped she'd forgotten how he'd never actually answered that question. He had come to loathe lying to this woman. "I rode shotgun for Wells Fargo for awhile. Did some troubleshooting for the Central Pacific. Guess it just sort of followed."

"Where were you a special deputy?"

He hesitated. What if Devlin knew a lawman from wherever he might mention? "Here and there," he hedged.

A fortuitous knock sounded on the front door. Chase breathed a sigh of relief. Abby stood, but Winnie had already reached the outer door. "Why, Mr. Perkins," Winnie said, "what an unexpected pleasure."

Chase grinned at the woman's less than approving emphasis on unexpected. One of these days Perkins was going to take the hint.

"Oh, dear," Abby sighed, and Chase knew the man had seen her in here. "Please excuse me, Chase." He

247

counted her footsteps and knew she'd joined Perkins near the front door.

"I just came by to make certain everything is all set for tomorrow morning, Miss Graham," the man said.

"It most certainly is, Mr. Perkins. You needn't have troubled yourself."

He cleared his throat. "If I may say, Miss Graham, I am finding it highly unpleasant to find you constantly in the company of that . . . that drifter . . . every time I come into this house."

"He lives here, Mr. Perkins."

"Precisely the point, my dear. A certain level of propriety is required of a person in your position. I hardly think being in a bachelor's bedroom constitutes appropriate behavior."

"This is my home, Mr. Perkins," Abby said. "And not that it's any of your business, but nothing improper has happened here. Now if that's all?"

Chase could only imagine the man's indignant exit. For a moment he feared Abby would simply go on to bed, but then he caught the rustle of skirts that told him she'd rejoined him. The chair beside his bed creaked as she sat down. "I probably shouldn't have been so blunt with him," she fretted. "I really can't afford to lose this job. I've been so looking forward to it."

He blew out a disgusted breath. "It's hardly improper for you to sit in a chair and read to a poor blind man," he said.

"I know, but . . ."

"Now this would be improper." He reached for her, catching her mouth in a quick kiss. He'd meant it as a joke, but he found it extremely difficult to let her go afterwards.

Quickly, Abby stood. "I . . . I think I'd best say good night."

"Abby, I . . ." He couldn't think of what to say, and so he said nothing, listening to her leave. He sat there, fighting a desire so fierce that his whole body trembled with the force of it. He had wondered if it was just the fresh air and sunshine this afternoon that had sent his heartbeat thrumming apace when he'd kissed her in the buggy. He hadn't been able to join her on her walk, because to do so would have scandalized her further. He had been stunned by how quickly his desire had fired. And now it had happened again.

But then he hadn't been with a woman for a long time, he told himself fiercely. That's all it was.

But he didn't believe it. Not for a minute. And the thought terrified him more than the darkness.

Chapter Fifteen

Heart thudding, Abby bolted out of bed. It was the first day of school. Trembling, she stood in the center of her room trying to shake off the aftereffects of a most unsettling nightmare. She'd dreamt she'd slept through the entire term, only to show up on the final day of school to discover she was to be tested by Hiram Perkins — on subject matter about which she knew nothing!

Grimacing, she raked her fingers through her cinnamon hair. Whatever the day had in store for her, it had to be better than her dream. Still, she couldn't quite steady her hand as she poured water into the basin and washed her face. She was grateful her first day of teaching here could only happen once.

Crossing to her wardrobe, she selected, then rejected dress after dress, finally deciding on a dark green calico, though she didn't feel quite right about that one either. She was just securing the last mother-of-pearl button at the base of her throat when a gentle knock sounded on her door.

"Abby, dear," Winnie called, "you're up, aren't

you? You don't want to be late your first day."

Abby looked at the clock and closed her eyes. She'd barely have time for breakfast. Where had the past hour and a half gone? "Be right there, Aunt Winnie." Quickly she pinned up her hair and hurried out to the kitchen. The smell of blueberry muffins and applecake hung heavy in the air. Winnie had made her favorites.

"Breakfast smells heavenly," Abby managed, though her stomach clenched nervously. What was the matter with her? She'd survived several first days of school back in Moline, in fact, looked forward to them. A new term meant a fresh start for teacher and students both. Then why this sudden stage fright about Willow Springs?

She gave herself a mental shake. She was being ridiculous. Some of her jitters of course stemmed from the supercilious Perkins. Would he stop by her classroom this first day and find her skills wanting? And what about Zeb Tucker? Would the boy be there? And if he wasn't, would Chase make good on his threat to break Harley Tucker's skull?

Such thoughts would sap anyone's spirits. But Abby was determined to give them short shrift. Her students were depending on her. And they were all that really counted.

Not taking time to sit at the table, Abby took a quick bite of muffin and a sip of milk. She would collect her lesson plans and be off. "I'd best be going, Aunt Winnie," she said, giving her aunt a swift kiss. "Did Uncle Ethan already go to the store?"

"Of course not," Ethan said, ambling into the room. "Do you think I'd miss wishing you good luck on your first day at a new school?" He picked up two muffins on his way over to her. "Have a fine day, sweetheart," he said and gave her a gentle hug. "Those kids don't know how lucky they are."

"Thank you, Uncle Ethan." As always, she found comfort in her aunt and uncle's warm support. She started out of the kitchen, then called back to her uncle, "Will Chase be going to the store today?"

"We haven't discussed it yet actually." Ethan grinned. "Does your asking mean you've forgiven him for being a — what was it? — boorish oaf about dear little Beth?"

Abby's mouth twisted wryly. "Yes, I forgave him. Barely. Just like I did you the time you did the same thing."

Her uncle was still chuckling as Abby returned to her room for her lesson plans. She was feeling better already. She would pick up the plans, say a quick hello to Chase and be on her way. She paused, feeling a sudden warm heat sift through her. Well, maybe more than a quick hello. As usual, she was astonished by just how much she was looking forward to seeing him.

She crossed to her dresser and frowned. The lesson plans weren't there. Nor were they on her night table. Maybe she'd absent-mindedly taken them with her to the kitchen. A quick check proved negative, as did a trip to the parlor.

"Blast!" she muttered, her agitation rising again. Why was all this happening this morning? In desperation she went to Chase's room, even knowing she'd never taken them in there.

He was dressed and just finishing shaving. He smiled in her direction, wiping the last of the shaving lather from his neck. "Looking forward to your first — ?"

"I can't find my lesson plans anywhere," she blurted. "What am I going to do?"

"I'll help you look," he offered, and she had to bite her tongue to keep from telling him how absurd that sounded. She ran about the house, getting more and more upset as the minutes ticked by and still she couldn't find them.

She was about to break down sobbing in frustration, when Chase came toward her carrying a sheaf of papers.

"You found them," she shrieked gleefully, coming over to take them from him. "Oh, Chase, wherever were they?"

"On the desk in the parlor," he said. "Right out in the open." He gave her a lopsided grin. "A blind man could've found them."

She leaned into him, so that he automatically raised his arms to steady her. "Thank you so much."

"My pleasure." His voice was warm, like melted butter.

She could have stood there like that all day, but she forced herself to straighten, self-consciously reaching up to fiddle with her hair. "I'd best be going. Thank you again."

"Mind if I walk with you?"

"I'd like that. I—oh, I almost forgot—" Quickly she went back to her room and collected her teaching certificate. She wanted to hang it on the wall of her classroom. She read the inscription to Chase, as they headed out the door. "Abigail Graham: Competent to give instruction in Reading, Orthography, Writing, Arithmetic, Geography, English, Grammar and History."

"Sounds impressive."

"I really do love teaching, Chase. I—oh, dear . . ." She stopped, her gaze tracking up the street.

Chase halted beside her. "Devlin?" he asked, his voice packing an amazing amount of hostility into that single word.

"He must want to wish me good luck, too," she offered cajolingly, wishing there was some way to ease the tension between the two men.

"Morning, Miss Abby," Devlin said, tipping his hat and coming up to her. "Thought you might need a friend on your first day."

"I'm fine, Sam. Thank you though."

Chase's tone remained belligerent. "How is it you're always just two steps behind Miss Abby, Sheriff?"

"Maybe it's you I'm two steps behind, Murdock. But don't worry, one of these days I'll catch up."

Abby frowned. That almost sounded like a threat. But that was absurd. Why would Sam threaten Chase, especially when Chase had once been a lawman himself? Though she was loathe to admit it, she supposed Sam could be a little jealous. He had shown an interest in her after all. But she hardly expected the two men to come to blows over her.

Embarrassed to even be thinking such a thing, she cleared her throat nervously. "I want to thank you both for being so kind, but I think I can make it the rest of the way on my own." She was dealing with enough butterflies about the day ahead without worrying about these two. Better to leave them alone to work things out. Without giving either one of them time to protest, she hurried ahead to the school.

Despite the morning's minor disasters, she'd still managed to arrive a good half hour before the children were due. She went inside, feeling a sudden eagerness now. The classroom felt fresh and alive, and Abby couldn't wait to get started. Within minutes she heard children's voices raised in play outside. Crossing to the window, she spied Molly O'Banion playing tag with another brown-haired urchin of about the same age. She smiled. It was going to be a good day after all.

At 8:50 she pulled the bell rope and about a dozen children of varying sizes stopped their cavorting and rushed up the stairs into the school, each one smiling and saying a polite "Good morning." Even Penelope. Abby's only disappointment was that Zeb Tucker was not among them.

Back inside she suppressed a smile at the friendly shoving match going on between two boys for a particular seat. Affecting a stern look, she clapped

255

her hands sharply. Both boys jumped away from their prize and retreated meekly to other desks.

"The class will come to order, please," she said, as she walked to the front of the room.

For the next half hour she took names, ages, and various information about each child's education to date. She seated the youngest children to the front, progressing to the rear of the room with the oldest — a fact which did not go over too well with Penelope Perkins, who wound up in the back of the room with the desk farthest away from the stove.

"I'm going to catch my death back here," she said, after raising her hand and getting permission to speak.

"You'll be fine, Penelope," Abby assured her. "Now if you'll all be very quiet for just a few minutes . . ." Abby arranged her seating chart, making quick notes to remind her of each child's current reading level. Mary Johnson, daughter of the hotel chambermaid, was ten years old and in the Third Reader, along with Molly O'Banion. Russell Perkins told her he was in the Second, but after the way he'd handled *Tom Sawyer*, Abby had an inkling he might actually qualify for the Fourth. Overall, she wound up grouping four students in the Third Reader, five in the Second, and the three youngest in the First.

"I seem to be a very lucky teacher," she said, "to have such bright and eager pupils." She told them how she intended to conduct class with reading, arithmetic and grammar lessons in the forenoon, followed by an afternoon of more reading along with history, writing and spelling. "When I'm working with one group, I'll expect the rest of you to be working on your assignments. If you ever have any questions, just remember to raise your hand. Now if the Third Reading group would pass to the front, please, we'll do some reading aloud."

Abby didn't miss a fleeting look of terror on Russell Perkins' face. No doubt he was thinking what would happen when it came time for him to read. Abby resolved to talk to him about it during recess.

Mary Johnson was just starting her third paragraph when the door opened and Zeb Tucker sauntered in. He wore his hat pulled low over his eyes so that the only part of his face Abby could see was an arrogant smirk that seemed to proclaim she should be glad he showed up at all. When the other students began to whisper amongst themselves, Abby tapped her pencil on the desk to restore order.

"You're late, Zeb," she said.

"I overslept." He crossed his arms in front of him, as though defying her to do something about it.

But that was exactly what she had to do. If she let him get away with being tardy, soon the other students would be late as well. "You'll have to stay after school tonight, Zeb. For now you can take that seat in the back next to Penelope's. Oh, and please remove your hat while you're in school."

For a moment Zeb didn't move, and Abby's mind raced to consider what she would do if the boy continued to openly defy her. But then suddenly she sensed his behavior no longer had anything to do

257

with defiance. With obvious reluctance he tugged the hat from his head. Abby stifled a gasp. He had the beginnings of a nasty black eye. She had to resist the urge to go to him, check the injury more closely, suspecting that to do so would only embarrass him further and force him to maintain his antagonistic posture. He seemed even more reluctant to take the seat near Penelope, but then he straightened his shoulders and did so.

Penelope instantly made a face and pinched her nostrils shut. "Does he have to sit by me, Miss Graham?" she whined. "He smells like a goat!"

"That's enough, Penelope!" Abby snapped.

For the tiniest instant the arrogance in Zeb Tucker vanished, though Abby doubted any of the children noticed. Despite the bluff and bravado, Zeb was a boy on the verge of manhood. Even the taunts of a spoiled child could cut deep.

"Just as I will not tolerate tardiness in this class," Abby said evenly, though her patience was long since exhausted where Penelope was concerned, "I will not tolerate rudeness either." Abby carried her copy of *Webster's Unabridged Dictionary* back to Penelope's desk. "Zeb isn't the only one who's going to be punished here, young lady. I want you to look up the word *rude,* write out the definition, then write a two page essay in your copy book to present to the class tomorrow about why good manners are important."

Penelope pouted furiously. "I will not!"

"Perhaps you'd like some time to reconsider in the corner," Abby said. "Now."

Her face burning a beet red, Penelope stomped her way to the corner. "Just wait until my father hears about this. You'll be sorry."

Abby could well imagine Perkins' reaction. But she couldn't worry about it now. If she didn't nip the girl's behavior in the bud today, it would be completely out of hand the rest of the term.

Though still fuming, by recess Penelope had decided she would write the essay, and so Abby allowed her to go outside and join the others. "Could you come here a minute first, Russell," she said.

The youngster shuffled shyly toward her desk. It seemed impossible Russell and Penelope could be a part of the same family.

"We need a couple of minutes to talk, Russell, all right?"

"C-can you c-c-call me Rusty, like Mr. Mur-Murdock does?"

"If you like."

He smiled, nodding.

"It's about your reading . . ."

His gaze immediately dropped to the floor. "Are you g-going to m-m-make . . ." His body hunched up with the effort to get the words out, but the harder he tried, the more the words wouldn't come.

Gently, Abby caught his hand. "There's no hurry, Rusty. You take all the time you need."

It took him five minutes, but he got it said, and it was precisely what Abby had feared. "I-I-I c-c-c-an't r-read out l-loud l-l-like M-M-Mary. The other t-t-t-teacher made m-m-me. And-and-and my-my father made me . . . and-and-and . . ."

"Shhh," Abby soothed, "I don't want you to worry about it. That's why I wanted to talk to you. If you don't want to read out loud with the class, you don't have to."

He seemed to visibly relax, though it was obvious he didn't quite trust that she meant it.

"I tell you what," Abby said, "I'm going to send a note home with your father . . ."

His eyes widened and she hastened to reassure him. "In the note I'm going to say I need your help a little bit every day before school. Can you be here a little early, Rusty?"

He nodded.

"You and I can have some private reading lessons. And you can take all the time you want, all right?"

He nodded again, this time more vigorously.

"All right. You go on out and play now."

Impulsively, he threw his small arms about her neck and gave her a fierce hug, then turned and rushed out the door. Abby blinked rapidly, swiping at a stray tear. She was certain Russell's speech would improve if the child was just allowed to relax. No doubt he'd had to rush to get in a word edgewise with Penelope as a sibling. And with his father's unyielding ways . . .

Abby pushed the thought away. She wasn't going to think about Hiram Perkins any more than she absolutely had to. Instead her thoughts turned to Chase. She wondered what he was doing right now, if he'd gone down to the store to help Ethan. She wondered, too, if she should tell him about Zeb's black eye. Surely, Chase hadn't seriously meant to do harm to Harley Tucker.

And yet she'd never seen him so angry as when he'd had Tucker by the shirtfront yesterday afternoon. If she hadn't been there, Chase might not have had to threaten Tucker. He might have broken his neck on the spot.

She shook her head. Things were not looking up, when even her thoughts of Chase proved depressing. She was grateful the fifteen minute recess was over. Rapping on the window, she called the children back inside and they continued with more lessons until lunch. Since the day was bright and beautiful she allowed them to take their lunch pails outside, but when she reached for her own, she discovered she'd forgotten to pack one. Her stomach rumbled its irritation. Considering her meager breakfast, she didn't think it wise to wait until supper to eat again. She could be home and back in no time.

She started toward the door, but stopped when she heard the familiar sound of Chase's cane tapping up the front steps. His broad shoulders filled the open doorway.

"Chase, what—?"

"Hungry?" he asked, holding up her lunch tin.

Flustered, she hurried over to him. She was achingly glad to see him, yet suddenly terrified to think of Perkins finding out. "Thank you," she managed, wondering how she could tactfully ask him to leave, yet wanting desperately for him to stay.

261

"Winnie was going to bring it over, but I convinced her it was good practice for me to be out on my own."

"I appreciate it." Abby wrung her hands together, hurrying to the window to try and gauge if anyone might have seen Chase come in."

"You know your aunt seems awfully anxious for me to be self-sufficient. Think maybe I'd better look into rooming at the hotel?"

"I . . . sure, of course," she said distractedly, her thoughts filled with a vision of Hiram Perkins walking into the room.

Chase straightened, looking at first surprised, then hurt. "If that's what you want."

"I . . ." Good heavens, what had she agreed to? Well, there was no help for it now. She had to get him out of here. "Thank you again for bringing my lunch."

"I brought enough for two."

"Oh."

"But you want me to leave, don't you?"

"Yes . . . I mean no. I mean . . ." She sighed helplessly. "If Hiram Perkins should come by . . . Chase, please understand."

"Fine. I'll try not to let the door hit me in the behind on the way out." He turned and stomped toward the door.

Abby closed her eyes. Now she'd hurt his feelings. Men! He hadn't been nearly so upset last night when he'd hurt hers! She caught his arm. "Can you come by later? Walk me home?"

"I don't think so. Your uncle wants me down at the store."

"Please?"

He fingered the smooth head of his cane. "Maybe." With that he was gone.

Abby sat at her desk, eating an egg salad sandwich, barely tasting it. "He'll be back," she said aloud, as though somehow in the saying it, she could make it true. "He'll be back."

Despite her distress about Chase, the afternoon raced by and four o'clock came much too soon. "Class dismissed," she said, smiling at how boisterous the children could still be at the end of a long day. She was exhausted. And she still had Zeb to deal with.

Even then the day wouldn't be over. She had little doubt Hiram Perkins would be on her doorstep tonight. Maybe she wouldn't even have a job to come back to tomorrow.

Outside, she looked for Chase, but there was no sign of him. Though disappointed, and not a little hurt, she supposed it was just as well. "Come along, Zeb," she said, "it's time you and I took a trip to the woodpile."

Chase tromped toward the school, tapping the cane in front of him as he walked. He knew he was late, but that was all right. Let her wonder if he was coming. He didn't even know why he was bothering, since she was so all fired worried about pompous

263

fools like Hiram Perkins and what they would think if she was seen with him! He told himself he needed the practice in getting around, that was the only reason he'd decided to come by for her.

"Hey! Watch it!" a young voice yelped, and Chase instinctively reached out as he felt and heard someone tripping over his cane.

"Are you all right?" he asked, helping the unknown youngster to his feet.

"Yes, sir," the boy said. "I'm sorry."

"It's okay."

"Don't you ever watch where you're goin', Isaac?" the boy's apparent companion chided. "Come on, let's get going. I can't wait to get home and tell my pa about Miss Graham takin' Zeb Tucker out to the woodpile."

Chase stood stock still. The sounds of the boys racing off receded to nothing, as he felt a sudden, sickened rage boil to life inside him. Abby was going to whip Zeb Tucker? For what? What could the boy have done to deserve a beating? Part of him was furious that she would hit the boy. But another part of him, a part that made him even more furious, worried that a boy that big wouldn't stand for any whipping, that Zeb just might hurt *her*.

Hurrying as fast as he dared, he made his way to the school, then paused to listen intently. He caught the sound of voices coming from behind the building. Abby was talking to Zeb in remonstrative tones.

Chase stormed toward her, shaking with fury. She must have seen him, because he heard the rustle of

264

her skirts coming toward him in a hurry.

"Chase, what is it? You look—"

He cut her off. "All of your sweet talk is just that, isn't it?" he raged. "Talk! Just talk. When the first thing goes wrong, you're no different than the rest of them. Your answer to bad boys—the woodpile!"

Abby blinked, startled, then indignant. "How dare you? Zeb Tucker was tardy this morning and he has to be punished . . ."

"I hardly think he needs to be beaten."

Abby gasped. "What are you—?" She noted the way he was holding himself. He was livid, seething with outrage. "Oh, my . . . the woodpile. Oh, Chase, no, no . . ." She caught his wrist, but he jerked away, his eyes blazing with fury, and, more amazingly, betrayal. "Chase," she said more gently, "please, listen. I would never hit a student, ever. Zeb is out here at the woodpile . . . to chop wood."

He straightened. "What?"

"We'll need it this winter. I thought it would be good exercise for him. And he was late to school. If I let him get away with it, the other students would expect to get away with it as well."

Chase started to say something, then stopped, seemingly unable to find any suitable words. Raking a hand through his hair he turned away from her. Abby stepped around him, saw the heightened color in his cheeks.

"I'm sorry, Abby. Jesus, I'm sorry."

"I do wish you wouldn't blaspheme, Chase Murdock. And I accept your apology. You didn't know."

She caught his elbow and led him over to a tree stump. She thumped it loudly with her palm so he would hear where it was. "Have a seat."

He sat. "Damn."

"It's all right," she assured him. "Honestly. I think it's wonderful you would be so concerned for Zeb that you defend him against me."

Chase was still deeply embarrassed. Maybe she should be angry that he would think her capable of hitting a student. But she remembered his own revelation about being beaten by a teacher. It was little wonder his emotions would have ruled his better sense.

He gripped his cane so tightly his knuckles showed white. "How I could ever think that you of all people . . ." He shook his head, his voice trailing off.

Abby curved her hand over his shoulder. "I know how hard it is for you to trust anybody. I wish I had that teacher of yours standing in front of me right now. I'd give her a piece of my mind, let me tell you."

"I'll just bet you would."

Abby told Chase about Zeb's black eye. "I don't know what to do about it."

"Tell him to get the hell away from that bastard."

Abby rolled her eyes, but decided against any further remonstrances against Chase's language. He was still too upset. "Do you ever think of your father? I mean think of where he might be right now, what he's doing?"

"If he isn't dead, he's dead drunk. That's all Clete

Cor—" Chase nearly bit off his tongue to stop the word. He scarcely dared breathe, wondering if Abby had noticed.

"His name was Clete?" she asked softly.

He only nodded, his heart still thudding with thoughts of what he'd almost done, said. But he detected no change in her.

"He hurt you enough when you were a child," Abby said, smoothing the hair back from where it had fallen across his forehead, "stop letting him hurt you now."

With a groan Chase caught her hand, bringing it to his lips, kissing the tips of her fingers. "If there was one wish I could have, one minute I could see again, only one," he said hoarsely, "it would be to look on your face, to see your eyes when you hurt for me." He reached up to gently stroke her cheek. "I've never known anyone like you."

"That makes us even," she said, smiling, because if she didn't she would cry, "I've never known anyone like you."

She became aware of the silence then. Zeb had finished chopping the wood.

"Can I go home now?" the boy asked, coming up to them. Alone she'd found he wasn't nearly so quick to put on the cocky act he used in front of the other children.

"You may. And Zeb, I was very pleased with your work today. You're a fine student. I'm glad you're going to give school a chance."

Chase stood. "Don't let your father keep you from

what you want out of life, boy."

"Did you mean what you said about bustin' my father's head?"

"Let's put it this way, if you ever have more than you can handle with him, you let me know."

"Why should you care?"

"I just do, that's all."

"My pa was so drunk, he couldn't even tell you were blind. But I knew. And you still weren't scared of him?"

Abby could hear the threading of admiration in the boy's voice and hoped Chase was aware of it as well.

"You just let me know, hear?" Chase repeated.

Zeb didn't say anything, but Abby could tell he was at least considering it. She watched as the boy started off down the road toward home.

"Between taking on his father yesterday," she mused, "and trying to stop an assumed beating today, I think you've made yourself a new friend. Though I doubt he'll be in any hurry to admit it."

"You let me know if he ever comes to school with more than that black eye. I mean it."

"I will. I promise." She grabbed his hand. "Come on. You came by to walk me home didn't you?"

"I don't know. Are you sure you want to be seen with me?"

She ignored the sarcasm. "I'm sorry about lunch. It was a long morning." She told him about Penelope. "How about if I make it up to you? We can go on a picnic Saturday."

He shrugged. "What would Hiram Perkins say about that?"

"I don't care what he'd say."

Chase blew out a long breath and faced her squarely. "Yes, you do, Abby. That's just it. You might wish that you didn't, but you do. You love this job. You want to keep it. And maybe that means spending less time with me, not more."

She didn't want to hear that. "We can work something out."

"What we'll work out is that it's time I was on my own. I need to think about moving into the hotel."

"No. You're not ready yet."

"I'm as ready as I'm going to get and we both know it."

"Can we talk about it later?"

"Later won't change anything."

"Please?"

Reluctantly, he agreed, but the walk home was grimly silent. Things did not improve when she reached the house. On her doorstep stood Hiram Perkins.

Chapter Sixteen

Abby paced furiously from one end of the parlor to the other, trying desperately to hold her tongue. Perkins had been insufferable ever since she'd led him into the house, but so far she'd let him vent his rage unchecked. She told herself it was because one of them at least should remain rational. But part of her knew Chase was right. She didn't want to risk losing her job.

As for Chase, he was showing remarkable restraint. He had seated himself on the divan. And while some of Perkins' vitriol was directed at him, so far Chase had said nothing. She suspected it was because he wanted to see what she would do first, to see if she really would stand up to this man for what she believed was right, no matter what the consequences.

"Never has my daughter been treated so abominably, Miss Graham," Perkins bellowed. "And I tell you it will not be tolerated."

"The child was rude," Abby said evenly. "She needed to be corrected." Abby was glad Ethan and

Winnie had not yet returned from the store. They didn't need to see this.

"You humiliated her. She was sobbing her sweet heart out."

Abby found such a scene hard to imagine. "Mr. Perkins, this really isn't something that needs to be a point of contention between us." She was trying very hard to be reasonable. "We both have Penelope's best interests at heart. Surely you can see the advantage of her getting along amicably with the other students. Her rudeness to Zeb Tucker was—"

"And that's another thing!" Perkins cut in. "That boy wasn't to set foot in that schoolroom again. I didn't want to tell you this, young lady," he waggled a finger in her face, "but he's the one who tore that room apart."

Abby took a step back from the finger, but otherwise stood her ground. "If you know that, why wasn't something done about it?"

Perkins turned away. "There was no proof."

"Then you don't really know that Zeb—"

"I don't want to talk about Zeb Tucker!" he gritted, obviously annoyed that he'd allowed himself to be sidetracked. "I'm here to discuss my daughter. And your very tenuous position as Willow Springs school teacher."

Abby straightened. "Is that a threat, Mr. Perkins?"

"It most certainly is."

"Well, then perhaps I should be just as blunt." She glanced at Chase, as though merely looking at

271

him could shore up her courage. Which it did. "You don't have to threaten my position, Mr. Perkins. I quit!"

Perkins jaw dropped, and he stopped in mid-tirade. "I beg your pardon?"

"I said, I quit. I hope you have a suitable replacement in mind. Or perhaps you'd like to repeat your own stint in front of the classroom."

Perkin's jowls puffed out. "You are a most exasperating young woman, Miss Graham."

"Thank you." She marched over to sit beside Chase. "I guess I'll be joining you in the store tomorrow, Mr. Murdock."

"I'll look forward to it, Miss Graham."

Abby warmed to the pride in Chase's voice, pleased that she had not disappointed him after all. No doubt her aunt and uncle would understand as well. But what about the children? a tiny voice niggled at her. Was she putting her pride above their welfare? She thought about Russell and the way his little face had lit up when she told him he wouldn't have to read in front of the class. Perkins would never continue such an arrangement. She groaned inwardly. How could she ever allow Perkins to teach those children? She bit her lip, knowing Chase's pride in her was about to plummet precipitously. But she had no choice. She had to get her job back. And to do that she would have to apologize. "Mr. Perkins, I—"

"Now just a minute," Perkins blustered. "We have

an agreement. You signed your name. You can't just up and quit, young lady."

"Excuse me?"

"You heard me. You cannot relinquish your position, Miss Graham."

"I can't?" She stood, adopting a defiant posture, though her heart thudded with a faint glimmer of hope. This might yet work out to the advantage of both the children and herself. "But if my performance is that unsuitable, Mr. Perkins . . ."

He took a deep breath, his belligerence now seeming a last ditch defense. "You shouldn't have been so hard on my daughter."

"I don't feel I was. Penelope is a bright young girl with a wonderful future in front of her, but I think we both know she could afford to practice a little diplomacy with others."

Perkins stiffened. Abby was certain that he wanted nothing more than to put her in her place once again. Instead he muttered, "I'll speak to her about it."

"Thank you."

"You'll be there to teach tomorrow?"

"I will." She gestured toward a chair. "Would you like to sit down? I could offer you a cup of coffee, some tea?"

The man blinked, genuinely surprised by her turnabout. "No, no thank you. I'd best be getting on." He headed toward the door. "I'll show myself out."

When he'd gone, Abby couldn't suppress the

shudder of relief that coursed through her. She still had a job, and the man had actually promised to talk to his daughter about her behavior. The outcome was certainly better than any she could have predicted. She stepped toward Chase. "How did I do?"

"I've seen a prizefight or two in my time," he allowed, "but none like that one. You had him on the ropes, but you missed going for the knockout. Why?"

"Why?" She stared at him in disbelief. "If I make the man grovel, then what happens to Rusty? Or Zeb? Even Penelope."

"I'm sorry. I didn't mean the question as a criticism. I was only curious."

She pressed her fingers to her temples, her head pounding now that the earlier tension had passed. "Forgive me."

"It's all right."

"I don't want the man as an enemy, Chase. He's arrogant and judgmental, but he's also father to two of my students and in his way I think he actually wants what's best for them."

"It's easier to catch flies with honey than vinegar, eh?"

"Something like that. I want his cooperation. If I attack him on a personal level, I'll never get it." Her head continued to throb. She crossed over to the desk and pulled open the bottom drawer, extracting a half-full bottle of amber liquid. "Ethan uses this to help him relax sometimes, when he can't sleep. Maybe it would work for me." She tugged the cork loose and sniffed the bottle's contents, making a face. "Then again, maybe not."

Chase returned to the divan. "What is it?"

"Whiskey. Would you like some?"

"I don't drink." His voice was angry, clipped. He blew out an exasperated breath. "I'm sorry."

She came over and sat beside him. "I'm the one who's sorry. I should've thought." She pulled his hand into her lap. "I wish I could undo what your father did to you, but since I can't, I wish instead that you would let it go."

"It's too late, Abby."

"Too late to put an end to the bitterness you feel toward a man you haven't seen in what . . . nearly twenty years?"

He turned his head. "Too late for a lot of things."

His mood had shifted abruptly and she wondered what veiled something lay hidden in those words. He seemed so lost, so vulnerable all at once.

"Don't look at me like that," he said softly.

She blinked, startled. "How do you know I'm looking at you?"

His voice was pained, the words slow. "I can feel it. Like you can see inside me. Like you can see every tiny part of what I am."

"Why don't you want me to see those parts of you?"

"Because there are things I've done in my life that

I'm not very proud of, things that are ugly, dirty. Things that should never touch you."

Her hand tightened over his. "Nothing you could have done could ever make me think less of you. I think I know you pretty well by now, and what I know I like."

He shook his head. "But that's just it, Abby, you don't know. You don't know the half of it."

"Then tell me."

"I can't." He had come as close as he dared and now he pulled back. She might think she could understand, but to Abby he was an ex-lawman. She had no way of knowing she was talking to an outlaw, a man with a price on his head, a man who could spend ten years in prison for the Willow Springs stage holdup alone.

If only he'd met her two years ago, before he'd made that fateful decision to cross over the gray line he had so long walked. He grimaced inwardly. Who was he fooling? He wouldn't have listened to her then. He wanted revenge against Breckenridge, and nothing and no one would have stopped him from getting it. The only thing that had stopped him at last, forced him to think, was being blind. Had he been able to see he would've been gone from this house the very day he'd regained consciousness. On the run again. On the run from what he sensed in Abigail Graham the first day—empathy and vitality and an abiding compassion that scared him to death.

276

"Chase, I know I shouldn't say this, that it isn't at all proper for a woman to . . ." She bit her lip, then plunged on, "Chase, I care about you. Very much."

His eyelids slid closed and he raked a hand through his dark, shaggy hair. "Damn."

She brought her left hand up to caress his jaw and it was as though she'd sparked some unseen fuse. He groaned, reached for her, pulled her to him, his lips claiming hers with a passion that turned her blood to fire. His hands twined in her hair, caressed the nape of her neck, her back.

"Abby, sweet Abby . . ." He lost himself in the wonder of holding her, feeling her passion build to match his own. And if they hadn't been in her aunt and uncle's house he would have pressed her down to the floor and taken her then and there.

But he thanked God they were. Because it would keep him from ruining her, from destroying her life. With sheer force of will he pulled away from her, her tiny cry of frustration like a knife to his vitals. "Winnie and Ethan could be home any minute," he rasped.

"The store doesn't close until six."

"Abby, please, I haven't done that many decent things in my life. Let me do this."

"Stay away from me?"

"Yes. Dammit, yes. I'm no good for you. I'm not a man for any decent woman."

"Why do you say that? You're a lawman . . . *were* a lawman. Is it because you're blind? You know I

277

don't care about that."

He rose to his feet. "Abby, go."

He heard her shuddery sigh and knew she was on the verge of tears. Damn. But she didn't say any more as she rose and left the room.

He felt for the liquor bottle, found it and picked it up. He'd tasted whiskey once years ago and found it vile, like his memories of his father. He raised the bottle to his lips, then swore and sent it shattering into the fireplace.

Abby rushed into the room. "What happened? Are you all right?"

"I'm fine. I'm sorry."

She crossed over to him, linked her hand in his once again. "I hate to see you hurting like this. I wish you'd believe me, trust me like I trust you. I feel I can tell you anything, Chase. I feel like . . . like we're friends. Like you're my very best friend."

"Friends?" he choked. "You think this is friendship?" He kissed her again, cruel, ruthless. "This is lust, Abby, all right? Lust, not friendship. I want you! I want you in my bed." There, he'd said it, crude and harsh. And now she could hate him and he could free her from the snare of lies that was his life.

She stood there for a long time, and he could tell she was trying to settle herself, to keep from sobbing. He had hurt her. Oh, God, he had hurt her badly. But he didn't take the words back. Wouldn't. Couldn't.

She would tell him to go to hell now, tell him to get out of her house, out of her life. It was what he deserved. Her words almost sent him to his knees.

"It won't work," she said, her voice shaking. "It won't work, because it is too late, Chase Murdock. You are my friend, and I am a person who does not take friendship lightly. Because a best friend can share anything—even anger and hurt. Do you want to see how far you can push me? To see if maybe there's a point where I won't come back? It can't be done."

I could push you, he thought despairingly, *I could send you away with one word. Cordell.* But he didn't say it.

"And if you really do want me in your bed," and he could tell she was making a conscious effort not to sound as agonizingly embarrassed as she felt, "I will tell you that I've entertained similar notions about you." With that she turned on her heel and fled.

He'd been trying to set her free, trying to end a relationship based on lies, and instead he'd discovered to his horror, to his joy, that it was indeed too late.

Heaven help him, he'd never felt this way before in his life. He hadn't even known what it was until now. Friends? Sweet God, he loved her!

Chapter Seventeen

Noah Gantry stared down into the lush green valley for any signs of activity at the Diamond B main ranch house. There was none. Nor did he detect any movement around any of the half-dozen outbuildings that flanked the two story structure. In fact, except for a handful of dozing horses divided between two corrals, there was no sign of life at all.

But he knew the Breckenridges were there. He'd seen the woman earlier this morning. She'd come out to toss hay to the horses. He'd taken a perverse pleasure in seeing such a beautiful woman in charge of such a mundane chore. Judging from the angry jabs she'd made with the pitchfork, she'd found no pleasure in the task at all. That she was even doing it only confirmed for Noah that the ranch was deserted. Most of the hands would be out on fall roundup, driving Diamond B cattle to the Cheyenne railhead. Any remaining crew was likely out on the range.

As for Luther Breckenridge, he'd come out briefly to sit in a chair on the front porch, but had seemed to suffer another one of his consumptive attacks and gone back into the house.

"This is almost too easy," Noah muttered. He wouldn't have minded a bit of a fight. Maybe Breckenridge would go for a gun, at least make it interesting — Noah grinned — before Noah killed him.

Noah eyed his three companions. "I'm going in alone," he said. "Wait here. I may not be back 'til nightfall." He had an idea what he was going to do with Felicity Breckenridge, and he didn't want to be hurried. Or interrupted.

"I don't see why we're botherin' with a ranch," a hawk-nosed Frank Brown complained. "How much money can they have before roundup's over?"

"I got me a feeling Breckenridge has lots of money all the time," Noah said. "Besides, if I say we do it, we do it."

The Kid and McKenzie said nothing. They'd already settled themselves in front of a boulder with a pair of dice. With a shake of his head Brown went over to join them.

Noah mounted. The Kid hadn't said much since Noah had put an end to Josey Vinson, but more and more Noah had felt a need to watch his back. Maybe he'd have to take care of the Kid, too, one of these days. Not that the Kid had the guts to do anything himself — including shoot him in the back — but the Kid might be putting too many wrong ideas into McKenzie's head.

281

Right now it didn't matter. What mattered was what waited for him in the Diamond B ranch house. Noah kicked his bay into a trot.

Ten minutes later he was tying off the gelding to a hitchpost in front of the house. He tromped across the porch to the front door, gave his Colt a quick check, then opened the door and went inside. Spartan furnishings gave the spacious main room a decidedly empty feel. A horsehair divan, rolltop desk and two straight-back chairs were the only pieces of furniture in the room. The only personal touch — and it could have been store bought — was the bearskin rug that fronted the fieldstone hearth.

"Who are you?" a feminine voice demanded.

Noah looked up to see Felicity Breckenridge standing in the archway that probably led to the kitchen. If finding a strange man in her living room frightened her, it did not show in those violet eyes. "No one answered my knock," Noah lied amiably enough.

"I didn't hear any knock," she snapped. "Now just turn yourself around and get out of my house." Those incredible eyes sparked with anger. Noah felt a flash of surprise. She had seemed meek, kowed in her husband's presence in Willow Springs. But she was anything but that right now.

"Actually, ma'am," he drawled, "I come by lookin' for work. I didn't see anyone outside."

"Everyone's out with the herd. Except my husband, of course." She added the last with a hint of warning, as though to keep him from getting any ideas. But it was much too late for that. It had been too late ever since that day in Willow Springs.

"I would've been here sooner, but I had some trouble with my horse. Maybe if I could talk to your husband?"

"He's resting upstairs."

"Feelin' poorly, is he?"

"He gets around." She held her ground in the archway, and in fact did not move back even when Noah closed the distance between them. "I think you'd better leave."

"Not until I talk to your husband."

Her eyes narrowed as he stopped some four feet away from her. He'd been careful to keep his left profile averted, but now he faced her squarely.

"I've seen you somewhere before," she said.

"Willow Springs."

She touched a finger to her lips. "After that horrible stage robbery, of course."

"You seemed calmer about it than your husband," Noah said.

"Luther lost over five thousand dollars that day. I thought he was going to have a heart attack." She took a step toward him. "Why did you come here?"

"I had me an idea that maybe you could use someone around your ranch who knew how to handle himself in rough situations."

"You?"

"Exactly."

"You know your way around guns, Mr. — ?"

"Gantry. Noah Gantry. And, yes ma'am, I know my way around guns."

A sudden eagerness sparked in those eyes, which she quickly shuttered. She was a cagey one, he had to give her that, damned cagey.

"Are you a scrupulous man, Mr. Gantry?" she purred.

"Any scruples I might have can be bought and paid for, Mrs. Breckenridge."

"I see." She gestured toward the kitchen. "Can I offer you a cup of coffee."

"I'd like that."

He moved to follow her, his gaze straying to the open door of a room off to the right. In plain view was a safe abutting the room's far wall. Noah unconsciously licked his lips.

Felicity poured him the coffee, as he took a seat beside the rough-hewn pine table. "Your husband fallen on hard times since the robbery, ma'am?"

"What do you mean?"

"I mean I've seen nicer furniture in a bunk house."

"My husband doesn't believe in spending any more money than he absolutely has to, Mr. Gantry."

"Doesn't sound like you're too happy about that."

"I wouldn't mind having some nice things." She studied him closely. "How did that happen to your face?"

He wasn't used to a woman being quite so blunt,

284

but he shrugged it off. "Shoshone," he said, a strange smile coming to his lips. "He paid the price. I cooked him over a slow fire."

Felicity's gaze wavered a little then held. "Maybe you're just the man I've been looking for, Mr. Gantry."

"How so, ma'am?" He was enjoying this, like a snake enjoys cornering its prey.

"Luther and I have been married four years," she began.

"I'm real happy for you, I'm sure."

"Don't be. I despise my husband, Mr. Gantry. I can't go anywhere, can't do anything. If I so much as look at another man . . ." She took a sip of her coffee. "Do you know I haven't had a new dress in two years. Not since—" She stopped.

"Since what?"

"Nothing. Never mind." She set the coffee down. "I want my husband dead, Mr. Gantry. I want him dead and buried and out of my life forever."

"You don't exactly pussyfoot around, Mrs. Breckenridge."

"Not any more."

"You want me to kill him?"

"He's upstairs, asleep. I'll pay you anything you ask."

"Why haven't you done it yourself?"

She shivered, and Gantry saw for the first time that much of her bravado was bluff. She could hire her dirty work done, but she didn't have the stomach for doing it herself.

"You've got the money here?" he asked.

"In the safe."

"You know how to open it?" This could be even easier than he'd hoped.

"No. I don't have the combination. But that doesn't matter. Luther will open it himself tonight. He always does. Every night he sits in that room for hours and counts his money, touches it, caresses it. It's like he makes love to it."

A smirk played at the corners of Noah's mouth. "And how do you make love, Mrs. Breckenridge?"

For just an instant revulsion shadowed those violet eyes as her gaze flicked to his twisted features, but it was gone so quickly he could've chosen to believe he'd imagined it. Except that he had not. She would do anything to rid herself of her husband it seemed. Anything.

He was surprised she hadn't already enticed a ranch hand to kill the man for her and he asked as much. "His men are hand picked," she told him. "Though it may seem strange to you, my husband inspires a fierce loyalty in his workers."

"But not in his wife."

"No, Mr. Gantry, not in his wife." She rose and crossed to his side of the table, running her hand along the unmarred side of his face. "But I can be loyal, Mr. Gantry. To the right man."

Gantry followed her upstairs to her room. She pointed toward the closed door at the end of the

286

hall. "The pain was too much this morning. He had whiskey for breakfast. He won't wake before three. That means we have two hours."

She clicked the door shut to her room, then crossed to draw the curtains. The dark fabric allowed little light to creep in. His stomach twisted, but he said nothing. Felicity Breckenridge could have him in her bed — but only so long as she didn't have to look at him. He told himself it didn't matter. He was hard and ready. And he didn't give a damn who she was either.

Their coupling was quick, primitive, animal grunts and groans the only sounds that passed between them. It was over in minutes. He lay back, sweating, spent, but he was ready again soon after. And again after that. He would make the most of these two hours.

At three o'clock he stood and dressed.

"I hear him," she whispered. "Be quiet and wait here. He opens the safe just after supper."

She stood at her door, dressed, every hair in place. Nothing about her gave the slightest hint of the raw lust they'd just shared. Without a backward glance she opened the door, then quickly closed it behind her. Noah remained on the bed, chafing, wondering how he would find the patience to wait three hours. But his interlude with Felicity Breckenridge provided the answer. In minutes he was asleep.

He woke to the sounds of voices raised downstairs. He rose and crept to the door.

"Get out of here, woman!" Luther Breckenridge shouted. "You know you're not allowed in this room when I'm counting my money!"

"I'm sorry, Luther," Felicity said in placating tones. "I just thought you might like a cup of coffee."

"Get out! As if I don't know what you want. I've seen it on your face ever since you got back from your little trip."

"I don't know what you're talking about, Luther."

"Slut! Don't tell me you didn't sleep with that lawman, Devlin. Anytime you get near a man, you can't keep your clothes on. I should never have let you talk me into sending you alone."

"But, Luther, that was over a week ago. Can't you just let it alone?"

Noah padded into the hall. He had no interest in whether or not they resolved their argument. Breckenridge had mentioned the money. It was time for Noah to join them. Felicity's next words halted him in his tracks.

"And what if it had been Cordell? Wouldn't you have wanted to know?"

"But it wasn't!" Luther shouted.

Noah frowned. Breckenridge had mentioned a little trip. Had someone found Cordell's body? And if that was so, why hadn't Felicity identified it? The woman certainly knew what Cordell looked like. Felicity said something then he couldn't hear. Frustrated, he tiptoed toward the top of the stairs. A board creaked.

"What was that?" Breckenridge demanded.

"What was what?" Felicity asked. "I didn't hear anything." Though it was obvious she had.

Noah ducked back in the hall, listening to the rancher's lumbering footfalls across the front room. Noah drew his gun. When Breckenridge reached the bottom of the stairs, Noah stepped into view and thumbed back the hammer. "Don't move," he said, as he descended the stairs.

"What the devil?" Paying no attention to Noah, Breckenridge whirled on his wife and backhanded her across the face. "Whore!"

She didn't blink, didn't cry. She just stared at him, defiant, circling around to stand at Noah's side.

"I hear he's been counting out his money for me," Noah said.

"For us," Felicity amended.

Luther's eyes widened in horror. "No! No, you can't have it. It's mine." His face purpled, his eyes bulging. "You can't! You can't!" He lurched toward Noah, but seemed to run into an invisible wall. He clutched at his chest, his breath coming in agonizing gasps. "Please!" He dropped to his knees. Noah and Felicity stepped past him.

"Felicity!" he wheezed. "Felicity, I beg you."

She turned. "You beg me, Luther? What about all the times I begged you?"

289

"I'll do anything you say . . . anything . . . Just don't let him take my money. Please." Tears streamed down his cheeks. He collapsed forward, his breathing seeming more painful still. "Please." Breckenridge clawed toward the bearskin rug in front of the fireplace.

Noah continued toward the far room. He crossed to Breckenridge's desk, whistling appreciatively at the mounds of paper money and gold. "There must be thirty thousand dollars here."

"At least!" Felicity cried, running her hands over the currency.

"Don't touch it."

"What?"

He smiled, catching her hand and leading her out of the room. "We've got something more important to do first."

"What's that?" Though somewhat uncertain, she gave him an answering smile.

Noah led her out to the bearskin rug. They had the time. He had the urge. Quickly they disrobed, coupling urgently not six feet from Luther Breckenridge's body. "Your husband seems to be dead," Noah said, when they'd finished.

"Thank you," she murmured. "Thank you so very much."

"And to think I'm going to get to blame all of this on a dead man." Noah tucked in his shirttail.

She frowned. "Luther?"

"No. A man named Cordell. You might remember his little run-in with your husband a couple of years back. I've heard tell you had a lot to do with it."

She grimaced. "If Cordell had had half the back-bone you have, I could've been a widow two years ago." She finished buttoning her dress. "But why do you say he's dead?"

"I killed him."

A light dawned in her eyes and a sudden wariness. "It was you who shot him?"

"We had a little disagreement a while back."

"When exactly?"

"Does it matter?"

"Maybe after a certain stage holdup?"

Noah straightened. "And if it was?"

She blinked, aware all at once of the danger inherent in such questions. She gave a quick laugh, but there was a nervous trill in the sound. "What you've done in the past is your business. But maybe you'd like to know about Cordell—since you obviously wanted him dead."

"I heard you and Luther talkin' about your goin' back to Willow Springs to look at his body."

"Not his body. Him. Cordell's not dead."

Noah's blood went cold. "What?"

She told him of her summons by Sam Devlin. "But your bullets did do some permanent damage. He's blind."

"Cordell blind?" Noah laughed. "Maybe that's even better than dead, eh? But why didn't you identify him?"

"Let's just say I owed him one."

"Then why tell me?"

"I owe you more. You killed my husband." She crossed to the window, staring out at the vast valley beyond. "All of this is mine now. All of it. The money, the power."

Noah wasn't listening. He was thinking of Cordell. Alive and blind. This he would have to see for himself. His gunhand itched. Finish the job.

"I've waited so long," Felicity said. "You can stay, Noah, share it with me."

"I'm not really good at sharing." Noah picked up his Navy Colt. "I'm not real fond of witnesses either."

Felicity turned, laughing. "Luther's dead. You don't have to worry about wit—" Her look of triumph vanished.

Noah smiled and fired the gun.

Chapter Eighteen

Abby clambered out of bed, mustering every ounce of her courage. She was going to have it out with Chase this morning. She'd tossed and turned all night, his harsh words ringing in her ears. *I want you in my bed.* He'd flung them at her to hurt her, to drive her away, but he hadn't even realized the depths of the anguish with which he'd spoken them. Whether he acknowledged it or not, he was hurting too.

There are things I've done in my life that I'm not proud of, things that are ugly, dirty. What things? What could be so terrible? If only he would tell her, they could talk about it, put it behind them.

She dressed quickly, then hurried to his room. The door was open. She stepped inside to find her uncle closing an apparently empty bureau drawer. Chase was nowhere in sight.

" 'Morning, honey," Ethan said, straightening, an unreadable look in his brown eyes.

Abby's heartbeat quickened. Her gaze darted about the room. There was something different about it. Something wrong. The bed had not been slept in. "You're overworking Chase," she chided with a forced lightness. "Sending him to the store this early. Really, Uncle Ethan . . ."

"He's gone, Abby," Ethan said softly.

Her heart turned over. "What?"

"I helped him move his things to the hotel late last night."

"No. No, you couldn't have. I would've heard you."

"He's gone, Abby," Ethan said again. "I was just making sure we hadn't overlooked anything."

"But why would he leave? The man is blind. He needs me . . . *us*," she amended quickly. "He needs — "

"He needs to be on his own," Ethan interrupted gently. "He's been dependent on us long enough, maybe too long."

She walked to the window and stared out at the steadily lightening day. "What do you mean?"

"I've got eyes, Abby. I've seen the way you two are with each other. To tell you the truth, I admire Chase for moving out."

Abby felt her cheeks heat. "We haven't done anything wrong."

"I know that. But you're tempting fate to spend so much time with him."

"I love him, Uncle Ethan."

He looked at the floor, then at her. "I know."

"You don't approve?" She made no attempt to

hide her disappointment. She thought she understood Winnie's reservations, but from her uncle, she realized now, she had expected, even hoped for, his blessing.

"I like Chase," Ethan said slowly. "I really do. But he's a man packin' secrets, Abby. Secrets that could get you hurt, and that I don't like, don't want."

"He won't hurt me." She said the words with a stubbornness she didn't feel.

Ethan's gaze was kind, but he cut her no quarter, gave her no place to hide. "He already has."

"No!" Tears rimmed her eyes.

"Abby . . ."

She straightened. "I'm going to the hotel. I'm going to talk to him."

"I don't think that's a very good idea."

"Uncle Ethan, I love him! Please . . ." Her voice broke.

He crossed over to her, wrapped his arms around her, arms that had soothed a thousand childhood hurts. But her pain this time was beyond even Ethan's gentle caring. Still she lost herself in the familiar comfort, sobbing quietly for long minutes. When she drew back, the shoulder of Ethan's shirt was damp with her tears. Reaching into the pocket of her dress, she withdrew her handkerchief and blew her nose. "What am I going to do?"

"Give yourself some time. Give Chase some time." Ethan pulled his own kerchief from his pocket and dabbed at the tears still tracking down her cheeks. "If it's meant to be, it'll happen."

"I need to see him, talk to him."

"Time, Abby," Ethan repeated. "Chase has had a lot happen to him the past couple of weeks. He needs time, even if you don't. He's got some hard decisions to make."

"About those secrets?"

"Maybe."

"Did he tell you what they were, Uncle Ethan?"

"No."

"You don't think—" she took a deep breath, "you don't think it could be anything too terrible, do you?" Her heart thudded as she awaited his answer.

But he skirted the question, saying instead, "I think he truly doesn't want to see you hurt."

"He's hurt me by leaving. He's hurt me by not saying good-bye."

"That wasn't easy for him, Abby. He did say one thing while we were walking to the hotel. He told me he met you two years too late. What that means, I don't know. But you've got to let him handle this his own way. If he thinks his past will hurt you, you've got to trust his judgment and let him go."

Abby crossed over to the chair and sagged into it. She had no strength to argue the point. "He's not leaving town, is he?"

"No. Not yet anyway. He'll still be working for me at the store."

Abby heaved a long, shuddery sigh. "I guess I'd best get ready for school."

"Are you all right?"

She stood. She didn't want her uncle to worry any more than he already was. "I'll be fine." She managed a smile, then headed back to her own room.

She sat on her bed a long time, thinking. Chase's abrupt departure had taken her by surprise. He'd talked about leaving, but she'd had no idea he'd meant to do it so quickly, so clandestinely. She supposed he thought he was doing her a favor.

And maybe he was. His crudely put announcement that he wanted to bed her had elicited her own response that she'd entertained similar fantasies about him. Perhaps he was being gallant at last, saving her from herself.

Well, no thank you, she thought grimly. She was no simpering prude, afraid of her own woman's body. Neither was she frightened nor ashamed of the sensual feelings Chase had stirred to life within her. In fact, she welcomed those feelings, embraced them openly. She was in love with him. And she wanted to share every part of that love with him, every part of herself. She'd spent a lifetime immersed in romantic dreams. With Chase she could make those dreams a reality.

Now all she had to do was convince him.

She gave her head a rueful shake. No small task, considering his apparent resolve to end even their friendship. But she wasn't about to let him get away with it. At least not without a fight. She recalled her own resolve to confront him and decided nothing had changed, except the timing of the confrontation. Instead of here and now, it would have to wait until this afternoon in the mercantile. But it was going to happen. They had to talk. It was the only way.

She forced herself to her feet. "Wherever you are, Chase Murdock," she grumbled, "whatever you're doing, I hope you're as miserable as I am."

Somehow she made it to school. Hours that normally flew by crawled at an interminable pace. Rusty's private reading lesson went well, but it was all she could do to concentrate. Penelope's essay on rudeness was actually well thought out and deserving of high praise, but at recess the girl again called Zeb Tucker a goat. And then at noon two younger boys—brothers—got into a wrestling match over a stickball game. Abby kept the two after school, then stared at the clock, thinking only of how their antics had delayed her meeting with Chase.

"If either one of you lays a hand on the other ever again," she fumed, pacing back and forth in front of the chastened youngsters, "you're each going to write 'I will not punch my brother' on the blackboard three hundred times a day for the rest of your natural born lives. Understood?"

The boys nodded in unison, their eyes wide as saucers as they took a collective step back from her.

"Now go!"

They practically fell over one another in their scramble to get out the door.

Suppressing a twinge of guilt, Abby gathered her things and hurried home. She stopped only long enough to drop off her books and lunch tin, then she marched toward the Graham Mercantile. She kept her head high, maintaining a tenuous hold on a confidence she didn't feel. What if he wouldn't talk to her? What if he wouldn't listen? She bit her lip. What if he'd taken the afternoon stage out of town?

"Were you just going to walk by without saying hello?" Sam Devlin's voice chided behind her.

Abby stopped, her heart sinking. Sam was the last person she wanted to see right now. Turning, she forced a smile as the lawman pulled his office door shut and strode toward her. The badge on his vest seemed shinier than usual.

"Haven't seen you for a couple of days," Sam went on, his normally buoyant smile tempered by an undercurrent of another emotion she couldn't read.

"I've had a lot of school work," she said, wishing to heaven she'd taken a roundabout way to the store. She had no patience for idle chitchat. She wanted only to see Chase.

"I've missed you," he said. "Can you stop in for a few minutes?" He gestured toward his office.

There was an earnestness in him now that made

299

Abby suddenly uncomfortable. She shook her head. "I have to be going. I have to get to the store."

"Please?" The earnestness grew stronger. "I have something important I want to ask you, say to you."

"I really should go."

He blew out a long breath, his gaze at once hurt and oddly concerned. "It's Murdock, isn't it?"

"Sam, please, I . . ." She didn't want this conversation.

"I know he moved into the hotel last night."

"He needs his independence," she said quickly. "He—"

Devlin held up a hand. "You don't have to say anything. You don't owe me any explanations, Abby."

Then why did she feel as though she did? Why did she know she was responsible for the pain in Sam Devlin's brown eyes?

"I suppose I shouldn't say this now. I'm not a man who needs his pride bruised up any more than it already is, but it's in me and it's gotta come out." He caught her hand. "I never set much store by fancy words . . ."

"Sam, please don't—"

He paid her no heed, the words spilling out. "I'm a forty dollar a month lawman, who never figured himself the marryin' kind—until I met you, Abby Graham." He swallowed hard. "I want you to be my wife."

Abby stared at him, stunned. She had known he was attracted to her, liked her, but never had she expected this. "Sam, I—"

"Don't answer now," he said, squeezing her hand. "Just think about it. All right?"

"No, Sam, please." Even her addled senses told her she couldn't leave things like this between them. She couldn't give him that kind of false hope. "Sam, you're a good friend, but . . ." She tugged her hand free. "I can't marry you. I don't love you."

He closed his eyes briefly, then opened them again, a kind of bemused sadness now evident in his face. "I knew you cared about Murdock," he said quietly, "but I guess I hoped to God it hadn't gone any farther than that. I'm sorry, Abby, but I've been a lawman long enough to trust a gut feeling when I have one. And I have a real bad feeling about Murdock. I don't want you to think I'm sayin' this because you turned me down. I can take that. But I don't know if I can take you makin' the mistake of your life with that man."

"I don't see it as a mistake, Sam," she said softly.

He shook his head. "Stay away from him, Abby. Please, stay away from him." With that he turned and disappeared into his office.

Abby stood there, her emotions roiling. Twice in one day, people she cared about had been less that subtle in their warnings that she stay clear of Chase Murdock. But what neither Ethan nor Sam seemed to understand was that it was too late, far too late

301

for her to back away. She loved Chase, loved him enough to overcome whatever it was he was now trying to wedge between them.

That is, if Chase himself would cooperate. He was the one variable she couldn't predict, though she was determined to try. Gathering her flagging courage, she again headed for the mercantile.

The bell above the jamb tinkled as she walked in. She inhaled the familiar mingled aromas of leather goods and coffee, spices and fresh fabric, feeling as always that her aunt and uncle's store was as much home as the house in which they lived. Not an inch of space was wasted here. Winnie and Ethan offered everything from groceries to hardware, from pickled fish to pitchforks. In the center of the store stood a potbellied stove, unlit now, but there to provide an island of warmth in the winter for any who dropped by to engage in a friendly game of checkers, the latest gossip, or both.

Winnie was straightening bolts of calico on one of the side shelves. Ethan was filling a grain order for Padriac O'Banion, Molly and Keefer's father. Abby smiled at them, but continued toward the rear of the store. The determination she'd carried with her all day dropped precipitously as she spotted Chase. He was standing at the back counter refilling two large glass jars. Even as short a time ago as yesterday, Chase's big hands wrapped about peppermint balls and licorice whips would have brought a teasing laugh to her lips, but today the innocuous task only seemed to mock her, accentuate the widening gulf between then.

He cocked an ear at her approach. "Can I help you?" He added a "ma'am," apparently guessing her gender by the lightness of her step, or perhaps by the absence of the jangle of spurs. His easy manner convinced her he had no idea to whom he was speaking.

"Less than a day," she murmured, knowing she was being unfair, "and you've forgotten me already?"

He stiffened, taking an unconscious step back. "Abby. What are you doing here?" His tone was now implacable, hard.

"You must have known I would come." She kept her voice low, taking care not to be overheard. "Or perhaps I should've gone to your room at the hotel?"

A muscle in his jaw knotted. "And wouldn't Perkins have loved that?" he gritted. "I thought I made it clear last night. We need to stay away from each other."

"And what if I have a different opinion?" She stepped around the counter, stopping bare inches from where he stood. "What if I don't think we should stay away from each other at all?"

He turned away from her. "Dammit, Abby, I'm doing this for you, can't you see that?"

"No, no, I can't. Not until you tell my why, convince me, instead of sneaking off like a thief in the night."

He seemed to wince. Abby caught his wrist. "All I'm asking for is the truth."

"Abby," he rasped, "you haven't got an idea in the world what you're asking for."

An odd feeling skittered over her, Sam Devlin's words echoing in her ears. *Stay away from him, Abby. . . . I have a real bad feeling about Murdock.* But she ignored the feeling, her hand slipping down to link itself with Chase's own. He did not pull away. "Whatever it is, you can tell me. You—" She noticed the quiet then, the unnatural quiet in the normally bustling store. She glanced around her. Winnie had stopped sorting bolts of fabric and was regarding her with an openly worried expression. Ethan seemed more resigned, as though he wished she hadn't come, but knew she would. Padriac O'Banion looked embarrassed.

Abby swallowed guiltily. She hadn't meant to upset anyone. "We can't talk here."

Chase pulled free of her, his resolve to put distance between them very obviously reasserting itself. "We can't talk at all, Abby. I'm going to be leaving Willow Springs."

His words were like a physical blow. "When?" she managed to squeak out.

"Soon. By week's end."

Her eyes burned with unshed tears. She could tell he'd made the decision in the heartbeat it had taken him to say the words. She had come here to get him

304

to talk to her. Instead, she'd somehow forced his hand, driven him to leave town. "You can't mean that. Not after what we said to each other last night."

He reached out, found her arm, then maneuvered himself around her. "Especially after what we said last night." He angled his head in Ethan's direction. "I'm going to open those crates of canned goods in the back room," he called out. "That okay with you, Ethan?"

"Fine, son," Ethan answered, though his now troubled gaze settled on Abby.

Abby looked away, catching Chase's arm before he could escape to the back. "Come by the house tonight between six and seven," she whispered, hating herself for the desperation threading her voice. "Winnie and Ethan have a church meeting. Come by the house, or I promise you, I'll come to the hotel."

He scowled, his lips thinning. He wasn't a man to field an ultimatum gracefully. But she'd left him little choice. Because he cared. Whether he wanted to admit it or not, he cared too much about her to let her be seen going to his room at the hotel. "I'll be there."

She let out a shaky sigh, then straightened. Forcing an overbright smile, she waved off her aunt an uncle and walked quickly out of the mercantile. She was a dozen steps down the street before she was at all certain her legs would support her the entire distance home. Chase was leaving Willow Springs. Leaving her. For her own good.

And she had only one hour tonight to convince him otherwise.

At home alone in the house she paced the floor of the parlor, jumping every time she heard the slightest sound. As it had in school earlier, time seemed to stretch endlessly past its normal bonds. The two hours she would have to wait for Chase seemed more like two days. In desperation she went to her bedroom and made an attempt to work on her novel, a once loved avocation she now scrupulously avoided. The attempt only added to her intolerable frustration. Nothing of Tex Trueblood's adventure seemed real to her any more. Chase Murdock had even muddled her imaginings.

She slammed the journal shut, then gasped to hear a knock on the front door. Chase. Her heart pounded. Fighting back a surge of panic, she hurried to let him in. "Thank you for coming."

"What choice did you give me?" His voice was surly, but she took heart that it at least seemed forced. Brushing past her, he tapped his cane toward the parlor.

"Have a seat," she offered.

"I'll stand."

She watched him from across the room, unable to take her eyes off him. He'd changed from the denims and blue chambray shirt he'd been wearing at the mercantile. Dark gray trousers hugged lean hips, his white cotton shirt accented by a black leather vest and string tie. Rich, mahogany hair brushed past his shirt collar, and her hands seemed to tingle as she thought of what it would be like to trail her fingers through the stray lock that tumbled across his forehead.

"You look very handsome," she said softly, even as she felt her cheeks grow warm.

"I wouldn't know. I haven't had much occasion to look in a mirror lately."

She wondered if the sarcasm was his defense of choice for the evening, or if he was as nervous as she was. Either way she would have to handle it. If this was to be their last conversation, she intended it to be a memorable one—for both of them. She would get some answers from this very close-mouthed man. Taking a determined breath, she crossed to the divan and sat down. Chase remained standing near the hearth.

"Sam Devlin stopped me on the way to the mercantile this afternoon," she said, pleased to see that the mention of Sam's name had its usual effect on Chase. He was instantly alert, wary.

"More questions about me?" He tried to sound casual, but failed.

"Actually, no." She waited a beat, then said, "He asked me to marry him."

A look of raw pain flicked across Chase's features, a look quickly shuttered away. But it had been there. And it gave her hope.

"What did you tell him?"

She could've drawn it out, gauged his reaction. But she didn't have to, didn't want to. She'd already discovered what she so desperately wanted to know. Chase Murdock was in love with her. He didn't want to be, but he was. "I told him no."

Chase fingered the end of his cane. "He would have made you a good husband."

"Would I have made your life simpler if I'd said yes?"

He straightened. "Did you ask me here to tell me about Devlin?"

"No." Her heart thundered. "I asked you here to talk about last night."

"It's all been said."

"I don't think it has." If she chose the most outrageous tack possible, perhaps she could fluster him, get him to lower his guard. She took a deep breath. There was only one tack outrageous enough to fluster Chase Murdock. "Last night you said you wanted me to go to bed with you, is that correct?"

"Abby, for God's sake . . ." He stalked away several paces, cursing low under his breath.

"Did you, or did you not, say it?"

He didn't answer.

"Were you telling the truth?" She stood and stepped close to him, catching the heady fragrance of bay rum. "Do you want me in your bed, Chase Murdock? Like I want you in mine?"

His breathing had grown shallow, and his whole

body was rigid with what it must have cost him to stand so still, to not back away from her. If he challenged her boldness openly, she knew she would be lost. She had precious little experience with an aroused male. And she was not at all certain she had the fortitude to brazen this out, if he so much as hinted that he would take her at her word.

Long seconds passed, the silence growing awkward, painful. He was so still, unmoving, it was as though he had turned to stone. And then she realized what he was doing. He was waiting her out. He would not touch her, nor would he retreat. It was she who had approached him. She would have to be the one to advance or back away. And she knew which move Chase expected.

Instead she lay a hand against his chest, felt his heart surge beneath her palm. "I've waited for you all my life, Chase Murdock. All my life. I love you."

He closed his eyes, a pained sound coming from his throat. "You can't love someone you don't know. And believe me when I tell you you don't know me."

She smoothed her hand along the side of his face, her fingertips tracing the line of his jaw. "I know all I need to know. I know I love you." Her lips brushed his. "I love you."

For the space of a heartbeat he held himself in check. Then with a groan he crushed her to him, his mouth raining kisses across her forehead, her cheeks, her eyes. He tasted of her, gloried in the sweetness, the warmth, the magic that was Abby. And he struggled against the words. God, how he fought them. But then he was saying them over and over and over again. "I love you, Abby. God help me, I love you so much."

Abby's heart soared with a joy so fierce she feared she could die of it. "Oh, Chase," she cried, her voice shaking, "everything's going to be all right. You can stay in Willow Springs, stay—"

With an anguished oath he set her away from him. "No. No, Abby, I can't." He made his way to the door. "Don't you see? It's because I love you that I can't. Not ever." And then he was gone.

Chapter Nineteen

Chase sat on the bed in his hotel room, trembling. Why in God's name had he told Abby he loved her? Why had he said it? Admitted it? Now it would only make things that much harder for her when he left town. Because he was leaving. On tomorrow's stage. He'd go to the mercantile first thing in the morning and tell Ethan. Abby's uncle would try to convince him that he should face her, not take the coward's way out, but Chase knew this was the only way.

To stand in the same room with her was to lose the courage he needed to get out of her life. To touch her was to never let go.

He lay back, surrounded by the darkness that was his constant companion and relived the feel of her lips on his, heard again the love that threaded her voice whenever she spoke to him. Desire burned hot in his loins, in his heart. He wanted her, wanted her fully, completely, like he'd never wanted a woman in his life. With Abby he could have shared what he'd never before had—the awesome wonder of intimacy with a woman he loved.

Could have. And now never would.

Tears stung his eyes and he swiped them angrily away, fighting off a sudden rush of embarrassment. He hadn't cried since the day Murdock died.

But then what had he had to cry over? He'd never left himself open, vulnerable to the kind of pain that would make a man weep—until Noah Gantry had left him for dead, and Abby had willed life back into his savaged body. But her gift of life had not been the one he'd known prior to Gantry's bullets, it was a life of gentleness and laughter, of family and love.

The pain his leaving would cause her seared him like acid fire, because he knew how easily he could spare her. All he had to do was tell her the truth—that he was an outlaw, a thief, a hired gun. Then she would hate him, wish him gone and be glad. But he couldn't do it. He couldn't destroy even the illusion of the love she bore him. He would carry it with him always, carry, too, the knowledge that he had at least saved her the grief of seeing the man she loved gunned down by a bounty hunter or led away in chains by the law.

Sam Devlin's suspicions grew more overt every day. Chase wouldn't be surprised if the man wired Luther Breckenridge to return to Willow Springs. What better way to eliminate the sheriff's competition for Abby than to put Chase behind bars?

No, any choices Chase might have had to stay,

take a chance on anonymity with Abby were lost to the lawman's jealousy. Devlin wanted Chase out of Abby's life. Toward that end he would use any legal means at his disposal.

Except that now he wouldn't have to. Chase would do the honors for him. He would leave like the thief in the night Abby had called him and pray God she would never know how close her words had cut to the truth.

As to where he would go, what he would do, he had no idea. Head east, he supposed. Depend on the pity of strangers to get him to a place where a blind man might be of use.

He hadn't given up the notion that one day his sight would return. But now when it happened, he would not see the one thing in the world he wanted most to see—the face of Abigail Graham.

Nor would he strap on a gun and track Gantry. In a perverse way he owed Gantry what small measure of life he had come to know. Not the acts of eating and breathing, but the sense of being alive that had been with him ever since he'd first awakened to the sound of Abby's voice.

A voice he would never hear again.

He closed his eyes, then opened them, the black void unchanging, and he saw in it his life without her.

Abby stared out at the eager faces of her students

and tried hard to keep her mind on the grammar lesson for her Second Reader class. But it was fast proving impossible. Her thoughts were consumed by an almost paralyzing fear that she would never see Chase again.

She'd had another nightmare last night. As with the previous dream Chase had been calling to her, and she'd tried desperately to find him. She was not blind this time, but it made no difference. She could see nothing. She groped her way through some sort of dungeon, deep in the bowels of the earth, a fetid hole without light, without hope. She'd found Chase there, a prisoner, shackled to dank stone walls.

"I can't be with you any more, Abby," he'd said in a voice devoid of emotion. "I want you to marry Sam Devlin. He'll make you a good husband."

Over and over she'd asked Chase what he'd done to be condemned to such a place, but he never answered.

"M-M-M-Miss Graham?"

Abby shook herself, surprised to see a worried look on Russell Perkins' small face. How long had the boy been trying to gain her attention? "What is it, Rusty?"

"The-the-the answer is-is-is a noun."

"Noun?" She frowned.

"The p-p-p-part of speech that names a p-p-p-person, place or thing is-is a noun."

"Oh. Very good, Rusty. That's correct." She

314

didn't even remember asking the question. As if her fears about Chase were not sufficient, her gaze fell again on Zeb Tucker's empty seat. She prayed Harley was not blacking the boy's other eye. Twining her fingers together to keep her hands from shaking, she managed a smile in Molly O'Banion's direction. "Can you give me some examples of nouns, Molly?"

"Proper or common, Miss Graham?"

"Common." She listened distractedly as the child began to recite, her thoughts again leapfrogging to Chase. Last night he'd held her, kissed her, told her he loved her, sent her world spinning with joy, and in the next breath he told her he was leaving. That it was *because* he loved her that he couldn't stay in Willow Springs, couldn't be a part of her life.

What sense did that make? What sense did any of it make? After he'd left the house, she went over it all again and again in her mind until she thought she would go mad. Then exhausted, she'd slept, only to be tormented by her dreams. And never did she find any answers, only more questions.

Secrets.

Things in my life I'm not proud of, things ugly, dirty.

Didn't he owe her the chance to make her own judgment about whatever it was he kept hidden from her? Or was that precisely what he feared? That she would judge him as harshly as he judged himself?

315

Abruptly she rose and crossed to the window. "Those were all fine common nouns, Molly," she said, though her voice trembled badly. She forced herself to take several deep breaths, fighting back tears. She did not want the children suffering her mood. "I know this isn't the normal schedule, children," she said, turning again to face them. "But I want all of you to take out your readers and read the next story to yourselves. Please begin at once."

There was the shuffling of slates and books, but the children themselves seemed subdued now, as if they too sensed something amiss.

He's leaving today. The thought struck her like a thunderbolt. *Today.*

She returned to the window, her fingertips touching one cool pane, as she looked northward toward the butte-studded plains rolling on into forever. How could everything seem so normal, so tranquil, when her whole world was falling apart? And how did a man who'd come into her life scarcely three weeks ago have the power to turn that world inside out?

"You're not leaving, Chase Murdock," she murmured fiercely. "Not without telling me the truth of why you can't stay."

Her thoughts tumbled one upon the other as she considered how a blind man could leave town on his own. He would have only one choice. The afternoon stage. That would give her time then to see him during lunch — even if it meant visiting his hotel room.

She felt a little better then, as though at least she could get through the rest of the morning. She would call up the first spelling group, have them— She frowned, squinting to see what it was that had caught her eye near the road. A man on foot? Lurching, stumbling. She peered closer. The figure collapsed.

"Stay in your seats, children!" Abby said sharply. "I'm going to be leaving school for a few minutes."

Gathering her skirts, she hurried out the door and up the road. She was no more than a hundred yards from him now. He was trying to get up, but his stomach seemed to pain him and he doubled over again.

My God! Abby's hand flew to her mouth. Zeb!

She was running now, tearing toward him. "Don't move, Zeb. Stay still."

He was on his knees when she reached him. She hunched down beside him, wrapping one arm around his shoulder to support him, using her other hand to lift his chin, see his face. Her stomach turned over, and she had to battle the urge to gag. His whole face was a swollen, bloody mess, all but unrecognizable. An anger such as she'd never known ripped through her. "Did your father do this? Dear God, Zeb, did your father do this to you?"

"He said I couldn't come," he gasped. "He said I was too stupid for schoolin'. He was crazy drunk."

317

Zeb looked up at her through the purplish slits that were his eyes. "I be fine, Miss Graham." He struggled to rise, but she restrained him.

"Don't move. I'll get a buggy, a horse."

"I can walk, honest." He brushed at her dress. "I got blood on you, ma'am." He looked stricken. "I'm sorry. I'm real sorry."

"You never mind that. Stay here, Zeb. I mean it." She ran back to the school and caught up the reins of Molly's paint pony, Pepper, then led the animal back to Zeb. The boy didn't utter so much as a moan as she helped him mount. He lolled forward listlessly as she led the pony back to the school.

Hurrying, fearful he would fall from the saddle before she could get back, she raced up the front steps and pushed open the door. "I'm sorry, children," she said, straining to keep her voice calm, "but Zeb's been badly hurt. I have to see that he's taken care of. School is dismissed for the day."

"Is-is . . . will he be okay, Miss Graham?" Rusty asked fearfully.

"He'll be fine." She said it, then offered a prayer that it be true.

The children filed out solemnly, even Penelope looking horrified at the sight of Zeb's bloody face. Abby took Molly aside. "Do you think it will be all right with your parents if you walk home today, honey?"

The girl nodded. "I'll get Pepper tomorrow. Zeb needs him now more than I do."

"Thank you, sweetheart." Abby gathered the pony's reins and tugged him up the street to the house. There, she did her best to ease Zeb down from the saddle, sparing him as much pain as possible. But he was a big boy for fourteen, and she could barely keep him on his feet as they made their way up to the front door. For once Abby would have been glad to see a smiling Sam Devlin coming up to her. But when Ethan and Winnie had arrived home last night, it was with the news that Sam had dropped by the store to announce he would be out of town for a few days. Apparently Sam had said nothing to them about his proposing to her, and Abby had decided to leave it that way. Nor had she asked where Sam was going. For now she was on her own with Zeb.

"I shoulda stayed with Pa," the boy said, his breath catching, his teeth clenched against the pain. "He usually lets me be after he hits me. I shouldn't 'uv come. I shouldn't 'uv . . ."

"Hush, now." Abby threw open the door and helped him inside. "I don't want to hear any more talk like that. The thought of you lying out there with no one to care for you—" She didn't finish. "Just a little further now, then you can rest." She led him into Chase's old room, where he sagged weakly onto the bed. "Lie still. I'll get some whiskey and bandages."

Over the next hour she did the best she could for him, feeling at once awed and somehow saddened

319

by how stoically he endured the pain of the whiskey on the score of cuts that marked his face.

"We'd best get that shirt off you, too. It's filthy."

"No!" He clutched at it, his fists knotting in the cotton fabric.

"Zeb," she soothed, "it's all right. I'll wash it out for you, see if I can repair some of those rents."

"No! You're not gonna see—" He turned his head away.

Abby stilled. She'd been so conscious of the battering his face had taken that she'd made little note of the rest of him. She spoke to him then, in quiet, reassuring tones, until at last he relented and allowed her to undo the buttons of his shirt.

He raised up a little, closing his swollen eyes, as she peeled the shirt away from his body. "Oh, my dear Lord . . ." She stared at the welts and gouges that marred the sun dark flesh of his back. "What . . ." She swallowed, tears for a moment blinding her. "What in God's name did he hit you with?"

Zeb did not look at her. He was rigid with embarrassment. "His belt, mostly. And . . . and he has this broken axe handle. I didn't want . . . I didn't want you to see."

Abby fumbled with more bandages, her hands shaking so badly she could barely hold them. As quickly as she could she cleaned up the cuts, wanting to spare Zeb any more humiliation. The helpless rage she'd felt earlier, when first she'd seen his face, doubled and redoubled until she could scarcely think.

She wanted Chase. She wanted Chase here now. To do something about this. To somehow fix it, make it right.

Instead she helped Zeb lie back, pulling the coverlet up under his chin, seeking to make the boy comfortable, take away whatever small part of his hurt that she could. Amazingly, Zeb blushed.

"Ain't nobody tucked me in bed in a long time," he mumbled. "Not since my ma died."

"And when was that?" Abby asked softly.

"I was five, I think. She got real sick. I remember Pa makin' her get up and make 'im his meals though. She could hardly walk, and he'd push her around. I tried to stop him, but he hit me. And I was too little, and . . . and . . ." A tear slid from one swollen eye. "I hated him though, I hated him so much. I still hate him." His lips—swollen, split—trembled. "I shoulda left a long time ago."

"What made you stay?" she asked gently.

A sob choked him. "I'm all he's got. Who'd take care of him, if I left? See that he eats . . ."

Abby held his hand and cried with him, but not for the same reasons. In her life she'd never wanted to do physical violence to another human being—until now. She could easily have put her fist in Harley Tucker's face—or worse.

"Your father's a grown man. He'll just have to do for himself, or not. That's his choice. But I'll tell you this, you're not going back there."

321

"I got no place else."

"You've got right here. I'm sure it would be all right with my aunt and uncle. In any case, you're not moving until you're better."

"I can't—"

"We'll talk about it later. You rest." She smoothed a hand across his forehead, trailing her fingers downward so that he closed his eyes. "Sleep."

She sat there with him, Chase's admonition thrumming through her that he wanted to be told if Harley Tucker ever did further injury to Zeb. She remembered, too, the look on his face when he'd said it. If Chase was planning to leave on the afternoon stage, word of what happened to Zeb would surely stop him. But she couldn't do it, couldn't tell him. Didn't dare. Not even to keep him in Willow Springs.

She had no doubt in her mind. Chase would kill Harley Tucker. She couldn't risk that. Not because she cared what happened to Harley, but because she cared too much about what happened to Chase. And Zeb. It would be better that she never see Chase again than—

She jumped, startled, the front door slamming open with thunderous force. Who—? What? Had Harley—? Abby rushed toward the sound, then stopped dead to see Chase storm into the room. Fury pulsed from every pore of his body, and though he must have sensed her being there, he had no sense of where she was, because he blundered headlong into her.

She cried out, stumbling backwards. He flung out an arm, making an instinctive grab for her. Somehow she caught his hand and managed to remain upright. He offered no apology, no inquiry as to whether or not she was hurt. "Where's Zeb?" he demanded. "Is he here?"

"Who told you?"

"Told me?" he gritted. "It's all over town. Rusty came up to me at the stage depot. Said Zeb had blood all over him. Dammit, Abby, where—"

"It ain't your business, mister," came a weak voice from the bed. "Just leave it be."

Chase made his way to Zeb's side, taking a seat on the bed. "I'm making it my business. How bad did he hurt you, boy?"

Zeb said nothing, though his slitted eyes looked wary, tense.

"I'm not going to hurt you." Chase held out a hand and reached slowly toward where the boy lay. Zeb didn't move. Abby watched, mesmerized, at how gently that hand feathered across the bandages on Zeb's face, his arms, his back. Chase applied an all but imperceptible pressure, causing Zeb no additional pain, but allowing Chase to sense every cut, every weal.

Chase stood then, his features ash pale. Abby could feel the rage coming off from him in waves. Without another word he stalked from the room.

Zeb pushed himself up. "Miss Graham, what . . . what's he gonna do? Miss Graham—"

"Shhh." Abby came over and gently, but firmly, forced Zeb back down onto the bed. "It'll be fine. I'll talk to him. Don't worry."

"Don't let him kill my pa."

"Of course not." Abby looked anxiously toward the open door.

"And don't let Mr. Murdock get hurt either. Not on my account. Please, Miss Graham."

"I promise. Now you get some sleep." She rose and hurried out, pulling the bedroom door shut behind her. She found Chase in the parlor, going through the desk. "What are you look—"

She stilled, her eyes widening in disbelief, as he extracted Ethan's Dragoon Colt and set it on top of the desk. He then continued to grope through the drawer, finding first a gunbelt, then a box of ammunition. With unerring precision he opened the cylinder and rammed a bullet into each of six chambers. Snapping the gun shut, he hefted the heavy weapon in his right hand. His thumb rested on the hammer, his index finger on the trigger guard, as he seemed to test its weight and balance. Satisfied, his face grim, he shoved the Colt into the holster, then deftly belted the holster around his lean hips.

Abby stood there, her heart pounding, disconcerted, horrified, at how natural he looked with that gun on his hip, how at ease. She had to force herself to move. "Chase, for the love of heaven, you can't do this. You can't fire a gun. You're blind!"

He headed toward the door, cursing when his knee collided with the edge of a chair. But he didn't stop, just stepped around it and kept walking.

Abby grabbed his arm. He pulled away.

"Blast it, Chase! Think!" she pleaded. "This isn't the way. Do you think Zeb will thank you for killing his father?"

He didn't answer, just jerked the door open and stepped outside. She hurried after him. "Where are you going?"

"To pay a call on Harley Tucker." His voice was cold, deadly.

"You're being absurd. You may be able to load that gun by feel, but you can't find the Tucker place." She was desperate, clutching at anything.

"I'll hire someone to drive me."

"Chase, don't do this." She again caught his arm. "Let the law handle it. Sam will—"

"Will what?" he snarled, whirling to face her. "This isn't the first time Tucker's used that boy for a punching bag. But, by God, it's going to be the last." He shook his head. "Jesus, Abby, I only felt what that man did. You *saw* it, saw it with your own eyes—the blood, the pain. How can you stand there and tell me to let the law handle it?"

"Because I don't want you killed! Harley Tucker may be a drunk, but he has two good eyes and a rifle. You won't have a chance."

He rested his hand on the walnut handle of the Colt. "I'll have all the chance I need."

She could see the determination in him, the blood fury held in check on a very frail lead. "Then at least let me be the one to drive you out there."

"No. It's too dangerous."

She straightened. "Then I'll follow you."

He cursed. "I suppose you would, wouldn't you?" He blew out a disgusted breath. "All right then, let's go."

She led the way toward the livery, then stopped by the mercantile long enough to get Winnie to return home and see to Zeb, manufacturing some white lie about an errand she had to run at the O'Banion place. Luckily, Chase had stayed outside the store. One look at his face and Winnie would have known Abby was lying. Ethan had been inventorying a delivery in the back room, and Abby had not seen him at all. Abby only smiled noncommittally when Winnie mentioned how well Abby seemed to be taking Chase's leaving Willow Springs.

As Abby drove, she tried several times to get Chase to talk, hoping to defuse the rage in him, but it was no use, and she soon joined him in a tense silence. By the time she reined in at the Tucker place, clouds were gathering and a storm was imminent. But it was not nature's storm that concerned her.

"I want you to tell me what Tucker's doing, where he is all the time. You got that?" Chase said, his voice terse, as he climbed down from the buggy.

She stayed seated, her fingers digging into her knees in an attempt to calm her shaking nerves. "I will."

"And for God's sake, watch yourself. If he pulls a gun, you get the hell out of here." He gripped her wrist. "Promise me that. Swear it."

"I promise."

Tucker had come out of his tumble-down shack and was stumbling his way toward them, his bleary-eyed gaze squinting up at Abby. "Git off'n my land. Now."

"He's not armed," Abby whispered to Chase.

Chase relaxed a little. "Good." He walked around the buggy and strode purposefully toward Tucker. Abby was certain Chase was again using the man's stench to pinpoint his location. Her own nose wrinkled distastefully at the combination of body odor, whiskey and urine.

Chase stopped some six feet shy of Tucker. "You're going to pay for what you did to that boy, old man."

"He's my son," Tucker snarled belligerently, and it was then Abby guessed the man was not as drunk as he tried to appear. His bloodshot eyes darted cannily about, as though seeking a weapon. "I'll learn him any way I see fit."

"And I'm going to *learn* you, you son-of-a-bitch," Chase gritted. "I'm going to give you some of what you gave Zeb and see how you like it." He unbuckled the gun belt and let it fall to the ground.

Abby screamed a warning as Tucker launched himself at Chase.

Chase side-stepped nimbly, bringing the back of his hand down across the man's back. Tucker yowled and went down. From the ground he crawled, crab-like, toward Chase. But Chase heard him and moved again out of reach.

Tucker snatched up a rotting fence post and while Abby shouted for Chase to watch out, Tucker swung it in a wide arc toward Chase's head. Chase ducked, then drove at the man's midsection, sending both men sprawling.

Tucker squealed like a trapped pig, grabbing up fistfuls of dirt and heaving them at Chase. Chase clawed at his eyes, but still recovered enough to send a crushing uppercut to Tucker's jaw.

Tucker's head snapped back. He cursed, screamed. Chase gripped Tucker's shirtfront and again slammed his fist into the man's face. Tucker sagged back, his head lolling like a rag doll's. Chase drove his fist home again and again.

"Chase! Chase, for God's sake!" Abby hurled herself against his upraised arm. "You're going to kill him!"

Chase's shoulders heaved with the effort it took him to stop. He sank back, still straddling Tucker's belly. His whole body shook, his raw, bloody fists clenching and unclenching. Slowly, deliberately, he dragged in deep lungfuls of air, fighting to bring himself under control. "I'm sorry. I warned you not to come."

"I didn't want you to kill him."

"His kind don't die, they just rot away an inch at a time, rot everything they touch." He lurched unsteadily to his feet, stepping past the inert Tucker. He made an attempt to tuck in his straggling shirttail, swipe the dust from his pants. Abby retrieved the gunbelt and handed it to him. Automatically, he settled the belt about his hips and began to buckle it, then he seemed to reconsider, winding the belt around its holster and handing it back to her. "We'd best get you back to town."

"What about Tucker?"

"It'll be raining in a few minutes. Maybe it'll wake him up. Or maybe we'll get lucky and he'll drown."

Abby gripped Chase's arm and led him to the buggy. He helped her up, then climbed in beside her. She put the gunbelt on the floor, then gigged the horse into a trot. For long minutes they rode in silence, until finally Abby could take no more of it. "That wasn't just Harley Tucker you were beating back there, was it?"

"I don't know what you mean."

"Yes, you do. You were trying to get even with your father."

"And if I was?"

"Did it help?"

He heaved a long sigh. "No."

"Did you father beat you like Zeb's . . . ?" Her voice trailed off.

"Sometimes he skipped Sundays." He laughed without humor. "But not out of any respect for the Sabbath. He was just too damned drunk from Saturday night."

"It must have been so awful for you. I can't imagine—"

"I know you can't." There was a bitterness in his voice that made her wince. Is that what made him feel so separate from her sometimes? That he didn't think she could understand the life he'd led, or the reasons he'd made whatever choices he now regretted? Choices that he felt put a barrier between them that could never be breached?

"You said you were at the stage depot when Rusty told you about Zeb. You were leaving town, weren't you? Without so much as a good-bye."

"It would have been better for you if I had."

"That's a lie, Chase Murdock," she snapped, the day's events putting an end to any pretense of subtlety she might otherwise have wished for. "You couldn't possibly want what's best for me, and not break my heart. I love you, remember?"

He kept his face straight ahead, his features impassive, but she knew she had scored a hit. The muscles beneath his shirt were bunched whipcord tight.

She reined the horse to a halt. "I wish you would believe me. There's nothing you can't tell me. Nothing."

He raked a hand through thick, dark hair. "Oh, yes there is, Abby," he said. "Yes, there is."

Thunder rumbled overhead, and despite the buggy's canopy, she felt the first few pelting drops of rain. But she ignored them, reaching toward Chase to trail her fingertips across his lips. "I love you," she said again, then kissed him, ever so lightly on either side of his mouth. "Tell me. Please, tell me."

With a groan half-prayer, half-curse, he pulled her against him, his mouth devouring hers. With his tongue he teased, tormented, tasted, revelling in the honey sweetness that was Abby. *Tell her . . . tell her . . .* his mind thrummed, taunted. *Tell her and have her know you for the bastard you are.*

Rain slapped harder on top of the buggy. Chase leaned back, breathing harshly. "I'd better . . . get the sides up . . ." He reached for them, fumbled with the straps.

Abby's hand closed over his. "Don't bother. I can see some kind of cabin a few hundred feet from here. We'll wait it out."

"No. We can make it to town."

She took up the reins and clucked the horse toward the tiny house, nestled amongst a copse of cottonwoods. Some pioneer's dream come to ruin long ago, no doubt. She hopped to the ground, the grass already damp, wetting the hem of her skirt, her shoes. She led the gelding to a small lean-to on the south side of the roughhewn building, then stepped back to the buggy and caught Chase's hand. "Come inside with me. Come inside where it's warm."

"Abby, you don't know what you're asking." His voice was tortured, pained. "You don't know—"

"I know all I need to, Chase Murdock. I love you."

Lightning split the cloud dark sky, thunder cracking close behind. Light rain became a downpour. Abby stood beside Chase, rain drenching their faces, their hair, their clothes. But she didn't notice, didn't care. She only cared that Chase gripped her waist, drew her to him, his body molding itself to hers. The hard heat of him pressed against the soft swell of her stomach, leaving her no doubt of his arousal, his need, his want of her.

But still he let her go, set her away from him, allowed her one more chance to back away. "Please, Abby," he said hoarsely. "Please, let me take you home . . . where you'll be safe."

"I'm already safe," she murmured. "I'm with you." She linked her hand to his and led him inside the waiting cabin.

Chapter Twenty

Abby stood in the center of the one-room cabin, clutching the blanket she had brought from the buggy. The coarse spun wool felt scratchy, but warm against the rain damp chill beginning to seep into her bones.

"I can hear your teeth chattering," Chase said. He was hunkered down in front of the fireplace, stacking what meager kindling she'd been able to scrounge from the woodbox outside the house. "You'll feel better once I get the fire going." He'd already had her check to make certain the chimney was clear. "And maybe you'd best get out of those wet clothes."

His voice carried no hint of the desire she'd sensed, felt surging through him just minutes ago, outside in the storm. He was obviously regretting his momentary lapse and seemed determined to resurrect the barrier between them.

What she had yet to decide was whether or not she was going to let him. He might be able to mask his passion in his voice, his words, but he could not know the subtle ways he betrayed himself to her eyes. The way his hands shook when he handled the firewood, the way he tensed whenever she came within two feet of him, the way those smoke blue eyes seemed to follow her everywhere, though he couldn't see her at all.

She clung to that threading of hope, however wishful her thinking, her shoes scraping across the wood plank floor as she circled the barren room. She hugged the blanket shawl-like about her shoulders, her gaze seeking out any remaining sign of the cabin's one-time human inhabitants. But she saw only layerings of dust and dead leaves and the small droppings of some four-footed creature who had objected briefly to their intrusion, then skittered noisily out a small hole near the floor of the north wall.

She wondered vaguely about the builders of the tiny cabin, about what could have driven them to abandon their home. Illness? A failed crop? Or perhaps a better opportunity somewhere else. So many variables, so many unpredictable turns in life, in a relationship.

"Maybe you'd best light the fire," Chase said, rousing her from her musings. "I don't want to burn the place down."

Abby crossed to the fireplace and took the match Chase held out to her. Instantly he stood and walked to the other side of the room. Abby gave her head a rueful shake. Some things in life weren't so unpredictable after all.

She lit the fire, then warmed her hands in front of the flames.

"I guess you didn't hear me," Chase grumbled. "I said, get out of those wet clothes. Winnie and Ethan would have my hide if I let you catch your death out here."

"Your clothes are wet," she noted saucily. "I don't see you taking yours off. Besides, how do you know I'm not naked as the day I was born?"

He stiffened abruptly. "Since when are you making fun of the fact that I'm blind, Abby?"

She flushed guiltily, horrified by his reaction. She'd meant no harm. In fact, she'd been flirting with the man! And yet, wasn't her courage to indulge in such outrageous flirting rooted in the very fact that Chase could not see her? Could not as easily discern her frightful inexperience in such matters? Not to mention the fact that she could scarcely compromise her modesty by disrobing in front of a blind man.

She hurried over to him. "I'm sorry," she said. "I didn't mean that the way you . . . I'm sorry. You know I would never make jest of your blindness."

"Forget it."

But she couldn't forget it, as she watched him back away from her yet again. She cursed inwardly. She had wanted to breach the barrier between them, but she had succeeded only in locking it more firmly in place. Miserable, defeated, she made her

335

way to the fire.

Chase slumped against the back wall of the cabin, his need to get away from Abby fired as much by her apology, as by her teasing suggestion that she could have already removed her clothes and he wouldn't know it.

He wasn't angry with her. In fact, quite the opposite. Gruffness had been the only defense he could muster against the brain searing image his mind had conjured when she'd even mentioned the word naked. He'd already been battling that very image since he'd held her in his arms outside.

And how could he have explained to her that he didn't need eyes to know she was still dressed? That if she were naked in this room, he would know it, even if he were robbed of all five of his senses.

"Come sit by the fire." Abby's voice carried to him, soft, melodic, hopeful. "We both need to dry ourselves, after all."

He didn't move, couldn't. Didn't dare.

Outside, the rain still hammered against the roof. It could be hours before they started back to town. Hours alone in this cabin with Abby. His wanting her was a given fact he'd never bothered to deny, even to himself. But *her* wanting *him* was something else again. Her passion unnerved him, even, at times, scared the hell out of him. Somehow he had accepted her delusion that she loved him, loved the man she believed him to be, not the man he was.

But he was a man used to quick couplings with women well paid for the privilege. He'd never even been with a respectable woman, much less a virgin. The women in his life had been takers, just as he had been. They used each other to satisfy a mutual lust, nothing more. He'd never wanted it any other way, even on the off chance that it might have been offered.

And now here he was. Chase Cordell, outlaw, besotted out of his mind over a Colorado schoolmarm, who probably didn't even know what went where. Hell, he'd heard tales of respectable women who bragged that their husbands had never in their lives seen them naked!

He swore explosively, slamming his fist onto the planked flooring. He heard Abby gasp, but made no attempt to explain. Who in the hell did he think he was anyway? Hadn't he already gone through this? No matter how much he wanted Abigail Graham—and dear God, had any man ever wanted any woman as much as he wanted her?—he could not give in to that want. Ever.

He was no romantic hero fresh from one of her novels. He was a flesh and blood man weighed down by too much backstory to ever have the slate wiped clean. No matter how he might have come to wish it.

Swallowing another curse, he pushed himself to his feet, padding the length and breadth of the small room. A woman like Abby didn't want a man for a night. She wanted a husband, a family, a future. He could offer her none of those things, only the prospect of a lover who could one day end up on the wrong end of a rope.

He paused, listening. The rain had slackened. He let out a long, grateful sigh. He would convince her to head back. Now. He crossed to the fireplace, hunkered down beside her.

"Chase?" Her voice was tentative. "I really am sorry. I would never hurt you."

"I know." Too late he realized his error. He should have gone to the door, called to her to join him in the buggy. He'd come too close, much too close for a man trying too long, too hard to honor intentions he had no real wish to keep.

And just like that his self-control crumbled, fell to dust. In the darkness that was his world, he reached for the light that was Abby.

Abby felt Chase's hand touch her arm, track upward to rest at the nape of her neck. One minute she had feared him angry with her, the next he was beside her, his body radiating with a heat more fierce than the fire that now glowed at her back. And in his touch she knew at last that there would be no more excuses, no more reasons, no more backing away.

And the fears she'd felt earlier—about her inexperience, her naïveté, disappeared in the butterfly touch of his lips on hers. This was what she wanted, ached for from the first minute she'd realized she was falling in love with him. "I want to please you, Chase," she murmured. "I want to make you as happy as I am this minute."

"You make me happy just being alive, Abby." He feathered kisses across her lips, her cheeks, her nose, her eyes, forcing himself to go slow, be patient, more patient than he knew how to be. For the first time in his life he worried that he wouldn't be able to be a man, because he wanted so much to be the right man for Abby.

He found her mouth again, a low groan escaping his throat. Sweet Christ, she tasted like honey, like light, like everything in the world that was good and fine. He had no right to touch her, no right to sully her with what he was.

"Someday," he said hoarsely, desperately, "some day when you look back on this and curse the day I was born, I want you to remember that I tried to stop it."

Abby only smiled. "Don't try to be gallant now, Chase Murdock. I've long since discovered it's not in your nature." She curved her arms around his neck, letting the blanket slide down to pillow beneath them. "But I love you anyway."

He leaned back on one elbow, smoothing her hair with his hands. "I wish . . ."

"What? What do you wish, Chase? Tell me."

"I wish to God I could see you, really see you. I'd give my soul to see your face. Just once."

She caught his hand. "See me with your hands, Chase. With your hands, with your mouth."

He dared glide his hand downward across the bodice of her dress, dared capture a breast with his palm. He felt the nipple swell, grow hard beneath the still damp fabric. Fumbling, trembling, he undid the buttons that hid her from him, his loins on fire with what touching her like that was doing to him. Over and over the thought pulsed through him. Never in his life had it been like this . . . never in his life . . .

He tugged free the ribbons of her chemise, the ripe swell of her breast now hot against his palm. He could see the rosy tip in his mind, feel it grow taut, pebble hard in his mouth. She gasped, her back arching, her fingers threading through his hair to hold him to his erotic task. He swallowed a groan, bolts of ecstasy coursing through him, sending more blood pounding into his already engorged sex.

"I love you, Abby." He said it again and again, as much for himself as for her. He wanted to hear it, savor it, sear it into his memory as fully as every curve, every line, every delicate inch of her satin smooth flesh.

He finished undressing her, undressing himself, wanting to pleasure her, pleasure her more than he wanted to be pleasured himself. He couldn't erase his past, couldn't foresee the future, but for this moment, for this tiny space of time, he would be the romantic hero of Abby's dreams.

His hands skated past the feminine curve of her stomach to the center of her womanhood below. He touched her there, felt her tremble, writhe, cry out. "Chase . . . oh . . . what . . . ? Oh, Chase . . ." The words subsided, replaced by soft moans, then quaking tremors that rocked her. And he gloried in the new world he alone had gifted her with.

A minute passed, then two. Her shuddering eased, and she lay still. He felt her stiffen ever so slightly, seek to close her legs against him. He knew at once she was embarrassed. Before she could utter a word, his mouth moved over hers once again, murmuring love words he didn't even know he knew, until she stilled, relaxed, grew bold once again.

"The same," she whispered. "I want it to be the same for you."

Her hands skated purposefully across his chest and down. He swallowed convulsively, his neck arching back as she dared circle his engorged flesh.

"Show me." She caressed the tip, the shaft. "Show me what to do."

His own large hand curved over her smaller one, his mind all but lost to the shattering ecstasy of what she was already doing to him. He moved her hand for her, once, twice, then his hand fell away, as he groaned, cried out, the blanket beneath them

341

knotting in his fists, as she brought him to the edge of madness.

Abby's eyes burned bright with tears. She watched him, watched his face, the agonized joy etched in every feature, every line. She continued the stroke he taught her, faster, faster. Then he startled her by pushing her hand away, his voice a desperate plea, "No more."

But before she could ask if she had done something wrong, he pressed her down upon the blanket, his whole length rising above her.

"Open yourself to me, Abby. Please, open yourself to me."

Instinct drove her now. Her thighs parted and her cry mingled with his as he thrust himself inside her with one powerful stroke. He lay there, unmoving for but a heartbeat. "Did I hurt you? Abby . . ."

She moved her hips, her head twisting from side to side. "I need . . . oh, Chase, I need . . . you. Hurry . . . please . . . hurry."

His body was fire, and she was match to his flame. He took her then to the world of her dreams, dreams woven of heroes and magic, dreams woven of love. And as his seed burst free inside her, her world spiralled outward, drawing him in, propelling them both into the rainbow-hued mists of paradise.

He lay there long after, shaking, spent. Awed. "Abby, sweet God, Abby." He said her name over and over, buried his face against her breast, the realization slamming home like a thousand sun-bright bursts of light. "I was blind all my life 'til I met you. Blind all my life . . ."

Abby nestled in the crook of Chase's arm, sated, deliriously happy. And for a time she slept. When she woke, it was to find him still beside her, holding her, as though he never wanted to let go. "I didn't mean to fall asleep."

He smiled. "I like listening to you breathe, feeling your breasts rise and fall . . ."

Her cheeks burned, and she wondered at this sudden rush of shyness after what they had just shared. But she couldn't seem to help it, fight it. "I . . . I suppose we should get dressed. Winnie and Ethan will be worried if we're much longer."

"I suppose." But he made no move to rise.

She turned on her side, her naked breasts now pressing against his chest. He growled, his lips curving into a lascivious grin. "Winnie and Ethan may have to worry for another couple of years or so," he teased.

She had to laugh, her embarrassment gone. It felt so natural to be here with him, so right. She wanted nothing more than to wake up with this man at her side for the rest of her life. But there was only one way to ensure that. And she knew he would never ask. For though she was certain of his love for her, she was also certain his past still lay lodged somehow between them.

Well, she thought bravely, it had been a night for boldness, had it not? Why not one more bold step? She lay her hand along the side of Chase's face, feathering her fingertips across his beard shadowed cheeks. "You are my true and special hero, Chase Murdock," she said. "You are my white-hatted knight in shining armor. Are you prepared then to do the honorable thing for your lady fair?"

He frowned, suddenly cautious. "And what might that be?"

"You have deflowered me, sir," she said. "Surely something comes to mind."

"Abby . . ."

She plunged onward, before her courage fled. "Will you marry me, Chase Murdock?"

He stilled. "What?"

"Marry me."

He caught her face in his hands. "What?"

"You heard me."

He felt stricken, sick. Every reason for not doing what they just did, together in this room rose up to haunt him. "I've got nothing to give you, Abby. Not as a husband."

"What we shared just now would be nice."

"I have to provide for you, take care of you."

"I'm a teacher. And you can work with Ethan . . ."

"I'm not a storekeeper."

"You can't very well be a lawman any more."

344

"That's not the point. Abby—"

"No!" She cut him off. "There's only one point. One answer I need. Not even a yes or a no to 'will you marry me?' But a yes or a no to 'do you *want* to marry me?' "

She felt him tremble, felt his heartbeat quicken against her palm. "There's nothing I want more in the world, Abby. Believe me. But . . ."

She pressed her fingers to his lips. "I know there's something you're hiding from me. It's past denying, Chase. I know it, feel it. But it doesn't matter. I don't care what it was, not any more. I only care about the Chase Murdock I know, I love. You never have to tell me what it is. Never."

He closed his eyes, felt tears scald his cheeks. Everything in him demanded that he tell her, tell her now. Prove that it did matter. It mattered to hell and back. But he couldn't, wouldn't. "I love you, Abby."

"We'll make it work. We will."

Cordell . . . Gantry . . . Breckenridge . . . Devlin. The names haunted, taunted. But he shut them all out. His passion blazed hot, fierce once again, as his hands branded her, seared her, made her his own. His wife. His love. His life. "I'll marry you, Abby. I'll marry you."

Chapter Twenty-one

Abby gripped Chase's hand tightly and waited for the explosion. Winnie did not disappoint her.

"A week from Saturday!" her aunt shrieked, pacing about the parlor, wringing her hands. "You can't get married a week from Saturday! That only gives me eight days to get ready."

Abby laughed with delight, giving her aunt a heartfelt hug. She and Chase had already weathered the initial storm—that of announcing their impending marriage in the first place. Winnie had taken it much more gracefully than Abby might have thought. And Ethan was genuinely tickled.

Of course, that was after they'd gotten over their initial upset that she and Chase had even been out in that horrific downpour. But all things had been quickly forgiven, when they'd learned of her engagement.

"We needed to be alone for a while," Abby told them. "We wanted to sort things out, make some plans."

"And maybe invite Harley Tucker to the wedding?" Ethan chuckled.

Abby rolled her eyes. Nothing got past her uncle.

"I'm just glad Zeb is doing so well," Abby said. Their first stop when they'd returned home had been Zeb's bedroom, but the boy had been fast asleep. She'd insisted that they not disturb him. Abby had yet to decide how she was going to break the news about what Chase had done to Harley anyway. She was happy to avoid it, at least for tonight.

"I knew you wouldn't be on that stage, boy," Ethan was saying, grasping Chase's hand and giving it a firm shake. "You and Abby are just two peas in a pod."

Chase looked uncomfortable all at once, his beard-stubbled cheeks flushing with color. "Never did much care for the ride in a stagecoach," he mumbled.

Abby's pleasure faded just a little. "Actually, Uncle Ethan, it was because of Zeb that Chase didn't leave Willow Springs."

"Bosh and nonsense!" Ethan snorted. "Chase wouldn't have got on that stage anyway. I'd 'uv bet the mercantile on it."

"Not while I have any say about it, old man," Winnie sniffed, giving Ethan a playful swat on the arm.

Was Ethan right? Would Chase have stayed? She bit her lip, studying that blush, and she was suddenly certain Ethan was right. She grinned, happier

347

than ever, if such were possible.

Ethan strode over to his desk and poured himself a small glass of whiskey. "I say a toast is in order, ladies and gentleman. Love is always a time for celebration. Isn't that right, Winnie, my dear?"

"Ethan Graham, you'd celebrate a tumbleweed rolling down the street, if you think I'd let you drink a glass of that odious liquor to do it!" Then Winnie shook her head, laughing. "But I guess tonight really is a celebration. Our little Abby is getting married." On the last two words her voice cracked and the tears came. "Oh, Abby, my baby!"

Abby rushed to Winnie's side, wrapping her arms about her, patting her back. "It's all right, Aunt Winnie," she soothed. "We'll still be right here in town. We're not going anywhere."

Winnie sniffled, drying her eyes on her apron. "But you won't be my baby any more."

"You'll always be my mother, Aunt Winnie," Abby said gently. "I love you and Uncle Ethan so much. And I'm so happy with Chase." She looked lovingly toward him, and she knew by the warm smile that curved his lips that he had heard.

"Can we get on with the toast?" Ethan complained merrily.

Chase lifted the glass of lemonade Winnie handed him. Abby and Winnie did the same. They all clinked glasses.

"To a long and happy life together," Ethan beamed, holding his glass aloft, "and to a whole passel of healthy grandchildren!"

Now it was Abby's turn to blush. Her uncle was definitely feeling his oats.

"You know, Chase," Ethan said, setting his glass on the desk. "I actually had Zeb helping me with cipherin' the accounts for the store earlier this afternoon. Seems I kind of fell behind, when I had to do more work in the store after my assistant went and quit on me this morning."

Chase smiled. "I hope you haven't filled that opening yet, Ethan."

"It just so happens I didn't quite get around to painting up a Held Wanted sign."

Abby watched, her heart near bursting with pride, as Ethan and Chase sat down on the divan and began talking over plans for the store. Though she knew Chase didn't see himself as a storekeeper, he was not at all patronizing to her uncle, but genuinely interested in anything Ethan had to say. For Ethan's part, her uncle already loved Chase like a son.

The evening bustled by pleasantly after that, until it finally came time when she had to bid Chase good night. She stepped outside on the porch with him, inhaling the night air still damp, heavy from the day's rain. "I'll miss you," she said, gliding her arms about his neck and pulling his head down for a warm, sweet kiss.

"Not as much as I'll miss you," he countered.

"Bet?"

He chuckled. "I don't think so." He pulled her close. "God, I never thought I could be this happy. Never. I love you, Abby Graham. I'll shout it from the rooftops. I love you so much."

"Eight more nights for you all alone in your hotel room." She sighed. "Eight more nights until I'm Mrs. Chase Murdock."

He kissed her again, long, deep. "The longest eight nights of my life, woman," he said, his loins tightening.

"We could find a place, maybe—"

"No." He shook his head. "I want to wait. I know I'm going to live to regret this. But I want our next time together to be our wedding night. Is that all right?"

"It's wonderful." She hugged him tight. "Every minute I love you more, Chase Murdock. Every minute." She kissed him one last time. "Good night."

The days that followed were a romantic idyll, Chase and Abby stealing away every chance they could to be alone together, take long walks, talk. Chase even opened up to her a little about his past—about the war and a major named Quinton who'd befriended him, even the heartwrenching fact that his father had once given him up for adoption, only to have the couple return him when they had a child of their own.

She'd watched Chase's face as he'd recounted the story, no particular emotion evident in his face.

And it was then she knew just how much it had hurt him. "I can't decide who was more cruel. Your father or those abominable people who—" She sat there, shaking, hurting so much for him, that it was he in fact who wound up comforting her.

"I think that's enough of my past for one day," he said, leaning back against a willow in the grove of trees on the south side of town. "I didn't tell you to make you sad."

"I know." She touched his face. "I just can't bear how much you've been hurt."

He caught her hand, kissed her palm. "It hurts less now that I've told you." He cupped her face, found her lips with his own. Long minutes later he pulled back, his breathing harsh, his entire body achingly frustrated. "Are you sure I promised no lovemaking for this entire week?"

"I was there when you said it."

He rubbed his temples with the tips of his fingers, rasping out, "Had I had a head injury or anything at the time?"

"Not recently." She giggled, gliding her hand tantalizingly close to the taut bulge in his denims at the apex of his legs. "Change your mind?"

He groaned, laughing painfully. "I'll be damned if I'm going to let you get away with that, woman." He pressed her down, his hand massaging her breasts beneath the thin cotton fabric of her dress. She sucked in her breath, the pliant mounds seeming to swell against his palm. "Chase . . . don't . . .

351

oh, please . . ."

He had done it to tease her, torment her with the same fire coursing hot through his blood. But he had only made his own too obvious condition that much worse.

"Is this what happened to you that day we first kissed?" she asked, sitting up, smoothing her dress.

He only growled.

"Why did we make that promise?" she asked, genuinely wishing that she had not allowed him to talk her into it. She missed the warmth of his body, the full measure of his loving.

He sighed. "Because it was right, Abby. And you know it. I want you as my wife, totally, completely on our wedding night. Not for stolen moments when we have to wonder if anyone is missing us, wondering where we are."

"I do love you, Chase Murdock."

Murdock. He had spoken of Quinton today, not telling Abby the major's last name. But how easily Chase had come to accept Murdock as his true surname. Cordell seemed a name from another lifetime, not his own. If only it could be so.

He frowned suddenly, blinking his eyes. "Is the sun setting?"

"Yes. Why?"

He shrugged. "It felt warmer earlier, I suppose." His heartbeat quickened. He knew he was facing west. He squinted harder. Did he see shadows? Edgings of light? Or was it some trick conjured up in

352

the deepest wishes of his mind? For if he could have but one, it would be as always to see Abby. He turned toward her. The dark seemed the same then, no change. His heart sank. He'd only imagined . . . No, wait. It was not as dark as before. "Abby—" He reached for her. "Abby, I think—"

"Oh, my heavens!" she cried, leaping to her feet, swiping at the grass clinging to her dress.

"What is it?"

"Sam's coming. He's seen us. I didn't know he was coming back tonight. Blast!"

"You don't want him to see us together?" he demanded, confused.

"It's not that. I just wanted to let him know about us first. I thought it would only be . . . kind."

Chase scowled, but relented. "I'll leave."

Sam reached them then. "Don't go on my account, Murdock. I know all about it." His gaze raked Abby from head to foot, disgust evident in every line of his body. "Your upcoming marriage was the first thing I heard about from the eight people who stopped me when I rode into town."

"I'm sorry, Sam," Abby said. "Honestly. I would have liked to tell you alone."

He stood there for a long minute, then lifted his Stetson and ran a hand through sweat-damp dark hair. "I know, Abby. I'm sorry. I guess I'm just not a good loser. I'm real happy for you, honest."

In a way she thought he was. Happy that she was

happy. But it was all too obvious he was not pleased with her choice. She grew more and more uncomfortable at the implacable look in those brown eyes whenever he looked at Chase.

"Where were you on your trip out of town?" she asked with forced lightness, though she had no real interest in the answer.

"I was just gettin' to that." Still he kept his eyes on Chase. "Rode up Wyoming way. But found out when I hit Cheyenne that I was wastin' my time."

"What do you mean?" Abby asked. She was more than interested now in what Sam had to say. Very obviously whatever Sam had done had something to do with Chase.

"Remember that stage robbery, Murdock?" Sam prodded. "The one you *almost* busted up, when you got your head near shot off?"

Abby winced.

"I remember," Chase said coldly. "It's hard to forget being blinded."

"You might recall I mentioned a couple of passengers on that stage name of Breckenridge, owned Diamond B up past Cheyenne."

"Might."

Abby watched both men now. Whatever Sam was doing, Chase was not caught unaware. He was on guard. But against what she had no idea.

"The Breckenridges had themselves a run-in with Cordell a couple of years back, you'll recall," Sam went on. "And I got to thinkin' what if I could get somebody up there to sketch me up a picture of Cordell. I could show it around. See if any folks in Willow Springs remember him in town before the robbery . . . or anytime at all."

"Sounds like a smart idea," Chase allowed. He stood there, wondering if all of his plans with Abby would go for naught right here, right now. Devlin seemed to be enjoying baiting him, trying to draw him out.

"You got your picture?" Chase prompted, when he could bear Devlin's silence no longer.

"Didn't work out," Devlin said. "Seems the Breckenridges up and got themselves murdered."

"Both of them?" Abby gasped.

"Yep."

Chase felt sick. He had no feeling about Luther's death, but Felicity didn't deserve to be murdered, no matter what she'd done. "They catch who did it?"

"Nope. But the law's after him."

Chase's heart thudded. He knew. He knew before Devlin said it.

"Gantry," the lawman said. "Noah Gantry."

"So there must have been a witness," Abby said.

"Well, it seems Mrs. Breckenridge wasn't quite dead when a ranch hand come by. She named her killer. Said somethin' else too. Somethin' mighty peculiar. I haven't been able to sort it all out yet. Pretty soon, though, I think." He paused a beat. "Pretty damn soon."

355

Abby felt suddenly cold. She wished to God she could read the undercurrents going on between the two men. She wanted to believe it was simple jealousy. But it wasn't. It was far more deadly.

"Congratulations again," Sam said, tipping his hat. "And good night." He strode back toward town, seeming inordinately pleased with himself for a man who'd just found out a woman he'd wanted to marry was marrying a man he despised.

"I'd best be getting back to the house," Abby said. "It's getting late."

"Can you walk yourself back?"

She frowned. "Of course. But why?" She stepped toward him. "I know Sam upset you. But I'm not going to ask any questions, all right?"

He pulled her close, kissed her deeply. "I love you. Abby, please always remember that, I love you so much."

He terrified her when he talked like that. As though he were leaving. As though he would never come back.

"I just need to be alone for a little while, all right?" he said, forcing a smile she knew he didn't feel.

But she didn't argue. "See you tomorrow?"

"Try to keep me away."

"Good night, then."

"Good night, Abby. I love you." He listened, as her skirts rustled through the grasses on her way back toward town. He drew in a steadying breath and tapped his cane toward the creek tumbling by just ahead.

It would happen any day now, he thought bleakly, as he walked. Devlin would find him out, arrest him. A prospect which left him with only two choices. To run, after telling Abby nothing. Or to run and tell Abby the truth.

He already knew which he would choose. He had to tell her, even though he knew it would destroy everything they had together. Better that she hate him, than feel herself deserted, abandoned by a faithless lover.

He inhaled the clean autumn air, cool now under the dwindling sunlight. How many more days would he have with her? How many before—

He cocked his head toward the creek. Had he heard something out of the ordinary? A twig snapping perhaps? He shrugged it off, his attention diverted by the same odd sensation of light he'd had earlier. Were there definite shadows now in his dark world? Lighter shades against the black? Dear God, was his vision coming back?

He wished he had a match. He wished Abby had stayed just a little longer.

And then he was forever grateful that she hadn't.

He whirled toward the sound of a gun hammer being drawn back, his right hand streaking instinctively for his thigh. But his Colt was not there. He stilled, waited, fully expecting a bullet to tear into his flesh.

"Just hold real still, Cordell," a gruff male voice demanded. "Keep them hands where I can see 'em."

"Who are you?"

"You don't know me. But I'd appreciate it if you'd come along peaceable."

"Whoever you are, you're making a mistake. My name's not Cordell. It's Murdock."

"Whatever you say, Cordell. Just move along straight ahead of me."

"Why should I?" Chase knew he had no real choice against a loaded gun.

"My boss wants to see you."

"And who might that be?"

The man's answer made Chase's blood run cold.

"Noah Gantry."

Chapter Twenty-two

Chase struggled against the rough hemp that bound his wrists behind his back. He felt his skin split, grow bloody, but still he fought the rope. He had no idea where he was, no idea where the man called "Buckshot" had brought him. He only knew that he was standing near the heat of a campfire, and that by voice count there were four men in the camp—Buckshot, the Kid, someone called Frank, and Gantry.

The first three sat sullenly nearby, maybe twenty feet to Chase's right. But Gantry stood just in front of Chase—barely spitting distance away—spinning the cylinder on his Navy Colt. Chase straightened, pulling harder on the rope, as the bastard spoke again.

"What do you think, Cordell?" Noah chuckled. "Feel luckier this time? Or is it unlucky?" He snapped the Colt's cylinder shut and drew the hammer back. Chase could sense the muzzle mere inches from his skull.

Click!

The hammer snapped home on an empty chamber. Though he tried with everything in him, Chase flinched yet again. A cold, dangerous fury built within him.

"I don't know how many times a man can tempt fate like you have, Cordell," Noah mocked. "What is that now? Five times? Six? Maybe I should add another bullet. Make it more interesting."

"How long you gonna keep this up, Gantry?" Buckshot McKenzie groused. "I thought we come to this town on business."

"This is business," Noah said. "*My* business. Me and Cordell go back a long way, don't we, Cordell?" He rubbed the barrel of the gun alongside Chase's throat.

Chase took the chance offered him. He rammed a booted heel where he guessed Gantry's arch would be. Gantry's yelp of pain confirmed he'd at least scored a hit somewhere.

But not without cost.

Gantry drove his fist into Chase's stomach, driving the air from his lungs, sending white hot shards of agony lancing through him. Chase collapsed to his knees. Gantry booted him in the ribs. Chase bit back a groan, tumbled forward face first into the dirt. Gantry kicked him again and again, vicious body blows to the stomach, chest, legs, groin. Chase felt darkness, deeper even than blindness, hover close.

He thought of Abby and prayed God Gantry would bury him deep. That way she would never know what he had been, though the irony of that thought did not escape him, even in the midst of the savage pain wrought of Gantry's blows. Scarcely an hour ago Chase was debating telling her himself. Now that death seemed imminent, it was desperately important that she continue to love the man she wished him to be.

"You want to kill him, boss?" Chase heard the Kid's voice, but it seemed far away, disembodied somehow.

The blows stopped.

"Hell, no, Kid," Gantry said, his tone placating, even amused. "I ain't gonna kill him. I got plenty more fun in mind for my old friend Cordell. Don't I, Cordell?" He slammed one more booted blow into Chase's stomach.

Chase choked, gasped, spat out dirt, blood, but he made no effort to rise. Breathing was his number one priority now. In and out. In and out.

"Blind," Noah sneered, stalking back and forth in front of Chase's hunched and beaten body. "I like that. I really do. I like it even better than if I'd killed you, Cordell."

"What the hell do you want, Gantry?" Chase coughed, spat more blood from his battered lips. "Why are you in Willow Springs?"

"Why to visit you, of course." Gantry continued to pace restlessly. "I been doin' some checkin'

361

around this nice little town you call home, Cordell. Or I guess I should say Murdock, eh?"

Chase's sluggish senses came alert. How long had the bastard been in the vicinity? How much did he know of the life he led here?

"Why I found out all sorts of interesting things today. I understand you're gonna be marryin' up with a little schoolmarm. Ain't that somethin' now."

Calm, Chase told himself. He had to stay calm, seem unaffected. It was bad enough the bastard even knew about Abby.

"Pretty little thing," Noah went on. "Real pretty from what I can tell. Ain't seen her real close up yet. Though I don't expect *you'd* know how pretty she is, since you can't see nothin'. Or are there other ways of seein' a woman?"

Chase struggled to his knees, his wrists raw, slick with his own blood.

"I bet there are all kinds of ways for a man to get to know a woman in the dark. Ain't that right, Cordell?"

Chase's chest heaved, the muscles of his arms bulging as he tore at the bloody hemp.

"I wonder if she'll get that same look in her eyes Felicity Breckenridge had when she looked at me." He laughed, a thoroughly evil laugh. "Right before I shot her."

Chase took a stumbling step toward Gantry. The campfire. The campfire was just to the outlaw's left. And what stunned Chase was not that he felt the heat of it, but that he *saw* it, or at least a blurred image of it.

"Careful now," Gantry jeered. "I wouldn't want you to *trip*—" Gantry's boot sent Chase tumbling to the turf once more, "over anything."

Chase again fought his way to his feet, keeping his face averted, lest any of these men guess he had even the vaguest hint of his vision back.

"Kind of gets to you when I talk about your woman, eh?" Gantry taunted. "Don't you worry. I wouldn't hurt a pretty little thing like her. At least not right off." He paced in circles now, caught up in the images of his own sadistic fantasy. "Why, the first thing I'd do is bring her back here, let you listen while I show her how a real man takes a woman. And takes her. And takes her. And takes her.

"And *then* I'll kill her." He laughed. "But I'll let you live. You can think about it, dream about it, remember what it sounded like when she screamed. And screamed and screamed."

"I'll kill you, Gantry!" Chase roared. "My hand to God, I'll kill you, if you touch her."

"Touch her?" He cackled. "I'll have my hands, my tongue, my teeth all over her body. Oh, I bet them tits are nice." He scratched lewdly at his crotch. "Then I'll stick my poker right up—"

With an insane roar, Chase launched himself at Gantry, his hands sliding free of the ropes that bound him. He slammed bodylong into the scar-faced outlaw, both men crashing heavily into the dirt. Chase grappled, fought, kicked, pounded, his own pain blotted out by his overwhelming rage. Somehow he found and held Gantry's throat, his hands squeezing, squeezing.

Gantry screamed, squealed, slapped, then tried to knee Chase in the groin. Chase avoided the blow.

Chase was winning; Gantry was dying. Chase could see veiled images, shadowy reflections of what was real. And he saw Gantry's eyes bulge out, his tongue loll to one side. Chase squeezed harder, harder, his fingers crushing the life out of the soft flesh.

He heard the footsteps, knew the others were at last bestirring themselves to aid their maniacal leader, heard at least one voice of protest that they not interfere, and then a pain exploded along the side of his skull. The darkness that had been his world for so long claimed him once again.

Chase came to, but didn't move. He was on his stomach, his hands once again bound behind his back, his whole body one massive bruise. He lay there, breathing harshly, listening. He heard voices, muffled, indistinct. He could recognize no words. But he'd heard the voices before, knew them somehow. And he knew he must be careful. On guard. Then he remembered. The voices belonged to Noah Gantry and his fellow killers.

Chase forced himself to concentrate, take stock of where he was. It was daylight now. He felt the sun on his swollen cheek. Evidently, he'd been unconscious all night. At least he hoped it was only one night.

Abby.

God, she must be out of her mind with worry for him. Probably thought he'd wandered off somewhere, gotten lost. "Abby. . . ." He murmured her name, the sound of it soothing, reassuring somehow. He shifted his fingers, tested the rope. He had to get out of here, warn her, protect her. Before Gantry had a chance to make good on his vile threat.

He knew the outlaws to be somewhere behind him and off to his right. Obviously they hadn't yet noticed that he was awake. He decided to keep it that way.

But he was also desperate to know if his eyesight was still improving, or if last night had been some cruel aberration, mirage. His heart thudding, Chase forced open his eyes, though only a little. He swallowed hard, forcing back sudden tears. It had been no mirage.

He could see!

Not well, but better. The blurred images of last night were a little sharper, a little more well defined. He could make out shapes of rocks, trees.

He could see, and the only thing around to look at was the twisted face of Noah Gantry.

Abby.

He closed his eyes, imagining the look on her face, her beautiful face, when he told her. God, he had to live to tell her.

Booted footfalls trod toward him across the hard-packed earth. He closed his eyes, controlled his breathing, keeping it measured, even. They had to think him still unconscious.

"What are we gonna do with him?" Frank Brown's voice. "I say put a bullet in him."

"Me, too." This one was Buckshot. "I don't want him tellin' anybody about our bein' here. When we pull that bank job Friday, I want us in and out of there clean and fast. If Cordell tells 'em we're around, they'll lock up the whole damned town tighter'n a virgin's—"

"Stop it!" The Kid's voice, more agitated than Chase had ever heard it. "You're both crazy. There's no reason to kill him. He doesn't know what we're doin' here."

"So what do you say we do, Kid?" Noah spoke for the first time. There was an undercurrent in his voice that the Kid didn't seem to notice. Noah didn't care what the Kid thought, didn't care what any of them thought. Whatever Noah decided, that was what would be done.

But the Kid rattled on, oblivious. "I say just dump him back at the edge of town. Get rid of him. He can't be lettin' anybody know about us. It would give away the fact that he's Cordell. He'd put himself in prison if he says one word."

"Maybe I don't want to take the chance." Chase heard the Colt slide from smooth leather, heard him thumb back the hammer.

Chase's heart thundered, but he didn't move, didn't do anything but breathe. In and out. *Abby, sweet God, I love you. I love you so much. Love you . . .*

Gantry let down the hammer and reholstered the gun. "Maybe not just yet. Maybe not just yet. I want him to hear what I do to his girlie. Take him over and tie him to that tree."

Chase felt himself being half-lifted, half-dragged by two men. He kept his body limp. They dropped him in some grass. Chase smelled the sharp tang against his nostrils. Someone strode away then, but the other stayed. Hands propped him against the base of the tree. Hands wound a rope around his chest and around the tree trunk.

The same hands slipped a knife into his palm.

"You were good to me once, Mr. Cordell," the Kid said, though Chase made no sign he was awake. "I figure that'll pay you back. It's the best I can do." The Kid stalked back toward camp.

Chase curled his fingers about the knife, his heart pounding. Through slitted lids, he did his best to make out the goings on of the four outlaws. They were drinking, passing around one bottle, then another. Chase had to wait an hour, then two. All the while he worked the ropes.

367

The outlaws fell, passed out, one by one.

The hemp split. He was free.

Chase didn't dare chance approaching them. One or more of them could stir. He had no gun. His vision was still too foggy.

There would be another time for him and Gantry. Another time.

Chase made his way to their horses, picketed amongst the trees only a few yards from where they tied him. He caught up the reins of one, hazed the others off, then rode toward town, judging the direction from the position of the sun.

His first instinct was to go to the schoolhouse, see Abby. But he didn't dare. Not in this condition. He had to clean up first, manufacture a story she might believe of where he'd been, how he'd gotten hurt.

He avoided Main Street, deciding to ride to the Graham house. It should be empty this time of day. Winnie and Ethan would be at the store. Zeb and Abby at school. The hotel would have too many prying eyes.

He threw open the door, enjoying the new measure of freedom even his foggy vision afforded him. He couldn't wait to tell Abby.

"Chase!"

Chase whirled, startled, to see Ethan striding toward him from the parlor.

"Chase, my God, boy, where have you been?" Ethan caught his arm, embraced him. "What happened to ya?"

"I . . . I got lost."

"We figured that. How'd it happen?" He gave Chase no time to answer. "When you didn't come into the store this morning, I got worried. Hotel man said you hadn't been in your room all night.

"I didn't want to worry Abby, but I thought maybe she would know where you were." Ethan rubbed a hand across the back of his neck. "I scared her to death, that's what I did. But I calmed her down, told her you were a big boy and could take care of yourself. Even blind, you know your way around this country better than most folks with two good eyes.

"I think you'd best get over there, though. Let her see you're all right for herself. I—" Ethan frowned, craggy brows that Chase could just discern, crashing together above his eyes. "Where's your cane, boy?" His eyes widened. "My God! My dear God! You can see, can't you?"

Chase nodded. "Happened last night. Real late. It's the only reason I found my way home." He forced a smile.

Ethan wrapped him in a big bear hug. "That's great, boy. Just great! You skedaddle over to the school right this minute and tell Abby!"

"I thought I'd better clean up first."

"She don't care what you look like. She just wants to know you're all right."

Chase tucked in his shirttail, then went to the

kitchen to at least wash his face, his hands. Most of Noah's blows had been to his stomach, so he supposed he could look passably unscathed to the unknowing eye.

"You look store bought wonderful!" Ethan pronounced, clapping Chase on the back. "Now git over to the school. Now!"

"On my way." Chase headed for the door.

"And Chase . . . "

Chase paused, glancing back.

"I want you to know, I'm real proud you're going to be my son-in-law."

Chase felt his eyes burn. "Thanks, Ethan. That means a lot." He stepped outside and took a deep shuddery breath, then strode toward the school.

It was all coming to an end. The thought struck him like a bullet. He wasn't going to be Ethan's son-in-law. He wasn't going to be Abby's husband.

Noah Gantry had put an end to that. And if he hadn't, Sam Devlin would have. Eventually. Chase had only been fooling himself that he could ever fit into a normal family life.

He would assure Abby he was all right, and then he would go to Devlin, tell the sheriff about Gantry. No matter how he tried to keep himself out of it, within five minutes Devlin would find a way to put him behind bars.

And that Chase couldn't allow. He wasn't about to wait for Friday to have it out with Gantry. He could find the outlaw now, track him, put an end to any chance Gantry might ever have to harm Abby. Even if it meant bending a gunbutt over Devlin's head to do it.

But he wouldn't think about any of that now, not yet. His pace quickened. He was going to see Abby, see the beautiful woman he already knew her to be. He took the school steps two at a time, then threw open the door.

He couldn't move, couldn't breathe, his heart threatening to burst from his chest, as he saw her for the first time—there in front of her classroom. Her dress was simple, blue, her very cinnamon hair was tied in a prim knot at the nape of her neck. And she was indeed beautiful. More than beautiful. She was the woman he loved, more than his life.

"Chase!" She dropped the chalk she was holding, and as he watched, she gathered up her skirts and in front of a room full of openmouthed children, raced down the aisle between desks and threw herself into his outstretched arms. "Oh, Chase, I was so worried, I—"

She took a step back, flustered, seeming suddenly to remember where she was. "Take out your readers, children," she managed, in her best schoolmarm tones. "And read the next story to yourselves." She then gripped Chase's arm and propelled him back out the door.

"Where have you been? What happened? I've been worried sick since Ethan came this morning and—" She stopped, her gaze tracking him from the top of his head to the tip of his boots. "You're a mess. And you don't have your cane."

"You're beautiful," he whispered hoarsely. "But then I always knew that you were."

Realization dawned in those hazel eyes. Her hand flew to her mouth. "You can see." The words were soft, filled with awe, wonder. And incredible joy.

He nodded, his eyes wet.

She gasped, one hand flying to her hair, the other smoothing self-consciously along her dress. "I . . . oh, no, I look awful. I . . . I was crying earlier, when Ethan . . . I . . . oh, no . . . not the first time . . . not the first time."

He caught her face, smoothing his palms across his cheeks. "You are so very beautiful, Abigail Graham. I love you."

She flung her arms around his neck. "I love you. Oh, Chase, I'm so happy for you." Then she stepped back. "But where in heaven's name were you? Are you hurt? Your face looks like it's bruised a little."

"I fell," he lied. Not the first lie. Damn, this should have been one of the happiest days of his life. Instead he was about to break the heart of the woman he loved. All because of lies, the stinking lies that were his life.

"Chase, what is it? What aren't you telling me?" She wrung her hands together in the folds of her skirts, her eyes suddenly wide, frightened.

He took a deep breath. Say it, Cordell. Just say

it. "I'm on my way to see Devlin. I . . . Abby, I'm sorry. But there's not going to be a wedding."

Chapter Twenty-three

Abby stood on the steps of the school and stared at Chase's retreating back. Her heart was hurting so much she thought she might die of it. No wedding? He had called off the wedding. Why? Why? She'd pleaded with him to tell her, talk to her. But he'd told her nothing more, only repeating that he had to talk to Sam.

Sam. What did Sam Devlin have to do with Chase cancelling the wedding. What did any of this have to do with Chase's disappearance last night?

She bit her lip, trying to keep more tears at bay. This couldn't be happening. Chase had regained his sight. He could see. And now he was walking out of her life. What kind of madness was that?

Her gaze skittered after him. She could still see him. He was taking the corner that would lead him to Main Street, to the sheriff's office. He carried no cane to guide his way. He was free.

Free.

No cane to fetter him down.

And perhaps no wife either? She recalled his saying once that if he'd been able to see, he would have ridden out of Willow Springs the first day he'd regained consciousness. Had he only postponed that ride?

No! She closed her eyes, tears rimming her lids. It wasn't true. It wasn't. There was more to this than anything he had ever told her.

Secrets. Things in his life he wasn't proud of. She wiped her eyes and walked back into the school. "Zeb?"

The boy looked up from his reading and turned toward her in his seat. "Yes, Miss Graham?"

"I want you to take charge of the class for a little while. I'll be back as soon as I can, all right?"

"Yes, ma'am." Zeb beamed with genuine pride. As did Rusty. Penelope looked sick.

Abby turned her back on all of it, even knowing she could be costing herself her job. Determined, and not a little angry, she slammed out of the school and marched toward Sam Devlin's office.

Chase strode purposefully up the street toward Devlin's office. His eyes never stopped moving. He noted every nook, every cranny of every building he walked by. He saw the garish colors of the sign beckoning customers into the Lone Tree Saloon. He saw the forest green and the sunshine yellow of the poke bonnets two lady shoppers were wearing. He saw the cobalt blue of the Colorado sky.

375

And he even sidestepped a day old pile of horse dung in the middle of the street.

He marvelled at it all, marvelled at being able to see again. And he wondered how short a time it would be before he again took it all for granted.

Perhaps much sooner than he might wish, he thought grimly. Living in a four stone-walled cage in a bleak gray prison would have to be the next thing to being blind.

His right hand flexed, dipped toward his right thigh. He should probably get a gun before he saw Devlin. He had to make sure he walked back out of that jailhouse a free man.

He had to keep Gantry from Abby.

Not that he would shoot Devlin. But he might have to draw down on him, tie him up to delay any planned pursuit. He stepped off the boardwalk, the free-standing stone jail the next building on his left. He stopped dead, his gaze catching an odd movement across main street.

A slouched figure lounged against the alley side of the false front building. The Kid.

The building was the Willow Springs Bank.

What the hell?

Chase crossed over to him. The Kid straightened, looked around wildly. "You can see?" the boy choked.

"Never mind that. What are you doing here?"

"Nothin'." The Kid toed the dirt with his foot.

Chase gripped his shirtfront and slammed him

back against the building. "I said, what are you doing here?"

"Noah's gonna take the bank," the Kid squeaked.

"Not 'til Friday."

"He changed his mind. He's takin' it in half an hour. Him and the others are ridin' in. They told me to come in first."

Chase's gut clenched. "What are you supposed to do?"

"What do you mean?"

Chase tightened his grip, pressing the Kid hard against the unyielding surface of the bank's outer wall. "How do you signal them everything's all right? That it's safe to pull it off."

"I . . . I'm supposed to be sittin' in the chair in front of the bank."

"And if they're supposed to ride out? Wait for another time?"

"I . . . I stand by the chair."

"Get out there and sit." Chase heaved him toward the boardwalk. "I want Gantry to think it's safe."

"I can't! Noah'd kill me. Jesus, Mr. Cordell, I saved your life!"

"You had a gun last night, didn't you? You didn't stop Noah from beatin' hell out of me." Chase shook his head. "I'm grateful. I really am. But I'm not letting Noah take this bank, take the people in this town."

"Josey always said you was too soft for this kinda work."

377

"Whatever happened to Josey? I figured you would have stuck with him."

"Noah killed him."

Chase stiffened. "And you're still ridin' with him?"

"He scares me." The Kid blinked savagely. "You don't know what it's like."

Chase snorted. "I don't? The man put a bullet in my head."

"There was times, a couple of times I stood over him in the night, my gun in my hand. But I couldn't do it. I just couldn't do it, Mr. Cordell."

"Don't call me that. It's Murdock."

The Kid's eyes were desperate, sad. "I want to go down to Mexico, you know. Start over. I want—"

"Go sit in the chair." Chase led him over to it, sat him down.

"What are you gonna do?" the Kid asked, his voice shaking.

"Get the sheriff. Get whoever we can to stop Noah. Can I trust you to stay here?"

"If you promise to kill him, Mr. Cordell. If you promise to kill him, I'll do whatever you want."

"I'll kill him, Kid. Count on it."

Chase started across the street, then groaned inwardly to see Abby striding toward him. He had to get her out of here. Noah could ride in early. There could be bullets flying everywhere in a matter of minutes.

She intercepted him in the middle of the street. "I

want to talk to you," she said stiffly, crossing her arms in front of her. "Now." She was obviously primed for a lengthy battle.

He moved to deflect her anger, laying his hand on one side of her face, caressing her cheek with his thumb. "I want you to go home. I want you to go home and wait there. I'll be there in an hour. I'll explain everything, Abby. Everything. I promise."

He could see the anger drain out of her, but there was fear, too, and uncertainty. They did not go away.

"Chase, please . . ."

"I promise, Abby. One hour. Then no more secrets, no more lies."

She unfolded her arms, letting them fall to her sides. "All right. An hour." She seemed to want to say something else, but decided against it. Without another word she turned away and headed home.

Chase let out a long, unsteady breath. He just hoped he could honor that promise. In an hour, he could be dead.

A glance back told him the Kid was still sitting in his chair. Chase hoped Devlin had an extra gun. The lawman was going to need all the help he could get.

Chase opened the door to Devlin's office and went inside.

The sheriff rose from behind his desk, an instant's puzzlement crossing his hard-angled features. But if he was at all curious about Chase's restored eyesight, he didn't ask. Instead he allowed an odd smile. "Now isn't this a nice little coincidence. I was just going to come lookin' for you." He drew his gun, slowly, levelling it at Chase's middle.

Chase stiffened. He could've asked what this was all about. An innocent man would. He didn't.

"I should've opened my mail last night," Devlin went on, stepping close to Chase, patting him down for a weapon, "before I came lookin' for you and Abby. Had a whole stack of mail that piled up while I was outta town. Some real interesting reading in this one." He held up an oversized piece of letter paper, turned it toward Chase. "Nice likeness. Eh, Cordell? I knew somebody, somewhere had to have a dodger with your face on it. Breckenridge had 'em made up special two years ago."

Chase felt as though the walls themselves were closing in on him, but he shook it off. "You can arrest me, Devlin," he said urgently. "I'll take any damned cell you want. Just listen to me for one minute." He checked behind him out the window, gazing across the street to the boardwalk in front of the bank. The Kid was still there, rocking nervously back and forth on the straight-legged chair.

"I don't want to hear anything you have to say. Not one word, Cordell. I'm getting you out of Abby's life right now." He tossed the reward poster back on his desk, then gestured with the gun barrel toward the door that led to the cells in the back of the building.

"The bank's going to be robbed, Devlin," Chase snapped. "You've got fifteen minutes, maybe less."

The lawman frowned, seeming to consider the words, then he straightened. "What kind of fool do you take me for?"

"See that boy across the street. The one in the chair in front of the bank. He's Noah Gantry's lookout."

"And how would you know?"

"Noah Gantry's the man who shot me."

Chase could tell that Devlin was trying to take this all in, sort it out. What he had to get the lawman to understand is that there was no time.

Very slowly Chase started to back toward the window. "Look for yourself."

"How do you know all this? About the bank. You set it up with them?"

Chase unbuttoned his shirt and showed Devlin the mass of bruises, scrapes across his upper body. "I overheard it last night, when Gantry and I were getting reacquainted." In short, clipped sentences he told Devlin everything the outlaws had said.

"Why should I believe you?" Devlin asked, when he'd finished.

"I don't know," Chase said. "I'm not sure that I would. But it's going to happen whether you believe me or not." Chase again looked out the window. He swore softly. "They're coming."

Devlin looked. "I don't see anything different."

"The Kid stopped rocking. He's looking at someone up the street. It's now or never, Devlin."

"All right. All right, I believe you." He crossed to his desk, pulled out an extra sixgun and stuffed it in his belt.

"Let me help," Chase said.

Devlin hesitated only an instant, then hefted the gun and tossed it to Chase. He opened the drawer again and threw him a belt full of ammunition. "I was going to have that thing repaired. The balance is off. And it's not very accurate. So be warned."

Chase eyed the gunrack on the wall, but knew a rifle would be less than useless at such short range. Quickly he checked the Smith and Wesson, making certain it was loaded. Then he strapped the gun around his hips. Warily, he hunched in front of the door, cracking it open barely an inch. He peered up the street, following the Kid's gaze. "Damn! This could be bloody. There's no time to warn anyone off."

"Can't be helped."

Chase pointed out Gantry to Devlin, then the two he guessed were Buckshot and Brown, though he'd never had a clear look at either of Gantry's new gunnies. All three were riding in from the south, but they were spread out, as though they had each ridden in alone.

"They know you," Devlin said. "You stay out of sight. I'm going to walk across the street. Real casual."

"Watch your back."

The sheriff gave him an unreadable look. "Don't worry. I will." He started out, then paused, his eyes still unreadable. "You love her, don't you?"

"I love her, Devlin." He flexed his fingers on the trigger guard of the Smith and Wesson. "But in about ten minutes she's not going to love me."

Devlin's mouth twisted ironically. "I wish I could count on that. But I don't think so." He took a long breath, his hand resting on the handle of his holstered Colt, then headed out the door.

What happened next, Chase was never sure. Whether the Kid panicked on sight of the sheriff, or whether he just panicked. But Noah, Buckshot and Brown had all reached the bank, when the Kid suddenly leaped up and began shouting: "It's a trap!"

Devlin drew his pistol and hit the dirt rolling all in the same motion. He fired three quick shots.

Buckshot's horse reared, its terrified whinny splitting the air louder than gunfire. The gelding's actions sparked similar panic in Brown and Gantry's mounts.

Gantry had his gun in his hand and was shooting at anything that moved.

Chase bolted out into the street. He fired once, twice, but missed because of Gantry's wildly wheeling mount. He forced a deep breath and fired again.

He swore. Another miss.

One of Gantry's bullets hit Devlin, then another,

sending the lawman sprawling backwards. He lay spread-eagled in the street, unmoving. Gantry's third bullet ripped a fist-sized hole in the Kid's chest. Deliberate, cold. The Kid slumped to the boardwalk. He had not even drawn his gun.

Chase dove for cover behind a horse trough, then came up firing. His eyes met Gantry's. The outlaw's face purpled with fury.

"Let's get the hell out of here!" Buckshot roared. He slammed his spurs into his gelding's sides, sending the terrified animal racing up the street at a dead run. Chase fired a wild shot. Buckshot tumbled from the gelding's back, dead before he hit the street.

Brown emptied his gun at Chase, then reined his horse to head out of town, reloading as he rode. Chase brought him down with another shot, then reloaded his own weapon.

Gantry drew a spare pistol, continuing to fire. "You're dead, Cordell!" he shrieked. "Dead! Do you hear me?"

On the street Devlin moved, heaved himself up to a sitting position. Chase saw him and fired again and again at Gantry with the faulty Smith and Wesson. Though Chase tried desperately to correct for the pistol's inaccuracy, the gun never seemed to do the same thing twice. One of his bullets grazed Gantry's mount. The horse bucked, but Gantry kept his seat.

With what seemed agonizing slowness Devlin

384

brought his gun to bear on the crazed outlaw. He squeezed the trigger.

Blood spurted from Gantry's leg. With a howl of rage the outlaw pumped another bullet into the collapsing lawman and spurred his horse out of town.

Chase dove for Devlin's gun. He grabbed it up, firing until the gun was empty, but none of the bullets found their mark. Gantry kept riding.

Chase swore savagely, then dropped to his knees beside the wounded Devlin.

From everywhere townspeople came now. The shooting had to have been heard all over town. Hiram Perkins was there. Chase noted he was already measuring Brown for one of his pine box specials. The Kid must have still had a few breaths left in him, because several men were carting him away with slightly more care than they would have given a dead body.

"A bank holdup?" Perkins asked, coming up to Chase.

Chase nodded, ripping open the buttons of Devlin's shirt, knowing at once it was hopeless. The man was dying.

"Sam! Oh, Sam, no!" Abby's voice.

Chase rose to intercept her, but he was too late. She rushed to kneel on Devlin's opposite side. Her eyes looked up imploringly at Chase. He shook his head.

Abby cradled Sam's head on her lap, stroking his

hair, tears streaming unchecked down her cheeks.

Devlin coughed, opened his eyes. "Abby!" He gasped, coughed again. "Abby . . . Cor . . . Cordell . . ."

Abby pressed her fingers to his lips. "Save your strength. Don't try to talk."

"Cordell," Devlin rasped, his lungs heaving with effort, as he tried vainly to suck in more air. "Abby . . . watch . . . yourself please . . . please . . . love you. Love you, Abby." A deep rattling noise sounded in his throat, the air expelling one last time from his lungs.

Chase reached over, praying Abby didn't notice how his hand trembled, and gently closed Devlin's unseeing eyes. From somewhere Ethan came, helped Abby to her feet, held her while she sobbed brokenly.

Chase wanted to be the one to be there for her. But there were too many people now, asking him too many questions. Yes, he and Devlin had learned the bank was going to be robbed. Again and again he recounted what happened, leaving out only those parts that would have brought in Cordell.

"You seem quite capable in a crisis, Mr. Murdock," Hiram Perkins noted, brushing imaginary dust from his blue frock coat. "Would you like Sheriff Devlin's job?" He held out the badge, he'd already appropriated from Devlin's vest.

"Don't you think you ought to bury him first?"

386

Chase gritted.

"It will be a lovely service, I assure you. But Willow Springs cannot be without protection, not even for a day. This horrible tragedy only proves that far too well. You've saved a good many of us from bankruptcy today, Mr. Murdock. What do you say, will you accept the position?"

Chase considered the incredible irony that he should be offered the job of upholding the law in Willow Springs. Devlin would no doubt be spinning in that grave of his. And perhaps Quinton Murdock already was. Nor was it lost on him that he had suddenly become *Mister* Murdock in Perkins' sallow eyes, instead of "that transient."

Even so, he took the badge. "I'll be your sheriff, Perkins," he said, "at least as long as it takes me to track Gantry." He pinned on the tin star, then excused himself and headed with what he hoped was nonchalance toward Devlin's office. He had to get his hands on that wanted poster.

He stepped inside, closed the door. And stopped in his tracks. Abby sat behind Devlin's desk, where Ethan had apparently brought her to get her away from the crush of people gathered in the streets. Ethan raised his eyes and cast Chase an oddly curious look, though he said nothing. Then he moved away from Abby, though not very far away, not very far at all.

Yet Ethan might as well have been in another country. Chase's whole world shrunk down in that instant.

Only he and Abby existed.

He and Abby and the reward dodger she held clutched in her fist.

Chapter Twenty-four

While he was blind Chase could only imagine the emotions in Abigail Graham's eyes. Imagine the compassion when he told her about his father. Imagine the fury when Zeb was hurt. Imagine the passion when they'd made love. Now he could almost have wished himself sightless again, never to have had to see the look that was in her eyes now.

Betrayal. Stark, cold, bitter betrayal.

Still gripping the poster, she stepped from behind Devlin's desk and crossed the room, stopping some three feet short of where he stood just inside the door. "This is what you couldn't tell me?" she asked, her voice laden with such pain that it was a knife to his heart. "The ugly things you've done in your life?" She crushed the poster, flung it at him. "That you're a thief—" her voice shook, "a gunfighter, a hired killer?"

He took a step toward her. She took a step back.

"How could you? How could you lie to me that way?"

"I didn't want to." He closed his eyes, the events

of the past twenty-four hours washing over him and he felt suddenly unutterably weary. "Abby, I warned you every way I knew how to stay away from me."

He resigned himself to that look in her eyes, resigned himself to her hate. There was nothing he could do to go back and change any part of what he had done or not done in his life. Turning away from her, he crossed to the gunrack and pulled down Devlin's Winchester.

"What are you doing?" she asked.

"Going after Gantry."

"Alone?"

He looked at her. "I work best alone."

Her gaze dropped to the floor. "I suppose you do."

From the other side of the room Ethan Graham cleared his throat. Chase had forgotten he was even there. Evidently, so had Abby. She looked at her uncle, her cheeks reddening. "I'm sorry you had to witness this, Uncle Ethan."

Ethan's normally ebullient manner was subdued, serious. "Are you all right, sweetheart?"

"I'm fine." She did not meet his gaze.

"Can you give me a minute alone with Chase?"

She looked puzzled and briefly hurt, but then she nodded, and went to stand by the door.

Ethan ambled over to where Abby had thrown the poster on the floor. He picked it up.

Chase waited.

Ethan came up to him, his careworn face rife

with sympathy, and not a little sadness. "I'm not going to ask you why you've done what you've done, boy," the old man said, folding the poster several times and stuffing it into his pocket.

In spite of himself, Chase felt his defenses rise. "That's good, Ethan. Because I'm not in the mood for handin' out answers just now anyway."

He stepped around the old storekeeper, stepped away from the kindness he saw in Ethan's gentle gaze and strode over to Devlin's desk. Slamming open drawers, he searched until he found a box of .44/.40 shells. He yanked the malfunctioning Smith and Wesson from his holster, unloaded it and shoved it into the drawer, then pulled Devlin's Colt from the waistband of his trousers. He took off the gunbelt and tugged the S & W's cartridges from the ammunition loops, substituting the .44/.40s., knowing he could use them in both the Winchester and the Colt.

Ethan followed, leaned against the desk. "I just got one thing to say about all this, son. Then you won't hear anything from me about it ever again."

Chase wondered if Ethan was speaking as much for him as he was for Abby, who hadn't moved from where she stood beside the door. She was looking toward the street, but he was certain she could hear every word her uncle said.

Chase punched another cartridge into the Winchester.

"Whatever man you were when you were left for

391

dead beside that creek," Ethan said, his voice as kind as his eyes, "is part and parcel of the man you are now. We all make choices, Chase. Some good. Some bad. But my feelin' about it is, sometimes we can learn a hell of a lot more from one bad choice than from a hundred good ones."

Chase buckled on the gunbelt, tied down the holster to his thigh, then hefted the Winchester. "I'll be using Devlin's horse," he said, knowing Ethan expected no response to what he'd said. "I don't know when—" he looked at Abby "or if, I'll be back." He held out his hand. "I'm glad to know you, Ethan Graham."

Ethan gripped Chase's hand. "Good luck to you, son."

"Thank you." He walked to the door. Abby backed away. She did not look up.

For just an instant the urge to reach for her, touch her, almost overwhelmed him. But he fought it off. Then he stepped past her out the door.

Abby stared through the window in Sam's office, watching as Chase mounted Sam's roan and rode north out of town. *I don't know when or if I'll be back,* he'd said. Did he mean he had no interest in returning to Willow Springs? Or had he meant the words more ominously? That his quest to find Noah Gantry could get him killed.

"He's a thief, Uncle Ethan," she murmured, her

voice breaking. "I was going to marry a thief."

"You were going to marry Chase Murdock, the man you love." He stepped up to her, put his arm around her. "Or should I say loved?"

She jerked away angrily, twisting to face him. "You're acting like I'm the villain here, like I did something wrong." She pressed her lips together, swallowing a sob. "Uncle Ethan, what am I going to do?"

He handed her his kerchief. "One thing you're going to do is talk to me. What are you feelin', girl? Tell me."

"I hate him."

Ethan smiled.

"Stop that!" she snapped. "I *do* hate him."

"So what you're saying is, he was lying a few minutes ago. That he never gave you any clues that it might not be the wisest thing you ever did to fall in love with him."

"That's right, he didn't," she said stubbornly.

"Abby, this is your Uncle Ethan you're talkin' to now. Not Winnie. You can pull the wool over her eyes every now and again. But this old sheepdog doesn't believe a word you're sayin'."

There was a woodbox in front of the window. Abby crossed over to it and sat down. Ethan joined her.

"How can I love an outlaw, Uncle Ethan? How can I?"

"Because he was no outlaw when you fell in love

393

with him. He was a man hurt and needin' help. And then he was a man who teased you and goaded you and made you laugh. Like you made him laugh. Like you made him cry."

"What are you talking about? I've never made Chase cry. What an awful thing to say."

"The man was crying in this room, Abby. Not five minutes ago, when he saw that poster in your hands. It tore his heart out to see you so hurt. A man doesn't have to shed tears to cry. You might do well to remember that."

"I remember too much already." She took in a deep breath and let it out. "Oh, Uncle Ethan, he did warn me away from him. So many times. But I wouldn't listen. I knew he was hiding something. I just never dreamed . . ."

"Good people can do bad things, sweetheart," Ethan said softly.

"Little things, maybe," she allowed. "But not murder—"

"You don't know that he's a murderer. My guess is, he isn't. A thief, yes. But not a killer. At least not a killer without good reason."

"But he knows right from wrong, doesn't he? Stealing is wrong."

"Why? Because you were raised up to believe it's wrong? And how was Chase raised? By tender hands, loving parents? No. What he learned, he had to learn himself. And who knows what pushed him over the edge to break the law that first time.

You don't know. You didn't ask."

"There's no excuse."

"If he's done bad things, he's a bad man. Is that it?"

She nodded, her own muleheadedness prodding her now.

"I think maybe it's time I tell you a story, Abigail Graham. A story long overdue."

"Oh, Uncle Ethan, for heaven's sake . . ." She started to rise.

"Sit."

She looked at him.

"Sit down, girl. Now."

She sat.

"You were three years old when your parents died. You don't even remember them, do you?"

"You know I don't." Why in the world was he bringing up her parents? How could their deaths possibly figure into what was happening with Chase?

"Winnie and I agreed, when Jonathon and Agatha died, to tell you they died of the cholera."

"Agreed?" Abby frowned, puzzled.

"Your parents were murdered, Abby."

Abby stared at him, uncomprehending. She didn't move, didn't speak, just listened, transfixed.

"We lived in Ohio then. Just a little town, nothin' special. Jonathon, Agatha, Winnie and I pooled our life savings and bought a rundown mercantile that was for sale."

Ethan's eyes misted. "Jonathon was eight years younger than me. I always felt more like his father than his brother. Agatha was the light of his life. They were in the store alone one night, checking inventory, when a couple of men broke in. Jonathon and Agatha told them to take whatever they wanted, that they had a little girl at home that needed her mama and papa. They shot 'em both down in cold blood.

"Jonathon died right away. A bullet wound to the head. It was Winnie who found the bodies." He looked at Abby. "That's why findin' Chase that day by the creek upset her so much. It reminded her of that awful night, when she'd found your father . . ."

Abby shuddered, but did not interrupt.

"Agatha was still alive, but there was nothing any doctor could do. It took her four days to die. She was in agony every minute.

"They caught the two men who did it almost right away. They were trying to sell off some of the goods they'd stolen from the store. They were tried, found guilty, sentenced to hang. They didn't even care. One of 'em laughed at Winnie in the courtroom when she asked 'em why they did it. Said they just felt like it.

"The mood in the town was ugly, real ugly. Folks were stirred up, crazy mad. It didn't seem fair that those two would get a quick easy death after what they did to Agatha.

396

"The night before the official hangin', a crowd stormed the jail, dragged them two men out into the street. Lynched 'em. But long before they died, that mob had those men blubber'n, screamin', beggin' for their lives . . ."

Abby could feel the agony in her uncle. Why was he torturing himself with these memories now? His next words answered her question.

"I was part of that mob, Abby," Ethan said softly. "And even though those men deserved to die, what I did was wrong. An unconscionable, immoral act. And there hasn't been a day that's passed since, that I haven't regretted taking part in it."

Abby felt drained, hollow. Ethan was ashen faced. And maybe a little afraid. That she wouldn't understand. But she did. Too well. "Good people can do bad things, Uncle Ethan," she whispered. "A very wise man told me that." She threw her arms around him and together they cried. "I want to understand Chase, Uncle Ethan. Honestly I do. If only he'd trusted me, told me—"

"You can't change yesterday, Abby. No one can."

She sniffled, blew her nose. "Do you think he'll be back?"

"He'll be back."

"I want to talk to him. I really want to talk to him, Uncle Ethan."

"He'll be back, honey. You just wait and—"

The door burst open. A wizened, buckskin clad codger, wearing a bodylong white apron sauntered

397

in. Abby recognized him as Ezra Weed, bartender of the Silver Nugget. Though they had never been officially introduced.

"Murdock here?" Ezra asked, scratching his beard-stubbled jaw.

"Not right now." Abby rose. "Why do you want him?"

"That young feller that got shot today in front of the bank is askin' for him over to my place."

"Why?"

He snorted impatiently. "I didn't ask."

"Maybe I can help," Abby said. She had heard people in the crowd saying the young man had once ridden with Cordell. She wanted very badly to talk to someone who knew Chase Cordell—the outlaw.

Chase reined in the roan and dismounted. He'd been after Gantry for five hours now.

He stretched his legs, keeping a wary eye on the landscape. He wouldn't put it past Gantry to hole up and try an ambush. Only when he was satisfied he wasn't being watched, did he hunker down and check for sign.

He frowned, studying the tracks in the hard packed earth. What he saw made no sense.

Rising to his feet, he stalked back to the roan. He tossed the left stirrup over the saddle and checked the cinch, thinking all the while. What in hell was Gantry up to?

At first the bastard had ridden at a hard run straight north, and Chase had no trouble picking up his trail. He even found the place where Gantry had stopped long enough to tie off the wound in his leg. About fifteen miles out of town, Gantry had grown cagey, his path more circuitous, almost zigzag cross-country.

But now. Chase double checked the sign. There was no mistaking it. Gantry had crossed his own trail, and he was heading south. Back toward Willow Springs.

Chase was certain it was no ruse to throw off any pursuers. The tracks would have been made only minutes apart if that were the case. He would not have stayed around to ride over his own trail an hour later, not when he could have put more miles between himself and Willow Springs.

And he wasn't holing up anywhere to shoot it out either. Or he obviously could already have done so. Gantry had to know Chase would track him. The outlaw wouldn't have to do anything but rein in to gain the vengeance he sought.

Then why bypass Chase and head back to Willow Springs?

Let you listen while I show her how a real man takes a woman. The sneering voice slashed across his mind.

Chase felt fear turn his blood to ice. The perfect vengeance for Gantry against Chase Cordell was not to hurt Cordell. Chase swung onto the gelding's back, raked his spurs along the animal's sides.

Abby!

Abby squeezed Cal Talbot's hand, speaking soothingly to the dying outlaw. "It's all right, Cal," she said. "You're not alone any more."

"They call me 'the Kid,' " he choked. "How come you can't remember that?"

"I'll remember." He was lying on a table in one of the upstairs rooms of the Silver Nugget. The beds were all occupied, Ezra had told her with a leering wink. The Kid seemed content and so she had not argued.

The mass of makeshift bandages on his chest dripped crimson with his blood. Abby tried not to look at them any more than she had to.

"Where did you get the name Kid?" she asked, liking the young towhead, wondering what had brought him to this.

"Not like Billy Bonney or anything, ma'am. Got it just 'cause I look like a kid, I guess." His breath caught, his face twisting, as he fought another spasm of pain. They came less often now. "Won't last out the hour," Ezra had told her. But then he needed his table back anyway, she remembered acidly. There was a big poker game tonight.

Abby wondered if she would ever get used to the casualness with which people seemed to view life and death out here in this vast, largely unsettled land. And then she realized that in a very real way that very devil-may-care attitude was part of the allure, the romance, of this beautiful country.

"I'm sorry Chase isn't here," she said, when Cal—she could not think of him as the Kid,—was resting more easily once again.

"Chase?"

"Mr. Murdock. I believe you called him Cordell." She had to lean close to hear him, his voice was growing weaker all the time. "Cal . . . I mean, Kid, I need to ask you something. It's about the Willow Springs stage holdup. Could you tell me how did Mr. Mur—, Cordell get shot?"

"Gantry went crazy . . ." he labored to get each word out "attack . . . woman . . . passenger . . . Cordell—Mr. Murdock—furious. Threw down on . . . Gantry. Made stage leave." Cal paused to catch his breath. Abby did not rush him. "Told Gantry to ride out. Gantry . . . hideout gun . . . shot Cordell—Mr. Murdock—like a dog."

Abby shuddered, vivid images of finding Chase all but dead flooding over her.

"Gantry . . . shot Josey . . . my friend."

"Shhh. Rest now." Abby frowned, looking toward the closed door. Had she heard someone pause on the other side? Quickly, she rose and went to the door. But when she opened it, it was to find the corridor empty. Deciding she was being foolish, she returned to Cal Talbot's side.

"Josey always said . . . Cordell no outlaw. Too

401

soft. Too damned soft . . ."

The Kid tried to catch his breath, couldn't. He gripped her hand, squeezing so hard she cried out from the pain. Then he seemed to relax, drift off to sleep. But his chest no longer rose and fell.

Abby blinked back tears, pulling the coarse wool blanket up over the boy's eyes, then quietly went down the back stairs to the waning sunlight outside. She was tired, but she felt too restless to just go home. Besides, she wasn't sure she was up to Winnie's overanxious concern. She knew her aunt meant well, but right now Abby just wanted to be alone. She had a lot of serious thinking to do.

Almost automatically, she found herself heading for the school. This time of night, it would be quiet, peaceful.

"Please come home, Chase," she said aloud. "I need to talk to you. Please."

She remembered the feeling of betrayal that had burned through her when she'd seen that reward dodger. Chase had seen it in her eyes. But she was wrong. Dead wrong. She knew that now.

He had not betrayed her. She had betrayed him.

Because when he needed her most, she had deserted him. Without allowing him so much as a word in his own defense.

"I'll listen, Chase. I promise. Just please come home. Please be all right."

She looked up, surprised to see she had reached the school already. For a moment she stood at the bottom of the steps, undecided about going inside.

Maybe she was ready for some company after all. And she didn't want Winnie to worry.

She started home, then remembered she'd left in such a hurry today, she'd forgotten her lunch tin. She would need it for tomorrow. Quickly, she climbed the stairs and went inside.

Even in the lengthening shadows, she did not bother to light the lamp. She knew her way around this room by heart. She was surprised then to bump into one of the children's desks, off line with the others in front of it.

She pushed it back into place, grumbling a little. Zeb must have moved it for some reason. She hurried to her own desk, slid open the bottom drawer.

She noticed the stench then, the fetid stench of an unwashed body. She made one, desperate lunge for the door. Lost.

An arm snaked out, a filthy hand clamping over her mouth to stifle the scream erupting from her throat. And then she didn't even think about screaming, as the cold blade of a knife pressed hard against her throat.

"Do exactly as I say, little schoolmarm," Noah Gantry hissed. "And maybe, just maybe, I'll kill you before you beg to die."

Chapter Twenty-five

Chase rode like the demons of hell were on his tail, but he couldn't escape the near crippling dread that raked him, tormented him that he was already too late. It was nearly dark and he was still ten miles out of Willow Springs. Gantry could have been there and gone over an hour ago.

Damn! Why hadn't he thought of it sooner? Why hadn't — ?

A bullet kicked up dirt to the gelding's left. The horse shied violently, but Chase was already leaping from the saddle, rifle in hand. He dove for a cluster of boulders and waited for a second shot to better pinpoint the shooter.

He felt oddly exultant. Gantry had holed up after all. Maybe the wound had slowed him. Maybe he'd decided to face Chase head on. The outlaw's reasons didn't matter. It only mattered that Abby was safe. Chase levered a cartridge into the Winchester's chamber, wondering now what was taking the bastard so long to fire again.

In the wavering light of a half moon, he guessed

the shot had come from a horseshoe shaped jumble of stone about a hundred yards over and to the left of where he sat hunched, waiting. From what he could tell looking into the mouth of that horseshoe, there were about five or six acres of level ground nearly encircled by the wall of rock. Gantry could hold off an army from inside that wall.

Except that one man couldn't stay awake indefinitely. Chase would wait. Maybe he'd get lucky and Gantry would bleed to death.

He frowned, sighting quickly down the Winchester, as he thought he detected movement within the horseshoe. There, on the level ground. A silhouette.

Gantry?

He'd never fired at something he couldn't see in his life. But his palm itched to do so now. Who else could —?

A lick of flame shot up from the middle of the horseshoe, turning almost at once into a roaring bonfire, sending flames arcing six feet into the night sky.

Why would Gantry build such a fire? Light the way for the man who would kill him?

Chase saw her then, limned against the red-orange flames at her back. Black rage ripped through him, a fury such as he'd never known. Standing next to her, his sixgun at her throat, stood Noah Gantry.

"Come on in, Cordell," Gantry called. "We've been waiting for you."

Chase corralled his anger, subdued it. If he went in there in a blind fury, ne would only succeed in getting Abby killed. Or worse. He had to play this out on Gantry's terms. And he would be lucky to get even one chance to save her. He had to be ready for that chance.

"Let her go, Gantry!" he shouted. "It's me you want."

"Just get in here, Cordell. Hands where I can see 'em. And they'd better be empty. Or I may have to start emptying my Colt into our little schoolmarm here."

A sickened hopelessness clawed at his insides. Dropping his guns where he stood, Chase closed the distance to the wall of stone. He walked through the gap, his gaze never leaving Abby's face. The terror he saw there almost made him forget how desperately important it was that he not do anything reckless.

"Don't hurt her, Gantry. For God's sake, don't hurt her."

"Hurt her?" Noah laughed, that thoroughly unpleasant laugh of his. "She's the guest of honor at our little party, Cordell. And I can't wait to see her dance, can you?"

Six feet still separated Chase from the two of them. Chase took another step.

Gantry knotted his fist in the hair at the base of Abby's skull. "That's far enough, Cordell. You get too close and you won't be able to see everything."

Involuntary tears sprang to Abby's eyes, but she did not cry out.

Chase stood there, feeling impotent, near crazed with fear himself that there was nothing he could do to stop this, nothing he could do to prevent whatever unholy plan Gantry had for Abby this night.

And he remembered all too well the betrayal in her eyes this afternoon, when she'd stood in Devlin's office and flung that reward dodger in his face. She'd wanted him out of her life. His lies, his sordid past. He'd tried to oblige her, though it hurt more than he thought anything ever could.

But his past had other ideas.

Abigail Graham, Colorado schoolteacher, was standing eight feet from a firepit in the dead of night with a gun held to her throat by a madman, because her life had crossed paths with an outlaw named Chase Cordell. If it cost him his own life, he would do everything, anything he could to spare her any more pain because of it.

A ghoulish cackle rose in the outlaw's throat. "Maybe I'll roast her, when I'm done. What do you think, Cordell? Nice 'n brown. Like that Shoshone." He grinned, loosening his hold on Abby's hair just a fraction. "Remember? I swear you turned green when I told you about it. But I only had me a coupla bites. Honest."

Chase's stomach clenched. But he kept himself loose, ready. He could see the look in Gantry's eyes.

407

The man was out of his mind crazy, so out of touch with the real world that he wasn't even aware that the filthy bandage binding his wounded leg dripped blood into the dusty ground with every beat of his black heart.

The sight of the wound gave Chase hope. If he could keep Gantry talking, preoccupied, perhaps he would lose enough blood to pass out before he could hurt Abby any more than he already had. If he could get Gantry to move about, the wound would bleed even faster.

Chase took a step to the right. Gantry shifted to follow him, maintaining his grip on Abby's hair. "Don't try nothin', Cordell."

Chase shook his head. "I won't. I swear, Gantry. I won't. Just don't hurt her." He took another step.

So did Gantry. The outlaw trailed his gun barrel along Abby's jaw. "It was real nice of her to come by the schoolhouse tonight, eh, Cordell? I was all ready to wait 'til mornin'." He placed the bore of the pistol against her throat and thumbed back the hammer.

Chase stood stock still, as though holding his own body steady could somehow keep Gantry's hair-trigger Colt from going off. "You're going to kill her, Gantry," he said. "Spoil your fun. You wouldn't want to do that, would you?"

Surprisingly, Gantry lowered the hammer. "No, we wouldn't want to do that. She hasn't danced for me yet. I want to see her dance." He let loose of her hair, backed away a step. The wound bled more freely. "Dance for me, schoolmarm. Dance!"

Abby didn't move.

Gantry fired his gun into the ground near her feet. "Dance, bitch! Now!"

Abby's body began to sway haltingly, tears streaming down her cheeks.

"It's all right, Abby," Chase soothed, not knowing if hearing his voice right now would make her feel better, or worse. "It'll be all right."

She continued to move her body, while Gantry cackled just behind her.

Hang on, Abby, Chase thought fiercely. *Hang on. Don't leave me. Don't give up now.*

A shift in the breeze brought with it the telling odor of coal oil. Now he knew how Gantry had gained his inferno so quickly. He also knew that Gantry must have slopped a gallon on himself alone.

"Let her go, Gantry," Chase said, though he knew it was useless. He wanted more time. More time. "Let her go and I swear I won't fight you. You can kill me any way you want."

Gantry seemed to consider it. "Any way I want?"

"Just let her go."

Gantry smiled. "You don't get it, Cordell. I can already kill you any way I want. I have the gun. And I have your woman."

"She's not my woman, damn you! She doesn't want anything to do with me. She knows I'm an outlaw, no better than you."

Gantry looked at Abby. "Is that true? You think he's like me?"

Abby stopped dancing. Chase watched her stiffen her spine, seeming to draw on some reservoir of courage deep inside herself. She looked Gantry straight in the eye. "I think you're pure pig, Mr. Gantry. And I think Chase is the finest man I've ever known." Before Gantry could react, Abby turned to face Chase. "I wanted you to know that. In case we both die here tonight. I wanted you to know—"

Gantry lunged at her, backhanded her across the face.

Chase was already moving. He drove himself bodylong against Gantry, grabbing for his gunhand as both men went sprawling into the dirt. Chase rolled, grappled, fought, slamming Gantry's wrist into the hard earth again and again until he let loose the gun.

And then Chase set free the bloodlust he'd held in check since first he'd seen Gantry's hands on the woman he loved. He slammed his fist into Gantry's face over and over and over again. He dragged the bastard to his feet, watched him sway drunkenly, then hit him again. Gantry collapsed into the dirt face first and lay still.

Abby was at his side, holding him, sobbing, sobbing. "I was so scared. I was so scared."

"Shhh." He held her to him, never wanting to let

go. "It's all right now. Everything's all right."

"No. No, Chase, you don't understand." She arched her head back to look up into his face. "I was scared about Gantry. But I was more scared that you would die thinking I hated you. I don't, Chase. I don't." She buried her face in his shirt. "I love you so much."

His heart swelled, threatened to burst inside his chest. He could scarcely believe his own ears. But he wasn't about to argue the point. He just stood there, held her close until her shaking stopped.

Long minutes passed. He kissed her hair, set her away from him. "I'd best get a rope. Tie this bastard up. After all," he gestured to the badge on his vest, "I am representing law and order now." He regretted the words, as Abby's gaze dropped away from his. So it wasn't all resolved. Not yet. He hadn't really supposed it could be. With a sigh he picked up Gantry's gun and handed it to her. "Keep an eye on him."

Chase retrieved the rope from his saddle and walked over to Gantry's inert body, lying just three feet from the base of the still-blazing fire. He grabbed one of the outlaw's slack arms and started to wrap the rope around it.

Gantry's whole body went tense. Chase tried to react, but Gantry let out an insane roar, suddenly seeming to have the strength of ten men. The outlaw spun over onto his back, grabbed for Chase's throat and hung on.

411

Shards of agony tore through Chase's brain, the world spinning crazily. He heard Abby cry out, but knew she didn't dare shoot. As blackness threatened to engulf him Chase groped blindly for something, anything to break Gantry's deathgrip.

He felt the heat of the flames, close, so close. He felt the end of something wooden, branch-like, jutting from the edge of the fire. His fist closed around it, raised it torch-like in the air. With a maniacal strength of his own he slammed the flaming end of the stick into Gantry's skull. The outlaw screamed, but held on.

Chase hit him again, sparks dripping onto Gantry's shirt. The coal oil ignited. Gantry shrieked, slapped at the flames with both hands, while Chase rolled desperately away. In the next instant the rest of Gantry's clothes seemed to explode, a fireball engulfing him, setting even his hair aflame. He rose to his feet, his inhuman screams splitting the night, as he lurched toward Chase like some hellish demon from the dark world itself.

Chase side-stepped. Gantry staggered on another twenty feet, his body driven now only by the spasming muscles of a dead man. Then Gantry collapsed, smoldering, blackened beyond recognition.

"Come on." Chase grabbed Abby about the shoulders, led her away from the horror, the stench of it.

He took her to his horse, grabbed up his blanket and settled it about her shoulders. Together they sank to the ground beside a large boulder.

"How do you feel?" he asked, knowing the question was scarcely adequate for what she had just been through.

Astonishingly, she smiled. "You should know," she said. "I'm always safe, when I'm with you."

His throat tightened. "Abby, I'm so sorry . . . I . . ."

"You saved my life."

"That bastard would never have touched your life if not for me."

"You're not responsible for him, Chase." She snuggled close to him, put her head on his chest. "None of that matters now anyway. What matters is that you're here with me. And that we talk about . . . about what happened this afternoon. Can you ever forgive me?"

"Forgive *you?*" he asked, disbelieving. "I thought you despised me. I'm the outlaw here, remember?"

She peered up at him, her eyes wide, serious. "Why are you an outlaw, Chase Murdock?"

How did a man answer such a question? He pondered it a moment, never having been forced to put it into words before. "I suppose because I was a fool," he said simply. "I let my anger, my need for vengeance against a man turn me into what he in fact was. A thief."

He sat there then, in the moonlit darkness and told her of Luther Breckenridge, and many other things he'd never shared with anyone in his life.

413

When he'd finished, he found her looking at him with those warm, quiet eyes. "What are you thinking?" he asked.

She kissed his jaw. "I'm thinking that you would still do very nicely for the hero of my book. I've been secretly working on a revised version, you know. I even sent off the first couple of chapters to Beadle and Adams."

He squeezed her tight. "I love you."

She looked at him, her voice laced with worry. "What are we going to do? Half the town probably overheard the Kid's delirium about your being Cordell. Hiram Perkins was beside himself when he discovered he'd pinned a badge on . . ." She looked away.

"An outlaw?"

"I'm sorry."

"Don't be. It's what I am, Abby. Or what I've become."

"But you're not, not really," she insisted. "At least not any more. What you did this afternoon has to count for something. A lot of people would have been wiped out if Gantry had succeeded in robbing the bank."

"That doesn't change the past two years."

"Then we'll leave, go away. To Mexico. Canada. Start over. We'll—"

"No." He shook his head. "I could never ask you to do such a thing. Live the life of a fugitive." He threaded his hand through her hair. "Maybe I

414

should give myself up. Maybe they would take this afternoon into consideration."

"No! They could send you to jail! You couldn't take the chance."

He arched his head back, staring up into the star-studded night sky. "When I was blind, I convinced myself that because I couldn't see, the law couldn't see me. That Cordell was dead, buried. He isn't, Abby. He never will be, until I face up to what I've done. And pay for it, if I have to."

She hugged him close. "I'm frightened."

"I'd be lying if I said I wasn't. But I can't ask you to run. And I don't . . . don't expect you to wait for me."

"Don't say that. Don't even think it. And no matter how long it is, Chase Murdock, I will wait. I will."

His mouth found hers and he kissed her, long, lingering, a little desperate. "I'll take my chances with the law, Abby. I have to. I can't ask you to run, and I can't seem to live my life without you any more." He set her away from him then and climbed to his feet. "We'd best get you home." He helped her up. "Winnie and Ethan are probably worried to death."

She nodded. But he could tell she was still very much afraid for him.

They arrived in Willow Springs just after day-break. Winnie and Ethan were overjoyed to have them home, safe. While Abby soothed a terrified

415

Winnie, Ethan took Chase aside. As always, he minced no words.

"Perkins sent for a federal marshal."

Chase felt his heartbeat quicken.

"There was one in the next town, ridin' through on the circuit. He rode all night, then came poundin' up to the house about four this morning, when Perkins told him you might be here. One look at him told me you got trouble, Chase. Vernon Jacoby doesn't give a tinker's damn what you did here yesterday. He only cares about the reputation he'll get for bringin' in Cordell."

"He doesn't have to bring me in, Ethan. I've decided to give myself up. Get it all behind me." His gaze shifted to where Abby still sat comforting Winnie on the divan. "She says she'll wait for me, Ethan. But I don't expect her to, don't want her to. Give it a couple of months . . ." he took a deep breath to steady himself, "then make sure she gets on with her life, will you?"

Ethan's eyes were unreadable, but he nodded and Chase relaxed a little. He strode over to Abby. "I'm going down to Devlin's office. There's a federal marshall there. I might as well get this over with."

Abby stood, a sudden wild terror in her eyes. "Don't! Please, Chase. No one knows we're back. Take the horse. Run. I'd rather give you up, than see you go to prison. In a little while you could send for me. You could—"

Gently, he cut her off. "I have to do this, Abby.

416

We both know it. I'll be all right. You'll see."

"I'm going with you."

"No. I need to do this alone."

He left her then and headed toward Devlin's old office, feeling with each step he took that a door was closing behind him, and that there was nothing he could do to stop it. And that the door was the door to a prison cell, where he could spend the rest of his life.

His palms were sweating when he reached Devlin's office. He took a deep breath and reached for the knob.

The door swung inward. A red-haired giant of a man stood framed in the doorway.

"That's him!" Hiram Perkins said, slinking up to stand beside Jacoby. "That's the desperado I was telling you about, Marshal. I always knew he was scum."

Vernon Jacoby held his Colt levelled at Chase's middle. "Come right in, Cordell. I've got a cell all picked out for you." He cocked the gun. "You're under arrest."

Chapter Twenty-six

Twelve separate charges of armed robbery. Marshal Vernon Jacoby enumerated each of them, as he led Chase to a cell in the back of the jail. "And that's just for starters, boy." Jacoby clanged shut the iron door and turned the key in the lock. "There'll be others. Likely worse. I know lawmen in four other states and territories that want to get their hands on you." Jacoby chuckled with genuine amusement. "But I guess I got ya first, huh?"

"I gave myself up, Marshal," Chase said, sinking down onto the stone-hard cot. "Remember?"

"That ain't the way I'm gonna tell it." The big man grinned and headed for the door that led back to the outer office.

"I suppose it doesn't count for anything that I didn't do any of those particular robberies you listed off."

"Doesn't count a damn, Cordell. You'd best get used to those walls. A jail cell's gonna be your home for a long time." Chase could still hear the man chuckling, even after Jacoby had closed the

418

adjoining door.

He sat there in the dim light of early morning that filtered through two narrow slits in the stone wall at his back, trying not to let the hopelessness he felt overwhelm him. He had thought to do the right thing by turning himself in. He wanted to clear the slate, so he could start life fresh with Abby. Even if that meant a couple of years behind bars. But how many years would twelve counts of robbery net him?

He shuddered, the walls seeming to crowd closer.

Even if he proved he was elsewhere for some of the twelve, he doubted he could account for his whereabouts for all of them. Any unsolved holdup over the past two years seemed to have been charged to the Cordell gang.

He raised his head at the sound of the connecting door opening again. He expected to see Jacoby. Instead Abby stood there, her hands twisting in front of her, her face pinched and drawn.

Chase rose and stepped close to the bars. "Go home, Abby," he said softly. "I don't want you to see me in here."

She blinked, her eyes overbright and he knew she was trying hard to be brave for him. She pulled the door shut and walked to the cell. "I had to come. Please understand."

"Everything's all right, Abby," he lied. "The circuit judge will be here in a couple of weeks, then it'll all be settled."

"Settled how? The marshal showed me . . ." Her face was pained. "Chase, you told me about Breckenridge and a couple of others. I . . . I . . . Chase, there are so many."

He blew out a long breath. "I didn't do any but the stage holdup, Abby. I swear it."

Tears streamed down her cheeks. "I didn't mean to ask. Forgive me. I should've known—"

"Don't cry, Abby. Please. Not over me." God, how he wanted to touch her, hold her in his arms. It struck him then that he very likely never would again. And he had to steel himself against the crushing pain of it, lest Abby see it in his eyes.

"I can't bear your being in this place," she said. "Not even for a day. I shouldn't have let you do this." She curled her fingers about the bars, struggling to steady her voice. "You should've run. I should have made you run."

"It's too late, Abby. And it was my choice, not yours. Even if I hadn't met you, I was damned sick of what I'd become."

"You saved this whole town yesterday! You shouldn't be in jail."

"Go home, Abby."

"If they convict you, if . . ." she bit her lip, "I'll help you get away, Chase. Just tell me what to do. Just tell me."

"No!" He paced to the rear of the cell and back, raking his hand through his shaggy hair. "Don't even think of it. Promise me!" He gripped the bars, wrapping his large hands around her much smaller ones. "Abby, if you were hurt . . ." He blinked rapidly, arched his head back, then drilled her with his gaze. "I want you to forget about me. Do you understand? Find someone who'll give you the happiness you deserve. A home, a family."

She pressed her lips to his fingers. "I want a family with you."

He groaned, pulling his hand away. "That can't happen. Don't you see? No matter how this turns out. If they don't get me for this holdup, they'll get me for another. Dammit, Abby, there's no help for it." His voice grew harsh. "I'm going to spend the rest of my life in prison."

"Don't say that!"

"The sooner you accept it, the sooner you can go on with your life." He turned his back on her and went to lie down on the cot, where he dragged one arm over his face. "Don't come back here again, Abby. I mean it."

Abby reached her hand through the bars, but he didn't notice, didn't move. Curling her fingers into her palm, she brought her fist to her mouth, no longer able to keep her tears at bay. Sobbing quietly, she returned to the outer office.

Jacoby was sitting at what had been Sam's desk. Stiffening her spine Abby marched over to him. "You're wrong about him, Marshal. Even though you have the law on your side. I can promise you, you don't have justice." Leaving the burly lawman

421

gaping after her, she walked from the jailhouse.

Back home she forced herself to get ready for school, though she had no idea how she was going to make it through the day. She was grateful to find Zeb still asleep, grateful to avoid giving him reassuring answers about Chase, when she felt only a numbing despair herself. Grateful, too, that after a long, anxious night Winnie was sleeping as well. But though she would have liked to get out of the house without answering any questions at all, Ethan found her in the kitchen. Abby paused in her preparation of a lunch she already knew she would be too upset to eat.

"How's he taking it?" Ethan asked gently.

She forced a deep breath, determined not to cry again, fearful she would never stop. "He told me not to come back, Uncle Ethan. He told me he doesn't want me to see him in that place."

"I can understand that."

"But two weeks? The trial won't start for two weeks, Uncle Ethan. How can I—" Her voice shook, broke, her force of will overridden by her fear for Chase.

Ethan drew her into his arms, held her as she wept.

"It's my fault," she hiccoughed. "If not for me, he wouldn't be in there."

Ethan lifted her chin. "If not for you, he'd be a dead man."

"That's not what I meant. After his sight came

back, he could've left, he could've run. It's because he loves me that he's in that jail.

Ethan's eyes were sympathetic, but his voice was firm. "It's because he robbed a stagecoach that he's in jail, Abby. And Chase was already a man tired of running, even before he met you. Otherwise, nothing anyone said to him would have mattered." He set her at arm's length. "You have to be strong for him, Abby. He'll need that from you."

She nodded, swiping at her tears. "I will be. I will be, Uncle Ethan. I promise."

The days passed, and somehow Abby made it through them. She assuaged some of the pain of not seeing Chase by sitting at her school desk at lunch time and writing him long, loving letters, which Jacoby obligingly delivered—after he'd read them. Whether or not Chase read them, she didn't know. He never responded. Not once.

As she wrote, she would imagine herself wrapped in Chase's strong arms, lying under a massive oak tree in a flower-studded meadow, where they would share special moments of each other's day. She told him of how wonderfully Rusty was coming along in his oral lessons, how Zeb had moved into the house and begun to prove himself a most gifted whittler. And how both boys had come to her to confess that it had been they who had vandalized the schoolhouse so long ago. They were both exceedingly sorry, but Rusty balked at actually confronting his father, and Abby had not pressed him.

423

She closed every letter with words that sang of her love for him, her faith that they would be together again soon. And then she would weep, terrified that it would never be so.

Evening hours were spent working on her novel, as she became almost obsessed with its rewrite. Spending time with her new hero kept her from going mad, as he clambered in and out of desperate scrape after desperate scrape, always to return to sweep the heroine into his arms.

It was only just before she fell asleep each night that she found no defense against the most shattering image of all. That of Chase, alone and afraid in his dark stone cage. In her mind, she would go to him, try to comfort him. But each time, he would send her away, his smoke blue eyes chillingly blank, lifeless.

Somehow, though, she survived the two weeks. The day Chase's trial was to begin dawned cool and crisp, the autumn sky an almost painful blue. Nervous, agitated, Abby rummaged about in her bureau, looking for a comb to catch up her hair, wanting to look her very best for Chase in the courtroom. Her fingers swept across a pink envelope. She picked it up. Lisa's last letter. After taking it out of her book, Abby had put it in this drawer, and until now, forgotten about it.

She smiled fondly, caressing the envelope. She'd all but memorized the letter's contents anyway. Still, she opened it, her heart caught up by words now more achingly poignant than when Lisa had first penned them.

Go west and live your dreams, Abby. Find a man worthy of how special you are. You deserve nothing less. Then build those dreams together.

"I pray we will, Lisa," she murmured. "I pray we will."

She took an extra minute to compose herself. This would be the first time in two weeks she'd seen Chase, and she had no idea what his reaction might be. She had to resign herself to the fact that she might not even get a chance to talk to him. That even if she did, he might refuse to speak to her.

And she had to think of Winnie and Ethan, too. They were beside themselves with worry for her, though they did their best not to show it. Abby had to be strong today, not only for Chase, but for her beloved aunt and uncle.

Straightening, her chin held high, she left her bedroom and went out to accompany Winnie and Ethan to the courthouse. Zeb, too, insisted on coming along.

Abby could scarcely believe the silence, as they headed up the street. Willow Springs had virtually shut down for the day. Everyone wanted to attend the trial. School was cancelled. The mercantile and several other businesses closed. When they arrived in the courtroom, it was to find the gallery so crowded, that Zeb was forced to find a lone seat, while Abby, Winnie and Ethan found chairs in the

425

back.

She had just seated herself between her aunt and uncle, when the main doors to their left opened. Her heart turned over to see Chase, his eyes staring straight ahead, the expression in them as coldly blank as her worst nightmares. She had to stop herself from crying his name, and then crying out in outrage, as she realized to her horror that he was chained, shackled hand and foot!

Though it cost nearly every ounce of her self-control, Abby allowed Chase to move by her without a word. But she didn't stop herself from catching Jacoby's shirtsleeve. "Why do you have to have him chained like an animal?" she hissed, just loud enough for the marshal to hear and no one else.

The marshal's eyes were not unkind, but he shrugged fatalistically. "I had a prisoner I trusted once, Miss Graham. He put a knife in my ribs. Never had an unchained prisoner since. And I ain't gonna start now."

Jacoby then nudged Chase toward the defendant's table to the left and in front of the rail that separated the main courtroom from the gallery.

Abby sank back into the straight-backed chair between Winnie and Ethan. In truth she wasn't certain that Chase wouldn't have tried to escape. Surely he must regret his decision to take his chances with the law. Even a year, two, now seemed too high a price to pay, even to never again have to look over his shoulder.

Chase had just seated himself, still looking straight ahead, when a door opened to the left of the judge's bench at the front of the room. The buzzing in the courtroom ceased. Chairs scraped back, as everyone rose to their feet. A black-robed, patrician-looking man in his mid-fifties made a casual sweep of the room over the rims of his wire rimmed spectacles, then walked over to take his place behind that awesome podium.

So this was Henry Lloyd Garrison, Abby thought. She had read about him briefly in a newspaper article last week. A fair man, a just man. The man upon whose shoulders her future now rested.

As the trial itself got underway, Abby took deep breaths to steady herself. Chase sat unmoving, impassive, almost indifferent, as a parade of witnesses from the stage holdup were called. None of them—not a woman passenger, nor her niece, nor the driver and shotgun messesnger—could offer a positive identification of the masked leader of the band of outlaws who held them up that day.

In fact, Abby almost thought she saw the older woman smile at Chase as she stepped down. Grace Thackeray had spoken glowingly of how kindly the outlaw leader had treated them, going out of his way not to frighten her or her young niece. The prosecutor had tried to shake her story, but failed.

As the day progressed, Abby's hopes dared raise a

little, even in the face of the ineptitude of Chase's own lawyer—a nondescript little man named Everett Simpson, who began nearly every sentence with "If Your Honor pleases . . ." until Garrison announced that it would please him mightily not to be so pleased.

The prosecutor, on the other hand, was an imposing mustachioed man named Lionel Adams. From his opening argument on, the man seemed bent on painting Chase as a malicious bandit and wanton lawbreaker.

By four o'clock nearly every witness had been called, and Abby's hopes soared higher. No jury could convict Chase on what had been heard here today. She found herself almost smiling, a thoroughly scandalous thought skimming through her mind. The man she loved had been a thief, a highwayman of the first order—and here she was, Abigail Graham, proper and law-abiding schoolteacher, thanking the stars about what a very careful, sensible thief he had been!

And then Lionel Adams looked out over the assembled gallery, something in his manner suddenly giving Abby pause. "I'd like to call my last witness, Your Honor."

"Proceed," Garrison said.

Adams' voice boomed. "The prosecution calls Mr. Hiram Perkins to the stand."

An audible gasp erupted in the courtroom. Abby stared as a thoroughly smug looking Perkins made his way to the witness chair. Her pulses raced, her palms sweating, even as she sought to convince herself that there was nothing the supercilious undertaker could say to hurt Chase.

"Mr. Perkins," Adams intoned, when Perkins had been sworn in and seated, "you were on hand, were you not, during the final hours of one Cal 'The Kid' Talbot?"

"I was."

Abby's heart skipped a beat.

"And could you tell this courtroom, please," Adams went on, "what precisely you heard this dying outlaw say?"

"Objection," Simpson put in. "Hearsay."

"Exception, Your Honor," Adams said. "Deathbed testimony is admissable."

"Admissable if this 'Kid' was coherent, not delirious, when he spoke," the judge said.

"He was quite coherent, Your Honor."

"Objection overruled. Proceed, Mr. Adams."

Adams gestured toward Perkins. "Tell us what you heard, sir. Tell us all."

Perkins turned a self-righteous gaze toward Chase, seeming to take especial pleasure in drawing out his testimony for full effect. "First of all, let me say, I was in the saloon that day in the first place, because I wanted to measure the poor unfortunate young man for one of my finest coffins. You see, if the fit isn't just right—"

"Yes, Mr. Perkins," Adams interrupted. "Please,

429

what you heard—?"

"Of course. Forgive me. It's always so tragic when the deceased is one so young, his whole life stretching—"

"Mr. Perkins." Even Adams was getting annoyed.

Perkins cleared his throat. "Yes, well, Mr. Talbot, er, 'the Kid,' was talking quite freely, you see, and . . ."

Abby remembered the noise in the hallway that day, felt the blood drain from her face.

"He was speaking of a man named Cordell, a man he identified as being part of the outlaw gang who held up the stage. He said Cordell was shot by a confederate named Noah Gantry. And, let me see now, I believe I recall his exact words: 'Cordell—Mr. Murdock—was furious' and that Gantry had a hideout gun and 'shot Cordell—Mr. Murdock—like a dog.' "

An audible gasp rocked the courtroom. In one sentence Perkins had inextricably locked Cordell to Murdock, and that by either name he had been a member of the outlaw gang who robbed the stage.

The judge rapped his gavel to restore order, but Perkins' smirk and Adams' triumphant smile already seemed to seal Chase's fate. Even the most sympathetic jury would be hard-pressed to find him not guilty in light of Perkins' damning words.

"Because of the late hour," Garrison said, "this court stands adjourned. We will begin again tomorrow at nine a.m. The prisoner is remanded to the town jail for the night."

Abby scarcely heard him, heard anything. Her whole world was Chase. She watched him push his chair back, listened to the harsh clanking of the chains that bound him. The corded muscles of his back strained against the fabric of his shirt, and she knew he was holding himself under rigid control.

Only for Chase's sake did she manage to gain a hold on the hysteria threatening to engulf her. For the briefest instant he had turned, looked at her for the first time. And she had seen such agony in his face that she had had to harden herself against it lest she hurt him more by shattering apart before his eyes.

Stone-faced, dry-eyed, she stood by her seat, as she watched Jacoby lead him out of the courtroom. She didn't remember being led from the courtroom herself by Winnie and Ethan, nor any of the walk home. Though later she recalled snippets of conversation amongst the throng.

"Really too bad." "He could get ten years." "I really liked the fella." "What a shame." "Fifteen years." "As many as twenty years."

For over an hour she sat in her bedroom and sobbed. Again and again her mind tormented her with images of what someone had called a tumbleweed wagon, a cast-iron abomination with one tiny barred window on its door, that had been parked beside the jail for nearly a week. They would use it to transport Chase to prison.

Abby shuddered. The thing looked like nothing so much as an oversized coffin.

Fifteen years? Twenty? It might as well be a lifetime. Chase would be lost to her forever.

Fighting an almost overwhelming despair, Abby dried her eyes, forced herself to leave her room, to assure Winnie and Ethan she was all right. She walked into the parlor, where Ethan sat, so deep in thought, that he did not at first seem to notice her. Then he shook himself, stood, coming over to grasp her hands in his.

She hugged him, accepting his grief to be almost as deep as her own. He loved Chase like a son.

Pulling away, she picked up the latest newspaper, now three days old, and stared at a front page saturated with stories about Chase, the trial. The overzealous journalist had even included a complete listing of all the crimes purportedly ever committed by Cordell and his gang.

"Look at this, Uncle Ethan!" Abby railed, crushing the paper in her fist. "They even mention that bank robbery in Rimrock. Chase was in Willow Springs and blind when that happened. I'm surprised they haven't linked him to the assassination of President Lincoln!"

"Give them time," Ethan muttered. "There are at least six others on that list he couldn't possibly have committed. And, because he tells me he didn't, I believe him innocent of the others as well."

He paced back and forth in front of the divan.

"This whole thing boils down to Chase's having pulled a handful of robberies over the past two years. He admits that, admits he was a fool for doing it, too. And I know he'd make restitution if he had the chance." He shook his head. "They could've put me in jail for the rest of my life for being part of a lynch mob. And what would that have done to Winnie, to you? Luckily, I didn't have the guts to turn myself in."

Abby longed to assure him he'd done the right thing, but she did not interrupt.

"I punished myself for what I did," Ethan went on. "And I think Chase has done the same. Yes, we need prisons to protect us from people who would do us harm. But Chase Murdock isn't one of those people. And in a way, he never was.

"Choices, Abby," Ethan murmured, his gaze thoughtful. "Ultimately, it's all choices. When we look in the mirror in the morning we want to know we did the right thing, we made the right choice. Maybe Chase deserves some prison time for what he did, but he doesn't deserve what Hiram Perkins would have them do. I just wish to God there was some way to undo what that pompous ass did today in that courtroom."

Abby suppressed an involuntary shudder. "I heard some people saying twenty years, Uncle Ethan. For a crime where the only thing taken was money from a man who owed Chase far more than he could ever pay."

Ethan sagged onto the divan, again murmuring, "Choices."

Abby returned to her room, her thoughts roiling. She had her own choices to make. If Chase were convicted tomorrow, he would be taken to prison for an untold number of years, locked away from her for what could be the rest of her life.

This could be his last night in Willow Springs, the last night she might ever be able to see him . . . touch him . . .

She walked to her bureau and opened the top drawer. For her there was only one choice. She made it.

In minutes she was on her way to the jail. Night shadows crowded in, but she found comfort in them, solace. She welcomed the darkness, the privacy she sought on this last night with Chase.

Jacoby looked up from his desk, startled. "Now, Miss Graham, we've been all through this. The man does not want—"

Without a word she handed the marshal two hundred dollars in paper currency. "It's all I have."

He stared at her, incredulous. "You're bribin' me to bust him out of jail?"

She kept her chin high, her words crisp, sharp. "I'm paying you to lock me into his cell and not come back for two hours."

She was prepared for his leer. Instead, he surprised her with a look of grudging admiration, and just a trace of envy. "I wish I had me a woman who cared that much about me."

He pocketed the money and handed her the keys. "I can't hear nothin' that goes on back there from out here. But I'll tell you this, Cordell comes through that door—" he pointed to the one leading back to the cells. "And I'll kill him. You understand that?"

She took up the keys and didn't look back. The cell area was even more bleak than she remembered, seeming more dungeon than jail cell. And she shuddered to recall the dream she'd once had.

Annoyed, she threw off the depressing gloom. She was here for perhaps the last stolen moments she would ever spend with Chase. She wasn't about to waste any of them.

He didn't even look up when he heard the key in the lock. He was lying on a crude cot jutting from the wall. Two blankets were the room's only adornments. Nothing else.

"You promised me a wedding night," she said, her voice throbbing with the love she felt for this man, "I'm here to take you at your word."

He bolted upright, but the joy she had hoped, dreamed to see on his face was not there. Instead she saw only rage, helplessness, and an abiding pain he tried to hide, but couldn't. "How the hell did you get in here?" he asked hoarsely. "I told Jacoby—"

"I paid him."

"Unless you brought a gun, go home."

"I don't want you killed. Chase, please, we'll get through this. Somehow we can . . ."

"Go home, Abby. For the love of God, get out of here. Have mercy, please." His voice shook, cracked. "You heard Perkins on that witness stand. I'll get fifteen years, if I get a day."

"You don't know that."

"Then they'll get me for something else."

She knelt beside the cot, catching his hand in hers. She felt it tremble, felt his whole body tremble.

"Get out," he rasped again. "Don't do this . . . I beg you."

She kissed his hand, held it to her lips, her tears burning like acid on his skin. "I love you." She brought that hand to the side of her face, held it, caressed it, then kissed his palm. "I lie awake, night after night and imagine your hands on me, Chase. Please, we have only this tiny space of time. Please don't cast it away . . . If they take away the rest of our lives. Don't let them have these two hours."

An animal sound of pain tore from his throat. "Abby, I can't . . . not here . . . not like this. Abby, please, leave me something."

"That's why I'm here. To leave you with something. To give you all that I have, all that I am." She bit her lip, desperate not to cry in front of him. "Please . . ."

She kissed his mouth. He did not respond. She traced her hands along his body, her movements at

436

first tentative, nervous. She was suddenly terribly afraid. Afraid she had made a dreadful mistake, that her being here was causing him more pain than if she had not come.

Her hands skated across his shirt, undid the buttons, finding his nipples, touching, tasting. She slid her hand under the waistband of his trousers, finding his sex, touching it, feeling it stir to life even as she knew he sought to quell it.

She stroked him, as she had that night, tearing at the fastening of his trousers, pulling them down past his hips. "I love you, Chase. I love you."

She tasted him and he dug his hands into her hair, his body convulsing. And then he dragged her atop him, his hands tearing, ripping the clothes from her body.

"Abby . . . my God . . . my God . . ." His tears burned her breasts, seared her heart. He drove himself inside her, thrusting, thrusting, spilling the essence of himself into her womb.

And then he lay against her, cradling her in his arms and wept.

She stroked his hair, kissed his chin, his mouth. "I love you Chase Murdock."

"It's Cordell, Abby. Just Cordell."

"No. It's Murdock. And it's Chase, the name you held inside yourself for so many years. The name a friend could call you." She held him close. "You are my very best friend, Chase Murdock."

He took her again, more slowly, savoring, tasting,

loving. It would be the last time. The last time he would ever touch Abby in his life. Even if he survived the years they would set for him in prison, he would not be back. He would not let her waste those years waiting for his ghost.

Yet in the shared moment of their release he was glad, achingly glad, she had come to him. Memories of these two hours would be all he would have to sustain him through the empty years that stretched endlessly before him.

She left as quietly as she had come, no final words, no false encouragements, only the tenderest of kisses and then she was gone.

The next morning Abby again shored up every ounce of her courage and made her way to the courtroom. Today the judge and jury would make it official. Today Chase would be ripped forever from her life. She sat again in the back row, Winnie to her left, Ethan and Zeb to her right. Her head throbbed, her temples pounding, as the pain of losing Chase built relentlessly inside her. But she gave no outward sign. This would be her last gift to him, that he would never know the agony that was all but crushing her soul.

Jacoby brought Chase in then, and her heart lightened the barest wisp, because for this last day she did not have to see Chase in chains. The marshal shrugged at her, smiling sheepishly, then ushered Chase off to his position at the defendant's table. Chase never once looked at her.

The judge entered and the trial was again underway. Everett Simpson reneged on his promise to call several Willow Springs citizens to the stand to extoll the fine character of the man they had come to know as Chase Murdock. He only mumbled that the defense rested, "if Your Honor pleases."

The defense and prosecution summaries followed, Simpson's deadly dull, and Adams' full of fire and brimstone retribution. Abby's heart ached every time she looked at Chase, sitting there, having said nothing in his own defense; nothing of the kind of man he was, had always been, except for a brief aberration, when he had allowed himself to believe the lies of his father, instead of the abiding truth about the goodness of the man Quinton Murdock had seen in him.

The jury would retire. Hiram Perkins would win his pathetic little victory. And Chase would be as good as dead.

Suddenly from next to Abby, Ethan stood and walked up the aisle. "I have something to say, Your Honor."

The judge banged his gavel. "You are out of order, sir."

"Is it out of order to save a man's future?"

"What are you talking about?"

"I want to know why I wasn't allowed to speak in Mr. Murdock's behalf?"

"We've already established his name is Cordell."

Ethan shrugged. "Only because of some negligible likeness on a wanted poster, which I have yet to see produced in this courtroom."

"You are still out of order, Mr. Graham. But I'm curious. What is your point?"

Ethan stood behind the rail and looked squarely at the judge. "My point is that Hiram Perkins was mistaken. Chase Murdock was not part of that stage holdup."

Abby's heart thundered in her breast, her gaze flicking to Chase. Chase didn't take his eyes from Ethan.

Ethan gave no one a chance to interrupt. "Cal Talbot was delirious, on the brink of death. He didn't know what he was saying. I should know. Chase Murdock—" and again he emphasized the last name—"couldn't have been there. My wife, niece and I found him badly wounded several miles from where the stage was robbed."

Abby couldn't breathe, so tensely was she holding herself. Choices. *Choices.*

"We know about your finding him," Garrison said.

"No, sir. You don't. Not all of it. We were travelling in strange country, it took us some time to get our bearings, find our way to town."

"Just what are you saying, Mr. Graham?"

"We found Mr. Murdock wounded, Your Honor—the day *before* the stage was robbed."

The courtroom erupted, everyone talking at once. Garrison nearly drove his gavel through his desk, as he called for order.

Chase sat still as stone for a long minute, then he turned his head away to bury his face in his hands. Abby could see his shoulders tremble.

Five more minutes passed before Garrison restored order, the gallery finally quieting. "Are you prepared to say that under oath, Mr. Graham?"

Ethan straightened. "I am."

"This is highly irregular, Your Honor," Adams blustered. "Besides, we all know there are plenty of other charges against the accused."

Zeb bolted to his feet, folding up the newspaper. "Not this one, Mr. Adams. Not the one on September twelfth." He pointed toward the paper. "He didn't do it because . . . because on that day, Mr. Murdock was with me. We went fishin'!"

"Your Honor!" Adams bellowed.

But Padriac O'Banion had left his seat. "And I'll swear Mr. Murdock was working for me when that gunsmith was held up in Clear Creek!"

One by one, in a spontaneous gesture that left Henry Lloyd Garrison and Lionel Adams speechless, the citizens of Willow Springs stood and said they were with Chase during one or the other of every crime on the list.

When the last had been accounted for, all eyes turned toward Hiram Perkins, who shifted uncomfortably in his seat, looking at first stubborn, then uneasy. At last Perkins cleared his throat. "It would seem I may have been mistaken."

Abby stood and glared at him.

"Yes, I was mistaken. I apologize, Your Honor. I misheard the Kid. I was standing out in the hallway, and I must have misunderstood."

Adams slumped into his seat, shaking his head. Garrison looked dubious, but oddly intrigued.

Abby waited.

"This is all highly irregular," Garrison said again. "But it seems Mr. Murdock can't be guilty, after all, since he's been so busy visiting with all of you over the past two years." His hard gaze drilled Chase. "You're an amazing man, Mr. . . . Murdock. With an uncanny ability to be everywhere at once. Stand up, please."

Chase stood. Abby held her breath.

"If you can promise me that you'll continue to use these amazing powers of yours—in other words be everywhere at once *except* ever again in my courtroom, I might be inclined to believe these people."

Chase managed to nod.

Garrison slammed down the gavel. "Charges dismissed."

The whole crowd seemed to surge forward then, to pound Chase on the back, congratulate him. Abby didn't even try to make her way through the mob. She would wait. Tears streamed down her face. She would wait to have him to herself.

"Oh, Aunt Winnie," she cried, giving her aunt a fierce hug, "he's free. Chase is free."

Winnie smoothed away her own tears, and Abby felt the briefest twinge, because she knew some of those tears were for Ethan. And for the lie. But most of them were tears of happiness for Abby. "I'm so pleased for you, dear. I know how much you love him. And I know he's a good man."

Again and again Abby overheard people telling Chase that if he wanted the job of sheriff, it was his. Even Jacoby stood to one side, grinning. She imagined he'd never been so happy to lose a prisoner in his life.

As the crowd began to thin a little, Abby made her way toward Chase. He was alone now at the defendant's table. She quickened her step, then stopped when she saw Ethan approaching Chase. Chase stood there, a hundred different emotions skating across his face at once—chief among them disbelief, gratitude . . . and love. He swallowed hard and stuck his hand out toward Ethan, who accepted it, then grabbed Chase in a bearhug embrace.

Abby saw the tears glistening in Chase's eyes, and she quickly swiped at her own.

"We'll see you two at home later, all right?" Ethan said, stepping away and coming over to give Abby a hug as well.

Abby could only nod, never taking her eyes from Chase. She listened as Ethan ushered Winnie and

443

Zeb out of the courtroom ahead of him. She was now alone with Chase.

The joy she expected to see in him was not there. If anything those smoke blue eyes looked more troubled, agonized than they had yesterday after Perkins' testimony. She touched his hand, curled hers over it, tears springing again to her eyes as she thought how close they had come to never again knowing even such simple pleasures.

He turned his hand over, and she saw the badge he held in his palm. "This isn't right. None of it." His voice was shaking. "I don't deserve—"

She pressed her fingers to his lips. "Don't." She kissed him. "Don't."

He crushed her to him, then just as quickly released her. "I'm sorry, Abby. I'm sorry. I need—" He dragged in a deep breath. "I need to be alone for awhile. All right?"

He didn't wait for her answer, instead heading for the back of the courthouse, slamming the door in his haste to be gone.

Abby sank into the chair at the defendant's table, the chair in which Chase had so recently been given back his life.

Alone.

He wanted to be alone. No. If there was one thing Chase Murdock didn't need at all right now, it was to be alone to set loose all of his father's old demons.

She rose to her feet, followed after him, but by

444

the time she reached the alley, it was to discover that he'd borrowed a horse and spurred it out of town.

But that was all right. She knew exactly where he'd gone.

It took her an hour to hire a buggy and drive out to the cabin where they'd first made love. She found his horse tied outside, but no sign of Chase.

She made her way through the still lush grass toward the creek tumbling by some hundred yards to the north. She found him sitting on its bank. She sank to her knees beside him. "Are you all right?"

"I don't deserve what Ethan did for me." He did not look at her.

"Yes, you do. And they all did it, not just Uncle Ethan. They all believe in you. Are you going to sit there and tell me every person in that town is wrong—except Hiram Perkins!"

He still wasn't looking at her. "Maybe."

"And Quinton Murdock was wrong?"

He said nothing.

"And I'm wrong?"

He looked at her then, touched her hair, her face. "Damn. Oh, damn . . . I love you, Abby. So much. But you deserve so much more than I could ever give you."

"You've given me more than you'll ever know." She cupped his face in her hands. "You've given me my full-blooded romantic western hero."

He tugged at a blade of grass. "Some hero."

445

She twined her fingers with his. "Beadle and Adams thought so."

"Who?"

"Those first two chapters I sent them—they want to see the rest of the book."

"Tex Trueblood? Abby, that's wonderful!" He smiled. "I know how much you wanted that."

"Except it's not exactly about Tex Trueblood any more." A breeze lifted the dark lock of hair that tumbled across his forehead and she reached to thread her fingers through it. "I have a new hero, you see? A kind of a Robin Hood sort of an outlaw, who falls in love with this truly wonderful schoolteacher."

He traced the outline of her face with his fingers, feathered her mouth with a kiss. "Tell me more."

She lay back, the heady scent of wildflowers drifting over her, and reached to unbutton the first button of his shirt. "He saves the town's bank from being robbed, and the townsfolk are so grateful, they make him sheriff. And Chase, that's the hero's name, Chase, tells Abby he loves her so very much. Abby, that's her name."

"Mmm hmmm." He opened her dress, undid the ribbons of her chemise, kissed her throat, her collarbone, the valley between her breasts. "And then what happens?"

She gasped, knotted her fingers in his hair. "He, uh, well . . ." her thoughts weren't coming too clearly any more. "They . . . they get married. And

446

they have a whole brood of wonderful children . . . and live happily ever after."

"Sounds like a fairy tale to me."

"A most wonderful fairy tale." She stayed his hand a moment, from where it had begun a most erotic exploration of her breast. "But it is my fairy tale, Chase. My book. I want you to know you're free to write your own ending. Free to go wherever you want, do what you want."

He looked at her with eyes that burned. "I'm not much of a writer," he murmured, skating his mouth up to where his hand had been. "I like your ending just fine, Abby. Just fine." He swept her up then in the magic of his loving, staking his claim forever on her heart.